HOOPLA

HOOPLA

HARRY STEIN

St. Martin's Press
New York

Library of Congress Cataloging in Publication Data

Stein, Harry.
  Hoopla.

    Originally published: New York: Knopf, 1983.
    1. Chicago White Sox (Baseball team)—History—
Fiction.   2. World series (Baseball)—History—Fiction.
I. Title.
[PS3569.T366H6   1986]   813'.54   85-30404
ISBN 0-312-38983-3

First published in the United States by Alfred A. Knopf, Inc.

10 9 8 7 6 5 4 3 2

FOR MY FATHER

I have often thought that the best way to define a man's character would be to seek out the particular mental or moral attitude in which, when it came upon him, he felt himself most deeply and intensely active and alive.

WILLIAM JAMES

There are only two families in the world, the Haves and the Have-Nots.

CERVANTES

HOOPLA

Introduction

(Forgotten, But Not Gone)

Southhampton, N.Y. September, 1974

For a great many years, I made my way through this life dragging accolades behind me like tin cans on a newlywed's jalopy.

"Luther Pond," came the introductions at banquets and on broadcast interviews, "America's most tireless reporter." Or "Luther Pond, journalism's bloodhound." Or, as my publisher often had it, in one variation or another (for he knew his business almost as well as I knew mine), "Luther Pond, Jack Public's favorite snoop in high places."

I rarely demurred in the face of any such assertions, no matter how exaggerated they became. So what if I did not actually have a source within Hitler's general staff? "The chief business of the nation, as a nation," as Mencken said, "is the setting up of heroes, mainly bogus." Hell, why shouldn't that be me?

God knows, there were few enough genuine men of distinction around. In a world so at ease with mediocrity as this one, the qualities I possessed in such abundance—energy, personal style, forthrightness, a sense of the dramatic—*were* exceptional.

So I was never one of those phoneys you'd find over at the Algonquin, crying in his bisque over the debasement of contemporary standards. I knew, and so did they, if they'd had the guts to admit it, that if contemporary standards had been any higher, we'd all have been in trouble.

Unlike some men, I did not have this altogether unsentimental view of the world handed to me at birth. My father, a Richmond, Virginia, attorney, held an exceedingly optimistic opinion of humankind, even in the face of the stark evidence to the contrary that abounded in his own profession, and I was unfortunate enough to inherit both his soft chin and his soft heart. As an eighteen-year-old, not only did I presume that every fellow who passed me on the street was capable of rational thought and informed discourse, but I had only the vaguest notion that he might be a sonovabitch. Having been raised to believe in the homilies, it came as a genuine shock to discover that the world is full of quietly unscrupulous men and, more important, that their shortcomings rarely lead to their ruination.

But I wised up thoroughly, and rather quickly. Barely a month into my first job, at the New York *Journal*, I was assigned to serve as the driver for a reporter named Brady, our task being to beat the *World* to the Long Island home of the family of a young woman lately decapitated. We were after a photograph of the victim (who, on the basis of a description of the head proffered by our man at the morgue, our paper had already described as "a beautiful blond"). As it happened, we screeched to a halt at our destination a bare moment after our competitor. Brady leapt from the car, took after the fellow and tackled him on the lawn, where they began grappling, pushing and gouging one another in the direction of the front door, through which they finally tumbled. The family was sitting in the parlor, quietly mourning. The reporters, oblivious, continued to struggle at their feet. But, abruptly, I spotted a portrait of the dead girl upon the mantelpiece, draped in black. Without a second's hesitation, I grabbed it and beat it out of there.

Even as a very young man, even in an age legendary for its hustle, even in a trade as relentlessly demanding as mine, I was a go-getter. From the outset, employers marvelled at my tirelessness and ingenuity, and rivals—I always had rivals—regarded me with barely checked frustration. Before I was thirty-five, I had grown used to hearing myself referred to as talented, brash, fearless, and I had long since stopped reacting, outwardly, to those other adjectives—petty, ruthless, treacherous—with which envious men smear their betters. I did not, I think, even then, lack for self-reflection. I knew as well as any man the mistakes I made. But the proof is in the pudding; most of those who so savagely assailed me have long since established their inconsequence far beyond my modest powers to add or detract.

What follows on these pages is the story of my professional beginnings, the tale of how, starting with little more than pluck and a keen sense of opportunism, I began making my way in the world; of how, indeed, within the space of a decade, I came to assume my place beside the other great popular journalists of the day—Runyon, Broun, Lardner, Swope.

It is, in a sense, an old-fashioned story. Ambition seems to have lately fallen as far into disrepute as wife beating, and damn few fellows come out for either in print anymore. Then, too, popular history is written in sand. The events I deal with, and more than a few of the individuals, have long since faded from public consciousness. I recognize that even I myself am no longer much on people's minds. (This last I have tried to accept with dignity; as one of the first men to fully grasp the dimensions of the general appetite for the ultimately trivial, I suppose I long ago forfeited my right to dismay over the possibility of falling, in turn, from circulation.)

I presume to maintain, however, that what I have to say is of considerable moment. Never before in my long experience has this nation been in such sorry condition as it is today. Never before have the values upon which I was nurtured been in such desperate need of affirmation.

But I am no hypocrite. For years I resisted all entreaties that I commit my memoirs to paper, and I do not pretend that my decision to do so now is entirely a matter of altruism. The inelegant truth is that having, in flusher times, dismissed the autobiographical form as the province of the has-been, having once noted, memorably (on the occasion of the appearance of the loathsome John Barrymore's memoir), that the publishers of such volumes always seem to be in a frantic race with the obituary writers, I was less than eager to resurface as so tempting a target.

But I am old now, older than once I dreamed it was possible to ever become. And I have at last been led to understand that it is time to move past a certain kind of pride.

At any rate, I have never been known to shy away from a scrap. In my heyday, I was pleased to be known, in print, over the airwaves, in life, as pugnacious, and I am pugnacious still. In the end, I regret my enemies not at all. Even on those occasions—and they ranged in time and substance from the aftermath of the investigation into the 1919 World Series to the reading of the Hiss verdict—when the accuracy of my reports was borne out by official finding, I found myself subject to vituperation, but always I prided myself on giving back at least as good as I got. And I stand as eager as I was fifty years ago to take on the world's self-righteous, those infuriating souls who believe they've got a corner on conscience and integrity and every other quality that might conceivably get a man into heaven.

No, I do not expect to be given my full due, now or ever. I moved beyond that kind of naivete before the First World War. But that, it seems to me, is no longer the point.

I vividly recall a visit, some twelve or thirteen years back, to the hospital where Westbrook Pegler lay dying. Heavily sedated, Peg was in a deep sleep, but as I stood watching him, he raised his hands and began rapidly moving his fingers, as if typing on a machine suspended in midair. A week later, when he expired, I remarked on that extraordinary moment to a colleague. "Sonovabitch was probably trying to write his own obit," he replied. "Now a lot of guys that hated his guts are gonna do it for him."

Well, dammit, that won't happen to me. There may be no immortality, but I'll be damned if I'll go quietly.

It was just yesterday that I finally made up my mind to go ahead with this thing. It was a lovely spring day here on Long Island and I was sitting on the porch, thinking about nothing in particular, staring out toward the pond, when Harriet, my latest nurse, sat down beside me and struck up her notion of a conversation. God knows, I try to be polite; I try to act my age. But suddenly I was aware that she was grinning too much and speaking in a gentle sing-song, and I went cold inside.

Doesn't anyone understand what the hell it is to be old? Doesn't anyone know that just because the limbs no longer do what one wants them to, and the head insists upon nodding, there still might be life within? This is Luther Pond here! Doesn't she know there was a time when men would have traded a year of their lives for five minutes of my time?

"Get the hell off your pretty ass," I told her, "and bring me a pencil and paper."

John L. and
the Golden Smile

It was billed as "The Fight of the Century," a seemingly preposterous notion given the fact that the century was only ten years old. But I'll tell you something, we all believed it. We were certain that very few events, and certainly no sporting event within imagination, could eclipse this one in significance.

And it looks like we were right. The century is pretty nearly eight decades old, and nothing else has even come close.

Show me another contest that stopped the whole country dead in its tracks for three weeks. Or one whose outcome provoked such widespread violence that people in twelve different states would lie dead in its wake. Or one that for years afterward would continue to be regarded as so inflammatory that motion pictures reproducing it would be banned from public display.

Truly, it was not so much a prizefight as a national morality play, a spectacle that in the public mind pitted good against an evil so vile that it became a palpable obsession that it be destroyed. The very existence of John Arthur Johnson, the Texas black man who had held the world's heavyweight boxing championship since 1908, was deemed by millions of his countrymen as an affront to every right-thinking white man. Of all the athletes I have known who routinely ignored convention, none strode upon it with quite so much enthusiasm as Jack Johnson; in an era when George Washington Carver was widely regarded as a radical, Jack consorted with white women—his distinct preference was for honey-haired prostitutes—raced expensive cars, drank the best champagne he could get his huge hands on, and said just about whatever he pleased. A great many people, including, I am sorry to say, several close relatives of mine, would've paid money to see Jack Johnson strung up.

But as the summer of 1910 approached, it looked like so conclusive a measure would not be necessary, for James J. Jeffries had at last deigned to personally assume the responsibility of destroying Johnson for them.

Jim Jeffries. "Jeff." The man held the nation utterly spellbound that season; if he'd announced that the flying machine was an optical illusion, the Wright Brothers might've been dragged from their shop; if he'd put himself forward for the Republican nomination for President, William Howard Taft would have engineered his bulky body into a courtly bow and stepped aside.

Jeff (we all called him that, as if the familiarity would make him accessible) was, as far as anyone could determine, the most awesome physical specimen that had ever existed. Six foot two, with an immense shaggy chest and limbs like redwoods, he had terrorized the heavyweight ranks for half a decade. Undefeated. Never even knocked down. With his unorthodox style—left arm extended, his incongruously boyish face (I always thought Gene Kelly, the moving picture actor, looked like him) buried against his shoulder— Jeffries was virtually unhittable, and deadly on the attack, boring in against opponents and beating them down. By 1904 there had simply been no one left to fight, aside from Johnson and a few other negroes, and Jeff, like every champion before him, drew the color line; and so, at twenty-nine, he had abandoned the title and retired.

But times had changed. Literally the very day Jack Johnson won the championship, knocking little Tommy Burns around an Australian ring, grinning so widely at the simplicity of it all that his six gold teeth shone in the late afternoon sun, the clamor went up for the great Jeffries to return. "But one thing remains," wrote Jack London from ringside. "Jim Jeffries must emerge from his alfalfa farm and remove the golden smile from Jack Johnson's face. "JEFF, IT'S UP TO YOU!" (I'll never forget those capital letters and that exclamation point; in all my years as a sportswriter, London was not only one of the greatest louts I encountered, but also one of the worst writers.)

But that, and a lot more like it, did the trick, for here was Jeff, a brief eighteen months later, as steadfast and sincere as ever, ready to take back the title that almost everyone agreed was rightfully his. "I'm doing it," he told us, "for the white race."

Not that the comeback trail had been lined with garlands. Jeff had brutalized his body in preparation for the bout, dropping more than sixty-five pounds. A country boy, a devoted woodsman and fisherman, he had even committed himself for three months to the strength-restoring mineral baths of Carlsbad, Bohemia, where he'd been forced to endure the empty prattle of a hundred European aristocrats, including King Edward VII of England.

But on his return to his homeland, the memory of the ordeal must have lifted instantly, for five thousand Americans stood on a New York dock shouting his name in tribute. And in succeeding weeks, scores of thousands more packed the nation's vaudeville theatres, at two dollars a throw, simply to shake his massive paw, advertised as "the fist that will lay the nigger low."

That the nigger would in fact be laid low seemed a foregone conclusion. The only questions were when and where. Into June of 1910, Tex Rickard, the ferret-faced promoter who'd arranged the match, dishing out ten thousand dollars in gold pieces as an advance to each of the principals, had had trouble placing the bout; San Francisco was the original choice, and the yellow pine arena on Market Street was already two-thirds completed when the governor of California bowed to pressure from anti-prizefight groups and banned the fight. Then Utah was considered. And Arizona. It was not until two weeks before Independence Day, the scheduled day of the fight, that Nevada's Governor Denver S. Dickerson invited the orphan bout to his state, no strings attached; Rickard immediately had the stadium dismantled and the timbers shipped to Reno. That was that, for even the most conscientious do-gooder would hardly bother to inveigh against sin in Nevada.

Finally, inevitably, Jeffries would face Johnson in a ring.

I was, at the time, the number four man in the five-man sports department of the New York *Evening Journal*. In fact, there no longer *was* a New York *Morning Journal*; back in '01, in the aftermath of President McKinley's assassination, the accusation had been widely made that the assassin, Leon Czolgosz, had been driven to the deed by the violence of the newspaper's anti-McKinley stance, and Mr. Hearst, indignant at having his patriotism thus impugned, had re-dubbed it the *American*. Still, by whatever name, the morning paper remained the pride of the New York operation. They would have no fewer than five reporters at ringside for the fight, while we would be sending only our top two men to Reno. As for myself, I had a pretty fair suspicion of where I would be on July 4; as punch by punch streamed in from ringside by telegraphic wire, the fight was to be reenacted by pairs of colored and white fighters at several locations around New York. I figured that, unless I had the extreme misfortune to be sent off to the Polo Grounds, I would be in Madison Square Garden or the St. Nicholas Arena, watching one of those sets of impostors square off.

It was not an unpleasing prospect, and I happened to be musing on it when a copy boy, only a few years younger than myself, tapped me on the shoulder and informed me that George McCullum, the managing editor, wanted a word with me.

McCullum did not like me; indeed, did not appear to like a soul on the premises. He had been lured to the *Journal* from the respectable *Sun* by a weekly wage said to be in excess of one hundred dollars and, like so many men at odds with themselves, he was bitter and resigned. In his presence I was always even more awkward than usual, had a tendency to stand before his desk, hands clasped behind my back, shifting my feet, like an eight-year-old.

"Yes sir," I said. "You wanted me, sir?"

He looked up from a piece of copy. "Oh yeah, Pond." He sighed, as if hating to proceed. "What're you doing on Independence Day?"

"Independence Day? I don't know, sir." I paused. "Going to the Polo Grounds?"

"No, you're not going to the Polo Grounds. You're going to be in Reno, Nevada, that's what you're doing Independence Day."

I looked at him blankly. "For the fight?"

He didn't answer, just sighed again. "We've got a problem. The *Times* has hired John L. Sullivan to cover this for them. The Yellow Kid is going through the roof."

"Mr. Hearst?"

McCullum sighed. "Yes, Pond. He just had this sent over." He thrust a small yellow newspaper clipping at me. THE BIGGER BRUTE WON read the headline, but he snatched it back before I could read further. "You know what that is? That's the *New York Times* story on a fight Sullivan fought fifteen or twenty years ago. He was the 'Bigger Brute.' And now the big lug is working for the bastards." He shook his head. "At least his name will be on the stuff. And the Great White Chief is after somebody's head because they've got him and we don't."

He fell silent and turned to stare out his grimy window. He stayed that way for an unbearably long time.

"Pardon me, sir. What exactly is it you want me to do?"

Wearily, he turned back to me. "I want you to cover Sullivan covering the fight. Wherever he is, I want you to be there. I don't want him to have anything you don't have. Not a thing. And if he does something that'll make him look bad, something dumb—drops a plate of food in his lap, *anything*—I want to read about it. Do you get that?"

"Yes sir."

John L. Sullivan. It was a name I'd heard all my life, a name spoken with the kind of reverence reserved for Abraham Lincoln, or Grover Cleveland. John L. Sullivan! I'd been only three or four years old when he'd lost the title, eighteen years before, but one of my most vivid childhood memories was of the color-tinted, life-size poster that hung in Atley's, the Baltimore barroom frequented by my Uncle Ned; there he stood, resplendent in blue tights and a red, white and blue belt, his bare dukes up, his strong jaw thrust forward. "John L. Sullivan, 'The Boston Strong Boy,' " read the caption, "America's First Heavyweight Champion."

But the caption, Uncle Ned said, had been modest. Sullivan was the first heavyweight champion *anywhere*, at least the first to fight by contemporary rules. But even that was only part of the story, for John L. Sullivan occupied a place in American life that was unique. He was a hero in a way no sports figure had ever been before, the way Sergeant York or Charles Lindbergh would be afterward. He was a titan, a superman. Children trailed after him in the streets; by the thousands, women who hardly knew what boxing was sent him indecent proposals. When Sullivan toured theatres around the country, offering a thousand dollars to anyone who could last four rounds with him, his coming could be an event for weeks in advance. (In his whole career, incidentally, only one man collected the money, and he did it only by clinching or dropping to the floor every time John L. threatened to unload.)

Even in retirement, legends clung to the man. Ned especially loved the story of the time Sullivan was arrested in Cincinnati for violating the local law prohibiting prizefights—and the judge acquitted him on the grounds that it hadn't been a fight at all but a footrace.

Sullivan had been, I was led to understand, a foul-mouthed braggart, a lecher and a drunk—the bartender at Atley's claimed he'd once downed fifty-six gin fizzes in an hour—but these qualities only added to his stature in the men's eyes. Jim Jeffries may have been a giant, but John L. Sullivan was a god.

I shuffled before McCullum. "I'm supposed to follow John L. Sullivan everywhere he goes?"

He nodded. "Yes, Pond, that's what I said."

"But what if he won't let me?"

From his scowl it was apparent he did not appreciate my dilemma. "Goddammit, boy, when the hell are you gonna become a reporter?"

I set out for Nevada the next day at noon, on the special express train commissioned by Harry Payne Whitney for his Wall Street friends, and arrived a bit more than four days later, late on the afternoon of July 2, 1910.

The scene I encountered as I walked toward Reno from the Southern Pacific depot, a half mile outside of town, was beyond imagining. The town itself was like all Wild West towns, at least as I'd always pictured them from the descriptions in the dime novels of my youth; with a few exceptions, the buildings were all one or two stories and built of wood; there were no sidewalks lining the dusty streets, but rickety planks; as I approached the town, I caught sight of a livery stable, and directly opposite it a saloon; the only concession to modernity in sight, besides the several brick buildings, was a set of trolley tracks laid down the center of a single street.

But I'd expected that. What startled me was the fact that on this wretchedly hot afternoon, this primitive cowtown was crawling

with life. It was like picking up a rock in a barren desert and finding
a huge, churning insect community.

The locals in the crowd were obvious; they wore flannel shirts,
denim pants, cowboy hats—some of them even toted six-guns—and
they walked with that particular lopsided gait of people accustomed
to riding astride, instead of behind, horses. Several of those horses
were hitched to posts off the street. But the natives comprised but
a tiny portion of the throng on Centre Street, Reno's main drag, this
afternoon. Suddenly this bleak outpost in the northern Nevada desert was as vivid a lesson in the variety of the human species, as
jumbled a melting pot, as New York City or anywhere else in the
nation. There were Chinamen in pigtails and silk smocks, who'd
made the journey from San Francisco; and Swedish dirt farmers in
coveralls, who'd come from Minnesota and Wisconsin; and Navaho
miners, many still wearing the grimy, bright red workshirts they
used on the job; the mix was stunning. But mainly, by the thousands,
from both coasts, their numbers increasing hourly as new trains
pulled in at the Southern Pacific depot, there were what my paper
habitually called "plain joes," men no more exotic than the straw
boaters or seersucker suits they almost all wore on this hot afternoon.
They had come to Reno for the sport and for the wagering, but they
had mostly come to be a part of history, to see that nigger shut up
once and for all.

As I waded into its midst, I immediately knew this was not an
angry crowd. They were simply a lot of people with plenty of time
to kill and nowhere to kill it. They meandered slowly, aimlessly
along, chunks of the crowd breaking off here or there to congregate
on the wooden sidewalks, other chunks turning up Commercial
Row, where the gambling houses ran nonstop and the honky-tonk
pianists all seemed to know only one song: "There'll Be a Hot Time
in the Old Town Tonight."

The noise on Centre Street, a roar composed of simultaneous
babble in a dozen languages, punctuated every few seconds by a
burst of raucous laughter, was deafening. Runners for the scores of
gamblers in town had long ago given up trying to shout out their
odds above the din, and had taken to approaching potential customers individually. "Jeff at ten-to-six?" one of them, a young man with
deep acne scars, shouted at me from a distance of two feet. "Or even

money for Jeff to take it in twenty rounds or less." I shook my head
and he brushed past me.

I grabbed the arm of a man in a boater, like many in the crowd
sporting a "Jeff, oh you kid" lapel button. "Do you know the way
to the Golden Hotel?"

He indicated he couldn't hear.

I put my lips to his ear. *The Golden Hotel?*"

He nodded and pointed to a red brick building, at four stories the
tallest structure on the street, located less than fifty yards away. It
had been hidden from view by an immense banner—"JAMES E. PEP-
PER WHISKEY, BORN WITH THE REPUBLIC"—that was strung up across
the street, affixed on one side to a balcony of the hotel and to the
marquee of a vaudeville theatre on the other.

It took me a good ten minutes to navigate the crowd and make
my way to the front desk.

"Excuse me, I was wondering if you have a room for me?"

The old man behind the desk eyed me with amusement. "Mister,
we don't got a room for no one."

I reached inside my jacket and pulled out my *Journal* card. "I'm
from the press," I said. "I believe my managing editor, Mr. George
McCullum, wired in advance."

He rose slowly. "Well, let's see about that." He turned and began
thumbing through a box of paper slips. "Yep, he surely did. Sorry
about that, Mr. Pond."

He came from around the desk and took up my valise. "Follow
me, sir." We walked up a steep flight of stairs, down a long corridor,
around a corner and into a . . . men's lavatory.

The deskman put down my bag on the tile floor, beneath a sink.
"Here you are, sir."

"But this is a bathroom."

"Yes, it surely is, sir. A new one, too, like everything in this hotel.
This is where you'll be staying." He nodded at a pair of cots, flush
against the wall opposite the toilet stalls.

I picked up my bag. "I'm not staying here."

He shrugged. "Suit yourself, but you won't find nothing else. The
town is booked up solid. Every private house with an extra bed is
taking boarders, and here we're using cots I didn't even know we
had. We got people staying in every bathroom in this hotel. Hell,

I hear there's people sleeping on the slabs in the morgue, and happy to get 'em."

I put down my valise and sighed. "All right, I'll stay."

He took it up again and started heading from the room. "Hey, where're you taking that?"

He turned. "You'd best not leave your things here unguarded. This ain't New York City, this is rough. And there's ten times as many rats around Reno this week as usual." He paused. "We'll hold this for you at the desk if you need something." He continued toward the door.

"Hey," I shouted after him, "do you know where I can find John L. Sullivan?" Even in those surroundings the name rang with a certain majesty.

He thought for a moment. "Try the tap room downstairs. All the boys from the press seem to pass their time there."

The tap room, a large, dark chamber with an oak bar against one wall, had, in fact, been turned into an unofficial press headquarters. In one corner, beneath a large ceiling fan that leisurely stirred the warm air, a pair of telegraph operators pecked away at their machines. The adjoining wall was lined with oak tables, in calmer times used by drinkers; now each bore a heavy black Underwood, for the moment all of them unused. On a round table in the center of the room sat, courtesy of promoter Rickard, the single element of the life that has always meant more to the sporting writer than anything having to do with mere words—the buffet table. This one was modest by New York standards (Giants owner Charles Stoneham sometimes produced caviar in the press room in the bowels of the spanking new Polo Grounds), but it would have to do; there was cool ham and roast beef, a platter of pickles, another of sauerkraut and, inevitably, a huge tub of potato salad.

This table was the focal point of the room, and around it, in small groups, were clustered nearly a score of my colleagues. I edged over alongside a pair of them, drawn by the intense agitation with which one of them was speaking.

The subject, it turned out, was Jack Johnson, and precisely *why* he was going to lose.

"Size has nothing to do with it," insisted the speaker, an earnest young man in wire-rimmed glasses who was rapidly losing his blond hair. "Johnson's problem is that he lacks that intangible something called heart. It's a characteristic of the race. He's yellow."

The other man, a small dapper fellow sporting a bowler and an extravagant handlebar moustache, took a puff of his stogie and shook his head. "No, sir. I've seen some niggers that's as brave as any white man. D'ya ever hear of Deadwood Dick? That nigger was as rugged as anyone you ever seen." He banged his gold-handled walking stick against the wooden floor for emphasis. "I mean, that nigger didn't scare." He paused and took another puff on his cigar. "Johnson'll lose cause Jeff's so big and strong, that's why."

"Folderol!" exclaimed his companion.

There was a momentary lull in the conversation. I seized it. "Excuse me," I said, reaching into my pocket for my *Evening Journal* card, "I'm Luther Pond of the New York *Evening Journal.*"

The man with the moustache extended a small hand. "Charmed. William B. Masterson of the New York *Morning Telegraph.*" He paused. "The *Journal?* When did you get into town?"

"Just this afternoon. I'm just here to . . ."

"The *Evening Journal?*" interrupted the intense young man. "You're not planning to instigate a racial war, I hope." He laughed, and offered me a hand. "Arthur Gillette of the *Times.* Do you honestly mean to tell me," he said, turning back to Masterson, "that you think negroes are just as brave as white men? As a race?"

Masterson shrugged. "I'm just sayin' it depends on the nigger. Most no, but some yes."

Arthur Gillette shook his head vigorously. "You're just wrong, that's all." He paused, then continued in a condescending tone. "You see, it's all in the chromosomes. Listen to this." He reached over for his jacket, hanging on a nearby chair, and removed a folded newspaper from its pocket. This is the *Times* of"—he checked the date—"June twenty-ninth. I just got it in today's post." He ostentatiously opened it and scanned the columns until he found what he was looking for. Then he cleared his throat and began reading: "Mr. Q. T. Simpson, a stock breeder of Chicago, appearing at a Boston meeting of the American Association for the Advancement of Science, declared today that it was only a matter of time before the darkest skinned Negro could be made as pink skinned as the Caucasian. 'By experiments with plants and animals, scientists have unearthed a great deal about the nature of the chromosome.' " Gillette paused to let the word register. " 'In a set of treatments with baths or injections, we shall be able to change the color of blacks' offspring by treating color controlling cells to war against the chromosomes.' "

He laid the paper aside and fairly leered at Masterson. This was not a terribly likeable fellow. "You see," he said, "characteristics of the different races are all determined by chromosomes. You can't have some yellow and some not yellow."

"With those women he runs with, I don't think we have to worry about Jack Johnson's offspring bein' black," quipped Masterson, who laughed for a full ten seconds at his own joke. When he caught his breath, he turned back to Gillette, still grim-faced. "Well, I suppose there's no arguin' with science. But I don't guess your stock breeder ever met up with Deadwood Dick, neither." He nodded his head at each of us—"Gents, I shall see you around"—and, chuckling softly to himself, turned and sauntered away.

Gillette scowled after him. "I'm pretty tired of him and his Wild West nonsense. All he ever did was hit people with that leaded cane of his. From behind, I'm told."

He read the surprise on my face.

"Sure. How do you think he got that nickname of his, Bat?" He paused and stuffed a pickle in his mouth. "And now that he lives in New York, all he does is wander around the saloons on Broadway, talking about what a hero he was."

I let a silence slip between us. "You said," I noted, "that you work for the *Times.* "

"Yes. The *New York Times.* "

"Well, I was wondering if you might be able to introduce me to Mr. John L. Sullivan."

"Certainly I could." Gillette's irritation instantly changed to self-congratulation. "I know him quite well. As a matter of fact"—he checked his gold-plated pocketwatch—"he should be here any time now. We're working together."

"Really? What kind of thing are you . . ."

"Ah, there he is now."

I turned, and could hardly grasp what I saw; the hard-muscled, clear-eyed gladiator of that poster in Atley's had become one of the most immensely fat human beings I had ever chanced to behold. As he waddled toward us, his bulky frame squeezed into a flannel jacket two sizes too small, a little cap perched atop his massive skull, he reminded me of nothing so much as Tweedledum. Not a soul in my long experience has ever aged worse; Sullivan was, I later learned, fifty-one years old.

"Guess who I just ran into out there?" boomed Sullivan to Gillette, his deep voice harboring the trace of an Irish accent.

"Bat Masterson," said Gillette drily.

"Yep, that's right," said Sullivan, not at all surprised by the response. He twirled one of the ends of his snow-white walrus moustache. "The little squirt picks Jeff to win it in ten. Says he'll win 'cause he's bigger."

"Yes, so he said."

"Yeah, well he don't know a damn thing," said John L. "Ever since I known him, the bastard always picks the bigger man to win. That's 'cause he's so puny hisself. He spent fifteen years bettin' against me." The fat man let out a sudden laugh. "I musta cost him a king's ransom."

Gillette glanced again at his pocketwatch. "You realize, of course, that you're late again. If you keep doing this, I'm simply going to have to put the copy over the wire without your seeing it."

"You can't do that," said John L. "My name's on it."

"But I write it," snapped Gillette. "So either you're here on time or don't bother to come at all."

I had been standing rather awkwardly off to one side since Sullivan's entrance and was not anxious to inject myself into this controversy. But since Gillette obviously had no intention of introducing me, I took advantage of the lull following the exchange to approach the great man.

"Mr. Sullivan, I'm Luther Pond from the New York *Journal*. I'm a great, great admirer of yours."

Sullivan eyed Gillette, shuffling through some papers at an adjacent table. "Oh, really," he said loudly, "it's always great to meet an admirer. Always great." He clapped me on the shoulder.

"Never mind that," called Gillette. "You'd better look at this stuff. It goes out in fifteen minutes."

Slowly John L. moved his huge bulk to the table, squeezed himself into a chair and took up the pages. Gillette rose and sidled over to me. "Look at him," he said. I glanced at Sullivan, holding page one of the text several inches from his face, staring hard at the first paragraph. "The idea that he could write his own copy is ludicrous! He can barely even read it."

At the table, Sullivan smashed a finger against the page. "Who the hell cares if Jeff had four porkchops for breakfast or not?"

"Your public," said Gillette sarcastically.

John L. abruptly rose, taking his seat with him for several inches before it dislodged and came clattering back to the floor. He tossed the papers on the table. "If that's the kind of claptrap you're gonna write, I *won't* read it." And, majestically, he began walking toward the exit.

I caught him halfway there. "Mr. Sullivan, sir, I was wondering if you'd permit me to accompany you during your coverage of the fight."

He lit up. "You wanna be with me? Well, hell, that sounds okay to . . ."

"Nooo," bellowed Gillette, dashing over to our side. "Absolutely not! He"—he pointed at me—"works for the *Journal*. He writes for William Randolph Hearst."

Sullivan drew himself up to his full five feet eleven and eyed Gillette contemptuously. "Hearst is a great American." He paused meaningfully. "My decision is he can do it." With his finger he began writing in the air. "Yours truly, John L. Sullivan." And he strode from the room.

That evening John L. offered to take me to dinner, an occasion that Mr. Gillette chose to pass up. We had very little to choose from in the way of cuisine; Reno had few restaurants and, though during the previous few days HOT FOOD signs had sprouted in the windows of laundries and barbershops and dozens of private homes, every table in town seemed to serve only pork and beans.

But merely appearing on Centre Street with John L. was an
adventure. Everywhere we went, he was an object of instant attention. Older men were particularly awestruck by his presence. When
we moved down the sidewalk, they would suddenly grow silent and
move aside, gaping at this fat man as if he was some storybook
creature come to life.

When we were at last seated at a back table of the Majestic Restaurant, having been hustled past a line of customers who'd been waiting for hours, the old man looked across the cheesecloth at me and
grinned. "A lot of real prizefight fans here, no?"

"There certainly are." I looked into his blue eyes and took the bait.
"And they certainly seem to idolize you."

John L. demurred. "Nah, they're bored, that's all." He paused and
smiled, almost shyly. "Yeah, I s'pose they do." He paused again.
"But this is some event here, no? A lot different than my day. My
God, when I fought Kilrain for the bare-knuckle title, we didn't
think a single soul would show up." He laughed and slammed a
meaty hand on the table. "People knew about it, all right. There
were placards all over the city of New Orleans advertisin' it. Trouble
was, since fighting was illegal there, none of 'em mentioned the time
or place." Sullivan shook his head. "My God, it's a wonder anyone
showed at all."

He looked down at his huge hands as if they were relics of another
age, then quickly back up at me. "But don't get the wrong idea, I
did all right. Not as good as these fellas today, but I made a livin'
at it."

"I know you did," I said. "My uncle talked about you often."

"Really?" He leaned forward on the table, pushing it slightly in
my direction. "What'd he say?"

Before I could answer, a frail waitress was hovering above us. John
L. ordered pork and beans for both of us and the waitress started to
retreat toward the kitchen. "And a beer," I called after her. Then,
glancing at John L., I amended that. "Two beers."

"No!" The sudden vehemence of this objection caused several
people at adjoining tables to turn toward us. John L. noticed them.
"Just one," he added, more softly.

"I don't imbibe anymore," he explained when the waitress was
gone. "Haven't for years."

I nodded.

"The stuff is poison. Once nearly killed me, gave me typhoid fever, and liver trouble, and the worst itch you ever felt in your life, all at once. I was laid up three months with it."

The explanation seemed like an obligation and it made me uncomfortable. "I understand, sir."

"It was my dear wife that finally set me straight. She's the one that showed me what a bloody waste my life was."

The waitress returned and set down our orders before us. I poured out my beer.

"Mr. Sullivan," I said, forcing a smile, "I'd hardly say your life has been a waste."

But he didn't want condescension. "What the hell do you know about it?" he snapped, his eyes ablaze. "My life's been a damn pisshole! I drank more liquor and did more women than any other bastard in the country, and now look at me. Writin' for some damn rag just to get a few bucks in my pocket." He paused. "So don't you tell me how good I'm goin'!"

"I'm sorry, sir."

We ate in silence for ten minutes. "Do you have a choice for the fight?" I ventured finally.

He looked at me and smiled, as if the outburst had never occurred. "Well, I'm not gonna pick a winner, if that's what you're askin'." He put down his fork and twirled one of the ends of his moustache around a finger. "I like Jeff well enough. He's a decent fella, on the level. It's that Corbett I can't stomach."

"Why do you suppose he got Corbett to manage him?"

"Oh, Corbett's a good fight man, all right, knows all the tricks better than anyone. It's the other stuff that bothers me, the name callin'. If he'd tried to use that on me, you can bet I'd have torn his damn head off."

Jim Corbett, in taking the championship from John L., had, in fact, waged a brilliant psychological campaign against him, whipping him into a blinding, debilitating rage before the fight even began, but it seemed an inopportune time to raise that. "What exactly has Corbett done that disturbs you?" I asked.

Sullivan's look expressed the extremity of his dislike for the man. "It was him that started all this talk of Johnson's 'yellow streak,'" he said. "Well, the way I look at it is that if Jeff didn't wanna fight him, he didn't have to. Hell, I never fought a nigger myself." He leaned forward on the table again. "But if he's gonna fight him, they should get on with it and cut out the name callin'."

"I think you're right."

"Damn," he continued, "there ain't no yellow streak in that nigger. The first time I ever saw him fight was twelve or fifteen years ago, down in Galveston. They got what they call 'Battle Royals' down there—six niggers in the ring all at once, and the last one standin' wins five dollars. Well, all them other niggers set on Jack first, 'cause he was the best, but he took 'em and dropped every last one of 'em." He paused meaningfully. "That ain't yellow."

"It certainly isn't," I agreed.

John L. slid his chair away from the table and clasped his hands behind his head. "Hell, if anything that nigger's foolhearty, the way he drives them fast cars and runs with them women and drinks all the time. I hear"—he laughed—"that he got arrested a couple of months ago up in New York for hittin' a barkeep who tried to serve him beer instead of wine."

"It's true," I said. "I live in New York." All evening long I'd had the vague sense that John L. did not quite know who I was.

"Hell no," he said, shaking his head slowly, "that nigger ain't yellow." He paused and reflected for a moment. "Fact is, that nigger reminds me of me."

I am not a light sleeper, but I had my problems that night in the men's room of the Golden Hotel. The fellow in the other cot, a reporter for the Denver *Dispatch,* was the loudest snorer I'd ever encountered, and every time I was at last about to drop off, someone would stagger in drunk, wanting to use the facilities. Almost seventy years later, it still saddens me to report that, when I awoke, the contents of several men's stomachs were stagnating beneath my cot.

It was, you will understand, a considerable relief to go outside and attach myself to the throng on Centre Street which, after having dissolved around midnight the night before, had magically reconstituted itself at eight that morning. The betting was even heavier than it had been the previous afternoon; runners were everywhere calling out their odds, which had abruptly jumped to two-to-one for Jeffries. The reason for this, I was informed by a small man carrying a wicker cane, was the information that George Little, until two weeks before Johnson's manager, was betting heavily against him. "The word is that the fix is in for sure," said the man with the cane. "Little knows something, or he wouldn't be throwing money around like that." He snickered. "Seems like the only ones betting on Johnson are the porters coming in with the trains."

The report seemed solid enough for me to lay down ten dollars, a full day's expense money, on Jeff.

At twelve-thirty, the appointed hour, I wandered back over to the Golden and took the new Otis Elevator up to Sullivan's room on the top floor. Arthur Gillette opened the door, and he made it clear that he was not pleased to see me. But John L. was plainly delighted by my arrival. "Hey, young fella," he called, waving at me, "c'mon over here." He patted the edge of his soft bed, in which he was sitting upright, finishing off what he assured me had been a pile of fourteen flapjacks.

I obliged. "Good morning, sir."

Gillette, from a straight-backed chair in the corner, eyed us with irritation. "We'd better go. We're expected at Moana Springs in half an hour."

The day's agenda, it seemed, called for the former champion to visit the opposing camps—first Jeffries' at Moana Springs, then Johnson's, up the road at the Willows—as the basis of a last-minute report on the attitudes of the contenders.

John L. slowly began shifting himself toward the edge of the bed. "All right, then," he announced, "I'm ready to do my duty." Maneuvering around me, he stepped to the floor and, in a quick, surprisingly fluid motion, whisked off his nightshirt, leaving him momentarily clad in the largest pair of striped shorts I'd ever seen. But an instant later he covered these with enormous pants, and then, in rapid succession, he donned his shirt, jacket and cap. Then, assuming a seat beside me on the bed, he yanked on his socks and shoes. "All right," he proclaimed, "let us depart."

Gillette looked at him as if he'd just defecated on the floor. "Aren't you going to wash up? Or shave?"

John L. shot him a withering glance. "For that bastard Corbett?

Not likely!" But he snatched up his shaving bowl and razor and moved out of the room toward the bathroom.

In the La Salle, heading toward Moana Springs, there was silence; Gillette, at the wheel, continually looked back at me with disgust, evidently hoping that his displeasure might persuade me to disappear. John L. sat beside him, staring straight ahead, mulling over his impending meeting with James J. Corbett.

It was a confrontation he did not relish. Their feud had been going on for more than twenty years, since the time when John L. had been the champion and Corbett an arrogant challenger, and it had been distinguished by several celebrated public incidents; there had been the time that Sullivan, who made a point of referring to the dapper Corbett as "that sissy," had agreed to meet him in an exhibition, and then at the last minute stipulated that the bout had to be fought in white tie and tails; and the time John L. had suggested a private meeting, ostensibly to effect a reconciliation, and then tried to break his rival's hand when he shook it; and the time that Corbett spotted John L. soused in a San Francisco tavern and sent for a policeman to have him arrested for drunk and disorderly.

But when we arrived at Moana Springs, a resort compound built to take advantage of the adjacent hot springs, we found Corbett in a conciliatory mood. He hurried over to the La Salle, a hand extended to Sullivan. "Welcome, John. Thank you for coming."

John L. took it fleetingly, and nodded.

This was the first time I'd seen Jim Corbett, and his appearance, too, was something of a surprise. With his lean frame and handsome face, topped by jet black hair fashioned into a famous pompadour, Corbett had, in his day, been something of a matinee idol. When, as champion, he'd toured in the play *Gentleman Jim,* his name had been linked with a dozen actresses, including the great Lillie Langtry, and he had ultimately satisfied the nation's storybook expectations by marrying the beautiful Vera Stanhope.

But Corbett could hardly pass for dashing anymore; he had a bit of a belly on him and, though his pompadour was intact, the face beneath it was leathery and deeply lined.

John L. nudged me with an elbow and nodded toward Corbett. "Must be touchin' up that head, eh?"

But Corbett refused to bite. "John," he said, drawing him aside, "let's have no quarrelling today. This is a time for men of our race to stand together."

Sullivan pulled away. "Where's Jeff?"

"Fishing. He's up at Wheeler's Lake, going for black bass. There's nothing more to be done on training, so I gave him the day off." He paused. "You can tell your readers he's in as good a condition as any man who ever entered a ring."

Gillette, standing nearby, wrote it down.

"I'll tell my readers what I damn please," snapped Sullivan.

Corbett smiled uneasily. "Would you like to see the camp, John?" He placed a tentative hand on the huge man's shoulder. "We've got amazing facilities, better than anything they had in our day."

Reluctantly at first, John L. allowed himself to be led around the camp. The training facilities truly were wondrous; a complete boxing ring, a dozen light and heavy bags, a fully stocked weight room, a medical compound, a handball court. For living quarters, the boxer and his staff had taken over a large Tudor cottage, ordinarily occupied by wealthy vacationers. Sullivan took it all in with mounting awe, his hostility toward his guide slowly dissipating. Corbett had more than a little to do with that, since every time they chanced upon one of the camp's employees, he introduced his guest as "my friend John L. Sullivan, the greatest of them all."

John L. was especially pleased to encounter, sitting on a stool in one of the far recesses of the cottage, strumming the jaunty "All Coons Look Alike to Me" on a banjo, the well-known vaudeville comedian Walter Kelly. Kelly (whose niece would one day be the Princess of Monaco) had been hired by Corbett to keep the camp loose, and he was delighted to hear that John L. knew of his work.

"I saw you in Boston," said the former champion. "You did that skit about the nigger in the courtroom."

Kelly nodded graciously. "It's called 'The Virginia Judge.'" He paused, then slipped into character. "But yo' honor, ah couldn't a don' took dat auto-mo-beeel, cos I'se jes a li'l fella an' das a big macheeeeeen!"

John L. roared. "That's it, all right," he gasped, wiping the tears from his eyes. "That's the one."

The conviviality was such that Corbett was moved to suggest that he and John L. pose, in fighting stance, before the motion picture camera that Rickard had stationed at the camp. A film was to be made of the bout, the promoter and the fighters to divide the proceeds, and Rickard wanted plenty of footage of both camps. "We're gonna need this film," smiled Corbett. "If Jeff knocks out the nigger as fast as I think he will, there won't be enough fight to last 'til intermission."

The two of them were sparring playfully before the camera, John L. poking and feinting with surprising agility, when a soft voice intruded on the scene. "Maybe you two oughta be doing the fighting tomorrow instead of me."

And there, suddenly, was Jim Jeffries. In the flesh, standing there in coveralls, a fishing pole in one hand, a pail of fish in the other, he looked less like a superman than an overgrown version of Huck Finn. John L. wheeled to face him. "Why hello, Jeff."

Jeffries put down his pail and shook John L.'s hand. "Pleased to have you here, Mr. Sullivan."

"Yeah, well here I am." He paused. "So tell me, Jeff," he added, adopting the weighty tone favored by journalists in Reno that week, "how do you feel for the fight?" Gillette edged in close.

"Good. Real good."

"He's in the best shape he's ever been in," interjected Corbett, "aren't you, Jim?"

"Yes sir, I am."

Corbett noted the intensity of Gillette's scribbling. "You want a quote? Write that Jeff says you can count on him to do the trick tomorrow. He knows he's going to lick this fellow." He turned to Jeffries. "Isn't that what you told me?"

"Yes sir, it is." But there was a decided lack of conviction in this. Jeffries turned back to Sullivan. "Have you been to Johnson's camp yet?"

John L. shook his head. "We're going there next."

Jeff hesitated. "Well, let me ask you something. How would you have fought this nigger?"

Sullivan was somewhat taken aback by the question. "I guess it's kinda late to be wonderin'."

"We know how to fight him," said Corbett. "All we have to do is bore in and he'll run. That nigger's yellow. We know it, and tomorrow Jeff's going to prove it."

The silence that followed this declaration was oppressive. Corbett finally broke it himself. "Hey, Jim, how about a game of hearts?" The game was the fighter's favorite.

So they repaired to a table set up on the lawn and began to play, with Farmer Burns, one of Jeff's trainers, joining the fighters as a fourth. For ten minutes the game proceeded without incident, Gillette, myself and several members of the camp standing behind the players surveying the goings-on.

But suddenly, visibly, Jeffries tensed; we all turned to him, then immediately to the man upon whom he had fixed his gaze. That gaze was so full of malice that it would have instantly set most men to trembling, but this man simply stared back at him. He was, I realized after a moment, Stanley Ketchel, the middleweight champion of the world. He had approached our group so quietly that none of us had even been aware of his presence.

"I don't want you here," said Jeffries finally, his tone as cold as his stare. "You've been fooling around with that nigger and you don't belong here."

Ketchel, a pleasant enough-looking fellow who indeed had been serving as one of Johnson's sparring partners, shuffled a bit but did not move. Jeffries looked at him a moment longer, then turned to Farmer Burns. "Put that fellow out."

Burns rose, grabbed Ketchel by the shoulder and led him, without resistance, past the cottage and toward the gate. But Jeffries remained agitated. "Enough of this game," he said with finality, tossing his cards on the table.

John L. struggled up out of his chair. "Well, we should be goin' anyhow. We've got to get over to the Willows." He started moving toward the cottage.

Corbett hurried over to his side. "Wait, John, before you go I'd like to ask you something." He smiled as warmly as he knew how which, I must say, was not terribly warmly. "Will you drink a toast of good luck to Jeff?"

Sullivan stopped in his tracks. "No, I'm sorry." He looked at his old rival and sensed that his words were being misunderstood. "I'd like to, understand, but we're in a hurry."

"Please, John, just a quick one." He paused and looked into John L.'s eyes. "Please, it'll buck the boy up."

Sullivan hesitated, embarrassed to acknowledge to this of all men the reason for his abstinence. "Oh, what the hell," he bellowed, throwing out his arms, "just one."

So Corbett ordered Burns to fetch a decanter of bourbon and three glasses from the cottage, and there, on the lawn, the three former heavyweight champions held their glasses aloft. "To Jim Jeffries," said Corbett, "who tomorrow will earn the gratitude of the entire white race."

Sullivan moved the glass slowly to his lips and took a tentative sip. He washed the liquid back and forth over his tongue before swallowing. Then he turned the glass over and downed its contents in a gulp.

He patted his huge belly. "Ah, that hits the spot." He turned to Jeffries. "Do you want another, Jeff?"

He shook his head. "No, I've got a fight tomorrow."

"How about you, Mr. Corbett?"

Corbett smiled. "No thank you, John."

Sullivan reached for the decanter, sitting on the table. "Well, I guess I will."

By the time we got on the road again it was late afternoon and John L. was in high spirits. "Goddamn sonovabitch," he kept repeating, "I can lick any of 'em." But when we were in sight of Johnson's camp at the Willows, could see the oil lamps burning in the windows, he suddenly straightened up in his seat and regained his composure. Indeed, when we entered the building, a ramshackle wooden structure known to the locals by the less pretentious title "Rick's Roadhouse," Sullivan marched up the stairs with the rigid solemnity of an undertaker.

The champion himself answered our knock at the door. "Hey, Captain John," he exclaimed, "real good to see you. Real good!"

John L. nodded gravely. "Charmed."

He was a striking figure, this Johnson, in his way more impressive even than Jeffries. He wasn't nearly so massive, but he carried himself like a great cat, with that same magical combination of dignity and grace. He was dressed this evening, as most evenings, in formal wear, a black suit and white linen; with his shiny bald head and gold-headed cane, he looked like an ebony Daddy Warbucks.

He ushered us into the chamber, bare except for a double bed, a dresser and one stuffed chair in the corner, into which John L. instantly collapsed.

Johnson flashed his famous golden smile. "Where you been at?" Sullivan jerked a thumb over his shoulder, like a hitchhiker.

"We've just come from Moana Springs," said Gillette.

Johnson nodded. "Ahhh," he said, as if that explained everything. He turned to the window and, leaning on the sill, stared out at the sunset, burning a brilliant amethyst against the bright blue of the desert sky. "I like it here," he said to no one in particular. "It's pretty."

I was surprised at how well-spoken Johnson was; the press had always had him speaking in rural negro dialect. But in the dark, he might almost have been taken for white.

Gillette cleared his throat theatrically. "Excuse me, Mr. Johnson, we're under deadline. Could we ask you a few questions?"

Johnson turned and faced him. "Who are you?"

Gillette paled slightly. "My name is Arthur Gillette, from *The New York Times*." He paused. "I work with Mr. Sullivan."

The champion glanced at John L., who blinked. "He's my 'sistant."

Johnson smiled. "I see. What do you want to know?"

"How d'you feel?" interjected John L. Gillette glanced at him with annoyance.

"Captain John," said Johnson, "I feel as good as I ever felt in my life."

Sullivan nodded meaningfully, indicating that he was satisfied, we could all go home.

But Gillette pressed on. "What did you do today?"

"I ran eight miles. That was all the training. Then I drove to Reno. I just got back a little while ago."

Gillette scribbled furiously. "What did you have for dinner?"

"Five porkchops."

"Do you have any statement to make on the fight?"

The black man took a seat on the edge of the bed. "Did Jeffries have anything to say?"

"Said he was gonna win," slurred Sullivan.

Gillette ignored him and flipped back through his notebook. "He said 'You can count on me to do the trick. I know I'm going to get this fellow.' "

Sullivan snorted. "That's what I said!"

"I'll give you something better," said Johnson. "Put down for me" —he thought for a moment, then dictated slowly—"I am going to win tomorrow and I feel so darn good over it that I'm just like a kid on Christmas morning." He paused. "That good enough?"

"Fine." Gillette rose and started heading from the room, then stopped. "Hey,"—this to me—"can you get the old man home all right?"

John L. turned to him, eyes ablaze. "Don't you worry, you sonovabitch, I'll get myself home."

"You can use my car," offered Johnson, smiling.

Gillette, as embarrassed as he was angry, said nothing, just turned and rushed out the door.

That left just the three of us in the rapidly darkening room. A minute passed. John L.'s chin, I noticed, had drifted down to his chest. I looked at Johnson, not knowing what to say, studying his profile in the window frame.

Mercifully, he broke the silence. "Let's go downstairs. You fellows look like you could use some partyin'."

It turned out there was a party in full swing just fifty yards away, in the tap room on the other side of the roadhouse. It included, I noted almost as soon as we entered, the most stunning collection of women I'd ever seen gathered in one place. "Who are they all?" I whispered to Johnson.

Even in the semi-darkness his teeth gleamed. "They're the 'divorced ladies.' " He waved a hand at the dozen or so beauties scattered around the large room, drinking champagne, talking to the male members of his retinue (among them, I noted, Stanley Ketchel). "They gotta do somethin' while they're waitin' for their divorce papers to come through."

At our appearance one of the women, a lithe creature with pale blond hair, ran over to his side. "All except this one," he demurred. "This is Mrs. Johnson."

I knew this not to be true. For weeks, the champion had been identifying each of a pair of blonds as his wife, and the members of the press, apparently unable to tell them apart, had faithfully referred to both as "Mrs. Johnson." One of them, Etta Duryea, would eventually achieve that distinction, but it was the other woman, Belle Schreiber, who stood before us now. John L. studied her with undisguised appreciation.

"Come, baby," she said to Johnson, "let me get you some champagne."

He pecked her on the forehead. "That's sweet, Mama, but not tonight. Tomorrow is *the* day." He glanced at John L., who was unable to take his eyes off her. "But why don't you take care of Mr. John L. Sullivan here. I'm sure he wants some."

She smiled, took Sullivan's arm and began leading him toward the bar. He followed her without a word.

Johnson looked after them. "That man looks like he could use a woman." Then he strode over to the player piano, rattling out "Oh You Beautiful Doll," and, with a finger to his lips, halted the fellow pumping it. Every eye in the room turned toward him.

"Ladies and gentlemen," he intoned, "in honor of tomorrow's"— he searched for the precise word—"festivities, I would like to play for you this evening a few numbers from my vaudeville act with Mr. Hammerstein."

This proclamation was met by raucous cheers from his staff and discreet, almost inaudible clapping of white-gloved hands from the ladies. Johnson rushed over to the corner, snatched up the bass viol of which he was known to be inordinately proud and, assuming a seat in the front of the room, began to play. The song was "By the Light of the Silvery Moon."

After several bars, he looked up at the crowd and grinned. "Some people think that paying a nigger prizefighter twenty-five hundred dollars a week to do this is too much. But did any of you folks ever see that play that Jim Jeffries used to put on when he was champ?"

"I did," called out one of Johnson's sparring parters. "It was about Davy Crockett."

"That's right," said Johnson. "He was up there in a coonskin cap, runnin' around so much you didn't know what was goin' on. And in the last part, big Jeff was romancin' an itsy-bitsy little girl—she couldn't of been more than ninety pounds—and he was clinchin' her so hard we in the audience thought he was gonna kill her." The crowd laughed loudly. "So next to that, this is *talent.*"

Johnson completed the song, then swung directly into another, "I Love My Wife, But Oh You Kid." It was a lively number which Johnson played with commendable gusto, and we were all enjoying it immensely. But suddenly, in the center of the room, there was John L., whirling around in circles with Belle Schreiber. They moved so rapidly, and the disparity in the sizes was so great, that he whisked her about like a rag doll. I'm not even certain her participation was voluntary; for a split second I caught her eye, and what I saw there was blind terror.

In an instant the crowd had gathered around them, shouting John L. on, urging Johnson to play even faster. He obliged, and soon Sullivan, unable to keep the pace, was perspiring and wheezing loudly. Finally he released Belle and began tottering back toward the bar. I ran over, cutting him off. Taking his large arm, I led him outside to the porch and deposited him gingerly in a wicker chair.

"Here, sir," I said, "why don't you take some air?"

He opened his eyes and looked at me. "Thank you, son. That's nice of you." Then he closed them again.

I returned to the party, where Johnson was still playing his viol. The tune this time was "Beautiful Dreamer," and he played it very slowly, as if it were a dirge. When it was over, he rose to his feet and, ignoring scattered appeals that he continue, placed the instrument back in the corner. "No time now," he said, heading out of the room, "there's a couple of other things to think about."

I lingered behind, watching the people in the room, the women, whom I was too timid to consider speaking to, and the men, who evinced no interest whatever in me. A good number of them, I noticed, were carrying long-barrelled guns in their belts. A few minutes later, leaving the room to check on John L., I caught sight of a singularly unsavory-looking character leaning against the bannister, holding what I took to be a double-barrelled shotgun.

I was surprised to discover Johnson on the porch, bent over John L., speaking to him softly, gently, as if he were an enormous baby. When he saw me he quickly rose. "You'd best get him home," he said. "I'll be needin' my rest."

I hesitated. "I saw your man with the shotgun in there."

Johnson nodded. "That's Cal McVey. Used to be a pretty good catcher in the National League."

"Do you really have to keep all those guns around?"

He laughed aloud. "Hell, boy, when we were trainin' in San Francisco, someone tried to poison me. They got one of my people instead. Now the talk is that someone is gonna shoot me." He shook his head. "I may be a dumb nigger, but I ain't ready to die, not yet."

He looked at John L. "Now, you'd best hurry with him. I already sent for my car."

I nudged the huge man on the shoulder. "Come on, Mr. Sullivan. We're going home now."

He swivelled his head and looked at me with a dazed smile. "He saw me fight," he said. "He saw me fight Paddy Ryan."

Johnson laughed. "Yeah, when I was a boy I saw him fight in Mississippi. That man was somethin' special, all right."

The car, a shiny Pierce-Arrow, appeared on the dirt road a hundred feet in front of us. I succeeded in raising John L. to his feet. "C'mon, Mr. Sullivan," I said, "we've got to walk down a little flight of steps here."

Johnson grinned at me. "I hope the *Times* is payin' you good for this."

"Oh," I called back, "I'm not with the *Times*, I'm with the *Journal*. I'm just covering Mr. Sullivan."

We had reached the bottom of the steps, but Sullivan was leaning heavily against me, barely able to stand. I paused for breath.

"Yeah?" said Johnson, intrigued. "What are you gonna write about the old man, that he got plastered?"

I looked at John L. his cap askew, his eyes half-closed, his noble mouth hanging agape. "Oh, hell, I don't know."

The next day, Independence Day, 1910—Fight Day—I arose early and hurried out to the arena, twenty minutes by foot from downtown Reno. Though it was five hours 'til fight time, and the doors would not officially open for another two, several thousand people already lingered outside the great wood structure.

Among them were the omnipresent runners, shouting out their odds, still two-to-one for the white man. I grabbed the first one that ventured near me and pressed a five-dollar bill into his hand. "For Johnson," I said.

"A fiver on the nigger," he nodded, noting the transaction on a pad of paper. He handed me a receipt.

My bet of the previous day thus effectively cancelled, I squeezed my way through the crowd toward one of the entrances to the stadium. It was guarded by a young man about my age in cowboy garb, one of the several hundred men deputized for the day by Governor Dickerson. A six-gun hung conspicuously from his belt.

"Doors open at eleven," he drawled when I was within five feet.

"Press," I said, reaching inside my jacket for my *Journal* card.

In a split second his gun was drawn, its long barrel aimed at my nose. "Don't touch that revolver!" he ordered.

I blanched. "No, no, you're making a mistake. There's no revolver." Slowly, I swung open my jacket. "See? I just wanted my newspaper card."

He lowered the gun slightly, so it was aimed instead at my stomach.

"My press card," I said. "Here, get it yourself." Cautiously he reached into my inside pocket and withdrew the card. He studied it intently.

"See? It shows I'm from the New York *Evening Journal*."

He dropped his gun and started to blush, the first person I'd met in Reno to be impressed by the card. "I'm sorry, sir. Go right in."

There was but one other person in the entire arena, a solitary figure in black sitting in the first row of the press section. On approaching, I discovered it was Bat Masterson.

"Hey, there," he said, rising to greet me. "You decided to beat the crush, too?"

I nodded. "Yes, sir."

He took a puff on his long, crooked stogie. "Smart boy, smart boy." He was, I observed, wearing a "Jeff, oh you kid" button. "Did you bring anything along to pass the time?" he asked. "The only thing I could find in my hotel room was this." He held up the current issue of *The Boy's Home Companion*. "Not bad, though. I'm readin' an article now on this new boy Jackson with the Cleveland club. He's leadin' the league in hittin', you know."

"Joe Jackson?" The name rang only the faintest of bells. The doomed Jackson was as new to his dirty business as I was to mine.

"That's the one." He laughed. "Only they call him 'Shoeless.'

That's 'cause he's supposed to be such a rube." He closed his magazine, leaned back and stretched. "Looks like it's gonna be a real hot one today, don' it? Bad for the fighters."

"Yes. And not too comfortable for us either, I guess."

Masterson scanned the rows and rows of empty benches. "Yeah. I hope the heat don' cause no short tempers."

"Do you really think there's a possibility of violence?"

"A possibility?" He grinned at the word. "Fella, at the Jeffries-Fitzsimmons fight in Carson City, me and Wyatt Earp checked everyone who came into that arena for a gun and we collected four hundred of 'em. They'll get at least twice as many today, and they won't catch half of 'em."

"Really?" I said, dumbly.

"Fella," Masterson continued, "I never in my life seen such a collection of low-life as they got in this town for this fight. In the last twenty-four hours alone, I ran into two of the best bank robbers in the whole country, Cincinnati Slim and that fella they call the Sundance Kid. I'm told they even got a Chinaman named Won Let all the way from Frisco; he's the executioner for the Hip Sing Tong, kills fellas with a hatchet. Not to mention every two-bit pickpocket in the country." He paused and patted his chest. "I got all my money taped right in here, every cent that ain't ridin' on the big fella. I figure all that trash didn't come here for the pleasure of watchin' a fight."

I myself had noticed several abandoned billfolds in the gutters along Commercial Row, but I hadn't known things were that bad. "That's awful," I said.

He puffed his cigar and shrugged. "It may be awful, but it's life." He paused. "If someone plugs the nigger in the ring," he mused, "I wonder if I collect on Jeff. What d'you think?"

"I have no idea."

He returned to his magazine. I turned to examine the slowly filling press section for familiar faces; the only one I noticed was Gillette's several rows behind us, but he studiously avoided my eye.

When the arena was at last opened to the public, the people entered in a rush, streaming down the aisles of the tiered stadium, clambering up and down the pine benches. In ten minutes, two thirds of the eighteen thousand seats in the place were occupied.

To my surprise, there were a fair number of women in the crowd. Rickard had thoughtfully provided a number of small boxes, shrouded by curtains, for the "divorced ladies," but in addition to these, hundreds of females sat on the stark wood planks, ordinary paying customers.

It was an unusually high-spirited crowd, a crowd more keenly charged up about the event at hand than any I'd ever seen. Even when a group of spectators objected to the presence of one of the two motion picture platforms, maintaining that it obstructed their view of the ring, the protest was entirely good-humored, and when Rickard ordered the platform dismantled, he received a five-minute ovation.

The most subdued section in the arena, as these things invariably go, was that holding the press, but even my colleagues displayed respect for the magnitude of the event; they were, almost three hundred of them, in their places a full hour before the scheduled start of the fight. All except John L. Sullivan.

I had been expecting the big man ever since one o'clock, the hour on which we had agreed the night before, after I'd tucked him into bed, to rendezvous at ringside. I had saved a pair of seats for him. But it was now well past two. I edged my way back to where Gillette sat, staring ahead into space.

"Hey there, Arthur," I said, "have you seen Mr. Sullivan this morning?"

He acknowledged me with a curt nod. "Why would I do that?"

"Well, you *are* working together."

He turned and looked at me with unveiled hostility. "I thought you were doing his baby-sitting now."

"Well, he's not here, and I'm getting a bit worried. Why don't we run over to his room?"

Gillette shook his head emphatically. "The fight's less than an hour away. You go if you want."

"Arthur, he's from your paper."

"I don't give a darn. I wash my hands of him."

When I returned to my seat, Masterson looked away from the ring, where a brass band was booming out patriotic marches, and noticed my distress. "What is it, fella?"

I explained about John L.

"Well, damn, let's go get him. They're gonna introduce all the former champions from the ring before the fight!"

Making certain our seats would be watched, we dashed out of the arena and ran—trotted, with an occasional interval of rapid walking, to be more accurate—all the way back to the Golden. We ignored the Otis Elevator, as agonizingly lethargic as it was stately, and climbed the stairs two at a time. The door to Sullivan's room was unlocked.

"Oh God," I exclaimed.

John L. was still in bed, his body a mountain beneath the covers, his head completely hidden by pillows. The story of his evening— two empty bottles of James E. Pepper—"Born with the Republic" —lay on the floor beneath his night table. The contents of a third formed a puddle beneath his bed.

"C'mon," said Masterson, "let's get him up."

While Bat rummaged through his trunk, searching for clothes appropriate to the occasion, I attempted to rouse the former champion; I nudged him, nudged him harder, then slapped him; finally I took a glassful of water from his washbasin and tossed it in his face. He blinked, snorted, and descended once again into a comatose state.

Masterson had found what he wanted, a somber three-piece suit.

"Well?" he said.

"I can't get him up."

"Damn, we'll just have to dress him as he is."

Slowly, we maneuvered John L. to the edge of the bed. For convenience, we decided to leave his nightshirt on, placing the pants, vest and jacket over it. We then yanked on his socks and shoes and, each of us taking a limp arm, dragged him to the elevator.

"How," I asked, down in the lobby, "are we ever going to get him to the arena?" We had noted on our dash downtown that the road to the stadium was clogged with automobiles and buggies, though the only remaining tickets were being peddled by speculators for two and three hundred dollars apiece.

"Horseback," said Masterson. "Wait here, I know the fella at the livery stable." He paused. "You do ride, don't you?"

"Yes," I lied, for there seemed to be no other alternative.

Getting John L.'s dead weight into a saddle was no mean task. It took four of us, the livery stable man and a Golden desk clerk, in addition to us, to hoist him up, and then one man had to stand on each side, preventing him from toppling off, as Masterson expertly mounted the horse from behind. I then boarded my animal, a huge black thing with angry eyes, and we set off. Even with his three hundred and fifty pound handicap, Masterson travelled so rapidly I was barely able to keep him in sight.

The moment of our arrival was opportune; the brass band in the ring was in the midst of "The Star Spangled Banner," and the crowd was turned in four different directions, facing the flags hanging limply over each of the four entrances. We thus caused comparatively little stir, despite the clatter every time John L.'s shoes hit another step as we headed down toward the press section. By the time we at last had John L. in his place, face forward against the long table intended for notepads, we were both spent.

But our respite was only momentary. As soon as the brass band had been cleared from the ring, the introductions of past fighters began, and the first of these was for John L. Sullivan. "At ringside today," intoned announcer Billy Jordan through a huge megaphone, "we have the most noble gladiator who ever strode the earth. Ladies and gentlemen, the Boston Strong Boy himself, John L. Sullivan!" Masterson and I each took up one of John L.'s arms and, like amateur puppeteers, raised them in the air in acknowledgment of the loud ovation. I realized, too late, that while his arms bobbed in the air, his head was hanging precariously forward, giving the impression to those in the vicinity that we were manhandling a corpse.

When the applause subsided, we gratefully replaced him in his former position, and the program continued; Corbett, in a white linen shirt rolled up to the elbows, was introduced; then "Ruby" Bob Fitzsimmons, who'd succeeded him as champion, then Marvin Hart, and after him, Tommy Burns, from whom Johnson had taken the title. Every man who had ever held the heavyweight championship was in attendance that afternoon.

But there was no time to dwell on portentous facts, for the moment the last champion had been announced, another roar shook the arena, this one far greater than any that had preceded it. I looked up and saw that both fighters were approaching the ring simultaneously, from opposite directions. Each was accompanied by an entourage of six.

Johnson entered the ring first, a striking figure in a black and white, velvet-lined bathrobe. He shuffled about the ring, testing the footing, bobbing, hitting at the air.

He turned his back when Jeffries, appearing more massive than ever on the raised platform, stepped into the ring. The white man was curiously dressed, in a bulky gray suit and gray golf cap, but he soon removed these with a series of vicious yanks, and stood, in a pair of tights of an incongruously gay purple color, staring sullenly across the ring at his opponent. Only when Jeffries began stomping the floor like an enraged bull, testing it for solidity, did the black man turn around, and then he gazed at Jeff with a bemused grin that seemed to mock the show of ferocity. Johnson too removed his robe, revealing a conventional pair of black trunks, and the fighters met in the ring with Rickard, who had agreed to serve as referee.

Then, quite suddenly, before any of us really had time to prepare for it, the bout was under way. I shook John L. violently. "Mr. Sullivan, the fight is on!" But he didn't stir.

In the ring, the fighters measured each other, Jeffries plodding forward in his crouch, Johnson feinting and moving away. So this was it, the event on which our lives had hung for weeks; it was, after all, nothing more than a prizefight.

And not, at the beginning, even a very stirring one. In the early rounds, Jeff shot an occasional right to the black man's body, each greeted by a cheer from the crowd, but Johnson's grin made it apparent they were ineffective. The most active figure in the vicinity of the ring in the early going was, in fact, Jim Corbett, who jumped up and down in his corner streaming abuse on Johnson. "You're yellow, nigger. It's showing now, you're yellow. Look at you run. Fight, nigger, this is supposed to be a fight!"

Johnson didn't respond at all until late in the second round when, abruptly, he stopped moving, turned to Corbett and smiled broadly, displaying all his gold. "You just hold on now, Mr. Jim, you'll get your fight."

In the third round, Johnson began to deliver; with a sudden brazenness he moved in close to the white man and shot jabs to his head. Jeffries, surprised, lunged forward and missed a couple of roundhouse rights. His opponent laughed, and responded with more jabs. Toward the end of the round, Johnson moved directly above us and looked out at Sullivan, draped forward on the table. "Wake up, Captain John, you're gonna miss *history!*"

That he was. From that point on, Johnson hit Jeffries at will, while his famous defense left him virtually untouched. I've never seen another fighter who could anticipate punches the way Jack Johnson could, and head them off so effectively. His defensive style has been likened to an outfielder snatching fly balls out of the air; he'd sense a punch coming, then snap a jab at the arm delivering it, cutting it down in midair.

By the eighth round, even Jeffries' most rabid partisans sensed the drift of the fight. During the action, Masterson, who earlier had been on his feet every time the white man had landed even a feeble blow, leaned over John L.'s prostrate form and looked at me, his thin face the picture of sadness. "What do you suppose the odds are on Johnson?" he asked.

I looked at the runners, still dashing around the arena taking bets. "They must be pretty heavy at this point."

It turned out, upon inquiry, that they were two-to-one on the black man, and rising rapidly; a great many other Jeffries bettors had also elected to hedge their bets. By the eleventh, the odds against Jeffries winning would be so great that the bookmakers would stop accepting bets entirely.

Jeffries, at first confused by Johnson's style, soon became desperate. He lunged, missed, lunged again. Johnson, parrying the thrusts with the ease of a veteran matador dodging a baby bull, finally just stood back and ridiculed him. "What you *doin'*, Mr. Jeff? Is that all you got? This is for the champeeenship!"

Jeff, pouring sweat from every pore of his massive body, said nothing, just kept coming, but he kept coming more and more slowly.

As his man visibly tired, Corbett's verbal assaults increased in intensity, as if he could thus compensate for Jeff's physical shortcomings. "You're *yellow*, nigger," he screamed, his face crimson, the muscles standing out on his neck. "*Yellow! You stink, nigger!!*"

But Corbett wasn't doing his man any good. With every new barrage of epithets, Johnson would simply pepper Jeff's face, already bloated, with blood gushing out of a deep gash beneath his right eye, with more blows. In the tenth, after Corbett made a particularly unkind reference to Mrs. Tiny Johnson, Jack's mother, the black man half-clinched, half-carried the exhausted Jeffries toward his irate manager. "That's fine, Mr. Jim," he said, smiling, "but where do you want me to put this?"

But even as he moved inexorably toward the pinnacle of his career, Johnson was aware of the hostility of the crowd. It was as sullen a mob as I've ever seen, a mob that felt victimized emotionally as well as financially. And Johnson could doubtless see the many bottles of James E. Pepper whiskey being passed from hand to hand among the silent men at ringside.

Following the tenth round, he dispatched one of his aides from the stadium, and the fellow came running back ten minutes later accompanied by the man I knew to be the local stationmaster for the Union Pacific; I later learned that Johnson was providing for a train to be available to make a hasty departure after the fight.

Quite obviously, the end was rapidly approaching. By the thirteenth, Jeff's movements were so lugubrious that it became doubtful whether he could last twenty rounds, let alone the scheduled forty-five. Indeed, there was general agreement among the press corps that Johnson could put him away any time he chose.

The black man seemed to agree. During the fourteenth, he positioned himself above the telegraph operators and commenced dictating their stories to them. "The Fight of the Century is over," he announced. "White hope Jim Jeffries has been outfought, outclassed and,"—he grinned in the direction of Corbett, sitting dejectedly on his stool—"outmanaged by Jack Johnson, the well-known nigger." With that he stepped forward and delivered three quick blows to Jeffries' face, completely bathed in blood now, and distorted almost beyond recognition.

"It's no good," Jeff mumbled to Corbett as he staggered back to his corner after the round, "I couldn't come back." They were the first words he'd spoken during the contest.

In the fifteenth, mercifully, Johnson elected to end it. He met the white man, toe to toe, in the center of the ring and hit him again and again and again, until Jeff stumbled backward like a drunken man and pitched forward onto his knees.

"Stop it," yelled a hundred voices in the crowd. "Don't let the nigger knock him out!"

But Jeffries forced himself up at the count of nine. His opponent was instantly upon him, smashing him full in the face with a hard left. Jeff crashed into the ropes right above us, and somehow ended up hanging out between the second and third strands. Several newsmen, Masterson among them, jumped to their feet and pushed him back in; Johnson accepted this infraction of the rules with a sardonic grin. As Jeffries came reeling toward him once again, he belted him with a right to the ear, then a left to the face. That did it; Jeff sank slowly to the ground, as if he'd been shot, and remained there, motionless. In an instant, not wanting him to be counted out, Jeff's handlers were in the ring, dragging him to his corner.

Suddenly there was pandemonium. Johnson allowed his arm to be raised, then, glancing quickly around at the throng, already on their feet, he bolted from the ring like a fullback bursting through a line, knocking aside more than a few spectators in his rush for the exit. A moment later the ring itself was besieged by fans; souvenir hunters would eventually dismantle and cart away the entire structure, the first time such organized destruction ever occurred in a sporting arena. In his corner, Corbett caught a whiff of the building frenzy, and ordered that his man, still unable to stand, be dragged from the ring. It turned out that Johnson's instincts had been deadly accurate; already the cries of "Get the nigger!" "Where'd the nigger go?" filled the arena, and the scent of blood would grow stronger into the night, not only here, but around the nation; eventually fourteen people would die in racial clashes, prompting Rickard to vow never again to promote a fight between a white man and a black man. And in his long career, he never again would.

In the midst of the chaos, John L. Sullivan abruptly started, as if an electric current had run through him. He raised his noble old head and looked about him with bloodshot eyes. "What the hell is going on?"

"It's all over," said Masterson softly, "the nigger won."

John L. was momentarily baffled by this information, then the sure light of knowledge dawned in his eyes. "Well, then," he boomed, "long live the nigger!" Laboriously he raised his hand and a pudgy finger etched the air. "Yours truly, John L. Sullivan."

Why I Am Writing This

by George D. Weaver

Chicago, Nov. 25, 1944

Well, guess what, I just found out that old Judge Landis kicked the bucket. Heart attack. The man on the radio says the old gent worked so hard on his Victory Garden, growing cabbages for the boys overseas and all, that his old ticker just gave up on him.

Personally, I believe this information to be propaganda. The way I dope out the situation, they just thought it would sound good, for the war effort and all, to put it in those particular terms. After all, it wouldn't impress hardly no one to say that Kenesaw Mountain Landis, commissioner of baseball of the world, just dropped off in his own bed, even though he was old. Everyone knows how he sent all those Wobblies off to jail for obstructing the war effort during the First War. What the hell better way could he do his bit this time except by dying?

That last part was meant as a joke, in case you didn't get it. I'm not really so glad that he died. I don't say I'm sorry, but I'm not so glad either. That's exactly what I told my wife Helen when we heard the news on the radio. We were right here in the parlor together when it came up in the broadcast and she just looked at me with big eyes. Helen knows me pretty good after all this time, that's why she didn't say nothing. So after a minute I said "Well, what about it?" And she still didn't say nothing, but she was looking at me like *I* killed him or something. So I said "I'm not so glad he kicked. I'm not sorry, but I'm not so glad either."

And just right then, the telephone rang. Helen was saved by the bell, you might put it. And who do you think it was? It was Joe Jackson, that's who, Shoeless Joe himself, the greatest ballplayer that ever put on a big league uniform, if you want my opinion.

You could have knocked me right over with an umpire's whisk broom. See, I had not spoken to Shoeless Joe for at least twenty years or more, and that's saying something. I guess he had been down in Greenville all that time, where he hails from, in South Carolina, and of course I was here in Chi. I heard he was running a liquor store down there. But that isn't the only reason I was surprised to hear from him. I was surprised that he even knew how to use a telephone.

That part I just said is also a joke, but not really. A lot of people like to make out that Joe Jackson was ignorant. Well, sure he was ignorant. But Joe was also stupid. He was stupid *and* ignorant. What I figure, now that I think of it, is that his wife must have gotten my number and dialed up, the same way she used to handle all Joe's contracts, which maybe was part of his problem in the first place. See, Joe couldn't count no more than he could write. I know that for a fact 'cause when Joe first came up north to the big leagues, he didn't have no idea whatsoever what the numbers on the houses were for. Or, rather, he knew what they were for all right, but he didn't know what they meant. Anyway, he sent a whole bunch of them, pretty silver ones, back down to his mother in the sticks, which is why for years afterwards, the little Jackson shack in the woods or someplace was numbered 1728. And that's the honest truth, too.

"Buck," said Joe, a little after I got on the line, "what you gonna do about this?" He was kind of shouting, on account of us being so far apart, I guess.

"Me? Why nothing at all, Joe."

"Nothing?" That stopped the rube right in his tracks. "You see, Buck, when I heard about the Judge, I couldn't think of no one in the world to ring up 'cept my old buddy Buck."

"Well, Joe, it's good to hear the old knowledge box is still working good as ever."

"It sure is. You see, I and Katie was thinkin' maybe you had a idea of somethin' to do."

"Like what?"

"Like what?" Suddenly there was a lot of bustle and hustle on the other end of the line, with Joe's wife telling him to give up the phone and him saying no, and the next thing I knew, there she was. "Mr. Weaver?"

"Mrs. Jackson."

"What I was figurin' was that maybe now if all eight of you boys made an appeal together, maybe you could clear up your names. It's been a long time. Folks forget. And now, with a new commissioner comin' in . . ."

"No, sir, ma'am," I interrupted, "you can just leave me out of that." I must have spoke up angrier than intended, because over on our side of the line Helen came over and put her arm around me, like I was miserable or something. Helen's funny that way. "I don't want any part of no appeal!"

The fact is, though I didn't say this right at the instant in question, I know very well that people won't forget. It's natural to think that they might, since they forget most everything else, and more historic things than this, too. From what I've seen, usually people only remember something if they was around personally at the time; or maybe if their father was around. When I was growing up, the Spanish war was about the biggest thing going, but there are kids around today who hardly even know the first thing about it. The same thing might even happen with the Great War. With this new one, it'll probably just be another "has-been."

But nobody ever forgets the "Black Sox," and that's the truth. Mention 1919 and it's the first thing that pops up in their skulls, the fix of the World Series, before the bolsheviki, or the League of Nations, or even Babe Ruth, who had a hell of a season that year. Every time new people find out my name, whether it be at the racetrack where I work or even amongst the company of friends, I see the same old look in their eyes. It's like I'm a devil or something. I seen that look a thousand times, and I don't care if I never see it again.

"But don't you want to clear up your name?" Kate Jackson asked me.

Well, sure I want to clear my name. Naturally I want to clear my name. Who did she think collected all those signatures on those "Reinstate Buck Weaver" petitions back twenty years ago, which was no easy task? Who else spoke up directly to Landis, like I did back in '27 at the gambling hearings? "Judge," I said after my testimony was done, and even a couple of the sporting writers said it was electrifying, "I don't feel I owe baseball anything, but baseball owes me something. I ask you now for reinstatement."

But I don't need no more aggravation. I don't need people's sympathy no more than their scorn. Sure, I'm sore about some things, like the way they cut short my career and all right in its heyday, and that it seems that no one knows anymore how I was the best third sacker ever to perform in the big show. But like my wife Helen says, what's done is done.

And now, with Landis dropping off and all, it's Rockefeller's roll to a nickel that it's all going to be dug up again. As a matter of fact, in about an hour that bum Luther Pond is going to pop up on that radio show of his, and me and Helen is just waiting for him to give tributes to the guy at our expense. That's how Pond likes to be, always the first to add heat to the fire. And in tomorrow's papers, there it'll be in the headlines, probably even pushing the war to the side, "Landis the first Commissioner, who saved Baseball from crooked ballplayers, Dies of Patriotism." And pretty soon the pencil pushers union will be at the door, asking questions like "How's things stacking up?" and "Are you bitter?"

Well, like I say, who says I'm bitter? I don't wish no one dead, not Comiskey, not Pond, not Eddie Collins, not even Judge Landis, and never mind all they did persecuting an innocent man. Fact is, in recent times I even got to think that the Judge was sort of funny. Actually, to be more precise about it, he made me think of Andy Hardy's father, all white-haired and wrinkled and stern, and *that's* what I thought was funny. Of course, Judge Hardy never went around growling or cursing like Judge Landis did, and he never banned anyone from his livelihood for life, but I think otherwise you will agree to the similarity. There is a story that once Commissioner Landis called Bill Klem, the great umpire, into his office to see him and growled "I hear that you have been going to the racetrack and gambling." And Klem said "Sure, I have been going to the track all my life and what's wrong with it?" At that Landis just backed away and added with a smile, "Why, nothing, Bill, I just wanted to hear it for myself." Well, for instance, that was something Judge Hardy also might do in similar circumstances.

"No, sir, Mrs. Jackson," I said on the phone, "count me out. I don't want no part of it. I've made my peace with the whole situation."

So she started to argue a little with me, but I just told her "Save your breath and save your money cause it won't do no good," and could she please put Joe back on the line for a minute, which to my surprise she did.

Now, the crazy thing is, I feel sorry for Joe Jackson. I always have. Of all the eight of us, he was not only the least well furnished upstairs, but also the most famous. Like, for instance, he's the one they hung that story onto, the one where a newsboy came up to him in front of the Cook County Courthouse and bawled "Say It Ain't So, Joe." Joe swears it never happened, and I'll bet he's right. I'll bet it was made right up by Hughie Fullerton or Jim Crusinberry and them other scribes that just wanted to sell papers from another man's misery. But Joe got stuck with it anyway, and he's never going to lose it.

"Well, Joe," I said, "how's tricks after all this time?"

"Never mind that," he came back, shouting again, not 'cause he was angry, just 'cause he was Joe, "what about the plan?"

"Joe, you been thinking too much."

That must've been a new one on him, 'cause it sure shut him up fast.

"Joe," I piped up again, "why don't you just let sleeping dogs sleep? Our names won't never be cleared by no new commissioner or no one else, so stop troubling yourself."

"Buck," he yelled, "I wanna get in the Hall of Fame."

"Well, who doesn't want that little thing?"

"I mean it, Buck. I earned it." He hesitated a little. "Maybe you did, too, but did you ever see anyone bust the old apple like me?"

"Not in this lifetime, Joe." I didn't, neither. "I'll bet you could go right on a big league team today and show the boys a thing or two."

I heard that cackle of his that I had not heard since the days of my youth. "Hot diggety, you're right about that. Just the other week I pasted one a country mile."

"You're still playing?"

"You ain't?"

"Sure I am, Joe. I manage a girls softball team Saturdays in Lincoln Park, and sometimes they let me toss the ball around with 'em."

"I mean hardball, Buck."

The man had me smirking like it was 1917 or something. "Well, not that, but I can still fit in my old uniform, though. You know what they say about me; I'd rather win than eat."

"You don't eat on account of that girls team?"

Then all at once came some scuffling at his end of the conversation, with Mrs. Jackson claiming he was pissing away dough again, and how they still had to ring up Cicotte and Felsch and some of the other boys, and Joe came back and shouted that he had to get off the line.

But all of it, Landis dying, and Joe phoning, and Helen getting funny like she does, it all got me to thinking that maybe it's time for yours truly to set down my point of view about how things were. About my career and the so-called scandal and all. I'm not saying it's going to do any good, but maybe it's time some individual set down the actual truth for a change, instead of the other way, just in case somebody may be interested. And that's how come I went out and found a candy store that was open, with pencils and paper, and it was not easy, this being the evening before Thanksgiving, and I wrote up what you see here.

I'm not fooling myself that it'll do any good, but who knows, maybe it just might. And I ain't had anything to lose for twenty-five years now anyway.

Nineteen Twelve

by George D. Weaver

My first introduction to the big show was in 1912, not a bad year for Democrats, which I was then and I still am. But it is not my intention here to dwell on politics. I will start this thing at the beginning, as they say, and then keep on going.

And the beginning, I suppose, was when Mr. Harry Grabiner, secretary of the Chicago White Sox Baseball Club, personally addressed to me a letter that winter at my house in Stowe, Pennsylvania offering me to come to Chi. I guess he knew I would do it, 'cause there was also a Pullman ticket in the letter.

See, for a fellow such as I was, there was no bigger dream in my head than playing big league baseball. And why not? Here I was, just a rube, and if I did not play ball, what else in the world would I do? Slave in the mines, that is what, like everyone else back in Stowe, and that includes my old man and my own brother Luther Weaver!

I did not have any doubts about if I could cut the mustard in the national game, not at all. From as far back as I could remember, I could lace the pill like no one you ever saw, at least not in Stowe. Of course, like I say, Stowe is not such a big place, but what I mean to get at is that I just always had faith in my own self. I was not a big head or nothing, I just thought it was a dead cinch that before too long I would be right up there with Wagner and Lajoie and Evers and all the other big pokes of the game back in the days I am telling about.

Still, when I got that letter from Mr. Harry Grabiner, I will

confess that it came to me as a shock. Don't get me wrong, I knew
I was all set for the fast company. Hell, I was brash as green paint.
The thing was, by then I had already been down in the minor
leagues a while, and I had hardly done so much yet to merit the
consideration. Sure, in my own eyes I thought I could outrun a
gazelle and outhit a bear, I guess you would put it, and then of course
there was my slick fielding. But I had not yet shown much of it to
anyone else. The only write-up I had ever gotten up 'til then, and
it's right here in the scrapbook with me now, the guy wrote that I
was "a scatter armed shortstop of indifferent skills and a batter of
little class." Now that I look at it again, I wonder what sort of a dumb
cluck I was to hang on to it all these years.

That article showed up in the San Francisco *Call,* which is where
I worked before the Pale Hose, which is another word for the Sox,
in case you didn't know, looked me up. Before that, in '10, I was with
the York club in the Tri-State League, and before then I played with
the Northampton nine up in Massachusetts.

It was a shame and a lie, by the way, to say what that bush league
writer said about my arm. My glove skills were not at all indifferent.
In fact, I'd say they were definitely different. After all, I was the same
guy the fans was to adore in later years. But it is true that I had not
yet sparkled in those early debuts, especially not the one with the
Massachusetts club. After fourteen games there I was batting only
.196 and was making more misplays than you can shake a stick at,
and one day after I had gotten whiffed twice, the manager, who was
a little Mick called O'Grady, walked up to me and said "Here's your
release, you're terrible."

But I guess the Chicago White Sox could see deeper than that, I
guess they could see that I had lots of pepper, and that's how come
they addressed me that letter. And so two weeks later, there I was,
done up in a woolen suit that I had shelled out eight bucks for, sitting
in an office with Mr. Harry Grabiner in Comiskey Park itself. It was
all beautifully fixed up and appointed, that office, with nice wood
and leather, even though it was the off-season, so one of the first
things I said was "You got a nice office." Well, that just made him
laugh, because it turned out it was not his office at all, but it belonged
to Mr. Comiskey himself, who was off hunting at his place in Michi-

gan with a bunch of big shots. That's what Mister Grabiner said. So he said it was up to him to deal with me himself.

"Well," he said, at which moment he suddenly looked down at a piece of paper there on the desk, "do you think you can help the White Sox, young man?"

"Yes, sir, I definitely do. No doubt about that." You see, I was not so much on the ball then as I am today and didn't know what was cooking.

"I see here that you batted only .278 in the Pacific Coast League."

"Yes sir, I guess that's it, all right. But I'm the sort of a player that does things that don't show in the numbers," which was true, by the way.

"And with York only .264?"

"Yes sir, but I'm better now, you can bet on that."

"What makes you think so?"

This was beginning to tense me up, 'cause actually I was not really so cocky like I made out. At the moment I was just a little more than twenty-one and five months old. " 'Cause I am. And you can put your money on it."

He looked at me close from behind his gold specs. "Is it true they call you 'Error a Day Weaver'? You got butterfingers or something?"

"Oh, that was teasing, is all. The boys didn't mean nothing at all by it." He just kept gazing at me. "You see, I made some wide heaves from time to time to the bag. That's on account of my arm being so strong."

"I see."

"I got a real strong arm."

"We know that. But you can't get away with that kind of sloppiness in the big leagues."

I didn't make an answer to that one.

"As for your stick work, they already call us the Hitless Wonders. We hardly need another empty revolver in the lineup." He pushed the little paper way off to the side of the desk. "But we do need infield help. What were you paid at York?"

"Two hundred a month."

"And at San Francisco?"

"Three hundred and fifty."

"That's very clever, Buck. You were getting one twenty-five at York and two hundred at San Francisco. Your salary here will be eighteen hundred dollars per annum. If we keep you."

All at once, there on the desk was a contract, all filled in already, and he was shoving a pen at me. I put down my john hancock real fast, so he wouldn't have a chance to think too much more, and that was that.

But once it was done, he was suddenly different, like Prince Charming or something. "Well, son," he said, pumping my paw, "it's nice to have you with us. Good luck."

And the truth is, at that particular instant I didn't mind none of the slights too much at all, not even the one about the butterfingers. There I was a big leaguer, which like I say is all I had cared about since I was nine or ten. When I got outside into the cold, and in case you didn't know, it can be quite cool in Chi in the winter, I didn't hardly notice, that's how happy I was. There I was outside the ballpark, walking around on Thirty-fifth Street, around near the viaduct, and there was nobody in sight, except maybe some coons that live there, and of course all the hot dog and popcorn joints were closed down on account of the winter and all. Looking at it, Comiskey seemed like the biggest ballpark in the world, which it just about was then, though of course later it got even bigger, and I admit I was a little scared at my prospects. But mainly I kept thinking how it was going to be a few months from then, with all the crowds pushing and shouting around the ballpark after a game, and there I would be amongst them, like a pig in shit.

Of course, dreams rarely work out as happy as planned, at least at the beginning. I do not know how much harm is done today to bushers by veterans, but back in the days of my time it was hellish. It was not good clean fun at all, quite the contrary, because these veterans that were about to lose their jobs didn't know how to do nothing else in the world, and second of all, because they did not know nothing about good clean fun in the first place. The definition of good clean fun to some of these boys was tricking a busher into drinking another man's piss, so that he'd die or something, or at least land up in the hospital.

No rookie of my knowledge escaped this torture, least of all some of the biggest stars. Ty Cobb, a ballplayer without comparison in my day, except maybe for Babe Ruth and Joe Jackson, may have had it worst of anyone, because even when he first came up he was brash as after shaving lotion, and had a nasty disposition to boot. The taunts at him were so hard to endure under, being both about his family and his Cracker origins, that finally he had to take on his own teammates. Day after day under the stands at Navin Field he battled them, one after the next, and he whipped them all, too, until he came up against Boss Schmidt, the big catcher. Nobody ever whipped Schmidt, not after he got mad enough to fight, and he gave Tyrus the thrashing of his lifetime. By then, Cobb had become so suspicious of his mates that he went on to pull a stunt that was as bughouse as anything I ever heard. One day in July, which of course is still pretty early in the season, he woke up with terrible pains in his tonsils. He couldn't drink soup even, let alone regular ballplayers' fare, which is meat and potatoes. But see, he was afraid to kick to anyone about it, including the manager Armour, because he thought that if they sat him down, even for a day or two, they might never let him play again. So he kept on with his work, even though after a week he was as feeble as Boston tea. In the matter of guts, Ty Cobb never took a back seat to no one, I will give him that. But things got so bad that finally he had to see a doc in Cleveland, and the doc told him "Ty, you have got to slow down. You have got to take to bed for a while and then have those tonsils operated upon." At which moment, without blinking an eyelash, Ty said "You can just go ahead and take them out right here." The doc protested, saying that he didn't have the right tools, nor even pain relief, but Ty started to make a fuss in that real nasty way of his, so at last the doc said "All right." And he cut out the tonsils right there and then, piece by piece, with a long scissors I guess. They had to stop each twenty minutes, so Ty could spit out blood and lay on the couch for a rest. After a couple of hours, when they were done, Cobb was so spent that Germany Schaefer, who was his roomie and the one guy he was on the up-and-up with, had to drag him back to the hotel. But the next day he was right back in the lineup, and he had a pair of singles to boot. All of that on account of the way the back numbers razzed the rookies.

Well, I'm not saying that what happened to me tops that, no such thing, but it was certainly no picnic on the grass, neither. When I got down to Fort Worth on the twenty-fourth day of February, which is where the ball club trained back then, the vets were laying for me. Of course, they were laying for the other bushers, too, but mainly they were laying for me. That is because Callahan the manager, and maybe Comiskey also, had slated me for a shot at the regular shortstop job, in the place of a fellow called Lee Tannehill.

Tannehill had been with the club almost from the start of its existence, which was ten years, and though I did not know him from Adam himself, this was the start of my woes. The vets were not willing to accept me laying down.

I should put in right here that, even though this was my big opportunity and all, I had another thing on my mind. See, back when I was working in San Fran, I had a girl there named Agnes. She was a danseuse, that is what she called herself, which is frog for dancer. I did not get it myself, either what she did or how come. After all, Agnes's old man was a bishop in some church in St. Loo, and had plenty of loot, and she did not have to do nothing at all if she chose, let alone running around on stages pretending she was a bird or the wind or other such things. But Agnes said that she did not care what people thought, for no one in this land knew beans about Art. She said people never said a word if fellows wanted to try great things, only girls. See, that was something else about her, she was a suffragist! Only do not get me wrong, she was no dog like you might expect, but a real peach!

Indeed, you might wonder how come such a girl, with her looks and brains and all, would be with a fellow such as myself, and so did yours truly. I even asked her one time, and she laughed like a hyena. "Buck," she came back, "you are so old fashioned. Don't you know it's a new world?"

And so, to make it short, I was planning in my head that one fine day me and her were going to tie the knot. But, the thing is, at the time in question I had not heard from Agnes for a month or more, not even a postal card, and I was worried out of my wits. Of course, this was not in the days when you could just ring up a person on the telephone as you can today, even long distance, and I wouldn't have done it anyway because it was her business to write me. I had other things on my mind. Naturally I was not planning that this would get in the way of my work but, like I say, I could not help but worry.

Which is why my reception in Fort Worth was even tougher to bear than usual. When I got to the hotel, which was the Bond Hotel right near the ballpark, I discovered my roomie to be no one else than Morrie Rath, who I knew by past feats. See, even though this was also his first go-around with the Sox, he had been in the fast company for years already, with the Philadelphia club and also Cleveland, and I was ready to look up at the guy. But he was as cool with me as ice, even despite my best efforts. So after a little bit I told him "Well, I guess I'll look for Callahan," who was the manager, just to say hello and all, and he just nodded like I was hardly there. Then in the hallway I bumped into some of the other vets, Sullivan and Zeider and Harry Lord, the third baseman, and naturally I presented myself, to which they just smiled and looked at each other. "Well, well," said Lord, "so you're him," and they just kept on down the hall.

The fortunate thing at this point, for I needed a pick-me-up, was that we were residing on the very top floor of the Bond Hotel, which was number eight, and they had a fine new elevator there. So I got in that elevator and had myself a few trips, and that turned the trick. And when I got out in the lobby, feeling fresh as morning, who should I find there but Nixey Callahan himself.

"Well, sir," I said, "here I am, and ready to play."

"Maybe yes, maybe no," he said. He was sitting there in a big chair, munching upon an apple.

"When do I get to show off my stuff?"

"Tomorrow." He bit into his apple. "Unless it rains. It's supposed to be beautiful, but it might rain."

"You'll want me at shortstop? I can also play third."

"Shortstop or third. Or the outfield."

This was a new development. "I'm game, all right, but I never played in the outfield in my life. I'm not so sure I would look too good out there."

He held up the apple, which by then was just the core. "This apple looks good, doesn't it? Well, maybe it is and maybe not. You can't go by looks."

See, this was the way with Nixey, as I was to find out. He was a good egg, he would never bull to you or get all miffy for no reason, but the guy would never say nothing for certain. There was no use trying to make him. If you said some girl was a lulu, he would come back with "She is when dry, but have you seen her wet?" If you said a horse you liked had a bum leg, he would say, well, maybe that's not so bad 'cause he still has more than you and me.

So after a little while more with Nixey, I went back up to the eighth floor, and there was Rath, giving me the evil eye once again.

"Well," I started, "I talked to Callahan."

He made no response, but only nodded at the dresser, where there was a piece of paper. "That came for you."

"What is it?"

But he was through gabbing, so I looked at it myself, and it was a bill. In nice, neat letters it said "7 elevator trips. Seventy cents."

"What's this?" I said.

"What does it look like? You were riding that elevator, weren't you?"

"Well, sure I was."

"So now you have got to pay for your fun."

I sat down on the bed, which I shared with this fellow, and looked real close at the paper. "I've rode elevators before, and I never paid for one yet."

"Where was that?"

"In San Fran. And also once in Sacramento."

At that he just started to laugh. "Those were minor league elevators, this is a big league elevator. A big league elevator you don't ride for free."

I thought about that a minute. "Well, I feel like I'm getting soaked. How did it get to be that way?"

"Listen, you may search me!" I could tell he was starting to get angry. "All I can tell you is that is the way it is. You have got to ante up to Walsh, because he is the captain and takes care of these expenses for the club."

This was indeed a sad thing to learn. I was not exactly well fixed for dough in the first place, being a rookie and all, and we were getting only a buck a meal for travel money. Plus Callahan had said you had to give a quarter a day to the waiter at the hotel, if you wanted to, and I figured you were supposed to want to. And there I was all the way up on floor number eight.

But there was just not a thing to be done about it. There would just be no more elevator rides for me, is what I made up my mind.

It turned out this was easier said than done. See, Comiskey was a stickler for tough work, and even though he was still up in Chi, it was his orders to Callahan for practices to start at nine-thirty all six days a week and go on 'til dark. They worked you like a mule at that place, and there was but an hour break for lunch back at the hotel, where the players might also wash up a little and relax. But for me, hustling up and down those stairs, the freshening up was harder than the workout. And at day's end, I was so bushed that a couple of times I just sat there in the lobby for a half hour or more before trying to make the room.

But the good part was that none of this got in the way of my work on the field, not one bit. I have always been a cat on my feet (and even now at my age I still am), but that spring I was just as smooth as sherry. Nothing could get by me at shortstop, and my heaves to the bag were straight and true, except for just a few times. And though back then I was not yet a wonder with the willow like I was to become, I was also powdering the pill pretty good. My very first contest, it was against the local Fort Worth club, I socked one for three bases that in later years, with the rabbit ball and all, would've taken a stroll four hundred feet.

And all the while my mates on the club, not the least my own roomie, were giving me precious little encouragement. In fact, for two weeks I got nothing at all but the dummy treatment from most of them, and it was not easy, for I am a man that gets lonely easily. Even now it is a wonder to me that I did not lose heart and do a fizzle, like so many other rookies in those days.

And all the while I could not stop thinking of Agnes. As the days passed by, I felt more heartsick than ever, which is why, one fine night, I finally decided to lay aside formalities and write to her myself. And I did so, two pages worth, all about my passions for her and my hopes for our bright future and also the dandy way I was playing shortstop. Writing up that letter was a good bit of tough work, and when I was done I left the room to walk outside and think a bit and smoke a cigar. Well, you can imagine my surprise in getting back to the room, all short of breath from the stairs, to find Rath sitting there on our bed reading my letter.

"Hey, what do you think you are doing there?" I came at him.

"It was right out there in the open," he came back, calm as anything, as if that was a good reason.

"It is not right to read a fellow's private letter."

"Well, if you don't want another fellow to read it, then you should not leave it laying around. Maybe in the minors you can do that, but not around here. In the big leagues, what is left laying about is fair game for prying eyes."

What he was saying was applesauce and I knew it! "Well," I said firmly, "you had better never do it again." And then I snatched up the letter from him and folded it up into my pocket.

Rath raised himself off the bed and walked over by the mirror and started changing his collar. I could tell he was planning to go out on the town again, as he had every other night with the other ballplayers. "Well," he said after a little bit, looking real close at some little mark on his face, "it sounds to me like the same old tale. Some girl has given you the bag."

"That is no concern of yours. You just stay out of my mail!"

"Well, I don't mean to get you peeved. I just figured you might want to talk about it. I do know a bit about skirts, you know."

And so, to make a long story shorter, I decided to open up my soul to him. Hell, if a fellow cannot confide in his roomie, then who can he? I told him all about Agnes, and how I had bumped into her in a restaurant in San Fran, and stole her from another fellow out there that was a writer and had actually wrote a whole book, and our future plans and all. He took it in with a real serious face, and then he gave his opinion, which was that there were other fish in the sea. "Why don't you let me and the boys fix you up with some other girl, Buck?" he said. "We know most of them that there is to know in this burg."

Naturally I said "Sure," being that I did not know any myself, and it would serve Agnes right, and also it seemed a possibility to buddy up at last to some of the vets. And that is what happened. The very next day I sat at lunch with Rath, and Lord, and Big Ed Walsh, and even Tannehill himself, who was a fine fellow face to face. They told me that they had put all their heads together and thought up a girl for me, all right, and she was something. Well, as it turned out, you could certainly say that again.

I made the acquaintance of Louise that very night, after practice, right in the hotel lobby. I'll never forget, she was wearing a shiny blue dress, down to the floor as the fashion was, with big yellow and green flowers on it. Her face had on it a couple of different colors, such as red for the cheeks and blue around the eyes. And yet she walked all prissy, like she did not have bodily functions or something, which I like in a woman.

And she seemed to care for me also. Dough was nearly not an object that night, as we painted the town red from head to toe, going dancing at some joint and afterwards to a saloon called the Golden Nugget, where in the back they also had gambling. Louise was a woman who knew how to listen to a fellow's woes, and though we had just been acquainted, I let her know all about Agnes, who I was through with anyway. And she knew about baseball, which Agnes did not. All in all, I didn't get hardly a wink of sleep that night.

Well, the next day that might have shown up a little bit on the ballfield. We were playing the Cincinnatis, and I muffed an easy one in the third that I should have had with my eyes closed, which I guess they almost were. But I also went in the hole to spear one, and I did some good stick work, so it was not too bad.

And when I got back to the hotel, there was Louise waiting for me, and that sure chased the wearies out of me. I ran up to the room two steps at once, and got all fixed up, and then I took her out on the town all over again, and to the same places, too. Only this time we ended up at her house, which was right there in the town. And after a couple of stiff ones, we just went right ahead and nuptialized, as they say. It was pie, just like I'm telling it to you, and it made me a most happy fellow.

Of course, I did not get home to the Bond Hotel 'til after dawn. It was lucky for me that Callahan was not then keeping no curfew. As it was, I was as beat as a fellow who had just tossed a tripleheader, and I do not know how I played ball at all that day. It was a wonder that I was not beaned, and I made a sap of myself in the field and also at the bat. Around the fifth frame or so, Big Ed Walsh, who was hurling for us that day, sat down next to me on the bench.

"Well," he said with a smile, "I guess I don't have to ask about you and Louise." I must have looked to him like an alki stiff or something.

"No," I replied, "you sure do not. And I certainly am grateful to you." Now, Ed Walsh was a wizard on the hill, and he had been pretty nearly my ideal since '07, when he had led the club into the World Series. And now that the Sox were a sad-looking bunch, I guess you would have to say he was the whole club by himself. It was an honor just that he would shoot the breeze with me like that. "Yes, sir," I added, "you fellows have made me quite a content man."

He screwed up his face funny. " 'Cause of Louise?"

"Yes, sir, Mr. Walsh. She is a fine woman, and no one knows it better than me."

The truth is, though I did not admit it at the moment, I liked Louise every bit as much as Agnes, who of course I had loved. I suppose you might say I was pretty much on the marry right then, on account of my starting fresh with my career and all.

By this time our side had been put down, and it was our turn to return back to the diamond. "Well," said Big Ed, as he started for the pitching slab, "don't do anything I wouldn't do."

But that evening something funny happened. Louise was not in front of the Bond Hotel at the expected hour, which was seven, and nor did she show up for four hours after that. In fact, she might not have shown up at all. I will never know, 'cause the four hours is all I waited. See, a little past eleven, Nixey Callahan walked right by me on his way into the building.

"Waiting for a parade, young man?" he said.

"No sir, I sure am not."

"Well, you never know when one might pass by anyway." He started for the door and then stopped. "By the way, you might want to know that you have got the shortstop job all wrapped up, unless someone better comes by the camp in the next three days."

Now right there was the best piece of news I had gotten maybe in my whole life. "That is wonderful, sir! I can't express to you how glad that makes me feel!"

A grin spread right across his puss. "Well, I would just advise you to lay off the hooks for a few days if you want to survive to enjoy it."

I didn't have any notion of what he meant by that one, so I made no response.

"A hook can be fine," he picked up, "but she can also be trouble."

"A hook?"

"A saleslady. Don't pretend with me, because I saw you with her two days running, not that I mind it."

"That was no hook, that was Louise."

"Well," he said, "it is possible she is no hook, just as it is possible I might call myself Smith tomorrow. But she was sure a hook a couple of weeks ago, I know that from personal experience and so does half the club."

But I hardly heard the end of what he was saying, 'cause in a shake I was heading up those stairs, getting madder each second. It kept rushing around in my skull that they must think I'm dead above the ears or something, and that I had given little reason to think different, and that now, just at the moment of my great opportunity, I might be coming down with cupid's itch or some other disease even worse. When I got into that room I did not hesitate, but leaped onto that bed like a banshee and right on top of Rath. He was not such a big fellow, not even as big as me by a long shot, and he was lucky to pull a Houdini before I brained him, that's how hot I was.

Well, it is all a long time ago now, so there is no reason to keep dwelling on it. But I will surely never forget the razzing I got, and Louise, and the elevator hoax and all of it, for it was harder on my spirit than anything I ever faced before and since, maybe even including the so-called scandal. But, like I say, in a few days it was already old news on the club. We headed up north to start the campaign in earnest, and then just a week into the season Tannehill got sent down, and there I was, the regular shortstop. Pretty soon I was everybody's buddy, just like Tannehill had been before, and no one hardly even mentioned his name anymore. See, they weren't bad fellows after all, only ballplayers. As Rath himself put it to me later, "Anybody who trusts a ballplayer is a fathead."

It certainly was good advice, and I would have been a lot better off if I had always kept it in mind, that's for sure. But, then, I have also found out that it is not fair to limit it just to ballplayers.

Introduction to
an Enigma

T y Cobb liked me.
    I realize that this is no longer a matter of concern to large
    numbers of my countrymen, but it is a fact that even now,
all these years later, makes me smile. This is not because I regard
myself as a particularly dislikeable fellow—I daresay that during my
lifetime hundreds of men have appreciated my company. I smile
because I am quite certain that over the course of the last six decades
of his life, through two marriages which produced five children, and
a business career that left him a millionaire nine times over, and the
most wondrous baseball career in the history of the game, Ty Cobb
liked no one else.

For those who never witnessed the man in uniform, worse, who
have grown up on modern athletics, it is perhaps impossible to grasp
what Ty Cobb once meant in this land. Though (baseball being the
most stubbornly backward-looking of games) he is still somewhat
with us, his remarkable statistical legacy still the standard against
which all his successors must be measured, gone is all memory of his
presence; of that lean, wild-eyed visage, day after day staring out
from the newspaper page; of that split-handed batting grip, for
decades as much a fixture in parks and sandlots as drinking fountains
and broken glass; of the very ring of that curious name which, hardly
realizing it, one was likely to hear spoken three or five or seven times
a day, by a stranger passing in the street, by a co-worker, in whispered conversation down the row at a funeral service. For fully a

quarter of a century, from the time of Teddy Roosevelt to that of Herbert Hoover, from the Russo-Japanese War to the eve of the Great Depression, Ty Cobb was always with us, in our air.

But gone, above all, irretrievably lost, is the sense of what Cobb once seemed to represent, of how much more he was than merely a ballplayer. His enduring fascination was never just that he hit so well, and ran so fast, and so routinely outthought his rivals. No, there was something unique in the *character* of his play, an obsession with excellence with which millions of his countrymen identified as eagerly as once they had identified with the grit of Alger creations. For Ty Cobb would do anything to win. Lip curled in a permanent sneer, eyes ablaze, he played with a reckless, almost unholy abandon. "I never saw anyone like Cobb," recalled Casey Stengel years later, "no one even close to him. When he wiggled those wild eyes at a pitcher, you knew you were looking at one bird nobody could beat. It was like he was superhuman." No matter the score in a particular contest, no matter his team's position in the standings, he thrust himself furiously, often violently, into the fray, taking endless risks on the basepaths, in the field, at the bat, seeming to taunt his opponents, always ready, if need be, to cut down those who got in his way.

Indeed, watching him play, it was possible to speculate, in defiance of logic, that winning was not his only concern; that Ty Cobb was consumed by another, more primitive objective: to annihilate the egos of other men.

Understandably, those whom he faced on the diamond tended to return his implicit contempt very much in kind. Among those who knew him in the flesh, this giant, this god (his face as recognizable as any president's, his achievements held in far higher esteem) was regarded with a loathing I have never since encountered. Around the American League, reasonable men would go so far as to sacrifice themselves in the service of causing him pain. During one memorable doubleheader at the tail end of the 1910 season, when Cobb was involved in a desperate battle with Napoleon Lajoie of the Cleveland Indians for the league batting championship and the Chalmers automobile that went with it, the St. Louis Browns allowed Lajoie eight hits in eight times at bat so that he might beat out the despised Cobb; Red Corriden, the Brownies' rookie third baseman, actually played

his position from the outfield grass. Even Walter Johnson of the
Senators, perhaps the gentlest man ever to appear on a ballfield and
certainly among the most competitive, used to routinely feed Cobb's
teammate and rival, Sam Crawford, fat, easy pitches, simply because
it so irked Ty to see Sam succeed.

Little of this was common knowledge at the time, of course. Less
known still was the fact that Cobb's penchant for violent confrontation was by no means restricted to the diamond; that, in fact, since
coming to the majors, he had twice actually been charged with
assault, on one of those occasions slashing a night watchman at the
Euclid Hotel in Cleveland with a knife. As political writers would
later know to ignore the indiscretions of Warren Harding and
Franklin Roosevelt, so it was understood in sporting circles of that
day that the more unsettling specifics of Tyrus Raymond Cobb's
makeup were not to see print. So, while the rest of the world accepted the facts as written—that Cobb's custom of sitting on the
bench before games, noisily sharpening his spikes with a file so that
they'd slice like razors, was aggressiveness; that his habit of maiming
second basemen was old fashioned, hard-nosed play; that his tendency to brood for days on end over imagined slights was intensity
—those few of us who knew better were left to wonder: What made
this man so utterly different from the rest of us? What was the fire
that raged so furiously within him? Was he, in fact, insane?

I myself initially encountered Cobb in the wake of the famous
Luker incident. This is May 1912 I am talking about. As it happened,
the preceding month had been the most difficult at the *Journal* since
my arrival on the premises, nearly three years before; indeed had
been marked by a sense of self-doubt unprecedented in the sixteen-
year life of the paper. You see, the *Titanic* had gone down April 15,
and we had—there is no longer any need for equivocation—botched
the story. Our initial headline on the disaster, a tragic spectacular
featuring fifteen hundred dead that might have been designed by
God Himself for our front page, appeared on the afternoon of April
16: ALL SAFE ON TITANIC.

There was, of course, an explanation; an erroneous wireless report
had been intercepted by one of our more enterprising men and,
under the circumstances, checking the report had been given even
less consideration than usual. We were, after all, at war, had been

from the instant we had first received word that the ship was in peril —and not just with the *Evening Post*, and the *Sun*, and Pulitzer's *Evening World*, our principal rival in the afternoon circulation battle, but with the *American*, our arrogant, well-heeled brother publication, upstairs at 232–238 William Street. Indeed, with the *American* most feverishly of all.

That evening, as the dimension of the sea tragedy began to become clear, the size of our own error brought activity in the office to a virtual halt. The paper's news editor, T. Arnold Cline, doubtless having already heard from Hearst himself, retreated to his office and passed the entire night in his swivel chair in a state of paralyzing melancholia; feet atop his desk, hands behind his bald head, staring glassy-eyed at the bookshelves opposite.

Incredibly, though, the lapses in our *Titanic* coverage continued. It was almost as if, having committed the original gaffe, we were grimly determined to see the happy side of the *Titanic* story through to the end. 868 SAVED announced our banner the following day, above a grainy photograph of icebergs, purportedly North Atlantic ones, that had been pulled from the files; EVERY WOMAN SAVED went the one after that. Both would prove wholly inaccurate.

Not that we ever acknowledged error, of course. When the *Carpathia*, bearing the *Titanic* survivors, at last pulled into New York harbor, we descended upon those unfortunates as rapidly as any paper in town, and printed the same tales of heroism and craven cowardice that they so willingly offered; the descriptions of Mrs. Isidor Straus, elderly wife of the Macy's magnate, refusing all entreaties to save herself, choosing instead to stand arm in arm with her husband amid the rising panic; of the four Italians from steerage who were shot by ship's officers as they tried to claw their way onto a lifeboat; of Benjamin Guggenheim, the mining tycoon, proclaiming as the ship began to list that "no woman shall be left on this ship because I was a coward"; of J. Bruce Ismay, the President of the White Star Line, pushing aside women and children to save himself.

But this was, in large measure, going through the motions, for the damage done to our morale in those first days had been inestimable. To have been merely beaten on this, the great disaster story of the ages, would have been devastating enough; we had humiliated ourselves.

Indeed, it was only the appearance, late in the proverbial day, of the *Titanic* waifs, that rescued for the *Journal* even a shred of dignity.

The waifs were a pair of tots, French or Swiss, aged approximately two and three and a half, who had been tossed from the second deck into one of the last lifeboats by a bearded man, presumably their father, and had been taken under the wing of one of the lifeboat's occupants, a certain Miss Margaret Hayes. Upon reaching New York aboard the *Carpathia*, Miss Hayes, who happened to be a second cousin of our advertising manager, had taken them to her West Eighty-third Street home. Thus it was that we were not only to announce to the world the presence of "Lolo" and "Lump" on these shores, running a prominent photo of the two "crinkly haired, fat-legged babies" on the front page, but that, for the two days thereafter, we were able to bar rival reporters from getting a look at them at all.

Understandably, we continued to run strong with the waifs for the next two weeks, even after they had been identified and their mother (from whom, it turned out, they had been surreptitiously taken by her estranged husband) had set out for New York from their home in Nice; indeed, even after most of the rest of the press had dropped the entire *Titanic* story from page one, we kept on giving them the treatment, daily describing what they wore, what they ate, the games they played in their new refuge at the Children's Society. Let the *Tribune* chronicle Taft and Roosevelt slugging it out in the Ohio primary. Let the *Times* worry about the revolutionists in Mexico. Let the *Sun* dwell on the death of old King Frederick of Denmark. The waifs were ours.

On the afternoon in question, May 18, we were gearing up for what looked to be the grand finale. The children's mother, Mme. Navritil, was due in town the following morning on the *Oceanic*. I was sitting in the newsroom when Joe Trumbull, in other times an excellent crime reporter, returned from a visit to the French Consulate.

"I am goddamn sick of those waifs," he announced, in greeting.

I nodded. "Who isn't?"

"I'll tell you something else," he continued, "they don't give a damn about them over at that Consulate. Never did."

"Really?"

"Those frogs had me cooling my heels for two hours before the Assistant Consul would even talk to me. And when he did, you know what he said? He said, and this is direct"—he flipped through his notebook until he found what he was looking for—" 'We offer our thanks to your fine Children's Society. Please tell your readers we are delighted with the treatment your government has accorded *all* the French survivors.' " He shut the notebook with a snap. "They washed their mitts of the whole thing at the beginning. And if you ask me, they were pretty smart."

"That's some story," I observed. "People don't much like the French to start with."

"Not this week, pal."

He stepped back and framed the headline with his hands. "FRENCH LAUD UNCLE SAM." Trumbull smiled wanly. "What about you? They don't got the sporting department on the waifs?"

"No. I'm just waiting for the scores to come in." It was an assignment the junior sporting men at the *Journal* were each obliged to handle two weeks a month during the baseball season. I was to take the line scores of games in progress off the wire, or, if a contest was of particular importance, by telephone, and prepare them for the late edition. It was early afternoon, and nothing much had come in yet.

"The Brooklyns playing today? Or'd they cancel in honor of the waifs?" Trumbull wasn't much of a baseball fan, but he lived in Crown Heights.

I laughed. "They're in Saint Louis."

The phone rang. "Pond, Sporting."

"Luther, it's Harry Glaser." Harry was covering the Yankees game against Detroit up at Highlanders Park.

"Yeah, Harry. What do you have?"

"Listen, Luther, there's big doings up here. Cobb just went into the stands and attacked a fan."

"You're not serious!"

"Tell copy I'll need ten inches, at least. Seems he hurt the guy pretty bad. He's on his way to Bellevue Hospital right now."

"What happened to Cobb?"

"Silks Laughlin's the ump. Booted him out of the game." He paused. "Listen, can we get a man over to Bellevue?"

As it happened, the only other sporting writer in the office was William Kirk, several desks away, composing a story on a promising East Side lightweight named Knockout Brown. Kirk was an amiable enough fellow, and not without talent, but he was the other junior man in the department and thus my principal rival. I got a copy boy to take my spot at the phone and hopped a trolley for Bellevue myself.

And, sure enough, in the antechamber outside the emergency room, there were two men, one of them a very large fellow who sat, doubled over, head in hands. One of his pants legs was torn halfway down. Dried blood soaked the material. His companion was beside him, a protective hand upon his broad back.

"Excuse me," I said, "but have you men come from Highlanders Park, by any chance?"

The injured man did not stir.

"Who are you?" asked the friend.

"My name is Luther Pond. I write for the *Evening Journal.*"

The friend beamed. "The *Journal?* This gonna be in the *Journal?*"

"Maybe."

He pounded the injured man's back. "Hear that, Claude? You're maybe gonna be in the *Journal.* How about that?"

The other slowly lifted his head to look me over. The man's face would, under ordinary circumstances, have been merely an unpleasant one. Now, however, although he was smiling, it was downright sinister, for the flesh around one eye was bloated purple, and a deep gash extended from the cheek to the chin. Slowly, he extended his hand. "Claude Luker," he said in a hoarse whisper.

I reached for the hand, then drew back involuntarily. Instead of digits I had grasped a claw, a mangled thumb and forefinger attached to a stump. I was as incredulous as I was repulsed. "You're the man Ty Cobb went after?"

The friend waited a moment for Luker to answer, then nodded vigorously. "Show him the other one, Claude."

With the claw, Luker gingerly lifted his left sleeve. The limb ended at the wrist. "He used to be a pressman at the *Times,* " explained the friend. "I still work there, but Claude, he had a run-in with a paper-cutter a few years ago. Ain't that right, Claude?"

The friend offered me his hand. "My hand's okay. I'm Tom O'Neill. What can we do for you?"

"Just tell me what happened at the ballfield, Tom."

"Well," he said, "it's the fourth inning, you see, and we're sittin' there, minding our business . . ."

"What the hell does it look like?" cut in Luker in a whisper. "The bastard attacked me."

"Just like that?"

"That's right," replied O'Neill pleasantly. "Went after a defense-less man. Me and the graycoats hadda pull him off. Claude's gonna have the law on Cobb and go to the finish."

"There wasn't"—I hesitated—"any razzing going on?"

"Sure there was a little rooting," said O'Neill. "Cobb made an error in the second, you see. We got a right, after all. We paid our fifty cents."

"What was said, exactly?" I pressed.

Luker gazed at me malevolently with his good eye.

"It's a free country," said O'Neill, "that's the point. Anyways, after it happened, me and Claude came down here. Tom Foley'll take care of this."

"You know Tom Foley?"

"Know him? Big Tom and Claude is like brothers. They was raised together."

"Like this," growled Luker, crossing his thumb and forefinger. "So you make sure you write it right."

"That's the reason me and Claude came all the way down to this hospital here," continued O'Neill, "because it's in Big Tom's dis-trict." He winked. "Free of charge."

I nodded and took out my notepad.

"Well," I said, "I'd still like to find out what was said at the ballfield."

"He told you," said Luker, "*nothin'.*" He forced himself into an upright position and glared at me menacingly. "*Nothin'!*"

"He said you were getting on Cobb about an error."

"Nothin', you goddamned little sheeny!"

I pulled back and gazed at Luker. "Excuse me," I said, "but I'm not Jewish."

"Nothin'," repeated O'Neill reasonably. "We got a right, after all."

Abruptly, the door across from us swung open and a young doctor in a long white smock strode briskly past us, wiping his hands on a towel. He was followed by an anguished young woman, a recent immigrant, in a bulky peasant skirt and babushka. In her arms she cradled a child whose head, however, was wholly obscured, having somehow gotten wedged within a kettle. The child was whimpering.

"Come with me, Mrs. Szusca," said the doctor gently, "I'll have that off in no time."

He paused and nodded at us. "I'm sorry gentlemen, I'll be with you shortly."

"What the hell is this?" demanded Luker, all at once regaining a booming voice.

"Go on in there, Mrs. Szusca," said the doctor, easing the frightened woman toward the adjoining room. "Go on, go on . . ." Then he turned and gazed at my companion. "You must be the fellow from the baseball game."

"He's hurt pretty bad, Doc," offered O'Neill.

The doctor approached and quickly looked over the facial wounds. "Not really. Keep your shirt on, big fellow. You're not the only patient here."

"You can't treat me this way," exploded Luker, "I'm a pal of Big Tom Foley."

"I suggest," said the doctor calmly to us, "that you take your friend elsewhere." He turned and headed out of the room.

"I ain't goin' elsewhere!" screamed Luker after him. "You're gonna pay for this, you sheeny bastard!"

"Keep your trap shut, Claude."

And there, at the entrance to the room, stood a large, moustached man in a three-piece striped suit, whom I immediately recognized from news photographs as Big Tom Foley, the former sheriff of New York County and the Tammany leader of Lower Manhattan.

"What's the matter, one beating a day ain't enough for you?"

"Hello there, Big Tom," said O'Neill. "No, I guess it ain't. You know Claude."

"All right, Big Tom," agreed Luker sullenly.

"And who might you be?" asked Foley, turning to me. "Another good samaritan?"

"My name's Pond. I'm with *the Evening Journal*."

"The *Journal*, huh? Never supports me." He smiled. "Very neat work. You the only newshound around?"

"Yessir."

He nodded. "Well, I have a statement on this matter. Take it down."

I opened my pad. "Were you there, sir?"

"I didn't have to be there, I heard all about it. And Claude Luker works for me."

He paused and stared for a moment at the floor, composing. "My statement is: 'I am shocked by today's incident at Highlanders Park. The folks in my district don't believe in a trained athlete assaulting a cripple, and neither do I.' " He paused again. " 'Ty Cobb is getting nine thousand a year to play baseball; he should be accustomed to rooting.' "

He watched me scribble the last of it down. "Got that?"

"Yessir," I said. "In other words, you don't feel that Mr. Luker bears any responsibility at all for what occurred?"

"Read my statement, young man. That'll tell you what I feel." He smiled. "You've seen Claude. You musta' drew your own conclusions, no?"

I started to write that down, but he snatched the pencil from my hand. "That, my boy, is *off* the record. Isn't it, O'Neill?"

"It sure is, Big Tom."

When I got back to the office, Harry Glaser was feverishly attacking his Remington. There were new developments. It seemed that Ban Johnson, the president of the American League, happened to have been in the stands at Highlanders Park and had witnessed the incident. Following the ballgame, he had met briefly with chief umpire Laughlin, and then informed Detroit manager Hugh Jennings that he was suspending the star outfielder indefinitely.

"Let me tell you," added Glaser, never glancing up from the page, "those Detroit fellows are none too happy about it. They say Ty gave Luker just what he had coming."

"Oh, yes? What exactly was it that Luker said?"

"Nothin' that'll ever see the light of day in this family newspaper."
Harry guffawed. "And that Luker has a voice, too, I'll tell you that.
I could hear him way back in the press section."

I headed for my typewriter a few desks away to compose my
sidebar on the scene at the hospital. "Yeah, that Luker is a mean
fellow, all right. Wait'll you see what I got." I took my seat and
flexed my fingers. "But I guess this'll be the end of it, right?"

Harry stopped his pecking and looked over. "Who knows, some
of those Detroit ballplayers were talking pretty tough. Said they
were going to see Johnson to get Cobb reinstated. There was even
some strike talk." He thought it over for a moment. "Probably just
chatter."

But it soon became apparent it was much more than that. Denied
an opportunity to meet with Johnson, the players fired off a telegram
to him, reiterating their support of Cobb. That night they left for
Philadelphia. After playing the first game of a scheduled three-game
series with the Athletics, Jim Delahanty, a part-time second baseman
acting as team spokesman, announced that the players would not
play the following day unless Ty Cobb played with them.

At the *Journal*, I took the report of the Detroit players' threat off
the wire myself, and I immediately grasped its implications. The
attack on Luker had itself been generally written off, both in the
press and in the streets, as an aberration; though the great man had
certainly lost his head, it had apparently been in the face of considerable provocation. But this business of players taking baseball law into
their own hands was more than unseemly; it constituted revolution.

Not that even so extreme a position should have been wholly
unexpected. For years, indeed, since the dawn of organized baseball,
players had complained about a system that left them subject to the
whims of management. They resented the provision in all of their
contracts that enabled owners to release players, in the event of
injury, on ten days' notice, without further compensation; and the
fact that, as in this case, athletes could be indefinitely suspended
without even the benefit of a hearing; and, most of all, that they were
bound to their teams by the reserve clause, to be sold, traded, released
—and paid as much or as little—as their employers saw fit.

Lately, players had been more forthright in their opposition to such conditions than at any time since 1890, when disgruntled members of the old National League had actually attempted to launch their own Players League. With the tide of trade unionism rising everywhere in the land, with public opposition to the trusts assured, with the cry for reform having been taken up by all political factions, the talk of a new Players Brotherhood had become insistent. Though they lacked leadership, though they were, in fact, as uneducated and ill-disciplined a bunch as any group of potential unionists on the continent, the players had long seemed poised for collective action. All they'd needed was an opportunity.

And now, in this seemingly trivial incident, involving as it did the game's greatest star, they seemed to have found it.

Within minutes I was on the phone, trying to track down Albert Gordy, the *Journal* sporting editor, in Cincinnati, where the brand new Redlands Field was to be inaugurated the following day. No luck; he wasn't at the ballpark, nor in his hotel, nor in the back room of Whitey's, the bar adjacent to the old Redlands Field and long favored by sporting writers. But barely a quarter of an hour later, he happened to call in himself. I filled him in on the Cobb developments.

"Say, Albert, let me cover this story."

The connection was weak and I wasn't sure he had heard me. "That's not in the budget," he said finally. "I'm the only one that goes on the road. Anyway, they're blowing out their ass. They're not going to strike."

"C'mon, Albert. Did you see my story on Luker?"

"I saw it."

My report from the hospital was, in fact, causing something of a stir in its own right, being the story that most effectively challenged the self-portrayal of Cobb's victim as an innocent. It had, in fact, proved something of a pick-me-up for the whole paper.

"Listen, Pond," said Gordy, "we'll get the story off the wire."

"Why not get it first hand? The *American* will." I stopped. "I promise you, Albert, I'll give you loads of color."

"I'm sure you will." There was a muffled laugh. "What're you after, Pond, *my* spot?" He thought it over for a long moment. "All right," he said finally, "but those Detroit bastards had better go out."

I caught a train to Philadelphia two hours later and arrived at the

Aldine Hotel, where the Tigers were staying, at around ten o'clock. The man I was looking for was Hugh "Ee Yah" Jennings, the Tigers' manager. Hughie had a reputation as a character, and though I had heretofore only seen him from a distance, it appeared fully earned. Often, while coaching first base, Jennings would launch into a routine designed to distract enemy pitchers, leaping in the air and yelling, like some kind of deranged cowboy, the phrase "Ee yah, ee yah." On certain occasions—always, for example, when the great Rube Waddell took the mound against the Tigers—Jennings would add another wrinkle, falling to the ground and commencing to play with a rubber snake, a tactic that effectively left Waddell unable to pitch.

But, for all of that, Jennings was a sound baseball man, extremely devoted to his players, and Harry Glaser, who knew him well, had assured me he'd offer an honest slant on the situation.

The man at the front desk, however, informed me that Jennings was not in his room. He'd rushed out just half an hour earlier in response to a telephone call, probably, I surmised, to a meeting with the club executives holed up at the Bellevue-Stratford. So I wandered aimlessly about the lobby, and from there into the hotel bar. A good choice: at a corner table in the nearly deserted room sat four strapping young men, each with a beer before him.

"Excuse me, are you fellows with the Tigers, by any chance?" I asked.

They looked up and studied me. "Maybe," said one, a large moon-faced fellow.

One of his companions moaned. "Christ almighty, Judge, you really do know how to throw 'em off the track, don't you?" He turned back to me. "You a scribe?"

"Luther Pond, the New York *Evening Journal.*"

He nodded. "I'm Jim Delahanty. This genius here is Ralph Works." He indicated the other two. "That's Tex Covington and that's Del Gainor." He paused. "And none of us is talkin'."

"You can call me Sheriff," observed Gainor pleasantly. "That's my name, *Sheriff* Gainor."

Though none of the four was at all prominent, I was acquainted with all the names. Especially Delahanty's. In addition to being the apparent leader of the strike action, he was one of five baseball-playing brothers. The oldest and most gifted, Big Ed, had made banner headlines in my own paper some years before when, on a training trip with the Washington Senators, he'd stepped off a Pullman train stalled at Niagara Falls for a breath of night air and plunged two hundred feet to his death.

"It's good to meet you all," I said.

"That's nice," replied Delahanty, "but we still ain't talkin'."

"Why not?" demanded Gainor. "I ain't had a single story writ up on me yet. I been up here three years already."

"Because we're already in the soup as it is," said Delahanty. "Wise up. These press boys aren't your friends. They sniff around when they need you."

"I won't use any names," I said. "All I want is a few facts."

"Hell, go ahead and use my name," said Gainor. "I want you to."

"Use mine too," said Works.

"Mine too!" chimed in Covington. "The folks back home don't hardly even believe I'm in the big time." He paused. "I got a brother that plays ball, too. Put him in. Same name as me—Tex Covington."

I grabbed a chair and pulled it up to the table, avoiding Delahanty's eye. "Well," I said, "maybe I will. It depends on what you have to say."

"We ain't talkin' about the Cobb situation," said Delahanty emphatically. "We'll do our talkin' tomorrow." He looked around the table at the others. "And that's final."

I shook my head. "Darn, Jim, what do you think brought me all the way down here from New York? The whole world knows you boys are mad as hell over what happened."

There was a silence.

"You could call me Judge," said Works, finally.

"Pardon me?"

"In your story. That's my name, not Ralph. Hardly nobody calls me Ralph."

I nodded at him. "Well, Judge, how'd you like another drink?"

"Sure thing."

"How about you, Tex? Don't worry about a thing, the New York *Evening Journal* has deep pockets."

"It have to be a beer?" asked Covington.

"No."

He looked at me in surprise. "No? And your newspaper'll foot the tab, no matter what?" He hesitated. "You sure you know who we are?"

So I ordered a fifth of bonded whiskey, and then a second, and, one by one, they told me. Covington and Gainor, one from rural Tennessee, the other from West Virginia, were best friends; each frequently interrupted the other with what he believed to be pertinent details. Works, a curveballing righthander, had been suffering arm trouble of late. Delahanty, who was a far softer touch than he tried to appear, soon joined in and was, before long, waxing downright sentimental over the departed Big Ed. Indeed, after a few minutes, I noticed that his eyes had misted over.

I was, by now, more than a little soused myself, and I tossed a comforting arm over his shoulder. "So, just tell me this, Jim," I said, "why so silent about what's going on?"

He gazed at me uncertainly, still unsure. "No reason," he replied.

"You fellows are big news. There's no telling what could come of this." I paused. "Word is, you've been talking with players on the other clubs."

There was a silence.

"Could be," answered Delahanty finally.

"Think the Athletics might go out, too, tomorrow?"

He made no reply.

"Sure, they will," blurted out Gainor.

"Could be," said Delahanty finally.

It was apparent that, even in his current state, there was little to be gotten from this man. I turned to the others with a smile. "Well, I just want you to know that as far as I'm concerned, it's pretty impressive, how loyal you boys are to Cobb."

Gainor looked up from his drink and gazed at me quizzically. "Who is?"

"That's right," added Covington, "not us."

"Hate 'im," chimed in Works, the most fully plastered of the bunch.

"But look how you're standing up for him."

Covington shook his head, a sudden smile on his lips. "Hell, I figured folks'd say we was *selfish*. After all, how many games we gonna win without Ty Cobb?"

"It's true," agreed Delahanty. "I thought the same thing."

"The four of us here ain't got the skills ol' Ty's got in his left nut," said Gainor, laughing. The rest of us joined him. "I mean it, too. We're terrible. We're a *terrible* team." He waited a beat, like a practiced vaudevillian. "And some of them teams we play is real *good.*"

That broke us up for real. In an instant, all five of us were doubled over.

"And, Cobb . . ." I tried, tears streaming down my face.

"If you ask me," interrupted Delahanty, now as loose as any of us, "I *liked* what that cripple said." He grabbed my arm. "Know what he was yelling out there? First he says that Cobb is half coon. Then, he starts up that Cobb fucks his own mama! Can you beat that?" He dissolved in laughter again.

"And, Cobb . . ."

"Ol' Ty, he just kept gettin' redder and redder, like he does," interrupted Gainor. "I was right next to him on the bench myself."

"Sheriff *lives* on the bench," cut in his pal Covington.

Gainor nodded agreeably. "It's true, it's true. And . . . and the cripple just kept up that razzin', and Cobb got more and more bug-eyed, and pretty soon he started shakin', and . . . there he went!"

The ballplayers laughed again, and so did I.

"Oh, me," said Covington, putting a hand to his forehead, "I am bamboozled."

"Me, too," said Gainor. "Strike comes at the right time, don't it?"

Works, whose head remained on the table, had not spoken a word for ten minutes.

"I guess I better hit the sack myself," I said. The room was, in fact, beginning to move in a slow, wide circle before me.

Delahanty clapped a hand on my shoulder. "Well, I guess you got your facts, anyway. We may look thick, but we got beliefs, same as everybody else. They do this to a big shot like Cobb, then what about us?" He paused and gazed at me with damp eyes. "You just make sure you don't get us in hot water. With Cobb, I mean."

"Queer thing," I observed, "how everybody's going around saying you fellows are so hot on Cobb's behalf."

Gainor grinned at me idiotically. "That's really what they're sayin'?"

"Ain't so," said Covington.

"People say lots of things," noted Delahanty, quite suddenly all business again. "But you watch out you don't write that. We gave you your facts. Don't you go sayin' that we're doing this 'cause we like Ty Cobb."

"That's right," said Gainor gravely, though his grin remained in place, "don't ever."

The following day I treated myself to a healthy dose of bicarbonate of soda and made it to Shibe Park early, before noon. I was approaching the visitors' clubhouse beneath the third base stands when, abruptly, the door flew open in my face, followed by Ty Cobb himself, rushing out of the room. I jumped out of the way and barely avoided him.

"I'm sorry," I said.

He stopped. "You should be, you little sonovabitch."

Ty Cobb was not a handsome man—his features were too sharp, his complexion mottled—but up close, even in street clothes, he was taller than expected, and far more powerful in build.

Words deserted me. I nodded dumbly.

"You watch it, boy. Nobody does that to Ty Cobb."

I hesitated a long moment. "I'm sorry," I said again.

"Okay, Tyrus, that's enough."

And there, in the clubhouse doorway, stood Hughie Jennings, hands on hips, dressed only in his long flannel DETROIT shirt. "You hear me, Ty?"

Cobb looked at him. "He ran into me, Hugh," he said. "He could've killed me."

"Yeah, well, never mind that. This man is a reporter. Mess him up and they'll suspend your ass for a year."

Cobb made no reply, merely glared at me a moment longer, then turned on his heel and stalked away.

I looked helplessly at Jennings. "Really, it *was* an accident."

He grinned. "Sure it was an accident. What does that have to do with it . . . what's your name?"

"Luther Pond. From the New York *Evening Journal*."

". . . Mr. Pond." He laughed. "You're the one that wrote the story on the cripple. Ty liked that."

"Oh?"

"Sure. Don't mind Ty, he's just touchy right now."

"I can understand that."

"Cobb takes things personal."

"I see."

"Sure. You met the cripple, you know how Ty feels."

With a sweep of his hand, Jennings motioned me into the club-house. I instantly noted, with relief, that I was the first reporter on the scene. Around us, nineteen men stood before wooden stalls, slowly donning their uniforms. Jim Delahanty was in the corner, half dressed, rubbing some goo into his small infielder's glove. He did not look up at me. I had often been in major league clubhouses before, and had grown accustomed to the raucous, often vulgar banter and schoolboy antics that in baseball circles passes for socializing. But this clubhouse was grim as a church.

"Is there somewhere I might have a private interview?" I asked Jennings.

He smiled. "I can trust my boys."

"No, what I mean . . ."

"That's a gag," he cut me off. He looked at me gravely. "Tell me, Mr. Pond, where'd your paper get the inside dope on the *Titanic*?"

I hesitated. "You mean the story about . . ."

"Another gag," he said, erupting in a huge grin. "Come with me."

Jennings led me down a narrow corridor toward the office of the visiting manager, and pulled open the door. To my astonishment, the tiny room was as packed with sporting writers as a five o'clock subway car; evidently, Jennings had been in the midst of an impromptu press conference when he'd been called out to fetch me.

"Say, fellas," called out Jennings in greeting, "you guys owe me one. I just spared another baby sporting writer the wrath of Cobb."

The men in the room laughed, as Hughie made his way through the throng and took a seat behind the oak desk in the corner. I hung back at the edge of the crowd, attempting to look somewhat less foolish than I felt. Not, of course, that anyone else present gave me a second thought.

"So," started up Jennings, "here it is five minutes later and I still have no idea what's going to happen. You boys ready to leave me be?"

"C'mon, Hugh," called out a writer, "they haven't told you anything? That's kind of tough to believe."

"You saw for yourself," retorted Jennings, "they made me leave the clubhouse when Ty was in there with them. He's the ringleader of this thing. He's the one you should be after."

"You know that Cobb's not talking."

"Well, boys, that's *your* worry today. Welcome to it."

"The other team gonna show up?" shouted out someone else.

Jennings eyed him indulgently. "You from Philadelphia?"

"You bet," responded the reporter.

"And you haven't figured out where to find Connie Mack yet? Why, he's right across the way, in the *other* clubhouse."

We laughed.

"And if they do, will you field a team?"

It was I who had called out the question, somewhat to my own surprise. Jennings looked back at me a moment, displaying, it seemed to me, a trace of respect.

"My direct orders, from Mr. Frank Navin, are to play a ballgame today," he replied. "He's the owner of the club and I do what he says. If I don't, we not only forfeit the contest and get fined five thousand dollars, but"—he paused—"Hugh Jennings gets tossed out on his ear. And what'd you boys do for fun then?"

For a long moment there was only the whisper of pencils scratching pads.

"Listen," added Jennings seriously, "a lot of you fellows know me. I sympathize with the boys. Don't print this, but if I was still a player, I guess I'd be with them."

"But how in the world are you going to get up a team now?" someone asked. "The game starts in a couple of hours."

Jennings said nothing.

"You must have made some plans."

"Mr. Jennings!"

The voice was high-pitched and urgent, that of a teenager.

"Mr. Jennings!"

"What is it, Ben?"

The sea of reporters parted, leaving the manager face to face with his clubhouse boy.

"The players just left the park. Delahanty told me to tell you they'll be ready to play, if Cobb is in the lineup."

Jennings nodded. "There's a surprise, huh, Ben?" He glanced around the room with what seemed to me a sudden small smile. "Well, boys, this is going to be something, isn't it?"

That it was. Within half an hour word had spread throughout the stands and into all those parts of Philadelphia where people interest themselves in such matters, that Hugh Jennings of the Detroit Tigers intended to recruit a team from amongst the spectators in attendance at Shibe Park. The Athletics, for their part, had apparently agreed to play. The city was instantly astir, as a thousand men reached the simultaneous realization that a lifelong fantasy was suddenly within reach. To play in a major league game! Against the world champions! I don't mind admitting that I found it a sore temptation myself, probably, under other circumstances, would have run right onto that field and offered myself up.

When, an hour before game time, Jennings finally gave himself over to the task of inspecting the volunteers, he found no fewer than seven hundred men, several in their sixties and one in his seventies, arrayed along the foul lines. Since testing their prowess individually was obviously out of the question, Hughie merely marched before them like a drill sergeant inspecting a ragtag army, and tapped on the shoulder the men who most *looked* like athletes. These were informed they would be paid fifty dollars for their services and sent hurrying into the Detroit clubhouse to put on the team's spare road uniforms.

I watched the selection process with field glasses from the wooden press stand behind third base. There were several dozen of us there, bantering all the while in that playful but studiously superior manner sporting writers so often assume when discussing amongst each other the men they write about; on the agenda at the moment were speculations as to cruel or unusual punishments that Ban Johnson might cook up for the striking ballplayers. Suggestions ranged from obliging them to do an honest day's work in a factory, to arranging for their batting averages and earned run averages to be foreverafter

published in bold type, to forcing them to attempt to spell each
other's names in public.

But after several minutes of this, I became uncomfortably aware
that the man beside me had remained altogether silent. When all the
volunteers had at last been selected and disappeared into the clubhouse, I turned and introduced myself.

"I know who you are," he said. "I read your story."

He was, of course, referring to the Luker sidebar; as far as any of
my colleagues seemed to be concerned, those four hundred words
were the only ones I'd ever written.

"What did you think?" I asked.

"Obviously," he said, "you hadn't yet met Mister Cobb when you
wrote it."

"I have now."

"I heard." He smiled faintly. "I'm Joe Albers of the Detroit News."

I was, of course, familiar with the by-line. Albers was a good
deal older than most of us in the press box that afternoon, but it
was not merely his patrician bearing or his sober three-piece suit
than made him more distinguished. He had covered the Tigers
since the team's inception a dozen years before—had, indeed, covered the original Detroit National League franchise back in the late
1880's—and within the trade his prose was much admired for its
clarity and wit.

"I hope you don't mind the kidding," I offered.

"No," he said. "But, you see, it's different for me. I care about
those boys."

"You're against the strike?"

"To the contrary, I am merely for the strikers. And I'm afraid that
they're starting to think of themselves as heroes."

Albers had the reputation, in fact, of being something of a father
figure to the ballplayers. It seemed they were frequently invited to
his home for dinner, and routinely sought his advice on personal
matters. When I asked him about that, he smiled. "Oh," he said,
"that depends. Some of them are pretty far from home, you know."
He paused. "I'll never get involved in their finances. I always tell
them that Mister Cobb's the one making all that money in the
market, not us newspaper stiffs."

"I was talking with some of the Detroit players last night," I said.

"Drinking with them," he corrected. "I don't approve of ball-players doing that kind of thing. Or sporting writers."

I paused, stung by the reprimand. But he did not appear to bear me any ill will at all. "They don't," I ventured, "seem to care for Cobb."

"No."

"Why not? I understand he's difficult, but he is the star of the club."

"For one thing, he's beaten the daylights out of almost every one of them."

"He has? His own teammates?"

"That's one of Mister Cobb's ways of welcoming new men to the club. Charlie Deal, the new third baseman, had his lip split open just a few weeks ago." He stopped and glanced out at the field; the men in Tigers uniforms were spiritedly tossing baseballs to one another.

"You don't seem to like Cobb much," I observed.

"Mister Cobb and I do not speak. But I am as fascinated by him as any ten-year-old boy in the bleachers. He wasn't like this when he came up, you know. He was only eighteen, and as scared as they all are. But he had all that talent, and so the veterans went after him more mercilessly than I had ever seen in all my years in the game. They ridiculed him, and splintered his bats, even intercepted his mail from home. And I don't think Mister Cobb has ever really trusted anyone but himself since then."

Suddenly, there was a stirring in the stands. The Detroit Tigers, the real ones, were trooping onto the field, in uniform, through the centerfield gate. At their head was Ty Cobb, who assumed his normal position in centerfield, staring defiantly at the impostors on the sideline. His teammates, in turn, began to move toward their habitual spots on the field. But within seconds, the home plate umpire was running toward the outfield, signalling with his hand for Cobb to remove himself from the field. He instantly did so, simply opening a door in the left centerfield wall, stepping into the grandstand and taking a seat. He was followed by every one of his teammates.

Albers and myself watched this scene in silence, while all around us our colleagues hooted it up.

"You and Cobb never talk at all?" I prompted.

Albers turned back to me. "Not a word. And the strange part is that I believe he used to like me tolerably well. Not that you ever know with Mister Cobb, of course." He paused. "Anyway, one day —it was a *slow* day, I'm sure you've run into them yourself—I made the mistake of calculating in print that the previous year he had been paid the extraordinary sum of forty dollars and sixteen cents for every base hit he had made. Since then I've been in his Sonovabitch Book."

"His what?"

"Yes. He really keeps one, you know."

As it turned out, not all of the young men selected by Jennings were to be starting players. Two had been told that they constituted the Detroit bench, and in their stead Hughie inserted into his starting lineup his two coaches, Deacon McGuire and Joe Sugden.

This turned out to be a wise move. Though both were in middle age—Sugden, with his snow-white hair, might have passed for sixty —and both in their prime had been catchers, and decidedly mediocre ones at that, they at least knew their way around a baseball diamond. During the game, each would score a run.

Those two runs would, however, be the only ones the Tigers would mark that afternoon—while their opponents would tally twenty-four. And, truth be told, the Athletics allowed the two old catchers to score their runs, shooing them around the basepaths like housewives chasing loveable pets from the kitchen.

And that is the way it went. Beforehand, when Jennings' collection first appeared on the diamond in their ill-fitting flannels, most of us in the park believed the game would be a lark, a nine-inning farce as hilarious as any show on the boards. Indeed, that prospect is what had inspired the presence of a great many of the twenty thousand fans in attendance.

But it wasn't that way at all. By the third inning, hundreds of patrons had already departed, and scores more were demanding their money back. For, excepting their hijinx with McGuire and Sugden, the Athletics played it completely straight, seizing this opportunity as the gift it was. Men who the day before had had to face fastballs travelling at ninety miles per hour and curveballs that snapped like whip ends, now found themselves opposite Aloysious Travers, whose only previous experience as a pitcher had been on behalf of the St. Joseph's College nine. This individual was made to pitch the entire game, though he yielded more than thirty hits and, in one particularly gruesome three-inning stretch, sixteen runs. Chief among those bedeviling him was Philadelphia's combative second baseman Eddie Collins, a thorough professional, a future member of the Hall of Fame, who actually seemed to play harder than usual. Collins not only collected five consecutive hits, but also saw fit to steal four bases, at one point provoking the amateur catcher to toss a ball into the stands in frustration.

Aside from Hugh Jennings, who somehow found it within himself to put on his customary show from the first base coacher's box, the real Tigers, witnessing the rout from the bleachers, appeared to be the only ones in the park enjoying themselves. But it is certain that no one was enjoying it less than League President Johnson, who had cut short a trip to the Redlands Field inaugural in Cincinnati to see if the Tigers would make good on their threat.

A huge, swaggering, pinstriped aristocrat, Johnson was nominally an employee of those eight captains of industry who owned fifty percent of the national pastime. But, excepting Charles Comiskey of the White Sox, who nursed an ancient personal grudge against him, the American League owners would as soon challenge Johnson as be caught lobbying for the Sherman Anti-Trust Act. They were businessmen, and Ban Johnson, a man more tenacious in the defense of profit than any of them, was superior business. "Baseball," he was fond of saying, "is the sinew and gut of the American spirit," and he regarded the game as a private preserve. Thus when, a few months earlier, Illinois Representative John Gallagher had proposed a Congressional investigation of what he called "the baseball trust," charging that players were "nothing more than industrial slaves," it was Johnson who had mounted the furious counterattack. "That man," he had gravely noted, and the message had been duly transmitted on the nation's sporting pages, "represents something alien to the American character."

So while the owner of the Tigers, Frank Navin, had greeted the strike with a gentlemanly appeal to his players to "trust the owners to get you justice," Johnson now, at last, hit back with everything he had. Within minutes of the conclusion of the contest in Philadelphia, he issued a pronouncement that every man on the roster of the Detroit baseball club was suspended forthwith. "There will be," his written announcement concluded, "no more farces in the American League."

That message reached those of us in the press stand by messenger, and we were staggered by its implications. The man was ready to banish twenty players—one full team of the sixteen that then constituted big league baseball—as an example to the others.

"Good Jesus," said Albers softly, "this is what I was afraid of."

Within seconds, he was on his feet, heading for the Aldine Hotel. Without asking, I tagged along.

We walked down the steep runways of Shibe Park rapidly, in silence. At ground level, he stopped and turned to me. "How old are you, young man?"

"I'm twenty-two." I wasn't exactly embarrassed by it anymore, but I realized it sounded damn silly.

"It isn't what you thought it was going to be, writing sports, is it?"

I hesitated. "It's not always this way, Joe."

His look was unexpectedly severe. "It just isn't always this obvious." He paused, then added more softly, "And it's getting worse by the year."

We caught a cab and ten minutes later were at the hotel. We found ten or twelve of the Tigers in a smoking room off the lobby, deep in soft chairs, happily reliving the late travesty. To be sure, they understood, in an abstract sense, that they should be miffed—the Athletics had, after all, gone yellow on them—but they simply could not help themselves. Indeed, when we came upon the scene, they were trying to decide whether any of Mack's faint-hearted men had *failed* to substantially fatten his batting average.

"Three hits," proclaimed outfielder Davy Jones. "I was counting. Every one of 'em got at least three. Including Boardwalk Brown."

Several voices rose in lusty assent.

"No sir," countered Sam Crawford, "Boardwalk"—the Athletics' notoriously weak-hitting pitcher was a native of south Jersey—"got only two. They gave him a fielder's choice on that ground ball."

That was so, spoke up two or three others immediately.

"Well," conceded Jones with a laugh, "that's still two more than he had last year. And, Collins, he . . . Hey, look who's here!" He waved in our direction. "Hiya, Jimbo, back from the circus?"

His mates greeted him with equal enthusiasm and Albers forced a smile. "You boys certainly turned things upside down, didn't you?"

"Enjoy that pitcher, did you?" asked Jim Delahanty. "Us boys thought up a nickname for him—Deadarm Dick."

I laughed at that, but Albers only nodded. "Obviously you haven't gotten the word yet." He handed Delahanty his copy of Johnson's statement.

Delahanty scanned the page quickly, then began to read aloud. "Every one of the Detroit players has automatically suspended himself. The Detroit Club itself will not appear on the field again until I am assured it has players who can compete with other teams in the league . . ."

He stopped reading.

"What's that mean?" asked Jack Onslow, a second-string catcher. "That mean we all sacked?"

"That is precisely what it means," replied Albers.

There was a long silence, as this information registered.

"Goddamned Athletics," spat out Sam Crawford. "Shouldn't even have been a game in the first place."

There was another long pause.

"What'd we do now, Jim?" asked Judge Works, softly.

Delahanty made no reply, just continued to stare at the paper.

"We ain't gonna give up, are we?"

Delahanty looked up with sudden irritation. "No, we ain't gonna give up. Why, do *you* think we should?"

"Well," spoke up Covington, "we made our point. No one can say otherwise . . ."

"We ain't out just to make some point!" countered Delahanty.

"Hell," said Davy Jones, "we didn't just make a point, we made history. People'll be talking about this for years." He stopped. "But maybe we *ought* to think about the consequences."

That was evidently what most of the men in that room wanted to hear. In an instant, six or eight of them were talking simultaneously, urging retreat. "He'll do it," shouted a player on my left, "Johnson'll do it for sure." On my right, a gangly young man, pitcher Ed

Willett, was on his feet urgently suggesting that a representative be
sent to negotiate with Johnson. It continued this way for a full thirty
seconds.

"Losing your guts, you fee-simple sonsobitches?"

Abruptly, there was silence, and every head in the room slowly
turned toward Ty Cobb, looming in the doorway.

Cobb surveyed the room, his blue eyes cold, his hawk features
sharper than ever. "What the hell you expect," he sneered, "that this
was gonna be easy? That that sonovabitch wasn't gonna try and
bleed us? What are you, *stupid?*"

The others simply stood there, gazing at him, reminiscent of
nothing so much as chastised children. It was a long moment before
any of them spoke.

"Well," said Works, "what do you say we should do, Peach?"

"Do?" came the booming response. "Not a damn thing. We got
the bastard by the nuts. All we gotta do now is squeeze. Johnson's
tryin' to scare you, same as he did with me."

To this, the only response was Delahanty's. "That's right."

"Use your heads, you morons!" continued Cobb, vehemently.
"You soft-boiled or something? He's bluffing! How the hell they
gonna come up with a major league ball club out of thin air?"

There was an awkward pause.

"I guess," suggested Sam Crawford, finally, with a tentative grin,
"they could always sign up Deadarm Dick."

The laughter that followed eased the tension in the room considerably. Even Cobb managed a tight smile.

"I'll tell you another thing," said Cobb, "if he tries to get rough,
we're gonna close down baseball, that's what! Damn the Athletics!
This ain't just a question of one club. It's Johnson's style to convict
a man and judge afterward. Well, if he tries to sack us all, he'll find
a hundred and fifty ballplayers walking out on him." He paused, his
gaze moving from face to face. "Don't you give a damn about right
and wrong no more? What are you, men or lousy slits?"

And slowly, as Cobb continued in this vein, the others began to
come around. As far as his teammates seemed to be concerned,
Cobb's grasp of the situation was, quite simply, firmer than theirs.
They might not have liked him, but their faith in his judgment
appeared boundless. Within five minutes there was a show of hands

and the decision had been made, unanimously: the players would hold fast for Cobb's reinstatement.

When it was over, the players began making their way out of the room in twos and threes, talking spiritedly, once again full of fight. I turned to leave also, with Albers. But, abruptly, there was a hand gripping my arm.

"Hold on there, friend, I'd like to have a little chat."

I turned and gazed into those fierce blue eyes. "Excuse me, Mr. Cobb, I've got a deadline to meet."

To my surprise, he offered a disarming grin. "Upset about that little incident before, are you? I just didn't know who you were, is all." He paused. "You did right by me, boy. Ty Cobb don't forget those things."

"I was only doing my job," I replied, altogether taken aback.

Cobb nodded solemnly. "I know it, I know it. But you're about the only one of the sonsobitches that did."

Albers, smiling faintly, continued on his way.

Despite myself, I was more than a little flattered.

"Well," I repeated dumbly, "I did my best." I hesitated. "He *was* a sonovabitch, that Luker."

Cobb looked at me closely. "Am I wrong, or do you hail from my part of the country?"

"From Richmond, Virginia." Though I had, over the previous several years, tried hard to lose my accent.

He let out a little whoop. "I *knew* it. I knew I liked you, boy. C'mere."

Cobb flung an arm over my shoulder and led me to a couch.

"Now you tell me how come you left a nice town like Richmond for some goddamn Yankee stinkhole?"

So I told him, more or less; Cobb had little trouble grasping ambition as a motive. And when, with seeming earnestness, he pressed for details about my family, I offered some of those, too, placing special emphasis on my Great Uncle Samuel Pond, who had distinguished himself at Antietam.

But there was less calculation in this than there might have been. In fact, to my surprise, I very soon found myself feeling oddly at ease with the great man. For, as is so often the case with the exceedingly arrogant, beneath the forbidding veneer (and, in this instance, not very far beneath) there was a striking vulnerability. It would be imprecise to say that Cobb was awkward, even verbally, or shy; his time in the big leagues had moved him well past that. What I saw, rather, was a hunger for affirmation.

I saw in him, indeed, a kindred spirit.

Sooner than I had any right to expect, he was talking with surprising intimacy about his own past; about his own struggle to become a ballplayer; most particularly, about his late father, a teacher of mathematics and Georgia state senator, whom he had apparently regarded with overpowering affection, and whose opposition to the trade he had had to overcome. And, it was the queerest thing, as he went on, his Southern accent seemed to become thicker, as if, in the simple relating, he had moved from the tempestuous present to that other, better time.

When, at length, we both had to be going, it was with the promise that we would talk again the following day.

"Thank you, Ty," I said, offering my hand, "I'd like that very much."

He took it and, unexpectedly, he grinned. "What'd you think, I was a lousy bastard like all of 'em say?" He indicated vaguely over his shoulder. "Hell, I want 'em to think that. Keeps the sonsobitches off balance."

"Like Johnson?" I said.

Before the words were out, I knew I'd made a mistake. Abruptly his face got hard, and when he spoke, it was with the voice I'd heard earlier. "That bastard's gotta learn, same as all the others. You don't pull no shit on Ty Cobb."

Cobb's scenario for the evolution of the situation had, we soon learned, been somewhat optimistic. Support of the strike was indeed widespread; among the hundreds of laudatory telegrams that reached the players at the Aldine, there were even declarations of support from Detroit's Mayor Thompson and the entire Georgia delegation to the U.S. Congress; I received a wire myself, from Gordy in Cincinnati, instructing me to continue giving the strikers favorable coverage—it was selling papers. But the men upon whom the Detroit players had been most heavily counting were considerably less forthcoming. On Sunday, May 20, Delahanty, who had passed much of the previous evening wiring players on each of the

other fifteen clubs, began finding their replies amidst the fan mail:
not one team was prepared to publicly endorse the walkout, let alone
join it. Moreover, as the day progressed, comments on the strike by
a number of prominent individual ballplayers began reaching Philadelphia. Christy Mathewson had been quoted in New York as saying
that the move was "a terrible mistake." Johnny Kling, player-
manager of the Boston Nationals, stated flatly that Cobb had been
wrong in the first place, and the Detroit players were just as wrong
to stand by him. Napoleon Lajoie out in Cleveland made it known
that in his estimation the strikers were "off their nut." Even Athletics
manager Connie Mack, who the afternoon before had made himself
unavailable to the press, now decided that the strikers were "just
quitters," who had chosen to revolt only because their team was
lagging so far behind in the standings.

When these reports reached the strikers, they felt, as might be
expected, an overwhelming sense of betrayal. They had, to be sure,
expected massive pressure to be applied to their fellows; but they had
also made themselves believe that there would be at least a token
show of solidarity. Soon, however, their anger turned to discomfort,
and then to alarm. In mid-afternoon, sensing the moment, Alex
Moore, Johnson's executive assistant, arrived at the hotel. One by
one, he took the dissidents aside and made clear, in most graphic
terms, the consequences of continued resistance. Ty Cobb, he
pointed out, had little to worry about in the long term: his career was
secure. Only their own were in jeopardy. And over what?

" 'Beliefs,' is what I'm told Jim Delahanty answered to that," Joe
Albers informed me, when I ran into him late that afternoon in the
lobby. Albers sighed; he looked like he hadn't slept since I'd last seen
him. "Most of the boys are ready to throw in the towel, but Jim and
a few others apparently believe the whole trade union movement is
on their shoulders. I've entitled my piece for tomorrow 'The Charge
of the Light-Headed Brigade.' "

I laughed. "That's good. Maybe I'll borrow it."

He looked at me sharply, decided I was ribbing him. "I think,"
he continued, "that Jim actually expects the I.W.W. to come riding
to the rescue. He's been in touch with them, you know."

"He's got a long wait," I observed.

He gazed at me levelly. "You would do them all a service, Luther, if you would pass that information on to your friend, Mister Cobb."

In fact, I had not seen any more of Cobb that day than anyone else. Among the reporters on the story, rumors as to his whereabouts had begun to swirl like leaves in a windstorm. He was, it was said, at the Bellevue-Stratford, hammering out a compromise with Johnson and the league owners; he was in seclusion, considering an announcement of his retirement from the game; he was, in actuality, passing the day far more pleasantly than any of us, in the company of a Philadelphia lady friend.

So I was, finally, like the others, left to rely on the available facts. I filed my story as per instructions, reporting that, in spite of Ban Johnson's best efforts, the strike had not yet been broken, throwing in a couple of rumors to flesh it out, and waited.

At seven-thirty that evening I was still waiting, but I was at least waiting contentedly, having moments before taken a seat in the hotel dining room. I had just ordered a rye and soda and was looking through the previous day's edition of my paper, which a colleague had been kind enough to carry from New York, when I started. There, on the sporting page, beside my own story from Philadelphia, was a verse by William Kirk!

> Gather 'round me, players all;
> Players pudgy, players tall,
> Players lean and players fat,
> Let us have a little chat.
>
> Players, never lose your heads,
> Taft's is lost and so is Ted's;
> Folks that pay to see you shine
> Pay your salaries—AND MINE!
>
> If the rooters in the crowd
> Want to yelp in voices loud
> Words and names too foul to hear
> Let their yelps bounce off your ear.

There was more—those damn rhymes always went on forever—but I did not wade through it. This was *my* story he was treading on, *my* province. And treading so clumsily!

In an instant I was on my feet, heading toward the telephone in the lobby.

Then, just as abruptly, I came to a halt. For standing by the door, ten yards away, scanning the room, was Ty Cobb! Instantly forgetting my pique, I began signalling him, waving and smiling. He paid me no heed, however, just continued, grim-faced, to survey the room, then turned on his heel and strode away.

I went after him, nearly bowling over a negro busboy in my headlong dash across the room, and got to the lobby just in time to see him move away from the front desk to the adjacent staircase.

If, as a spectator, I had often marvelled at the man's speed, I was flabbergasted by it now, as I struggled to stay near him. Ascending the steps three at a time, he was, within a flight, out of sight, and I was obliged to try and track him by ear. Gasping, light-headed, I at last pulled open the door off the fifth-floor landing, where his footfalls had seemed to cease, and stepped into the wide, carpeted hallway. Sure enough, thirty feet away, violently pounding on a door, stood Cobb.

I reached his side just as the door, number 514, slowly swung open. Judge Works looked at us uncertainly. "Hello, Cobb," he offered softly, "c'mon in."

"Try and stop me," sneered my companion, who pushed the door open and brushed past Works. Wordlessly, I followed.

And there, lounging on the bed, leaning against walls, perched atop the dresser, sitting on the floor, were all the rest of the Detroit Tigers. Standing before them, dressed, as was his custom, in an expensive three-piece suit, a gleaming gold watch chain looping down over his generous belly, was Ban Johnson. His man Moore, half a foot shorter, was at his side.

"Well well," boomed Johnson, "look who'th here!"

I had not been aware that Johnson spoke with a lisp; it had certainly never been reported. But, in this situation at least, the fact made him no less imposing.

Cobb looked around frantically at his mates. "What's he doing here?"

"I invited mythelth," said Johnson. "Thith hath gone on quite long enough. Your friendth and I have dethided that they will be on the field Wednethday in Washington, in uniform. That right?"

"Yessir," came several desultory voices.

"And you, Cobb," added Johnson, "shall obey the league rules in the future, or you shall pay the conthequentheth."

"Without me?" said Cobb, looking at Delahanty, a sudden note of desperation in his voice. "You decided without me?"

"You wasn't around," said Delahanty. "Strike's over. It's final. Mr. Johnson is letting us off with only a hundred dollar fine."

"You look at me when I addreth you, Cobb," said Johnson sharply.

Cobb wheeled toward him, his face contorted with rage. But, somehow, he held his tongue.

"I happen to know where you were thith afternoon," said Johnson. "I know you were with R. L. Richard."

The others looked at him in surprise. Richard was the president of the United States League, an upstart organization composed largely of washed-up major leaguers that was in the midst of its first, and what would turn out to be its only, season.

"What of it?" demanded Cobb. A vein in his temple had begun to throb.

"If you want to join them, you go right ahead. You may not believe it, but Organithed Batheball will get along quite well without you." He paused and eyed Cobb coldly. "But don't ecthpect to take your teammateth with you. Ith that underthtood?"

Cobb said nothing, just stared back at him with murderous eyes.

"I think," said Johnson to the others, with a large smile, "that it ith. Good evening, gentlemen. I have an appointment for thupper."

And, with Moore in tow, he swept majestically from the room.

A moment later, still without having spoken a word of response, crimson with anger, Ty Cobb departed, too. He would remain suspended another ten games, which punishment he would continue to bitterly resent the rest of his days. Anyone else might have considered himself lucky; Jim Delahanty, for one, would be dropped from the team before the end of the season, never to hold another job in Organized Baseball.

To say merely that labor peace had been restored on the baseball front would be to grossly underestimate the impact of that week's events. So thoroughly had the will of major league ballplayers to resist authority been obliterated that less than a fortnight later, National League President Thomas Lynch, a Johnson protégé, felt safe in publicly stating that the players would *never* organize into a protective association. "Baseball players have no thought for business," he said, "their minds in that direction being only concentrated on the semi-monthly pay envelope." And, indeed, the notion of a players union would not again be seriously considered for five decades.

That was not, of course, the angle I chose to attach to my account of the strike's end; my readers did not wish to be depressed, nor, it had been made abundantly clear, did my editors. "The Detroit Tigers left Philadelphia this morning claiming a moral victory," began my story. "'Tis true they have agreed to return to the playing field and to accept a small fine, but the way they are talking, the grand old game has been changed forever.

" 'President Johnson has promised there will be no more rowdyism from the bleachers,' speaks Delahanty, just before the club's departure from the North Philly station, 'and that's good enough for us. From now on, you'll catch us calling ourselves the T.A.R.'

" 'What's that?' pipes up an unwary scribe.

" 'Why, the Tigers of the American Revolution,' he replies with a laugh.

"As for Cobb, he has nothing but kind words for his mates. 'They were set to go through to the finish with it,' says the Georgia Peach, 'but I didn't want those good fellows to get fired and blacklisted and all that just on my account. I told them to get back into the game and play for Mr. Navin—and win. And you bet I'll be back with them soon!' "

Nineteen Thirteen

by George D. Weaver

They called Charles Comiskey, who is the guy I want to tell you about here, The Old Roman. Back then the newspaper writers always gave the magnates names like that. Comiskey was The Old Roman, John McGraw was Little Napoleon, Frank Chance was The Peerless Leader, Connie Mack was The Tall Tactician. Hell, Mack is still The Tall Tactician, even despite the fact that his club has been stinking up the league for ten years now. But us players, we were always Buck and Happy and Knuckles.

Not that I did too much thinking about the meaning of that at the time. That's just the way things was, and if you did not like it, which anyway I did, you could lump it.

See, my first couple of seasons or so, I was just happy as a lark to be up performing in the big show, especially since I did not exactly set anybody on their ears. My first year I only hit for a hill of beans, which was .224, and then the year after, in '13, my glove work, which had been a little shaky to start out with, suffered from the famous sophomore jinx. I guess my arm was still too strong for my own good.

But I have to admit that even back then I had other qualities that count for something. As Ray Schalk, the little catcher, put it to me one day at Detroit after I had marked the winning tally all the way from second base on a bunt single (which is no easy feat to do), "Buck, I have never seen another ballplayer hustle as you do. You seem to feel you have not earned a day's pay unless your uniform is black at the end of it." In other terms, I was what they used to call a fireplug, and what they call a sparkplug today.

I know that on some clubs this would not count for too much, but let's face it, on our club it was one of the few things we had going for us. This was pretty embarrassing for The Old Roman, who was about the worst loser you ever saw. The word was that back when he was a ballplayer and then a manager, his clubs won almost all of the time. But now that he was a magnate, he had gotten used to defeat, all right, and then some. The Sox had been the champions but once, and that was in '07. Indeed, at the time in question, the Cubs were the big act on the boards in Chi and, like I say, we were a crowd of mutts. That is why I think Comiskey took a shine to me.

I found out that this was so back in my first year. We were up against the Athletics at home one day and Coveleski—Stanley the righthander, not his brother Harry the southpaw—was tossing for them and he was giving it to us good. This bird had about the most alarming dropball you ever saw, even though he was only a rookie, and we could not hit him for all of the tea in the world. Plus, it was August and real no suspenders weather, and the boys on our bench were dragging their tongues on the ground. Well, around the fifth inning I got a notion in my head, and it was to razz the rube in his own lingo, which was Polack. See, back where I come from, in Stowe, Pennsylvania, they got lots of them there working in the mines, as my own father did. It was from them that I picked up Polack razzing on the ballfield.

I guess I should add that by then I had myself become about as good a needle as anyone on the club. Earlier than that, in that same season I had even pulled the old Pullman sleeper hoax, on Lefty Schulz, who was a good-looking rook with the New York club. I walked over to the busher on the sidelines where he was heating up and made the introductions. "By the way," I said, "it looks to me like your soupbone is pretty sore today. Didn't you get a good rest last night?" which of course I knew he had not, 'cause his club had been on the overnight train.

"Well, no," he said, all concerned. "They gave me an upper berth," which naturally they always do for rookies, "and there was not too much room up there."

"Well," I said, "you put your arm in the little hammock by the window, didn't you? That is what it's for."

So he hemmed a little, and finally he said "Sure," 'cause he didn't want to look like a simp in my eyes.

Well, to make a long story shorter, I found out later that their next trip on a sleeper, the busher nearly suffocated himself to death on his pillow trying to work his left arm into that hammock, and of course after that it was so stiff he couldn't toss for a week or more.

So, anyway, there I was on the bench, and Coveleski had us flivvered, and all at once I start screaming "Vera-gava nay-doh-bray, ver-seek-nay-doh-bray," which means "You are a bonehead," or some such thing. In an instant, Coveleski forgot all about the fellow at the plate and looked over at me. "You shut your trap," he yelled.

"Nay-doh-bray vera-gava," I came right back, and that did it! He came charging over at me like a bull in a china shop, and if our coacher Gleason had not stopped him halfway in his tracks, he would've doomed me right there for sure. But instead he was made to go back to the pitching slab and try to get back to work, and by then he was so rattled he could no more find the plate than I could find the North Pole. He went ahead and issued five passes in a row, before The Tall Tactician finally figured it out to give him the can.

All the while, over in his private box behind our bench, which the sporting writers said looked just like the emperor's box in the old days in Rome, or at least it was supposed to, Comiskey was cracking up. There he was in that big gray hat he always had on and his fancy suit, even though it was a furnace out there, surrounded by all the other big punches, and he was carrying on like someone had just farted in a church or something.

After the contest, which we won in fine style, he came right up to me in the clubhouse. "Young man," he said, "where in hell did you learn that?"

So I told him just like I told you.

"Well, I might just give the whole club lessons in French, I-talian *and* Polish. That way we would win the pennant hands down." And he went off laughing to himself and shaking his noggin.

Now, it is not so easy to put across what an honor this was. Comiskey was no ordinary fellow, even for a magnate, but a man that was beloved by the public and press alike. It was almost like he was a god or something, the way people talked of him. Not only was he one of the fathers of the national pastime, as they already put it back then, but never before was there an owner that was such a man of the people, nor so generous and full of good humor. So now maybe you can see what I'm talking about.

Of course, at the moment in question, I figured he was joking about the lessons, which it turned out he was, but it was still pretty certain to me that he liked me. And around near the end of the '13 season I found out for sure. One fine day after we had played that same Philadelphia club, and had got skunked by Eddie Plank, The Old Roman came up to me in the clubhouse again and said "Well, Buck, it's too bad Connie has stopped throwing Cove at us." See, after the last season, they had sent him right back down to the boonies to get his head screwed on right, and he was not to show his face again in the big time for three more years.

"It sure is," I joked right back. "I don't think Plank talks a thing but English, and not all that good, neither."

"He's some pitcher, though. I certainly wouldn't mind having him with us on the round-the-world tour."

I waited just a moment here, 'cause there was something I wanted to get off my chest, but I did not know if this was the right time. "Well," I finally came out with it, "I would not mind being on that round-the-world tour myself, if there's a place for me."

That was sure the truth. For weeks a fellow had not been able to pick up a paper without gawking at some new write-up about the great tour that Comiskey was getting up with John McGraw of the New York National club. The plan was that the two teams would go off globe-trotting around the planet, playing each other in every two-bit country they could find. It was all for good will, that's what the newspapers said, and not for the purpose of making money, and it even had the okay of President Wilson. The only thing was, it was not really going to be the White Sox at all that were playing, even though that is what their uniforms would say. No sir, Comiskey was going around picking up some big stars from other ballclubs to fill up the roster, like for instance Tris Speaker of Boston and Wahoo Sam Crawford with Detroit. I guessed he just did not want the Chinks to think the Sox were a bunch of stiffs.

But, anyway, that had sounded like real bad news for yours truly.

Some fellows that was not going to get asked along said they didn't
care to go on any tour in the first place, which was mostly just sour
grapes. Of course, there were also fellows like Ping Bodie on our
club, who was once sold to Indianapolis and did not want to report
because someone had told him he had to cross a couple of continents
to get there. But me, I wanted to go on that tour in such a bad way
that I could not even keep my mind on anything else. After the
papers started printing all those articles about it, there were some
days I would stand there at my post at shortstop, or sometimes they
also played me at third base, just dreaming about all those faraway
places with strange-sounding names, like China or Paris.

And there was also another reason I wanted to go, too. The buzz
was that The Old Roman was risking everything he had to make the
trip, even including the ballclub itself. I remember the *Tribune* had
one story where it said all of his rich pals were telling him not to do
it 'cause it would never work out. And Comiskey just laughed and
said, "It's too bad I was not told that before I handed over a check
for ninety thousand to the steamship company." See, this was his
own personal dream and he could not worry if it left him busted.
Whereas the first round-the-world baseball tour, which was done by
Mr. Spalding back in 1881, was mainly for the purpose of selling
sporting equipment to the people that lived there, Comiskey said that
since this one was just for the good will and all, he was ready to face
the music. This is what the papers said. Well, I figured if the ballclub
was about to be a cadaver, I at least wanted a little fun while it was
still around.

So that is why I spoke up to Comiskey like I did, and to my
surprise he just beamed happily. "Well, young man, that is a coincidence, because that is exactly what I've come down here to talk to
you about." He stuck out his paw. "I expect you'll be able to show
those foreigners a thing or two about hustle, won't you?"

The rest of the season, which anyway was just a few weeks more,
passed by me like a locomotive. We ended up down in fifth place,
and I was sorry about that, but like I say, my head was too full of
plans to worry. I had lots of letters to send off, which is not so easy
for me even at this late date and back then was even tougher. Plus,
there was a whole list of items for me to buy, including a mess of
new shirts, two pairs of patent leather shoes, and a full monkey suit,

which by itself set me back forty-two bucks. This was on Comiskey's order, on account of us being good will ambassadors and all.

But finally, on October 16, 1913, we set off aboard a special train that was named the Diamond Special. The scribes said the Diamond Special was magnificent and that it was as fancy inside as anything, but I'll tell you the truth, it was not really so magnificent at all, just regular, except maybe the car the scribes rode in themselves. That car had a bar in there, all full of hooch for them to suck up.

We did not leave the U.S. of A. right off the bat, by the way. By no means. What we did was spend nearly a whole month on board that train, halting almost every day at some town or another on the way west. And just about every place we stopped, we played a contest in front of the locals, because most of these rubes had not laid eyes before on a big league ballplayer no more than a Jap or Chinaman. They would all show up at the depot as we pulled in, and usually there would be a band playing Sousa or some damn thing and then the local mayor would give a speech, and maybe McGraw too, but not Comiskey 'cause he was timid about public oration. Sometimes, though, Nixey Callahan would get up there instead and say a word for our side, which was pretty comical to see, since usually he would praise the town and then right away kind of take it back. And then we would all march over to the diamond, and every bug in the county would pay something to get a look at us working, and that was that. Afterwards, and this happened in almost every locale we went to, there would be some kind of banquet for the ballplayers. I will tell you the truth, I have never punished my teeth as I did then on that tour. We ate our way through Albuquerque and Dallas and Tucson, and by the time we made my old stomping grounds in California, we had almost all of us put on a few pounds, including me.

The biggest feast of all was about the last one we had, and it was a breakfast, too. It was in a burg called Oxnard, which was full of genuine cowboys. What they served us was roasted ox heads, that they had baked in big holes in the ground for the whole night before we ate them, and also plenty of beer. We just ate and ate 'til around noon, and then took a little rest, and headed right over to the field there, which really was just a field, not a diamond at all.

But I will show you now the sort of rubes we were dealing with.

Around the fourth frame or so, they had to stop the game, 'cause some of the bugs over on the sideline were causing a ruckus. They had been taunting the ballplayers that a horse could beat a man around the bases, and they were making a fuss to see it done. Also, many of the ballplayers themselves were ready to put a wager on it. So Hans Lobert, who was really a Phillie but was here with the Giants squad, he got himself set beside home base, and next to him they brought over this little horse that was supposed to be good at cutting corners, and someone fired a six-gun in the air and off they went. The Dutchman had him beat most of the way, too, for he was a fellow who had swiped forty-one bases that year. But at the last second, Hans made a dive for the plate and so did the horse, who nipped him by a nose. All in all I enjoyed this spectacle, for I had wagered on the horse myself, though only a measly dollar, and, after all, the Giants were our rivals.

It was just a couple of days after the six-legged race, as one of the scribes put it, that our bunch, of which there were sixty-seven people in all, set across the sea aboard the *Empress of Japan*. The trip across was no piece of pie, neither, as ten days out we ran smack into a storm that the crew said was about the worst in twenty years. There were waves sixty feet tall out there, and the boat bounced around like it was in a bathtub or something. I don't have to tell you that all of us were sick in fourteen languages, and I kept wondering if maybe old Ping Bodie was right all along. It was sure some relief to sail into Yokohama, which took more than two weeks to get to!

I do not see much purpose in going into the first part of the trip here, except the highlights, especially with us now being at war against the Japs and some of these others. But I will point out that the eats over there in Japan was so bad that I do not know how a person can live on it, let alone fight a war or play ball. But we played a couple of contests against a Jap college team named Kioko, and they were not half bad, except they did not have someone who could pitch. Still, I have to admit that the best thing that happened there was in the hijinx department. In a town called Nagasaki, the Jap police would not let us back on the boat because there was a billiard ball missing from a joint where some of us had been playing. Well, it turned out that Merkle of the Giants had put it in his pocket, and he said it was a mistake which the Japs did not buy for even a minute, and finally they had to get some guy from our consulate there to smooth it out.

From there it was on to China, where it rained spikes the whole four days we were there, and then to the Philippines and Australia, Ceylon and Egypt, and you can imagine what it was like. There we were working in front of all these odd ducks, and I don't think most of the time they even knew what the hell was going on. In Egypt, the khedive himself, who was kind of like the king there, came out to see us, and he had his back to the field the whole time. Some of the boys got a little miffy at this, so Heinie Zimmerman went over to see what was up, but he came back with a big grin across his map. "It's okay," he said, "he means us no disrespect. It's just that with so many ballplayers around, he's worried about his harem."

I guess you could say that was the way it went all over. We ballplayers had a high time, and no one meant us no disrespect, but no one could really figure out what we were up to out there. Oh, they would show up to look us over, all right, kind of the way you might take a trip to see a bearded lady or something, but most of the time they just stood there like dummies. For instance, one time in Ceylon, we were playing on a pretty nice field that usually they used for cricket, and Speaker made about the best grab of the spheroid I ever clapped eyes on, diving after it like a fiend and then rolling over a few times and still hanging on to it. Well, I'm telling you, it was just as quiet at that place as a nigger stealing corn. So when he came in I said "Nice grab, Tris." And he just smiled and said, "Oh, did you notice?"

There was plenty of good will, there's no denying that, but it was mostly amongst us travelling tourists. It was kind of curious, because there we all were together, the ballplayers, the scribes and the big cheeses, all of us there in the same boat. So we had a feeling between each other like we had never had before, and would never again after. Hell, even Bill Klem, who was there to umpire the games, almost ended up one of the boys. It turned out that Klem had this awful fear that the towline of the boat was going to hook on the equator at low tide and we would go down, so one night we woke him up and told him his fear had occurred. You should've seen the fellow running about, packing his bags. After that it was hard to look at him the same awesome way as before.

In fact, just about the only bird on that tour who did not fit right in was Jim Thorpe, the famous redskin, who was a clam if ever there was one. You could light a cigarette under the guy and he would not say nothing. And he did not get on much better with any of his teammates than with me. See, Thorpe had not yet played no big league ball at all, but McGraw had picked him up for the tour anyway on account of his being famous from the Olympic Games. But when it came right down to it, he was not only not friendly, but also a big bum on the diamond, for he did not know how to hit a curveball. But there he was with his new wife, who he called by the handle Snooks, and the two of them went about quiet as mice, always wearing a real somber look on their Indian mugs, and they gave all us white men the jumps.

But the important part that I have been meaning to get to is that this was also the time when I really came to have a close-up gander at The Old Roman. At the start, during the crossing and for a few days after, the old gent was about the sickest of the bunch, and so he kept out of sight. But by the time we got to China, and then most of the rest of the way, he was as full of vim as anybody, even despite his years. There he would be every day, all chummy with the Chinks or Aussies, depending on where we were at the moment, acting like an alderman or something. Of course, it is no happenstance that I say that, since that is what his old man had been, Honest John Comiskey of the seventh ward. The Old Roman even made out that the foreigners knew what was up with the game. "The fine points move them like an electric shock," I heard him tell one of the writers one day that was always following him about. "I cannot understand what they say, but their gestures tell a story of bewilderment and delight." I suppose he thought he had to say that, because I promise you, Comiskey was not no moron.

And every night he would still be going, sitting up on the deck of the *St. Albens*, which was the boat we took after we left Japan, holding a highball in his paw and gabbing 'til the cows came home.

It was pretty interesting gab, too. Most of his tales were about the time when he was a busher himself, back in the seventies and eighties. He talked about those days like they were just as fresh in his dome as yesterday, which I suppose they were, and every night a whole crowd of us, even including most of the sporting writers, would sit out there with him, taking it in. He would go on and on about how rough it used to be, how when he was with the old St. Louis club he used to kick runners off the bag when the ump wasn't looking and slap the ball right down on their conks to put them out, stories like that, and also about how easy us modern ballplayers had it, with our woolen uniforms and nice hotels and all. But he could take chaff just as well as give it. A few of the fellows, especially the ones on the Giants, would come right back at him that he was just an old-timer and good riddance to the days he talked of, and Comiskey's old puss would grow red, but he would laugh right along with them.

There was only one time when he seemed to get a little miffed. It was when we were anchored right in the Suez Canal, the night before we left Egypt. He was telling about the first time he invented the modern way of playing first base, which he had done at the old Polo Grounds in New York at 110th Street and Fifth Avenue, against the New York Mets. "I had had it in my head for weeks," he said, "that perhaps it made sense to play away from the sack, so as to cover more ground, instead of directly on it, as was the custom then. When I took this position, the spectators immediately commenced hooting at me, and the umpire himself approached me and asked what I was doing. But I persisted, and by the end of nine innings, I had changed the game of baseball." He stopped right there and looked around at us real slowly in the light of the silvery moon. "I revolutionized baseball, and I was making a wage of seventy-five dollars a month at the time."

"So what of it?" piped up Heinie Zimmerman. "I hear that some of your players are still making seventy-five a month."

"That's not true!" said Comiskey, suddenly real loud, with veins popping out all over his noggin. "I pay my players what they deserve."

"That's right," spoke up one of the scribes by the name of G. W. Axelson. He was with the *Record-American* back in Chi and he was always sucking up to the old man.

But Comiskey was not content with that. "Isn't that right, Buck?" he said.

It was pretty dark out there, but I could tell every eye in the place was eyeing me. "Yes sir, I suppose it is." After all, I was making two thousand five hundred per annum, which may not have been too much, but it was only my second season.

"Damn right," he came back. "I am good and tired of players snivelling that they're going to quit the game if they don't get more money. When I was playing, I was always afraid the game was going to quit me."

And even though he did not work for Comiskey, Zimmerman did not make no response to that, and neither did the others, 'cause we could tell how hot the old man was.

Well, that pretty much ended that evening right there. A little while after, goodnights were said, and most everyone went off to their cabin. But I stayed a little bit behind, and then when I saw Heinie was alone, next to the railing, I walked right over to him.

"Well," I said, "I guess you're sorry you said that to him?"

"Who?"

"The Old Roman."

"The Old Roman is full of shit!"

I had never before in my life heard such perfumed talk of The Old Roman, especially from a fellow ballplayer. "The Old Roman is full of shit? You must be off your onion."

But he didn't get mad or nothing, just paused and spit down in the Suez Canal. "How much did you get paid to come on this tour, Weaver?"

"Why, five hundred fifty dollars, of course, same as everybody."

"That's right, for five months of work. And how much do you think the magnates are making off of it, Comiskey and McGraw?"

"I don't have no idea. But I do know that Comiskey is risking his whole ballclub."

"You believe that hogwash?"

"Certainly I do."

He laughed, not that he really thought it was funny or anything. "Listen, Weaver, Comiskey is rich as a bank. They'll make enough from the motion pictures alone to pay all our salaries, and then some. Do you think they had us out there by the Pyramids just for kicks?"

What he was talking about was a thing that had happened a few days before that. See, there was this fellow Frank McGlynn that was on the tour from the Electric Film Company, and we had all gone out to the Pyramids with our gear, and he had told us to play a little ball there, even though there wasn't hardly any room. He even got Ivy Wingo of the St. Louis ballclub to toss the ball all the way over the top of the Pyramids while the cameras took it all in. "Well," I said, "I don't know why I should believe you. Comiskey has always done all right by me."

"It's all the same to me. Advice that ain't paid for ain't no good, I suppose." And off he went to his cabin.

Now this bothered me a little bit, but I let it pass by for the instant. I am not the sort of fellow that goes around dishing my boss. It was not 'til we got to Paris, France, which is where we went after Rome, Italy (where we got to meet Pope Pius the Tenth in the flesh), that I really got a notion of what a skinflint Comiskey was, after all.

See, Paris was one of the biggest stops of the whole tour. We had four contests we were supposed to play there in some big park, and the word was they were selling tickets like ice blocks in August. Search me as to how come. From what I could tell, the frogs know even less about baseball than the wops, which was flat nothing. The ones I tried to explain it to, most of them seemed to think you played ball with your feet.

But the thing was, it was pouring rain so hard when we got there, we hardly even wanted to leave our hotel, which was the Paris Latin, let alone play ball. So that's what we did. For the whole first day, we just hung in the lobby of the hotel shooting the breeze, just like back home, and stepping outside only to try the local eats and then go over to the follies. That's how steady it was coming down.

Well, around the second day, who shows up in the hotel but one of the frog promoters, wanting to know what's up. Naturally Comiskey and McGraw just pointed out of doors, where the water was running down in the street like a flood. But the promoter, he wasn't buying that. He wanted us to work anyway, like I guess the association football players did, even in such conditions. So it went back and forth like that for a while, with the promoter making a fuss that no one could even understand, and then the three of them went up into McGraw's room to chew it over like businessmen.

And then, after a bit, they all came out again, and the frog left. Comiskey took us all into the dining room and he said, "Gentlemen, we have decided to give them a couple of games, in the cause of good will and true sportsmanship."

Well, you can guess how much ice that cut with us players. Good
will is fine and all, but a fellow can break his legs working in water
like that, not to mention what it will do to his glove and spikes. I
was not about to speak up, but Zimmerman and Wahoo Crawford
and some of the others did so, and we all backed them up.

You could tell that Comiskey and McGraw got pretty hot on
hearing this, but of course they knew we were right themselves.
Even Callahan stood by us, without changing his mind or anything.

"You young men are being extremely unreasonable," said The
Old Roman. "We have a contract with these people, and I'm afraid
we are obliged to live up to it."

"There's nothing we can do about that," said Wahoo, who was
a college man himself, just like Comiskey. "We didn't play in China
in the rain, we shouldn't have to here."

"We didn't have a contract in China," came back McGraw, who
was a tough little guy.

But we would not change our tune, not that day, nor the next day
when the frog papers started saying that we were dodging the games
for the gay life in Paris, nor even when Comiskey brought over
Ambassador Herrick to the Paris Latin Hotel to talk us into it.

So finally The Old Roman had to throw in the towel. He told the
frog promoter he would pay him back some dough (which I don't
know if he ever did) and off we went to our last stop, which was
England.

Now, I do not know how much you know about the English, and
I did not know too much myself before this, but it turns out that
being polite is very big over there. Even the bugs that go to sporting
events in London know to be polite. They do not shine mirrors in
the eyes of foes as they do at ballgames here, nor even give them the
raspberry, which is a natural thing to do. But what happened over
there tested how polite they were, all right.

It all started the very first morning after we got there. We were
put up at the Hotel Cecil, and my roomie was "Death Valley" Jim
Scott, who was a southpaw with our club that had also been my
roomie back in Cairo at the Heliopolis Hotel. Anyway, we got to
talking there in our room and figured out it had been seven weeks
since we had seen a single word printed in our own native lingo, and
of course this now was our big break. So we called for one of the

boys that worked there and told him to bring us up a paper, which he did double quick. It was called *The Pall Mall Gazette*, and you can imagine our surprise to see a write-up right there on the first page about us world tourists.

And it was sure not a good write-up, I can tell you that. From what I could make out, as soon as we got off the boat, Comiskey and McGraw must have started gabbing to the local scribes, 'cause there it all was in black and white, the two of them putting the rap on the English. And it was no puny slight they were handing them, neither. The Old Roman had come right out and said that we Americans made much better soldiers than the English, and the reason for it was baseball. He said that the national game was good for both the mind as well as the body, and then added that if England knew what was good for them, they would take a tip and start playing it too.

"Well how in hell do you like that?" I said to Scott, when I had finished reading it to him out loud. "This is not good will in my book."

"I should say not," he said. "It may all be true, what they say, but I would not have said it myself."

Later on in that day, when we went outside to take a stroll on the town, none of the English people we saw made a remark about it, on account of them having such good manners and all, but in their own way they seemed pretty cool with us. And why shouldn't they? After all, they take their wars as serious as the next fellow. But of course me and Scott, and all the other ballplayers also, we were in a tight squeeze. We did not like the impolite statements in question ourselves, but then again, it was tough to talk up against The Old Roman to foreigners.

But you will not believe this, the very next day we picked up *The Pall Mall Gazette* and there was Comiskey at it again. He and McGraw had gone out to a show of *Broadway Jones*, which is what they called *Little Johnny Jones* in London, even though it was still the same show by Cohan and all as they had in New York, and some of the local sporting writers had caught up with them there and asked them again about what they had said. According to *The Pall Mall Gazette*, right there in the lobby of the show, The Old Roman pulled out of his pocket an old article, what they call an editorial, from *The New York Times*. The article was all about how baseball was

not any good and a dying game, and that cricket should take over
in the States instead. "Cricket will probably become as popular here
in the course of a few years as it is in England," is how it ended, and
Comiskey read it right out to those English news hounds, "and we
shall be contented to play a game worth playing, even if it is English
in origin, without trying to establish a national game of our own."
And then he stopped reading, and looked those around him right in
the eye, and slowly tore the article up, piece by piece. "Gentlemen,"
he said, "that editorial was written in 1881. I have carried it with me
all these thirty-two years, waiting to do what I just did."

Well, that really did it. No matter how polite a person may be,
he has his limits, even an Englishman, and us ballplayers were really
up a tree. Me and Scott did not even risk to go out of doors that day
until the afternoon, and when we did we got right in a taxi. See, I
don't think I said this yet, but when we walked around in these
foreign countries, we had to wear our White Sox sweater. That was
the rule, so it wasn't so easy to hide from the people that lived there.

Anyway, at the moment in question, we had it in our noggins to
ride over and gawk at the palace where the king lived. We were
heading that way and just starting to relax a little bit, when all at
once the bird doing the driving pipes up. "You blokes are with the
Americans?"

So we said sure, what of it, like we didn't know what he was
getting at or something.

"If you ask me," he said, "you ought to be ashamed of yourselves."

"Well, who asked you?" I came right back.

After that he kept his trap shut for a while and just kept driving.
Only when the car stopped, I saw we were not at the king's place
at all, but right back in front of the Hotel Cecil.

"What the hell's going on here?" I started. But then the guy
turned around and I saw that he was mad as a bedbug, with his puss
all red and little lines popping out in his nose. "Get out," he said,
"I don't want you in my vehicle." Then he stopped. See, he was so
polite he could not help himself. "There will be no charge."

Well, you can just guess how bad me and Scott felt after that one.
And the worst part was, we did not know what was up with the
magnates any more than that driver, except maybe to figure that they
were trying to get even with us for what happened in Paris. The fact

is, we had not laid eyes on those two ourselves since we blew into town, since they were not at the Cecil, but were being put up at some ritzy digs called the Savoy.

But then suddenly things changed. The next day, which was the day before we was to play our contest, Comiskey showed up again in the papers, and this time he laid it on thick about how sorry he was about all the bad feeling, and that it was all a misunderstanding, and he certainly did not want no international incident or nothing, and how he hoped that every English guy in the world would show up at the game. And to prove it, he had sent over Jim and Snooks Thorpe with a personal invite to King George, and also a tiny little White Sox uniform for the king's grandkid. And this was not even all. Later on in the day, the ambassador of the United States, who was named Page, also went over to the palace for a chat with the king, just to be sure for certain that things was smoothed out.

Well, this will show you how polite the English really are, for it worked like a charm. The king said sure he would show up, and suddenly every bird out there in the streets was grinning at us and pounding our backs like nothing had happened at all, and naturally they all wanted to come and see the game on account of good will and the king being there. So at the very last moment, they moved it from some park where they were supposed to hold it to the biggest place they could find, which was a cricket stadium that could hold thirty-five thousand English people.

And I do not have to tell you that the next day that place was packed like sardines. And King George was there, all right, with the ambassador on one side and The Old Roman on the other, both of them explaining in his ear the whole time and him smiling and nodding. Of course, these English did not understand what was going on out there no more than any of the others, and indeed the thing they liked best was the uniforms, especially the catcher's gear, that they thought was a big part of the game. But we put on a good show for them anyway, maybe the best of the whole tour, and the contest went an extra frame before Tommy Daly at last won it for us with a four-bagger to right. So all the locals went back to their homes ignorant as hayseeds and happy as clams.

Two days later, on March 21, 1914, we were finally on our way back home on the *Lusitania,* and when we got to New York, The

Old Roman was ready with plenty to say to the pencil pushers on the dock there. Like, for instance, "Baseball has advanced a hundred-fold in popularity as a result of the trip," and "We have built bridges across the seas as sturdy as the national game itself." He did not mention what the tour had brought in for him personally, which I later heard was seventy-five thousand dollars, or even about all the fuss in London. But I guess no one in the States gave a hoot anyway. See, Comiskey was once again a hero, like always, and heroes do not have to give answers like that.

The fact is, even years later, when we got ourselves into The Great War, he was still pitching the bull about the tour. "I flatter myself," he told some scribe, after we got into the mess Over There, "that it is no coincidence that of the ten political entities we visited, all are found on the side of the Allies in this great test."

Well, I guess that shows that The Old Roman knew where his bread was buttered, all right. Right up to the end, he was a fellow that always had a method to whatever he was doing. But I'll tell you the truth, 'til this day I do not know if he cared for any other person but himself.

Nineteen Fourteen

by George D. Weaver

No one could ever quite figure out the right way to say Eddie Cicotte's name. The announcer at the ballpark (who back then just yelled into a megaphone, so hardly no one could hear him anyway), he said it "Sy-Cotty." The bugs in the stands, they either had it "See-Cotty," or else "Sy-Cott," which is also how us ballplayers said it. I cannot say why no one ever asked Eddie himself how to do it, but I guess no one did. Indeed, I myself did not find out the right way, which was "See-Cott," 'til years later when I was sitting on trial next to the fellow. But I suppose it didn't matter. Most of us boys just called him Knuckles in the first place.

See, Cicotte was not one of those ballplayers that gets sore over a little thing like a name, or any other little thing. He was never no crybaby and usually a good sport. Knuckles was fine by him, even an honor, being as he was the first twirler to invent the knuckleball.

Of course, you might also say that as fine a character as Eddie was, in his early years it was an honor for him to be remembered by any name at all, for the truth is, at first he did not set the league in flames. By the time the Sox got him, which was a little after they got me, he had been in the fast company five years and two clubs had already given him the bird. That was not for lack of stuff, for Knuckles always had plenty of that, even despite the fact that he was a little guy and sort of fleshy, but rather because of his ups and downs. One afternoon he might look like a worldbeater out there on the slab, with his knuckleball jumping about like a burrhead in a minstrel show, and the next he would blow up and get the can before he had set down two batsmen.

Now there are those who said back then that the trouble with Cicotte was just that he had too much dog in him. Before I bumped into the fellow, I said it a couple of times myself, and maybe even after I already knew him. But see, it turned out there was a lot more to it than that. He had some dog, sure, but at the same time he had a heart so big you could pop it with a pin. He had both right at the same time, that was the curious thing about Knuckles. And the one kept getting in the way of the other.

Anyway, by the time we got to be pals, which was in '14, it did not look like he would ever be anything but a journeyman ballplayer, as they used to put it. It looked like he might kick around a couple of more seasons, and then you would never hear that queer name of his again, or clap eyes on his chubby body.

And that is why you would have to say that coming over to our club from the Bostons was about the best thing that ever happened to him (even if it also turned out to be the worst). For in the end it was the spitball, added on top of his knuckler, that did the wonders for him, and that was a lob he would surely never have picked up nowhere else. With the Sox, though, you almost could not help but learn it, on account of Kid Gleason being on our side, and also Big Ed Walsh, the greatest spitter artist of them all. After a little while, just about every hurler on our club learned to fling the wet one. I even learned it myself, and what the hell did I need it for?

Now it is a famous legend that spitballers are all dimwits. People think that because first of all what they do in their work is not exactly healthy, and also because there have indeed been a few of them that were bats. For instance, Bugs Raymond that used to pitch over with McGraw for the Giants. The Bugs could put away more hooch than anyone you ever saw and after he had been at it for a while, he could not control himself no more than a wild beast. The scribes loved this, 'cause it gave them good write-ups, but it was not so good for Bugs. I guess he was an alki stiff, if you want to know the truth, and he was pissing away his natural talent. So finally Mac got him sent to some swank place called the Keeley Institute here in Chi for the cure. Well, pretty soon The Bugs was up to his old tricks. He must've gotten some giggle soup in there, for after he had been there a week he was nearly tossed out for almost slitting the throat of his roomie, who was some old millionaire, while trying to give him a shave in his sleep. And a week after that he went to the can right out in the hallway. But when The Bugs finally did get out, he was very proud of his time there. He even wore a class button, and he carried around a book with snapshots of his schoolmates, as he called them. And even though Bugs checked out for good just a couple of years after that, when he was in his prime and only thirty years of age, people still thought it was the spitter that made him like he was.

Well, like I say, they had it all wrong. Spitballers were definitely not like southpaws, who are indeed a queer bunch. The proof was Big Ed Walsh himself, who was not only the supreme hurler of the day, except maybe for one or two others, but he had his noggin screwed on tight as a drum. In fact, I have never seen no pitcher who used his wits so much. Big Ed even learned how to cross his eyes to confound baserunners, which was some trick. There is a story about a time he was called upon to pull a rescue stunt in the ninth inning after the other club had sprung a rally and was just a run from tying up the score. There was a man on third and only one down when Big Ed joined the fray. His first two tosses were wet ones, which the batter did not offer at, 'cause he thought Walsh was looking at the runner. Then, on the third pitch, the runner took a big lead, thinking Walsh was eyeing the batter. Suddenly Big Ed shot the horsehide to third. The batter took a big swipe at nothing and the baseman caught the runner off the bag. "Batter out! Out at third!" came the ump, and that was that.

Now I cannot say if that story is straight, but you can see what I'm getting at about Walsh's smarts. And, like I say, he was such a decent egg, he would show anybody his tricks, even if you didn't ask him.

But when he first came over to the Sox, Cicotte was one of those fellows who would not take help from no one at all. It was not that he was swell-headed, not a bit. Old Knuckles knew that he had been something of a bum in people's eyes and that he was not living up to his talents. No, the thing was that he was timid in front of a great hurler like Walsh, and did not want to bug him, even despite the fact that Walsh did not mind.

This might sound funny to some, a ballplayer in the big show acting like that, but when you are only a second-rater, as Cicotte was then, you could be as full of awe looking at the big shots as a little tyke or someone of that nature. I personally was not so stunned at Walsh, because I had been on the club with him for a while and anyway he was a pitcher and I was not, but my eyes would get pretty big looking at some of the batsmen on the other clubs we played against. I even had some broken bats they had used. Other players got up collections of postal cards from places they visited, or pipes, or string, and one fellow I knew even had a pile of rugs from his travels, but me, I would get those busted bats and then get the fellows that had held them to sign them to me. I had lumber from Cobb and Lajoie and Speaker and even Shoeless Joe, who was still with Cleveland then, though of course he did not sign his bat on account of some bull he gave me about being late somewhere.

What I am getting at is that this was Cicotte's real problem, this thing they call confidence. It is definitely a thing a great ballplayer must have, or even a pretty good one. Knuckles just did not have that belief in his own self, and it showed in his work, but it looked like he just did not want to do nothing about it. His ball may have gotten pickled more than it should, but there he was in the big leagues and who could argue with that? Nobody at all, that's who, so why risk doing things a different way? That is how you start figuring when you do not have that thing called confidence.

Cicotte had so little of it that he spent half his time thinking up a new line of work. In his head I guess it was as sure as four aces that baseball was about to give him the bird for good, and then he would be up a tree. So on the road, while the other boys was out on the make and other such tomfoolery, including yours truly, usually he would sit by himself in his room reading about other jobs he might do and other ways he might improve himself, and all the time he was sending off for more free booklets from the papers. He had booklets telling how to learn law by mail, and bookkeeping, and good public speaking, and even how to dress up like a success. Around the time I got to know him, he was especially interested in learning how to do electricity, which was getting pretty big right then, always carrying around a big book about it and making drawings of wires and so on.

When the scribes would ask him about this, Knuckles would just smile in this way he had, showing off the hole in his front teeth. "I don't know how many times I've been asked for contributions for the widows and orphans of ballplayers who have not left them provided for," he would say. "I'm not going to be one of those players that goes to the poorhouse when a little hard luck comes my way."

I guess I should tell you here, in case you didn't know, that Cicotte had a wife named Rose and also a couple of girl kids.

I admit that some of the ballplayers razzed him about all this, and I was one of them. See, I could not understand what good these booklets might do a ballplayer in the big show in the first place. After all, I myself did not have no other trade to fall on, and what the hell did I need one for? And for another thing, it must be said that he was hurting the club's chances with thinking like that. I ask you, how many types of things can a fellow have in his noggin at once and still do them right? Just one, that's how many!

To make matters worst of all, Knuckles was a fellow that never fretted after he had gotten the old heave-ho from a ballgame, even if he had gotten pelted for ten runs. To the contrary. Now I am not saying that a pitcher should be a glum pot every time he has been made a fool in front of the spectators, or even go around booting his locker. Such things are just the breaks of the game and must be accepted. But this guy Cicotte, he would act like he did not care a bit. Indeed, sometimes he would even act happy to himself.

Well, this last part was just too much for a sparkplug such as myself to bear. One day, after he had gotten beat by the New Yorks, and on a two-bagger by their pitcher, no less, by the name of Slim Caldwell, there was Knuckles, sitting by his locker, and he was whistling.

"What the hell do you think you're doing now?" I suddenly piped up, so loud that in a flash every puss in the place was eyeing us.

Knuckles stopped. "I happen to like this tune." And he went right back on with his whistling. (The tune was called "Where the Black Eyed Susans Grow," in case you're interested.)

I walked over to him. "Well, just shut your beak."

"Why?" he said, real earnest.

"Shut your beak or I'll shut it for you." I held up my paw to show I meant business. "There are some of us on this club that don't take losing so light."

"Sock him, Buck," piped up Jim Scott, "powder the stiff."

But Cicotte, he just smiled back at me. "It wasn't me that booted that ground ball in the sixth," he said.

"Anyone can pull a bone once in a while," I came back. "At least I'm no second-rater."

To that he said nothing, but he kept right on with his smiling.

Well, that did it. In a flash I was on top of the fellow, and had him by the neck. I would have done some harm, too, if Big Ed Walsh had not popped in right at that moment to break it up.

As you can imagine, I did not lose too much love toward Knuckles after that one. None at all, in fact. Almost every time we got face to face, and it was the same with some of the other boys, too, such as Scott and Reb Russell, we would eye him like he was a leper, and someone might come out with a crack about how he was canary yellow out there on the mound.

But, like I say, there was not too much satisfaction in such tactics, as it all washed right off Cicotte. That is how come we decided to pull the other thing. What happened is that one day, when the club was on the road in Detroit, Scott and me slipped into his room and swiped all of his booklets. That night, when Knuckles shows up in the dining room, there are a bunch of us boys sitting together, and we had one of those booklets right on the table in front of us. This booklet was all about how to be a traffic manager on the high seas, telling boats where to go and such, and the moment Knuckles spotted it he turned red as a herring.

"All right," he said, real quiet, "give them back."

Now, of course, such a thing was not possible, as we had already shucked the others.

"Give them back," he said again, and he was getting hotter by the second.

But, see, instead of answering, what we did is all at once start grabbing our guts and making puking noises, real loud, pretending like we were all traffic managers on the high seas, tossing up our toenails.

It was actually quite comical, a lot of guys said so, but not Cicotte.

He just turned and walked out of the room. And for at least a week he did not come near any of us, even in the locker room. I do not know for sure if he ever put it together that I was one of the ones that pulled the deed, but I suppose he must've had his suspicions.

But this was an amazing thing about the fellow, I have never seen anyone like him on the question of bygones. Even later on, after we became pals, he never spoke a word to me about it. It was like it had not happened to him at all, but to someone else.

And that is the next part of the tale, how we soon became buddies, after all. It happened quite by coincidence. See, after Detroit, the club went back to Chi for a homestand, and one night I happened to walk into a place on Decatur Street called Conway's, where I had never even been before. This was a saloon, but they also had eats there. And there, in the corner, sat Knuckles with a couple of ladies.

Now, naturally, I did not plan to go over and talk with him, being as how he could not stand my guts, but I had to admit that these two were not so hard on the eyes, and especially one of them. So after I thought it over for a while, I decided what did I have to lose, and I strolled right over and made the introductions.

You should have seen the stunned look on Cicotte's puss when I did this but, of course, he was not a guy to cook up a stink. So, before he knew it, I just took myself a seat and joined in.

It turned out that one of the ladies was Knuckles' own wife, Rose, and the looker was her girlfriend, by the name of Helen. Well, pretty soon, the four of us were having a regular gabfest. "Say," I said to Helen after a while, "what else do you do, aside from going out on the town with these slobs?"

We all had a laugh over that one, so it took her a minute to answer back. "I work for the Salvation Army, over on Division Street."

"Oh," I said, a flash in my eye, "where I come from they call that the Starvation Army." I was one slick citizen that night.

So then I started to get into some details about me, like for instance the kind of season I was having, but all at once Knuckles cut me off.

"Don't listen to Weaver," he said with a laugh, "everyone on the club knows he has a swollen cranium." And I had to laugh right along, if not I would have looked like a gink in Helen's eyes. "Anyway," added Cicotte, "Helen doesn't care about our ballclub, do you, Helen?"

"Sure I do," she spoke up. "I'd like very much to hear what Mr. Weaver has to say."

"Ah, that's just soap," said Cicotte, "isn't it, Rose? You told me that Helen was strong for the Cubs and didn't give a hoot about the White Sox."

Actually, now that I think about it, you might say that Knuckles was maybe a little miffed at me, after all. But, still, I did not mind so much, not with a peach like that sitting there next to me.

You see, the fact is, I had not struck up with a classy girl like this in quite some time. I suppose maybe my heart was still out in San Fran in Agnes's pocket, for even though I had not heard a peep out of her, I still gave her a lot of thoughts. Indeed, just about the only skirts I had been seeing were hooks, like Louise who I already told about. After that time in Fort Worth, it seemed pretty clear that a fellow could not trust a girl and ought only have them about for fun. Besides, all the hooks I hung with were easy on the eyes, so a ballplayer did not have to hide his face being seen with them, and they did not get weepy when you went off with the club on the road or even home for the winter. Of course, I was a little jumpy about coming down with a disease, which is easy to do, so I always made sure only to step out with the ones that had the okay from other ballplayers. And one of them, Marjorie, even gave me a special rate, only three bucks for a night instead of five, after she found out who I was, which is a lot less than you end up ponying up for a wife.

But now, here was Helen, and she was different. Well, to make a long story shorter, by the end of that night, I had already taken a real shine to her and I guess she felt the same. In fact, when we said goodbye, I did not even try to buss her, which I could not have anyway, on account of Knuckles and Rose. And then I saw her two more times over the next four days, at which time the ballclub had to blow town.

By then I suppose I was already deep in love. But, see, I was also jumpy, as I did not want to feel like a simp again, or even appear like one, especially with Cicotte on the scene.

It was the psychological moment that the highbrows talk about, and I felt in a fix. It took me days before I at last decided what to do, which is what a ballplayer is supposed to. I went to my manager with the matter.

We were in Cleveland, and I found Nixey in the lobby of our hotel there, the Ohio Hotel, playing cards all by himself.

"Okay if I sit down?" I started.

"If your rump can take it. Maybe it can't."

"Listen, Nixey," I said, "I got a matter to discuss with you."

He kept looking down at his cards. "Do you play solitaire, Buck?" he spoke up finally. "It's not much of a game."

"No, sir, I don't." I stopped. "This is a personal matter. I think I am in love with a girl."

He did not look up from the cards. "A streetwalker?"

"No, sir. Her name is Helen and she's a pal of Knuckles' wife."

"Knuckles' wife Rose?"

"That's her. And I was thinking of asking her to be my wife. Only there are those that say such a thing is bad for a young player's thinking. And others that say it settles him down." I had been standing up all this time, ever since I got there, but now I started to take a seat.

"Don't sit down!"

"Why not?" I said. "You said I could."

"That was before." He gazed up at me. "I don't give advice like that, Weaver, I only take it."

"Well," I said, "thanks all the same, Nixey." I hesitated. "Keep this matter under your hat, will you Nixey?"

He looked back at his cards. "A fellow can always try."

Well, I'll bet it wasn't three hours before the other fellows on the ballclub were already razzing me about being stuck on a girl that I hardly knew at all, including even my pals. And they kept on with it through the whole road trip. There was no relief for me, none at all. They all made out like I was a sucker, and that Helen was just after my worldly goods and it was a sure thing that she would give me the bag. Even Jim Scott started saying I was a cluck, and he knew me better than anyone.

So what is a fellow to do? After a while he begins to wonder, that's what, if maybe it is so. By the time the club got back to Chi, I was so mixed up that I did not even give Helen a ring. For five days I sat in that town, and of course she knew I was there, too, since it was no secret, but that was her problem.

And the truth is, I might never have seen her at all if not for

Cicotte. See, one day in the locker room, he all at once comes up to my locker and invites me over to his place for dinner. Now, naturally I had my suspicions that something was up, but I went ahead and said okay anyway. That's how balled up I was.

And when I got there, something was up, all right, and it was Helen! But all at once, I didn't know what I'd been so worried about in the first place. Rose Cicotte had cooked up some ham for us, and we spent a wonderful time together, just like the first time, and it was dandy.

And that was just the start. After that, every time I'd turn around, there would be Knuckles saying I had to come by for some of Rose's roast beef, or some of her steak, and why didn't I bring Helen. Later on Helen and I figured out that this was their plan, to show me how cozy it was being hitched, how a fellow ate good all the time and always had somebody in his corner. I guess they did not know that Helen cannot cook at all. But, anyway, it turned the trick, for before too long I went right ahead and asked Helen to tie the knot. And when we pulled the stunt, which took place on August 27, 1914, right in the Cook County Courthouse, who do you think was up there next to us as the best man? Eddie Cicotte, that's who.

I might add what a fine friend he kept on being, too, for there was truly no other ballplayer like him. Most guys, if you have a problem, they will probably tell you to go to a bar and get sauced. But not Cicotte. Even if you were glum as midnight, he would never tell you to get lost, but always talk to you in that nice way of his. I guess you would just have to say that the guy was a champ.

In private, I'm talking about. Out there on the hill he was still the same old crumbbum. I no longer razzed him about it, of course, for what else is pals for, but sometimes it made me crazed as ever.

And one time in St. Loo, I just could not stand it no more. Cicotte had twirled for us that afternoon and had got the beans knocked out of him, much worse than usual. By the third frame, he had already given up six runs, and was gone, and the bugs in the stands was yelling that he had done a Brodie just so he could head over to the race track that was right next to Sportsman's Park. "Cicotte must have a hot tip," they kept on yelling.

Now, I should probably add one little thing here. The day before, when we had arrived in that town, there was a letter waiting for me at the Southern Hotel, and you will not guess who it was from. Agnes! She said she was there visiting her folks and maybe I could give her a ring!

Well, I guess I may have been a little bothered and hot, for I do not know how else to explain my actions. But that night, sitting in the hotel room and watching Cicotte, it was clear as anything that he did not give a hoot about what had happened on the diamond. He just sat there reading newspapers and, believe it or not, he was actually getting hot about *that.* Every once in a while he would look over at me and start reading out loud about some terrible thing the krauts had done in France, which is where his relatives were from.

"Knuckles," I finally cut in miffily, "why do you suppose there are so few frog ballplayers in the big show?"

He looked up from his newspaper. "What?"

"Why do you suppose there are so many more kraut ballplayers than frogs?"

"That's not funny, Buck."

"Who says it is? I'll tell you what I think. I think maybe the krauts on this side got more guts, too, just like in the war."

He eyed me real cold.

"I just want to say something. You have got plenty of talents; that is not the problem. I think the reason you're going so bad comes down to heart."

He was quiet a while more. Then, very tense, he added, "I think maybe you should do more thinking about yourself. About your scatter arm, for instance." He stood up. "I am taking a walk." And out he went.

"So am I," I decided. Only once I was in the lobby, there I was next to the telephone board, so I decided to give the hello girl Agnes's number.

"Well," I told her right off, "I almost did not call. I am now a married man, you know."

At that, she laughed. "Well, Buck, congratulations." That was a thing about Agnes, she was fairly cocky.

"So," I said, "that's that."

"That's nonsense. When can I see you?"

"Well"—I stopped—"maybe now. But I cannot stay out too late. I am a big leaguer now."

"Come over here." She paused. "Father and mother are in Kansas City until Friday."

Well, to make it brief, I went over there. After we shot the breeze a while, lapping up some wine, she explained why she had not written me the last time, which was because she knew my mind was on baseball and she did not want to have a broken heart. Then, pretty soon, things began to happen. She said, "Why don't we relax a little?" and before I knew it, I was running around that house in her old man's robes and pointy hat. This made me feel a little odd, but I enjoyed it and Agnes did even more. Finally she took me right into her old man's room, and we jazzed in there, under the cross, with yours truly still wearing those duds. It was a pretty warm time.

Anyways, it must have been midnight before I got back to the hotel, and I was bug-eyed to see old Knuckles sitting there on the bed, waiting for me. I did not know what to say, or even how to start, but luckily I did not have to.

"Nice walk?" he said with a grin.

I must've turned red as a cherry, for I was some sight. "Sure it was."

He laughed. "I was at a bar or two myself." Then he stopped. "All right, Buck, I'm listening. You think I have no guts on the diamond?"

Well, naturally I hemmed for a little bit, but at last I got my wits all together, and we started talking real earnest. I could tell he did not like some of the things I was saying too much, but he did not let on. Like, for instance, I said, "You throw the knuckle ball too much."

"The knuckleball is my best pitch," he came back. "What do you suggest I throw, bloopers?"

"Certainly it is, but if a fellow knows it's coming, it's pretty simple to powder it. If you're so clever, why don't you find another pitch?"

"Like what?"

"Like the spitter, for instance. I have one, and I'll show it to you. But I'll bet Big Ed is going bats waiting to show you his."

So we went back and forth like that for a while more and then Knuckles said, "Well, all right, maybe there is something to what you say. I'll talk to Walsh about it."

So, of course, then I had to say, "Well, maybe you're right about my heaves, too."

When I said that, Knuckles lighted up, showing that big hole between his ivories. "This is fine. This is good, speaking up to one another right out in the open. If everyone on the club did it, nothing could do us more good."

"Well," I said, "I guess that's Callahan's job, to get that going."

I said that in a serious way, but then Eddie caught my eyes and we both started breaking up, thinking of Nixey trying to put over what we were saying, and we laughed for a good minute or more.

We talked a lot more on the subject for the next few days, Knuckles and me, and then, when we got home to Chi, one of the first things we did was stick up a poem from *The Baseball Magazine* on the clubhouse wall in Comiskey Park, right up near Cicotte's locker.

> When you once have hit the ball,
>   Run it out.
> Though your chance be great or small,
>   Run it out.
> Many a fumble comes, you know,
> Many a baseman muffs a throw,
> But you're lost unless you go!
>   Run it out.
> Come the best, or come the worst,
>   Run it out.
> You are gone? All right, but first
>   Run it out.
> Here is one who thinks it wise
> Just to play for exercise,
> But he'll score more if he tries,
>   Run it out.
> In the game, or out, the rule
>   "Run it out"
> Is the motto of your school;
>   Run it out!
> Other Shakespeares might be printing,
> Other Titians might be tinting,
> If some constant coach kept hinting,
>   "Run it out."

The name of that poem, by the way, was "Run It Out." It was certainly good advice, too. But people do not change over one night, especially not ballplayers. Knuckles began right away working out with Walsh, all right, just like he said, but it was as tough on him as nails.

The problem was the same old one as before, and that was confidence. Walsh's wet one was so alarming, jerking and diving all over the lot, that Knuckles would watch it a little and right away get a look on his map like someone had just kicked the bucket, 'cause how could he match it. But Big Ed did not get this at all, being a fellow that did not know nothing about discouragement, and he kept after Cicotte to keep trying it. First they tried it with spit, like normal. Then they tried it with tobacco juice, the way Red Faber, the other spitballer on our club, flung it, only Knuckles could not stomach the stuff in his mouth. Then they tried chewing gum, 'cause Walsh thought maybe he was not getting up enough spit. Then they tried Cicotte drinking a brew before he tossed, which is something Big Ed had once heard about in the bush leagues. But none of it worked.

I knew this for a fact, 'cause I was the fathead they had out there ten mornings in a row at the ballpark to catch it. First Big Ed would toss his ball a few times, just to show the way, and the horsehide would do a flip and a wiggle, and I'd make a grab at it and half the time get smacked right in the kitchen. Then Cicotte would toss his, and nothing would happen at all, except that my paw would get as waterlogged as Niagara Falls.

After a while, I guess even Walsh started getting a bit weary of this, 'cause finally he just took the ball from Knuckles and shook his noggin and said "Maybe we ought to try pee." And I don't think it was all in fun, neither, cause Big Ed was not a fellow to make too many jokes, let alone of that nature.

But what we didn't know was that Walsh had something else in his head at the moment in question, and that was the state of his own soupbone. There was no way to guess what was up, because the whole time he was helping out Knuckles he just kept going right along like a champion, winning ballgames as usual. But the very next week after he said the remark about pee, the whole world found out about it. Walsh was tossing against Washington, and around the fourth inning he just could not pitch no more. It was simple as that.

He tried, all right, for there was never a fellow more game, but he could not hardly raise up his arm, so finally Callahan had to pull him out.

Such a thing had never happened before to Walsh, and we all figured it would right itself soon enough. But it did not. After a couple of weeks they got the idea to send him off to Bonesetter Reese in Youngstown, Ohio. Bonesetter Reese had gotten a rep for himself way back in '99, when he had fixed up the arm of Nig Cuppy that every other doc had said was dead as wood, and after that many a twirler in a pickle went to see him. But he did not have the answer for Big Ed, and neither did the other sawbones he went to see. The next season after that he would throw only three ballgames, and more with his wits than with his arm, and then, fast as that, Comiskey would ditch him. It was almost enough to make a fellow think that Cicotte had got it right all along about baseball not being so secure. (And the truth is, after that season, I took all my dough except a little and put it in a poolroom.)

But the most queer part of it all is what happened to Cicotte after that. Without Walsh the club had no one at all to win ballgames for them, and so all at once Knuckles was a big cheese in their eyes. It was right near the finish of the season, and since the Sox were heading nowhere but to sixth place, Comiskey and Callahan figured it was a good moment for Knuckles to show his new stuff. So one day against the Red Sox, Nixey told him to go out there and fling nothing but wet ones, which is what he did, and of course they blew him all over the park. Knuckles finally had to go back to his knuckler just so we could get home for supper.

But all along, over on the bench, our third base coacher Kid Gleason had been eyeing Cicotte's work real close, and after the contest he went up to him and asked what substance he was using on the ball. "Just spit," said Knuckles, which was the case, and he went on to tell all the different ways he had tried it out with Walsh.

"Well," said Gleason, "back when I was with the old Orioles, there was a hurler called Sadie McMahon that tossed the wet one with the same motion as you."

See, Gleason was a guy that had been around, and was as clever as an alley cat and also tough, and that is why Comiskey kept him with the club, even though he could not stand his guts. Indeed, the buzz was that the two old-timers were not even on speaking terms.

"Big Ed showed it to me this way," cut in Cicotte, for he did not want to rob poor Walsh of the glory.

"I'm not sure he would be so fast to admit that," came back Gleason. "Why don't you just dummy up a little and listen to me?"

And the Kid went on to tell about how this fellow Sadie McMahon had been a second-rater until someone showed him how to toss the spitter with soap.

"With soap?" Cicotte had never heard of such a notion and neither had nobody else, not in this century.

"Darn right, with soap. You keep a little bit with you and you mix it up with mouth juice."

So the very next morning, we were out there again in the park, with Gleason teaching and Knuckles tossing and me catching, and it was the damnedest thing, suddenly Cicotte's ball was dipsying almost like Walsh's.

"Well," said Gleason, after he had looked it over for a while, "I guess you should make the grade with that, all right. Your only problem will be to figure out where to hide the soap." He looked over at me, still down there behind the platter like a thickhead. "Say, Weaver, maybe I will make you my next pupil. It is a pity a fellow with your speed does not hit from the left side." And off he went into the clubhouse, just as happy with himself as a baby on a tit.

I suppose you might say that the rest after that is history, or at least it used to be. The very next season, Cicotte was a new fellow out there on the hill. We never did call him Spits, 'cause he kept on tossing that knuckler three pitches of four, but now that he could sneak in that wet one when he needed it, fellows that used to paste him looked like saps in his hands. Knuckles called his new lob the shine ball, and he had so much gray matter upstairs, not a single one of his foes ever could figure out how he loaded up the pill. One time in Cleveland, a bunch of ballplayers even swiped his uniform, cap and mitt and sent them over to a chemist for a check, but the professor could not find a thing either. Later on that day when the scribes asked him about it, Knuckles just laughed and said of course nothing could be found, since he did not throw any such pitch in the first place, but it was just something in the minds of the batsmen. That was how certain of his own self he got to be.

And in the years after that, he just went on and on, getting all the better with age. In '16 he had the best stats of any hurler in the league, except for Babe Ruth with Boston, and in '17 he had the best of anyone at all, and tossed a no-hit game to boot. In '19, when he was thirty-five years of age and had been in the big show longer than any other hurler in the league, he won twenty-nine contests and dropped but seven. That is around when the sporting writers started tabbing him the eighth wonder of the world, which I guess he was.

He might have gone on for years more, too, since both his two pitches were easy as pie on the old soupbone. "The only thing that might stop me," he would put it, "is one of those seven year droughts, such as they used to have in Egypt."

But of course some other things came up in '19 also, and pretty soon they made Eddie leave the game, just like the rest of us. For a long time after that, I would always feel pretty sad when I got to thinking of Knuckles. And the saddest part of all was that with all of his triumphs and all, he never had gotten around to finishing up that course in electricity or any other trade.

Love and Opportunity,
Found and Lost

F reedom," a sporting writer of my acquaintance once remarked over drinks, "is a guy being able to pull out his
checkbook and, without a second thought, buy the winner of
the Kentucky Derby."

Another companion at the trough gave that but a moment's
thought. "No. Real freedom is buying the damn horse—and then
eating him for dinner."

I myself never placed great importance on money. Things financial bore me and so, in general, do those adept at finance. When I
made my own fortune, it was by inadvertence, and it altered my
routine not a jot.

But from the very beginning, I have always craved racehorse for
dinner.

For that I offer no apologies. My saving grace—and it strikes me
as sufficient justification for all but the most egregious of excesses—
is that I am interesting, my life has always been interesting, and
almost everyone else is boring.

Moreover, it is to that trait, to my insistence upon abiding by my
own rules and my impatience with everyone else's, that I owe my
very standing in the world. I would, indeed, venture the opinion that
every celebrated man I have ever known has been similarly self-
seeking. There are only so many hours in a lifetime, and those who
intend to make a mark on the world must early on determine,

consciously or unconsciously, that they will nurture themselves, or their reputations, in lieu of nurturing others.

My profession has, of course, always attracted a disproportionate number of men who have made such a choice. Artfully practiced, newspapering is perpetual motion, an endless series of small but gratifyingly public performances, building, if one is fortunate, to recognition or even acclaim. The conscientious newsman has little use for reflection; it is more than time wasted, it is time ill spent. Any man who stops to sympathize, worse, to empathize with the objects of his attention—the suddenly newsworthy, who are allowed to be famous, or notorious, for a day or a week before being sent hurtling back to obscurity—is almost certainly bound for obscurity himself.

Do not think of me as cold-blooded. The truth is, most of those we write about are not terribly different from ourselves; they are grateful for whatever attention they receive. And, in any case, men like myself have our own peculiar burdens to bear. I, for example, have been assured by people I trust that I make quite a poor friend. I have known for many years now that I am all but useless as a family man.

I began to discover that about myself shortly after I discovered Edith Manning, an event which occurred in early December, 1912, in the Chambers Street subway station. I was, by nature, a romantic man, given to a paralyzing loss of certainty around women; in fact, I had never enjoyed a sustained involvement with one, sometimes even doubted whether such a thing would ever come to pass. But that afternoon, as I stood on the uptown platform of the IRT, my head full of office prattle, there was Edith.

I spotted her first from behind. She was wearing, in accordance with the fashion that season, a dress of wool that fell to within an inch of the concrete, one that fit snugly around the midriff, suggesting an alluring fullness at the appropriate places. From beneath her hat, of green felt and elegant in its sweep, fell a careless lock of blond hair.

But that is not what most interested me. What caused me to stare and, moments later, when the train pulled into the station, to follow her onto the last car, was the fact that under her arm she carried not a hatbox, nor a copy of *The Ladies Home Journal*, but a volume by the social reformer Jacob Riis.

The subway system, only ten years old at the time, featured

wicker seats in pairs on either side of the aisle. I took a seat at one end of the car; she faced me, half a car away. She was, from this perspective, not beautiful in any traditional sense—her nose was too prominent and her forehead too broad—but it struck me that hers was a face of character. When her eyes abruptly met mine, I instantly averted my gaze and so did she. Two stops later, at Spring Street, she got off.

I had almost forgotten her, was on my way home on the same line four hours later after an assignment at Madison Square, when I chanced to look up from my notes and realized, with a start, that she had just boarded the train and was taking a seat directly across the aisle from my own.

In spite of all that has happened since, I continue to think back on what happened next with wonderment. Without a moment's consideration, I found myself moving across the aisle and into the seat opposite her.

"It's fate," I pronounced.

She betrayed a flicker of recognition and went into a deep blush. "Yes," she said softly.

"My name is Luther Pond."

She hesitated. "I'm Edith Manning."

"You were on the train earlier."

She nodded and looked away, gazing out the window at the blackness rushing by.

"Ordinarily I don't ride the train during working hours. Ordinarily I'm in my office downtown." I paused. "Do you ride the trains often?"

Many women, of course, did not, for already the underground system had begun to acquire an unsavory reputation. Just the previous week, if my paper was to be believed, a wealthy young woman from Philadelphia named Mary Archibald, staying with friends on Fifth Avenue, had had her handbag torn from her wrist at the new Columbus Circle station; the assailant had been but fifteen or sixteen years of age, "probably Irish."

Edith turned to me. "I go everywhere by train."

Taking this as encouragement, I began jabbering away about the subway system. I, too, rode the trains often, in fact saw the subways as one of the glories of urban life; indeed, I had personally made the acquaintance of the city Commissioner for Public Transport, Mr. Smythe; though one of my colleagues had lately purchased an automobile, and several others were talking of doing so, the subway system suited me just fine.

She took it in politely, nodding often, and when after five minutes she stopped me, it was with a single finger, raised discreetly. "Mr. Pond, the next stop is mine."

"Mine too," I said with alacrity, though, in fact, mine was four stations down the line.

So I accompanied Edith from the train and out onto the Bowery. "May I see you to your home?"

"I can manage, Mr. Pond."

"In that case, may I invite you for a cup of tea?"

"I'm sorry, I'm already late."

"You live around here?"

"Right across the way." She nodded toward a handsome brownstone, three stories high, with ornate carvings on the facade. "Good day, Mr. Pond."

I stared after her dumbly as she hurried across the street.

It was, I think, as much the nature of that encounter as the woman herself that so quickly cost me my head. Within an hour, I dropped in the box outside of the door through which she had disappeared a note pressing my case for a rendezvous; to this she replied, enclosing, to my surprise, the number of her telephone. Within a week, I had taken to phoning up Edith daily, and soon after that, I was attempting to arrange to spend every free moment by her side. This was not easy, for Edith seemed to have as few free moments as I did. In addition to studying for her teacher's certificate at Wagner College, she was a suffragette, and a passionate union supporter, and she passed much time in voluntary service to organizations devoted to these causes. Indeed, the previous year, during the strike of the ladies garment workers, she had spent so many hours at union headquarters on Delancey Street that she had faced academic probation.

All of this I learned early on, this and much more. On our very first evening out together, I took her to see Harold Eltinge in *The Laughing Husband*, a musical entertainment enjoying considerable success that season. She did not hide her lack of enthusiasm. She had, she said, found the play "trivial." Edith, it seemed, was an admirer of Isadora Duncan and other representatives of what was just then starting to be called the avant-garde. Henceforth, throughout our courtship, when we attended a performance, we invariably found ourselves in a dingy hall, surrounded by bohemians.

None of this deterred me. Smitten as I was, I tolerated from Edith behavior that was, in fact, very nearly abusive. Like so many principled sorts, she saw the world in terms of stark rights and wrongs. Pragmatism, in her eyes, was a dirty word. And in me, an inhabitant of the most pragmatic, the most morally flexible, of worlds, she daily saw signs of taint. She objected to the readiness with which I tailored my writing to suit the tastes of my editors; and the intense ill will I bore certain colleagues; and my occasional lack of compassion for those about whom I wrote.

For a time, I was actually moved to obscure those traits, going so far as to give Edith's views weight in the reportorial choices I made. When, in January 1913, I was assigned to the story of Jim Thorpe's impending loss of the gold medals he'd won at the Stockholm Olympics for alleged professionalism, my initial reports fairly shouted with righteous outrage; and, when the accusations proved accurate in all of their particulars, I set to unashamed breast-beating. It was Edith's contention, her *conviction*, that since the slow-witted Sac and Fox brave had clearly *intended* no wrong—when, as a student at the Carlisle Indian School, he had passed a summer playing baseball in the Carolina League, he had done so under his own name and for a mere twenty-five dollars per week—the punitive actions of the Amateur Athletic Union were not only overly severe, but smacked of racial prejudice. I did not go quite that far, not in print. But, while many of my colleagues were taking Thorpe to task for having embarrassed the Stars and Stripes, I took the tack that this stoic young man, who less than a year before my own paper had described, in early reports, as a "savage" and an "aborigine," was the very model of right-thinking American manhood.

"Yes, Thorpe spent a summer playing the national game," I wrote. "Well, this writer would just like to know why it is a crime for a track man to perform on the perfect diamond. Did Jim's quickness with the bat propel him faster afoot in Sweden? Did his adeptness at the fine art of sliding make his javelin travel an inch further? Did, perhaps, his skill with the mitt ease him over the high bar? No, there was no crime committed that summer in the Carolinas, only a crime averted—by Jim Thorpe! And that is the crime a young man commits when he fails to exercise his God-given skills to the maximum!"

I had the liberty to go on so improbably, at such length, because I had lately been designated a columnist. More precisely, I had been named *co*-proprietor of a corner of the sporting page labelled "These Sporting Days," whose previous tenant, George Moulthrop, had moved his family to California, where he was later unearthed composing advertising slogans. On the three days a week I was not writing the column, it bore the by-line of my rival, William Kirk. There was no longer even the pretense of civility between this individual and myself; we disliked each other with enormous frankness. So vivid had the sense of competition between us grown, that it appears, indeed, to have been a prime motivating factor in the arrangement. When McCullum summoned us to his domain and presented the plan, he indicated that eventually one of us would fall by the wayside. "Good luck," he concluded, seemingly elated at the prospect. "We'll be watching."

Thus, it was not without some apparent risk that I wrote in a manner designed to please my beloved. It was, however, with less risk than Edith supposed. For, in the case of Thorpe, I sensed in my marrow that the public felt a good deal less betrayed by the duplicitous redskin than did the many newspapermen who had labored for six months to make of him a hero. And, in fact, that feeling was rapidly borne out by the enthusiastic reader response to my Thorpe coverage.

The simple truth is, where my work was concerned, my infatuation with Edith did not in the least impair my critical faculties. By then, I had already developed the quality that distinguishes a very few men from the mass—an unerring sense of timing—and it was as much a part of me as eggs for breakfast and after work with the boys.

Thus it was that, though I had long been contemptuous of the sporting columnists' trustiest friend, the idiot rhyme, and Edith viewed it with greater loathing still, I shortly discovered within myself a decided knack for the genre. In fact, my very first effort, dealing with an episode featuring the great Boston righthander

"Smokey" Joe Wood, actually earned me a congratulatory note from the dour McCullum.

> "Smokey" Joe, "Smokey" Joe,
> Throws the ball like a loco-mo.
> Clickety, clickety, clickety whiff,
> Now you see it, now you're a stiff.
>
> Home Run Baker took his cuts,
> Struck out quick and shouted "nuts!"
> "Take it easy," called he to Joe,
> "My pride is sufferin' an awful blow.
> If I were a pitcher I'd toss less hard,
> And make no batsman play the Bard."
>
> Joe just smiled and shook his head.
> "Sorry, Frank, to turn you red.
> But toss it easy? I simply couldn't!
> Joe without smoke is a definite Woodn't."

As a subject, I much appreciated Joe Wood. A year later, his magnificent arm abruptly went dead, affording me the opportunity for a second, far more memorable column, a melancholy essay on fleeting glory and lost youth.

By then, Edith's efforts to reform me had become considerably less spirited; soon they were to cease entirely. Quite unexpectedly, she had found herself in love with me, and the sensation brought to her a quality of softness that was, on the whole, quite distressing. I was, to be sure, gratified by her indulgence, but this was assuredly not the woman I had come to admire.

And when, nearly a year after our initial encounter on the subway, she one afternoon broke down in sobs and confessed she was expecting a child, I felt very little affection for her at all; what I felt was a rush of panic. But I had always considered myself an honorable man, and two weeks later, I did the honorable thing. We were married in the village of Saratoga Springs, by the mayor, whom immediately thereafter I escorted to the races. He was the subject of my subsequent column.

As man and wife, Edith and I had our difficulties from the outset. Though she had sworn she would be tolerant of the demands of my work, now that she was obliged to pass the days resting at home, she soon began chafing beneath them. Home was a brownstone building on West Seventy-third Street and, I will allow her this, Edith decorated it splendidly, and made a point of befriending the local merchants. But when I missed dinner, which I did with some frequency, sometimes without notice, she would brood. And if I was obliged, or chose, to work late into the night, I could anticipate a womanly outburst of unsettling proportions.

So it went into that fall, through the gridiron season and into the following winter. My work, at least, continued apace; I appeared to be building a small reputation for myself as a stylist, while poor Kirk, with his tedious verses and endless celebrations of home runs hit and fifty-yard touchdowns scampered, was building a larger one as a hack. Not that I was by any means satisfied. The town was full of sporting columnists who knew how to string words together—Lieb at the *Press*, Rice at the *Mail*, Trumbull at the *Sun*, Runyon upstairs at the *American*. What I knew, what the others, their prose almost uniformly unburdened by content, seemed incapable of imagining, was that there was enormous room to grow.

It was in mid-April that I heard from Ty Cobb. Though I had not seen the man since the abortive strike, I, like the rest of the country, was aware that, in the midst of a protracted hold-out, he was refusing to report to the Tigers' training camp.

Hold-outs were nothing new for Cobb, but this one had grown particularly nasty. The great ballplayer was reportedly demanding the staggering sum of fifteen thousand dollars annually, and Detroit owner Frank Navin had come back swinging. Indeed, the enraged Navin was saying he was not sure he wanted Cobb on his team at any price. "Cobb is a threat to the harmony of this club," he said. "Money is not the issue, discipline is."

"If Cobb is waiting for anyone in the American League to pay him fifteen thousand dollars," concurred an equally heated Ban Johnson, "he might just as well stay down in Georgia and pick cotton."

It was to this situation that Cobb addressed himself. "How," he wrote simply, "would you like to come down here and write the truth about me for a change. Wire yes or no. Your pal, Ty Cobb."

McCullum was as instantly enthusiastic at the prospect as Kirk was shellshocked; such an offer from the volatile Cobb was quite without precedent; I could probably wring three full columns out of it; if they were juicy enough, they might even be flogged on page one. Edith, who was expecting the child shortly, was considerably less pleased. To her, I was obliged to pledge that I would pass no longer than a couple of days in Augusta, by the great man's side.

The train departed the Pennsylvania Station shortly after three in the afternoon, scheduled to alight in Augusta at precisely seven-fifteen the next morning. And, indeed, the first leg of the journey, into the nation's capital, proceeded strictly on schedule. But as we moved into my own home state of Virginia, and then deeper still into the old Confederacy, the observation that we remained two separate nations, distinct not only in values and modes of behavior but in development, became manifest; south of Richmond, the old sleeper began to move at a creep, shaking and groaning on ancient, rusted rails. The Southerners among the passengers greeted this extraordinary circumstance passively, but after an hour or so, a number of the Northerners, who actually had *appointments,* became agitated and made inquiries of the conductor. "Nothin' to be done," we were assured, with laconic certainty. "Don' worry 'bout nothin', we'll get there, all right."

This state of affairs persisted throughout the remainder of the journey, the rattling of the cars precluding all but the most fitful sleep. By the time we pulled into Augusta, it was past one in the afternoon.

I descended the car in something of a panic—I had wired Cobb that I would be on his doorstep before ten—and, grip in hand, hurriedly made my way into the depot. The locals within did little to restore my equilibrium.

"Where," I demanded of the attendant, "would I find a city directory?"

He looked up from the business at hand, a week-old newspaper.

"The city directory," I repeated. "Please, I'm very late."

"What is it you want, young fellow?"

"A city directory."

"Oh. We had one, but it's gone." He cleared his throat and assumed a businesslike air. "You just get in on the seven-fifteen?"

"Yes. Do you know where I might find another one?"

"Well, I s'pose not." He plucked a pencil from behind his ear and scratched at his nose with the dull end, then spotted a luggageman. "Say, Walt . . ."

The luggageman offered him a winning Southern smile. "Say, Robert . . ."

"Walt, you seen the directory?"

"The what?"

"I'm looking for William Street," I offered in exasperation.

"Where?"

"That ain't in Augusta," observed the attendant.

"It's where Ty Cobb lives."

"Ty Cobb!"

"Ty Cobb! We think a good deal of Ty around here."

At length, I was directed to a trolley stand, and told to forget William Street and simply repeat the magic name to the driver of the first car that happened by. This method worked admirably. Though the horse drawing the carriage moved with no greater alacrity than anything else in the region, I was, after forty-five minutes, summoned forward by the conductor. "See that," he said, pointing toward a large white house several hundred yards away, through a stand of trees, "there it is, one of the greatest spots in Augusta."

It was indeed (though I am not sure this is what the conductor intended to indicate) a striking residence, three stories tall and encircled by a veranda, the sort of home reserved, in the mind's eye, for Southern colonels and other literary creations. I hurried up the steps and onto the broad front porch, but before I could put my hand to the bell, the front door swung open. There stood Ty Cobb, in linens.

" 'Bout time."

"It's not my fault. The train . . ."

"Hell, boy," he interrupted with a sudden grin, "I'm ribbin' you." Then he began to laugh—the only time, I believe, in our entire relationship, I ever witnessed such an outburst. "Forget about your damn clocks down here. Take off your Yankee drawers, let your balls breathe."

He led me into the house, through an imposing entryway and into the dim, cool library. Cobb threw himself into a chair and waited for me to do likewise. Quite obviously, my physical needs were the furthest thing from his mind.

"Get out your notepaper," he snapped.

I wrote my initial Cobb column—in the absence of telephonic equipment, I was to have all of them print-ready upon my return—that very evening, after bidding Cobb goodnight.

AUGUSTA, GA. Ty Cobb might never admit it himself, for he is in plenty of trouble with the hometown rooters as it is, but there is only one spot on earth where he feels truly at ease—and that spot is not fair Detroit. No, it is to Augusta, just a stone's throw (if you happen to have Tris Speaker's right arm!) from his birthplace in the backwater of Royston, that the Georgia Peach flees at the finale of the annual campaign. Here he finds waiting his oldest friends and his fine old manse. Here are his hunting dogs and his automobiles. Here, as nowhere else, he can "let his hair down."

It is often observed that those with the greatest natural gifts in life are the least likely to advertise the fact, and Cobb certainly bears out the dictum. He is a man of exceeding modesty, usually preferring to let his bat do his talking. But Ty is no blushing violet, either, and when the occasion arises, as lately it has, he can make himself heard as well as the next man.

It was recently this reporter's privilege to journey down to this thriving burg of sixty thousand on the River Savannah, in order to obtain first-hand Cobb's slant on the Great Hold-Out, and Ty wasted as little time getting to the point as he does going from first to third on a bingle to left. "This whole thing has been bent up and down and sideways by the press," he told me. "I am not out to be the best paid man in baseball, as Navin claims. I just want a fair wage. I do not understand why Navin has put this on a personal basis. It is business, pure and simple."

"What justification can there be for a hold-out?" came the query. "Doesn't that just cheat the fan?"

Tyrus considered for a moment. "The rooters have given me my place in the world and I shall always be grateful. But I know enough of fame on the diamond to realize it lasts just as long as the ability is there to win it. I am no hog, but a ballplayer should be paid his full worth for the few short years he has. It is the old story of labor and capital."

"And if you do not get what you are after, then what?"

Cobb smiled. "Then, nothing at all. I shall be quite satisfied to remain right here."

That he most certainly shall be. And why not? Looking around Ty's library, the evidence is everywhere that he has already accomplished more in his seven and twenty years than most men do in a lifetime. There are the seven silver cups commemorating his league batting championships, scrolls and plaques too numerous to mention marking his memorable moments on the diamond, a large photograph above the mantel of Mr. Cobb with President Wilson taken during the late campaign.

Then, too, there are other objects in the room that indicate the fuller dimension of the man. There are framed musical compositions, figurines gathered on his playing tours and innumerable books, many of them on history. "I am a bug on Napoleon," said Ty, showing me the one he is reading at the moment. "I have all the books on his life I have ever heard of. I made a resolve to read two hours a day." For, in spite of his Dixie origins, Cobb is a man of culture, and, unlike many a diamond slave, he is kept plenty occupied by those other aspects of life.

Nor is he strapped financially. Later, when we went on a tour of the environs in his handsome motor car, Ty seemed to stop every two minutes to point out this or that land holding. "I like real estate and bank stock," he explained. "I have studied these matters as well as I have studied any hurler, and I admit I have had a bit of luck."

To a man, Cobb's friends are urging him to hold fast against Navin. That afternoon we stopped at the office of a local dentist where several of same hang out, and one was more vociferous than the next in defense of Ty's position. It was the same at the Country Club where he regularly hits the links, and at the music store of which he is a frequent patron. "You just stay down here with us," said the proprietor of the establishment. "We'll keep you pretty busy, all right."

Ty laughed. "I just might do that. Anyway, I have often wished I could become a composer." He winked at his friend. "Now there's a trade where a man can become immortal."

I composed that piece entirely by candlelight. Cobb had been feuding with the local electrical company over a bill of some four dollars, and the week before his service had been terminated. "The sonsobitches'll rot in hell before they get a nickel out of me," he swore. "And if they try'n come near here, I'll blow their fuckin' brains out."

This was, I'd initially assumed, the reason for the absence of Mrs. Cobb and the two small Cobb children. However, I soon gathered that they had not been on the premises all winter; in fact, Cobb had not seen them since departing Detroit five months earlier.

Mrs. Cobb's presence was sorely missed, by me if not by her husband. There was virtually no food in the house, a result of Cobb's highly idiosyncratic notions on diet and nutrition. I had picked up a ham sandwich at the aforementioned Country Club, but for dinner, Cobb had offered only salt crackers and a fifth of bourbon. The bed I was given was situated in the corner of what appeared to be a storage room. It was without linen, devoid even of a pillow. When I asked my host if I might possibly borrow one of his—for I had noticed six or eight piled on his own bed—he made it clear that he needed them all. "I'm a ballplayer, goddammit, I need my rest. You're jus' a fuckin' pencil pusher."

For, in truth, the rapport between us, what rapport there had been, seemed to have vanished into the dusty air the moment I had entered the house. The fact is, Cobb had been seized by a kind of desperation; improbable as it seemed, he half-believed that Navin would let him go, and the prospect, the very intimation of it, terrified him. Repeatedly, in calmer moments, he sought reassurance, not only from myself, but from local friends, even acquaintances. "Don't be silly, Ty," he would hear over and over again, "you're the greatest player in the game." But five minutes later he would need to hear it again, from someone else.

As I was re-reading my column, hunched over the single candle I had been given, he abruptly burst into the room in a nightshirt and stocking cap. "Look at this," he announced, waving a fistful of papers in the semi-darkness. "I want you to see this."

But almost instantly his interest was diverted. "What's that?"

"It's my first article."

"Hand it over."

There was menace in the command and I did so without hesitation. He moved close to the flame and began to read. I watched with a curious mixture of trepidation and pleasure; for better or for worse, this was, after all, the great *Ty Cobb* reading my stuff.

After a few minutes, he laid the pages aside and rose to his feet. "Just change the end," he said with a curt nod. "I already *am* a composer." And he stalked out of the room.

I picked up the papers he had left behind and, resuming my place at the candle, now barely half an inch high, began to leaf through them. They were Western Union telegrams, sent by Cobb to himself from locales around the country during the previous baseball season as part of an elaborate scheme to ascertain whether Navin, suspicious that Cobb might be contemplating a jump to the new Federal League, had been intercepting his correspondence. Apparently, in fact, Navin *had* been doing just that.

I put the papers aside, next to my story, blew out the candle and, laying my head upon the bare mattress, tried to coax myself to sleep.

When I awoke the next morning, Cobb was gone. Although I had not been directly informed of the fact, I assumed he was hunting; the afternoon before, at the dentist's office, he and a couple of the yokels loitering about the place had engaged in an animated conversation on the subject of a dog that one of them had just obtained, and Cobb had seemed as eager as the owner to witness the beast in the field.

Grateful as I was to find my host departed, I was preoccupied by another, more pressing matter: hunger. There was, as far as I was able to ascertain, not a morsel in the house. I had finished off the last cracker the evening before, had even, discreetly, sucked up the crumbs. Nor was there much hope of easy relief. The estate was isolated and under no circumstances would I have considered borrowing one of Cobb's prized automobiles. I had all but determined to head back to the trolley line, was rummaging one last time through the bare kitchen cupboards, when out the window I spied in the distance a ribbon of smoke curling from a corner of a dilapidated shack. On closer inspection, this proved to be the residence of a certain Uncle Joe, the caretaker of the property, who at that very moment was preparing some kind of stew. I introduced myself and asked if I might join him.

Instantly, fear shone out of the old negro's eyes.

"Mistuh Ty, he know you here?"

"He won't find out."

The old man reached hastily into a wooden box, pulled out an empty tin can, scooped it into the simmering kettle and held it out for me. "Now, scat."

A short time later, fortified, I took a seat in the library and began writing.

AUGUSTA, GA. Ty Cobb, the game's most famous player and currently its most embattled, is often asked to speculate as to the reason for his remarkable record on the diamond. Is it his natural skills alone that enable him to so dominate his fellows? Is his mind especially agile? Is it good old American (never say Yankee to Tyrus!) grit in pursuit of perfection?

Well, Mr. Cobb, who says that "life is too short to be diplomatic," will tell you that it is a bit of all three. But, he is quick to add, it is also something else—he keeps himself one hundred and ten percent fit.

At this juncture, dear reader, you are likely to exclaim "What else is new?", but it is a revelation to learn just how few ballplayers do that very thing.

"Up 'til now, baseball has been my profession," says Ty, a real music buff, "and I have treated my body like a professional violin player treats his trusty instrument. But since I may be giving it all up, maybe I'll let some others in on my secrets."

The most important point, according to the Georgia Peach, is to eat sparingly. Even in the off-season, he himself will devour, at most, two meals a day. "If I need no more than that when I am playing nine innings in the St. Louis summer," asks he logically, "why should I when lousing around?"

Just as vital, notes Cobb, a ballplayer must abstain from certain beverages. "Coffee is very hard on the eyes. Ditto sweet milk. I myself rely on buttermilk, which is very cooling to the system and seems to clear a man's eyes."

Though he advises the young ballplayer against alcoholic drinks, the magnificent Georgian is no teetotaler. "Above all," he asserts, "a man must know his own system. Many a man can drink ale or even whiskey without being harmed. Sometimes, if a man knows his limits, a little alcohol in the system can throw off those little ills."

As to the old question of exercise, Cobb warns against too much of the stuff, whether the man in question is an athlete or just an ordinary joe. "Light workouts are always best," he says. "In the winter, I keep in shape with hunting, a few rounds on the links and some light gymnasium work. The man who is truly fit will take care never to harden his muscles. Last year Player Louden on our Detroit club conditioned himself so fine that he became muscle-bound."

Cobb adds that, for ballplayers, excessive training can take a further toll. "My idea is that the player must store up nervous energy during the wintertime," he says, "for he will lose it fast enough during the season. By summer, you can always pick out the men that have worked too vigorously in the off-season by their pale miens and drawn expressions."

Considering its source, such advice is likely worth its weight in gold. This reporter, for one, has lately taken up buttermilk—and it is not so bad! But, as an aside, let me add emphatically that it is far too early for Tyrus the Great to assume the role of teacher. We can only hope that he will soon be back in uniform to instruct us, not by words, but by example!

Cobb returned home late that afternoon half-soused, and almost immediately fell into a deep slumber in his room. He had not, I glumly noted, brought home a dead animal for dinner—nor even a bottle of buttermilk. When he awoke and summoned me to his side, it was past seven. We seated ourselves in rockers on the front porch, a fresh bottle of bourbon between us, and stared out at the brilliant crimson of the early evening sky.

"You got a girl?" he asked suddenly.

"I'm married."

"Hah! You don't look it."

Unsure, I made no response.

"Tell me about this wife of yours."

So I did—told him, at any rate, of our magical first encounter, embellishing the story, as I generally did, to heighten the romantic element.

"Christ," he muttered, when I was through, "those lousy slits, struttin' around, pretendin' like they don' shit or piss." He paused. "An' then she got you to marry her, right?"

"Yes."

"You got any kids?"

"Not yet."

"Well, jus' lemme tell you somethin', don't! 'Cause when she starts poppin' 'em, that'll be the end."

It was I who paused this time. "What do you mean?"

Cobb leaned forward in his rocker and caught my eye. "What do I mean?" he sneered. "What are you, a simp? You ever try 'n do your work with some li'l bastard bawlin' all night long? The year Ty, Jr. was born, it knocked twenty-five points off my average! Li'l Shirley knocked off eighteen!"

To this I said nothing, just refilled my glass.

He snorted. "I cut 'em out, that's what I did, the both of 'em. Crossed 'em right off my list."

The diatribe came with considerable vehemence, but, it seemed to me, the rush of words bespoke not so much anger as a deep anguish. Once again, I sensed in this man a terrible vulnerability; once again, I felt in him a kindred spirit.

"My wife is pregnant," I admitted. "She's due any time now."

"You'll see. If you're smart, you'll pull the same stunt I did."

We sat there for a long while in silence, until it was dark, drinking. With the house behind us black, a sliver of moon gave off the only light. Beside me, Cobb lit a cigarette.

"Ty," I said at last, "I suppose it doesn't mean much, but I never told you how much pleasure it's given me watching you play. I just wanted to tell . . ."

"Tell it to Navin," he cut me off sharply.

"He'll give you what you want," I reassured him. "The man may be a tightwad, but he's not crazy."

"I told you, save your fuckin' pity!" he screeched, shattering the calm like a sudden blast of buckshot. Though I could no longer see his face, I knew it was beet red, the eyes full of murder. He flung the burning cigarette into the night. "How dare you come to my home and insult me!"

I sat stone still, my heart racing. Perhaps, I told myself, it was the liquor that had seized him, for we had consumed most of the bottle, and on empty stomachs. My own head was reeling. But, no, of course it was not that.

I said nothing, just waited. But when, a couple of minutes later, he at last spoke again, it was with seeming calm. "When I first left home to play ball, my daddy sent me a wire. He hated baseball, my daddy, but he wired 'Don't come home a failure.' And I didn't." He hesitated. "I ain't no failure, sir, you'd be proud of me."

He sighed, and began rocking back and forth, his chair creaking rhythmically. "I showed 'em, Daddy. An' I ain't done. You watch, I'll get even with 'em all!"

Four feet away, I remained motionless, feeling something very much like terror. At that moment I might have traded anything— my worldly possessions, my future—to be far away from this man.

He fell silent. I listened to his heavy breathing, to the creaking of the chair. "You just watch me, sir," he said again. There was a moment's hesitation, then he cleared his throat. "You with me, Pond?"

"I'm here," I croaked. Momentarily, I was at a loss for words. "He must have been a great man, your father."

I knew little of Cobb's father, except that he was reputed to have been a man of some standing in this backward region, an educator of some kind.

"He was like a god to me." Cobb stopped, then abruptly spat out a postscript. "He was killed. By a member of my own family."

I waited for more, but there was nothing. After a couple of minutes, I was aware that his breathing was heavier and, then, heavier still, and that he was asleep.

I did not say goodbye to Cobb the next morning, instead left him an appreciatory note on the table in the library; it was early, before seven, and the snoring from the bedroom into which I had dragged him was almost as forbidding as Cobb awake.

In any case, my mind was racing, had been for ten hours.

"How," I asked the familiar attendant at the station, "does a fellow get to Royston?"

"Royston, Georgia?"

"Yes, of course."

"You cain't."

"Why not?"

"No depot in Royston."

I sighed. "What's the nearest depot?"

"Elberton. Or maybe Carnesville."

"When's the next train there?"

"Cain't get to there, neither. Not from Augusta."

"All right." I dropped my grip to the floor. "Please tell me where I can get to from here that is close to Royston."

He rubbed his cheek. "Athens?"

Athens it in fact was, although that town, nearly four hours from Augusta by slow coach, was itself some twenty-two miles from my destination. When I alighted from the train, I was obliged to hire a local to take me the rest of the way by horse and wagon.

But the expense—fifteen dollars, round trip—troubled me little.

As we approached Ty Cobb's hometown, the intense excitement I felt was mitigated only by an undercurrent of apprehension. Driving through the north Georgia countryside, freshly green on that sunny spring day, I was keenly aware that the story that awaited me could well be my proverbial special break; might, indeed, prove of national consequence.

Royston itself was very much how one would imagine such a place. It consisted of ten or twelve dozen clapboard houses, varying in size, shape and hue, but identical in character, lining a series of unpaved streets; the great majority of Royston's official population of some thirteen hundred resided on the outlying tobacco and soybean farms. The village's focal point, and its business district, was a small square, at the center of which stood a Civil War memorial, a vigilant Confederate soldier watching over a stone trough.

It was before this object that we came to a halt. I stood on the buckboard and gazed about me. Not a soul was in sight, just several other horse-drawn vehicles hitched before business establishments. However, I noted, one of those establishments was the office of the Royston *Record*.

The editor, the only soul within, a small pink man I guessed to be in his late forties, identified himself as Mr. J. P. Smalley. A cursory inspection of the premises told me more than I needed to know about the man—that he was one of those Southerners who, having moved somewhat beyond the ignorance and provincialism endemic to the region, was determined to prove his sophistication to all who happened his way; busts of Plato, Caesar and Voltaire peered down at me from high pedestals in the corners; beside bound volumes of his newspaper sat the collected works of Shakespeare and Milton. I had known several such men in my youth.

Smalley brightened at the appearance of my *Journal* card. "Ah, New York, a capital city."

"You've been there?"

"Yes, of course. Two times."

He insisted on describing both visits at some length, and it was a good fifteen minutes before I could take the lead in the conversation. But when I did so, he was immediately forthcoming. Yes, he said, of course he'd known Tyrus, he'd known all the Cobbs. They lived in that large white house right across the way. "That," he noted, as if stumbling upon an original notion, "is what makes Royston so very different from a place like New York. Everyone knows everyone else."

I found it considerably more difficult, however, broaching the precise subject of my inquiry.

"The family moved away, have they?" I asked.

He nodded. "Up to North Carolina. We haven't heard a whisper from them since."

"Ah."

"It's hard to blame them, after what happened."

"Oh?"

"As I say, sir, Royston is a mere dot on the map."

"By which you mean?"

"The murder. Mr. Cobb was murdered."

"Ah." I nodded, feigning nonchalance, not knowing exactly how to proceed. But Smalley solved that problem for me.

"Officially," he said, "that remains a matter of conjecture, of course. But I myself hold strong opinions on the subject. I happen to have thought a great deal of Herschel Cobb." He smiled. "He was the owner of this newspaper."

"Was he?" I paused, glancing around the place with fresh eyes. "What happened, exactly?"

"Sit down," he said, indicating an empty chair in the corner. "You just sit tight, young man."

He disappeared into a back room and returned a couple of minutes later with a handful of newspaper cuttings. "Now, you take a look at these," he said. "I wrote them myself."

The cuttings, all dated the second week of August 1905, were in chronological order.

AUGUST 9   Ex-Senator and County School Commissioner W. H. Cobb of Royston was fatally shot last night by his wife. It seems that he came home late in the night and was mistaken for a burglar. He was unconscious until his death at 1:30 this morning.

Mr. Cobb was shot twice, one shot taking effect in the head, the other in the abdomen. A coroner's investigation is under way.

Accompanying the story was a brief account of the dead man's life. "Mr. Cobb," it read in part,

had been prominent in political and educational affairs both in the county and state. He was senator for the 31st senatorial district in 1901 and 1902 and was county school commissioner of Franklin County at the time of his death.

Mr. Cobb, about 43, came to Georgia from North Carolina about 20 years ago and began teaching mathematics in Banks county. He married the daughter of Captain Caleb Chitwood, of Banks county. Three children were born to them. They are Tyrus, the oldest, now a member of the Augusta team of the South Atlantic League; Paul, about 16, and Florence, 11.

A second article followed a day later.

The coroner's jury in the case of the homicide of County School Commissioner W. H. Cobb, formed a verdict of voluntary manslaughter against Mrs. W. H. Cobb today and ordered her arrest tomorrow. The warrant was held up until after the funeral today.

Witnesses were introduced who testified that there was a considerable interval between the shots, sufficient time for a person to walk back and forth across the room. Dr. J. O. McCrary, the first physician on the scene, produced a revolver and rock found in the coat pocket of the deceased.

Mr. Cobb had gone to a farm he owns near town and left his buggy and walked through the fields back into Royston. He was seen on the street at about 10 o'clock, but seemed, it is claimed, to hide his identity.

It is said that sensational developments will follow the investigation into the killing of ex-Senator Cobb by his wife. According to statements made in this city today, Mr. Cobb had received notice about two weeks ago that he had better watch his home. Before the night of the tragedy, it is alleged that there had been more than one disagreement between himself and his wife and owing to the various rumors it is expected that sensational developments will follow.

Mrs. Cobb's statements that she mistook her husband for a burglar are doubted by many. No other person, as far as is known, was seen at the Cobb home on the night of the shooting.

I glanced over at Smalley, sitting upright at his own desk. He was staring at me with bright, moist eyes.

> Mrs. W. H. Cobb, who was arrested under the coroner's warrant, charging her with voluntary manslaughter in killing her husband, whom she allegedly mistook for a burglar, quickly gave the $7000 bond required by Justice Jordan. The court to which this is returnable will be held the fourth Tuesday in September.

I looked up. "There aren't any more articles?"

Smalley nodded. "That's all."

"Why not? What happened?"

"Professor Cobb was an important individual around here," he replied, "and when he died, Amanda Cobb was quite a well-to-do woman. If you follow me."

"She was acquitted?"

"The case never got to trial. There was some"—he hesitated—"*explanation* offered that the court calendar was filled. It was left at that. And, as I say, shortly thereafter the family left town."

Smalley was, in fact, anxious to assist me with my research. A half hour later, when I exited the office, it was with a dozen pages of notes and the names of two other individuals, both located conveniently within the town itself, whose testimony might further advance the project. Each of them was, it turned out, equally cooperative. Far from finding the subject distasteful, Roystonians actually seemed to relish the opportunity to lead an outsider through the mucky terrain that, even years after the event, they had obviously not tired of exploring on their own. Indeed, it occurred to me that the only reason I had not read about all of this already was that no national reporter had bothered to make the trip to this town.

Brett Hubbard, who as an eighteen-year-old neighbor of the Cobbs had heard the shots and dashed over to discover the body, re-created the murder scene enthusiastically. " 'Fessor Cobb was lyin' there, all bloody 'n all, on the second floor terrace. See, Mrs. Cobb, she had been in bed when she heard him tryin' to get in through a window an' she popped him. She was still in her nightie. When I showed up, she was alone, of course. What else could you expect? But, if you ask me, that bed looked like there had been some pretty big goings-on in it."

Dr. J. O. McCrary, whom Hubbard had roused and led to the Cobb home, described the state in which he discovered Mrs. Cobb —"I had to administer calming pills"—before offering a number of ancillary observations of his own. "What I never got," he said, with a cocked eyebrow, "is how come the two Cobb children that were still at home, Paul and little Florence, how come they had been sent off to stay with friends that night." He paused. "And just tell me this, what was Herschel Cobb fixin' to do with that pistol I found in his pocket?"

But by far the most illuminating information, for my purposes, as well as the most poignant, came from one Joe T. Cunningham, to whom I was referred by the good doctor. Following McCrary's directions, I found this individual in his place of business, up a path from the center of town. MORTICIAN-FURNITURE read the sign above the door.

It was not, of course, as a furniture salesman that he initially interested me. "Yeah," said Cunningham, a taciturn young man with alert blue eyes, "I handled the body myself."

"Do you believe it was murder?"

He looked at me with some surprise. "I wouldn't know. Weren't no trial."

"From your examination of the body, I mean."

"I ain't no coroner, I jus' dress 'em up."

"I hear some talk that Mrs. Cobb might not have been alone that night," I pressed.

"It's a damn lie," he shot back, his voice suddenly louder. "Amanda Cobb's an honest woman."

I managed a smile. This line of questioning was clearly fruitless, not to mention somewhat degrading. "I'm just saying what I heard."

He nodded curtly. "Folks'll say any fool thing makes 'em feel important." He paused. "But no one knew that family like me. Ty was my biggest pal. Me 'n him growed up together."

And thus it was that slowly, through my incessant prompting, this mealy-mouthed hayseed came forth with the most intriguing view of the great ballplayer I had ever heard.

On the face of it "the cockiest, haughtiest li'l boy in the state," young Ty was, in fact, according to his friend, possessed of a highly "artistic temper, 'specially where his daddy was concerned." So sensitive was he that when the elder Cobb, a strict, sharp-tongued Baptist who harbored for his oldest child ambitions as a doctor, lashed out at him for his persistent obsession with a child's game, Ty would go silent for weeks on end. " 'Fessor Cobb was where the sun rose and set for Ty," said Cunningham. "He worshipped him and was scared to death of him all at the same time."

Herschel Cobb tried his damndest to make something of the boy, by regular beatings, and stern lectures, and honest work; in the summers, while other young men of his class loafed, Ty was forced to spend entire days "keepin' company with a mule's ass, plowin' the family land—and the Cobbs had the fartinest mule in Franklin County." But when, at eighteen, in spite of it all, the boy determined to make his living playing baseball, the father gave him his reluctant blessing. Over the next year and a half, while working his way through the minor leagues, Ty assiduously planted items about himself in the Atlanta newspapers he knew the Professor read; unbeknownst to the son, the father, never a sporting fan, clipped these items and carried them in his billfold. They were found on him at the time of his death.

"I'll never forget Tyrus at the 'fessor's funeral," continued Cunningham. "He was white as a nigger's teeth. He might've been dead himself. When we started to put his daddy in the ground, coverin' him up and all, he got to his knees and started screamin' and sobbin' and pullin' up the grass." He paused. "An' he never come back to Royston in all the time since."

I made it back to Athens late that night and, the following morning, on the train to New York, I began to compose the column.

ROYSTON, GA.   For years a question has been posed, in whispers, by Ty Cobb's fellow players, by sporting writers, by those rooters with a knowledge of the "inside game." The question is: what makes Cobb tick?

Until now, there have been no answers, only guesses. But this reporter, on an expedition into the very heart of the Georgia Peach's

home region, has uncovered a personal tragedy so monstrous, so un-
forgettable, that it may be seen as sufficient explanation for every one
of the great star's notable "quirks."

I paused and glanced out the window at the scenery rushing past.
It was uncanny, the locomotive seemed to be in as great a rush as
I to escape this damnable region. Was it, I wondered, a policy of the
line to have their trains move at twice the speed heading north as
they did going in the other direction?

"One line space," I wrote in my pad.

Professor Herschel Cobb, Tyrus' sire, had all the gritty determination so well known in his son. A latter-day pioneer in his backward region, he rose from a humble instructor of mathematics to
the principalship of a high school and finally to a seat in the senior body of his state's legislature. It was there, as a Georgia State
Senator, that he earned his crowning achievement, waging a long
and successful fight for a system of country schools throughout the
state.

His eldest son, whom he named for a great Phoenician general,
loved him like a god.

But on August 9, 1905, less than three weeks before Ty made his
debut in a Detroit Tigers uniform, his illustrious father lay dead in a
pool of blood, cut down by two shots from a revolver.

The trigger had been pulled by Ty's mother . . .

When we at last reached the Pennsylvania Station, I hurried to a
taxicab and headed immediately downtown to my office. A considerable surprise awaited me there: it seemed that Edith had given birth
two days before. I had a son, Luther Pond, Jr., and my ignorance
of the fact was the source of much mirth among my colleagues when
I appeared.

But at the moment, I had no appetite for their good humor.
Accepting their congratulations with brisk civility, I made my way
to McCullum's office and walked straight inside.

He glanced up from a page proof. "So, Pond, decided to honor
us with your return, did you?"

"I want you to read what I have," I said. "I think it's quite
important."

He knew I was not given to hyperbole. "Let's see it," he said gruffly, laying aside the page.

I waited outside his office while he read. Ten minutes later I was summoned back within.

"Is this true?" he asked.

"Yessir."

"Without any question?"

"No sir." I in fact had verbatim copies of the articles from the Royston *Record*.

He shook his head. "Quite a tale."

"Yes, it is."

"You realize, of course, we can't run it."

For an instant, I wasn't sure I had heard correctly. "Pardon?"

"This isn't news, Pond, it's back-fence gossip."

"But"—I hesitated—"you said it was a good story."

"Sure it is. I'll tell all my friends. But we happen not to be in the business of hero reduction at this paper." His look was suddenly severe. "People don't want to read about Ty Cobb *crying*, for Chrissakes. What the hell's the matter with you? They'll stone the building." He paused. "Show me what else you got. I hope to God you brought back something I can print."

Another man might have despaired at such a moment. I had certainly never had equal reason. But it has always been my experience that those who brood over lost causes, wasting their time retracing steps or plotting retribution, invariably lose sight of larger goals. I recognized, in any case, that the slight had not been personal; McCullum was simply a victim of his own limited vision. In the context of the world he knew, his might even have been the correct choice. I cannot say for certain that there was any other editor in town who would not have done likewise.

I handed him my two remaining columns and promised to have a third ready the following morning. Then I headed home to my wife and new son.

That evening, in the privacy of my study, I carefully labelled my research on Cobb and filed it away.

Nineteen Fifteen

by George D. Weaver

I t is a funny thing about this national game of ours called baseball, how quickly a ballplayer starts to queer in the eyes of others. By the end of the '14 season, there I was, only in the fast company a few short years, and already people were putting the old knock on me. Some of the scribes were writing that I was not stacking up as planned, what with my hitting and glove work that were not so regular, and of course when they print such things, the bugs just naturally follow along. There had even been some razzing going on from the stands to the effect that the Sox already had enough bums and ought to let me go. Naturally I did not let it get to me, being a strong-hearted fellow and pretty calm, but it was nothing to write home to Stowe about, neither.

And that is one of the reasons why after that season I tried out something Kid Gleason had said, which was to chop wood left-handed instead of righty. That is what some back number named Charlie Reilley had done to learn to hit from both sides of the dish, and Gleason said it might turn the trick for me also. It sounded like applesauce to me, but since I had to chop wood anyhow, I figured what harm could it do. See, there I was back home in Pennsylvania with my wife Helen, where it gets pretty cold, so there was always wood to break up.

And I will tell you something, the plan worked like a miracle! After two weeks or three, I could strike the wood even sharper lefthanded than righty. And when I got down to Fort Worth at the start of the '15 season, sure enough, I had a pretty good lefthanded stroke with a bat, too. Oh, it did not come the first time I tried it or nothing, but pretty soon I was smacking the horsehide nearly to the fence in right, which was three hundred and fifteen feet in that park, and the Kid would watch me, and grin, and say maybe I was not so much of a bonehead after all.

Naturally I was quite cheered up by this and eager to show my stuff against some real twirler and not just a busher, which is what Gleason had had throwing against me. But the thing was, aside from my special pals, like Cicotte and Jim Scott and a couple of others, no one else in the camp seemed to care what was up with me. Not that that was really so odd, since no one there seemed to care what was up with no one else either. Except for two guys. You see, The Old Roman had made some moves in the off-season, and they are the ones all the fuss in camp was about.

First off, we had a new manager, which everyone said was a good thing, 'cause even as interesting a character as Callahan was, he could not even lead an animal to water, forget about having it drink. The only trouble was, no one was too delighted with the new fellow neither, who went by the handle Pants Rowland. He had never been the brains in the big leagues before, but only in the bushes at Scranton, and had never even played in the bigs before. Everyone wanted to know why Comiskey had signed on a bird like that, except that maybe he wanted to call all the shots himself, for it was hard to know how the hell some manager who was not dry behind the ears could be commander-in-chief of a bunch of wild ballplayers like us.

But old Pants, he was just a sideshow at that camp compared to the other fellow, the world-famous Eddie Collins.

I probably do not have to tell you too much about Collins, for if you are any kind of baseball fiend at all, you already know how he was maybe the greatest second sacker ever, and how he spent all those years over in Philly right smack in the middle of the Athletics' "hundred thousand dollar infield," and how just the year before the Chalmers Automobile Company had given him a buggy for being the most valuable man in the whole league.

But what almost no one knew about, not then and not even so

much today, is how Comiskey came to pick him up from Connie
Mack. They always kept that part of it under the table, and for good
reason, too.

For it was on account of dirty dealings, pure and simple, on the
part of the magnates. See, just the year before that, the new Federal
League had started up, going up against Organized Baseball, and it
looked like it was doing just fine. Their very first year, the Feds had
gone out and signed a bunch of fellows from the big show, like Bill
McKechnie and Chet Chadbourne and Hap Myers and Long Cy
Falkenberg, and now they were after some of the big stars. The buzz
was that they were talking to Cobb himself, not to mention Speaker
and Shoeless Joe, and so it is no wonder the magnates were jumpy.
Our club had already lost our first sacker to the Feds' Buffalo club,
who was Hal Chase, a fellow that would chase after a dollar to the
moon, and Comiskey wanted to make sure it would not happen
again. One day around the end of the '14 season, he had even showed
up in the clubhouse, all red in the puss, and he had told us that if
anyone else was planning to be a traitor like Chase, he should know
he would never be let back into the big show again. He said that
pretty soon the Feds were going to flivver, he and the other magnates
would make sure of it, and when they did, they would count up who
their friends had been. And, sure enough, a few days after that, all
the owners got together and said the very same thing to the sporting
writers. There may have been a war going on in France, all right,
but for the baseball bugs, the real war was over here.

And the Feds kept coming right at them, that's for sure. Before
the start of the '15 season, they went to court saying that the major
leagues were a trust, which I guess they were, and that the magnates
were going around scaring us ballplayers spitless, which there was
no doubt about. It said in the papers, and on the front page, too, not
just in the sporting news, that there was some judge listening to the
case called Kenesaw Mountain Landis.

But Comiskey had it even tougher than the other magnates. See,
Chi was the only big league town aside from Brooklyn that the Feds
had took on face to face, and there was no way around it, the Chicago
Whalers was better than either us or the Cubs. In '14, they had ended
in second position in their league, just a game and a half from the
top, after a "whale of a pennant chase," as the scribes put it. Mean-

while, the Cubbies had dropped all the way down to fourth in the senior circuit, sixteen and a half games behind the Braves, and us Sox were even worse than that, back in sixth, thirty games out. And that was not even all. The Whalers also had got the famous Joe Tinker to manage them, and he was a legend in that town. Plus they were playing their ball in a brand new park, which is today called Wrigley Field. It is no wonder they pulled so strong at the gate. Hell, if I was just a bug back then instead of a ballplayer, I would have gone out to watch them myself.

So The Old Roman was in the soup, all right, no question of it. And that is how come it was fixed up for us to get Collins from the Athletics, though like I say, it was not 'til later that we found out the ins and outs. You see, it turned out that Collins himself had been thinking about jumping to the Feds, even despite the fact that the Athletics was a great squad and The Tall Tactician was like another father to him. I guess this father of his did not want to ante up what Collins could get in Newark. Nor was he the only traitor on that club, for Home Run Baker, who was the third sacker, was thinking of doing the same thing. That would have left only a fifty-thousand-dollar infield, and when Ban Johnson, the president of the American League, got word of it, he could have laid an egg right on the spot. In a day, he got it all set up between Mack and Comiskey in a manner to kill two birds at once. Collins was sold from Philly to Chi for fifty thousand, and never mind what I just said, that was quite a fabulous sum in those days, and then Comiskey sat down to try and sign up Collins, which he did—for three years at the rate of fifteen thousand per annum.

That is all anyone knew about it in that spring of '15, those salary numbers, and they are all anyone cared to know. No other man on the club was getting paid half so much, and I myself was pulling in but four thousand. And only a little before that, The Old Roman had been popping off in the papers that the raises in players' salaries on account of the Feds was an awful thing and would kill the game. "Salaries must be cut in half," he said, "and other expenses reduced accordingly."

Well, you might guess that some of the boys on our club took it all rather hard. No one had nothing against Collins, not then, for he was just a ballplayer grabbing at all he could, but you can bet that the gloom in that training camp was as thick as a fried egg sandwich. Nor was it a help the way the sporting writers were running around there like rats, only asking about Collins, except maybe for a question here and there about Rowland. Collins was a pretty quiet fellow, not like Cobb or Casey Stengel or one of them, and he had never got too much ink before, even despite his wonderful play. One of the scribes by the name of Hayner even told me, real hush-hush, that there was more "live" stuff to be written about King Kelly, who had been dead twenty years. But now, every time you picked up a paper, even the ones we got down there, there would be a write-up about Collins, on how he was a college man from Columbia, and how he had such fabulous hobbies as playing bridge and "Ask Me Anothers" and doing crossword puzzles, and how his wife Mabel and his kids was nearly as brainy as him. I am not a hard guy, and was even less then, but it was enough to make a fellow sick a few times over.

See, this is how the press is. If you are on top, as Collins was, they will suck up to you like anything, and of course it also works the other way around. Most of these ink wasters do not care for nothing at all except to get ahead themselves, and it is all the same to them if what they write is truth or falsehood. I know this from my own actual life.

At the moment in question, we had another cause for being miffed at the writers, too, and especially at one of them that went by the name of Lardner. You may be guessing ahead of me, and if you are, you are right, for there is only one fellow by that name. Us ballplayers did not call him Ring, but Old Owl Eyes. I guess you would know how come if you ever got a load of him. Anyway, he was a big tall bag of bones that had been writing up the club in the *Tribune* at the time I made the big show, and for a couple of seasons after. He was pretty deadpan all the time, so when he said something, a fellow could never be sure if he was getting the straight dope or getting his legs pulled, but aside from that, there had been nothing about the bird to kick about. Until, that is, he had begun printing baseball stories in *The Saturday Evening Post*. And now, in '15, he had gotten up a whole book of the damn things. The name of the book was *You Know Me Al*, and you can believe me, what he printed in there was not funny! It was all about some busher on the Sox named Jack Keefe, that could not spell right nor even talk plain English.

Keefe did not really exist nowhere at all except in Lardner's noggin, but there were also some actual fellows he talked about, such as Gleason and Cicotte and Walsh and Scott and yours truly, and we got the knock pretty good in there. For instance, there was a part where Keefe was sore over some contest he got blown out of. "Me loseing that game in Washington was a crime," is how it went, "and Callahan says so himself. This here Weaver throwed it away for me and I would not be surprised if he done it from spitework because him and Scott is pals and probably he did not want to see me winning all them games when Scott was getting knocked out of the box. And no wonder when he has got no stuff. I wish I knowed for sure that Weaver was throwing me down the river and if I knowed for sure I would put him in a hospital or somewhere."

Well, first off, like I say, this guy Keefe was not even for real, so tell me how could I have tossed a wide heave behind him? I did not make no bingles on purpose for no one, not even for a pal like Death Valley Jim. The way I saw it, there was only one reason anyone would print such a thing, and that was to make money! And that is what it was. I later heard that Lardner was getting two hundred bucks each for his write-ups in the magazine, and he probably got even more from that book!

Of course, that is not how the smart alecks were looking at it. When that book came out, there was all kinds of gas about how Old Owl Eyes was a great genius, and how fine it was that for the first time us ballplayers were not made out to be heroes, but just regular guys, and that in the book was what we were really like. Well, we did not ask to be heroes in the first place, but only got that way on account of the scribes themselves. And if there was ever any ballplayer like Jack Keefe, I sure never bumped into him, for even the dimwits in the fast company would never say what that fellow said about me. Indeed, if Lardner had still been hanging around with the club when we got our paws on "You Know Me Al," which he was not due to fortune and fame, he was the one that would've got put in some hospital.

But this is how it always was with the writers, anyway. They were the ones that were really simple-minded, not us. If you were going good, you were the berries in their eyes, and if you were going bad, even despite the fact that you might have a busted finger or something, you were a bum. It was cut and dry. They did not know about moods or anything else that was complicated. For instance, if a fellow had a comical side, they just could not get it that he might be comical and serious all at the same time, which is how a lot of us were.

Take the case of Hughie Jennings, who was a great ballplayer back with the old Orioles, and after that a pretty fair manager for the Detroits. These days no one recalls any of that about Hughie, for he was also a guy that knew how to have fun. In the eyes of the scribes, he was only a jokester, so now, all these years after, it is all anyone remembers of Hughie, even including baseball men.

But sometimes it gets even sorrier than that, and I am thinking now of the case of Ping Bodie, who was with the Sox when I first come up. Like I say, that Jack Keefe fellow that Lardner cooked up was not real, but everyone sort of figured he was taken from old Ping, for Bodie was indeed a character and a half. He was a little fellow in height, with a kitchen on him that stuck out three feet or more, and he ran as slow as a seven-year itch. One time when he tried to swipe a base, some scribe wrote down that "his head was full of larceny but his feet were honest," which is about how it was. And that is the sort of thing they were always putting down about Ping, that and about what a bragger he was, which I must admit was also true. He was a fellow that was always full of balloon juice about what he was going to do and how no one else could match him. I will never forget the time in Florida, on the way up north after training camp, when one of the writers saw a notice in the local paper about a travelling show starring "the world's greatest eater," who was Percy the Ostrich. Well, all of the scribes and some of the ballplayers, too, got together and had Ping challenge the ostrich in an eating contest. The next day the two of them got up in a boxing ring they had set up there and they started going at bowls of spaghetti, which was the eats Bodie had chosen for the contest. Well, sure enough, after eleven bowls, Percy the Ostrich got this sick look on his mug and wobbled away to his corner, and Ping was named the champion, and naturally the scribes wrote it up with plenty of ballyhoo.

Only, the thing was, there was another part to Ping, just like with Hughie, and it never got in the papers at all. See, he was not only a daffydil, but also a fellow with amazing skills. When he landed with the lumber, the horsehide took a regular expedition with Byrd. He could lace the ball as long as any ballplayer I have ever seen, even including the Babe himself. But he never got any kind of real chance to show off his stuff, on account of everyone taking him for such a bean skull. There was so much in the sporting pages about his stunts that finally Comiskey and Callahan just did not want to have him around no more. They figured the club had enough to laugh at without some diamond artist that was comical on purpose. And so old Ping was sent back to San Fran, where he had started out in the first place. He never did forget what Comiskey had done to him, nor the scribes neither, for he would tell anybody that asked him the same thing. "Those fellows just do not have no sense of responsibility."

And that was the size of it, all right. In that training camp in '15, all us ballplayers may have gone around saying "You know me Al," just like everyone else in the country, for it was just something a guy said to show that a thing did not have to be told in the first place. For instance, if a great hurler tossed a shutout and afterwards somebody asked him how he had done, he might just come back "You know me Al." But even though we said it, that does not mean we cared for the fellow that thought it up. To the contrary. And we had no more liking for most of the other scribes, the ones making such a fuss about Collins, printing all over the place that now all at once the Sox were going to be contenders and not saying a word about no one else. Those pencil pushers only want one thing, and when they get it, they leave you high and dry.

So there I was, doing my level best to become a lefty swinger, and I could hardly get no one in my own camp to pay notice. Finally, one fine day, Gleason said he would talk it over with Rowland, and a little after that Pants came over and looked at me hit a few. Then he said "Fine, fine," like I was hitting normal or something, and he went off on his way.

And when the club went up north to Chi, it was the same tune all over again. A couple of the writers may have raised their brows a touch when they saw what was up with me, but they sure did not write too many words about it, nor about no one else for that matter, even despite the fact that the club got off to a real fast start. Cicotte was hurling like a house in flames, and Scott and Faber, too, and we had a rookie called Felsch that was handling the centerfield patrol like Speaker, but still all a fellow heard about was Eddie Collins. I am not no sorehead, so I will come right out and repeat that he was a good ballplayer, covering ground around the number two bag and also doing good work on the basepaths, and even Gleason said he was a great ballplayer. But he was not the whole team on his own, that's for sure.

Still, none of us squawked about him right off the bat since, like I say, it was not really his doing and, anyway, it was indeed possible that with him on our side, we might be in for some World Series dough. No, the squawking did not begin in earnest 'til around the middle of June.

See, on a ballclub, you get to know a fellow pretty fast, and the more we found out about Collins, the less well we liked him. His nickname was Cocky, Cocky Collins, and that just about tells it right there. I am not saying he was a swellhead, not exactly, for he was not one of those fellows that would go around saying out loud that he had more moxie than other guys. It was not so out in the open as that. He would just walk around with a cock strut, and kind of eye the rest of us like we were simple. He would not go out drinking with the boys, nor even play poker, which is a thing we did a lot on that club, with a ten-cent limit. He would always just go off somewhere by himself to read, and not *The Sporting News*, neither, but a book. You can guess how we took that.

But it did not really get too bad 'til that time in June I want to tell you about. You see, the club had gone into a bit of a spin, and that day when we got back into the clubhouse in Comiskey after the game, all upset 'cause we had just dropped one to the Senators that we ought to have won, there was another poem from *The Baseball Magazine* up on the wall. It was called "Casey the Comeback."

The Mudville fans were sick and sore for many a summer day
And through the gloom in Mudville town there shone no cheering ray,
For the theme of every gossip, the talk in every hall,
Was how the mighty Casey had failed to hit the ball.

And Mudville scorned the mighty man who failed to win the fray
They found their golden idol was made of common clay;
They called him every epithet their scorn could conjure up,
And everybody shunned him from the mayor to the pup.

That same old club came back one day that beat the Mudville nine,
That same old pitcher graced the slab and smiled a smile benign.
The Mudville fans looked on aghast, as 'twas the aching heart,
For Mudville veterans didn't have a look-in from the start.

You see, this was a follow-up to another famous poem that you probably already know about, and it went on and on just like the first one, right on through the ballgame. And Casey came up in the pinch, just like before.

A deathlike stillness gripped the fans, and e'en the groans had died;
There were no cheers for Casey now, but only "Drat his hide!"
And again the pitcher loosed the ball, and again—but what was
    that?
It sounded like the crack of doom—but it came from Casey's bat!

Ten thousand eyes then saw the ball, as if it had been shot
From out some rifled cannon's mouth—and it traveled sizzling hot.
It swirled aloft o'er centerfield into the sky's clear blue—
It rapidly became a speck, then vanished from the view.

And then five thousand throats loosed up and yelled like men gone
    mad!
Ten thousand arms waved furiously, and hats went to the bad.
And from the blistering bleachers to the grandstand's swellest guy
They wept and laughed and cussed and blessed til all their throats
    went dry.

Oh! somewhere in our baseball land the shadows thickly fall.
The winds are sighing somewhere, and somewhere hangs death's
    pall,
And somewhere hearts are breaking, and towns are reft of fame—
But there is no gloom in Mudville, for Casey won the game.

Now, right away when they saw that poem, most of the boys figured it was me and Knuckles that stuck it up, like the last time. But it was not so. It was some poem, all right, and I would have liked the blame, but it had got up there another way, and that is what we told them.

So I read it myself, right along with the others, and when we finished, things got pretty emotional. While we were getting dressed, we sat around talking about old Casey, and how tough it must've been for him with all the bugs in the stands putting the knock on him, and how great it was that he pulled through anyhow. We talked about this for quite a while, comparing Casey's troubles to our own, and pretty soon it seemed that maybe things weren't so bleak for us as they looked.

But, see, Collins wasn't part of the bunch at all. He just stayed off on his own as usual, getting dressed in the corner, shaking his head and smirking at us.

Only, for some reason, this time Jim Scott spoke up. The fact is, Collins had had a pretty sloppy game that day himself, and might've used a pick-me-up as well as the next guy, I guess that's what Scott was thinking.

"Hey, Ed," he said, "how about you? You like the poem?"

Collins just gazed at him, cocky as anything. "Are you talking to me?"

"Who else do you think I'm talking to?"

"No."

"You don't? Why the hell not?"

Cocky looked at him like he was dirt on his feet. "I prefer the original." He stopped a second. "You do know the original? By Ernest L. Thayer?"

Well, I am sorry to say that that bottled up Scott pretty fast, for it's a pretty good guess that he had never heard of this Thayer, and neither had I, if you want to know the truth. We knew of the poem, but that was another story.

For a while no one said anything, we just went back to putting on our socks and such.

"This one is by Herman L. Shiek."

The guy who said it was Happy Felsch, the rookie centerfielder, and we all looked over at him in surprise. He had a big grin on his puss.

"Pardon me?" said Collins.

"This poem is by Herman L. Shiek." He paused. "It was me that put it up there."

Now one thing you should know about Felsch, he did not get his nickname for nothing. The fellow had as bright a disposition as any man in the game, and that includes Laughing Larry Doyle over with the New York club. It's only lucky the two of them were not on the same squad, 'cause seeing so much happiness all the time can ruin a lot of guys' days. Some of the boys thought Hap was simple, on account of his disposition and also because he was the worst draw poker player you ever saw. It was like he did not understand the game, for he would never retire from a pot, even if he had no chance at all. Also, he had once been a professional wrestler before he became a ballplayer. But if you ask me, he was no more simple than the rest of us.

"Herman L. Shiek wrote it?" answered back Cocky at last, with a smile. "Why he must be a genius. But I'm sure you agree that the original is still a tad better."

Felsch screwed up his map and started to think on that, but he did not get a chance to answer.

"The original was sure not better," interrupted yours truly. "How could it be better when Casey turned out to be a bum?"

That broke up the ice a bit, and all at once four or five guys spoke up, agreeing with me. Indeed, it was hard to know how anyone could say otherwise.

But Collins did not give a damn for the opinion of others. He just smirked and shook his noggin.

But I was one guy that wouldn't let him slip away so easy. "A poem like this is good for the ballclub," I added.

He looked at me in that way of his. At such moments Cocky looked like a weasel, for his eyes got real small and he had about the biggest ears on the club. "You really believe that?" he said.

"Sure it is," chimed in Felsch. "That's why I put it up."

Cocky touched the side of his dome with his finger. "You're very wise, Oscar, very wise indeed." See, Oscar was Happy's real handle, which everyone hated.

This was too much even for Knuckles. "What do you know about it?" he said to Collins. "You don't know everything, you know." I guess you can tell that by then he already had plenty of that thing called confidence.

Cocky gazed at him real calm and rose to his feet. He had finished dressing. "I know a lot more than you do, friend. I happen to be a student of psychology." He stopped. "I'll bet that you don't even know what that is."

"Sure I do," said Cicotte, in his quiet way, and I'll bet he did, too.

"Good," said Collins, "when I leave you can explain it to the others. You might also tell them that what they need is a good dose of mental discipline, not some idiotic rhyme." He turned and started strutting out of the room, then turned around. "Someday you fellows really ought to try reading something besides *The Baseball Magazine.*"

Well, you might say that that was not such a terrible incident. There was not even any scuffling. But the simple fact is, after that things would never be the same on that ballclub again. And why should they be? Most of us ballplayers had not been so sure how we felt about domeheads in the first place. It just did not seem right that a fellow fresh out of college, who was well furnished upstairs, would take a job smacking baseballs from an ordinary joe. Even some managers agreed with this. There is a tale about the time George Stallings, who ran the Boston club back then, sent a couple of college boys to pinch hit for him. First one struck out and then the other, at which point George, who had only been to sixth grade himself, walked over to where they were sitting glumly on the bench, stuck his puss an inch from their faces and started screaming "Rah-rah-rah, rah-rah-rah, rah-rah-rah!"

Well, I guess most of us felt just the same way. And this Collins had turned out to be the most smart alecky college man of all.

But we knew that having a beef with Cocky was not the same thing as being sore on some ordinary fellow, and not only on account of how much the scribes adored him. See, he was also the special favorite of The Old Roman, for Comiskey was a college man himself. He had been at a place called St. John's College in Wisconsin that his old man had sent him to, and though he did not talk of those days too much, he liked the brainy players as much as anyone.

So for quite a while we kept our traps shut about Collins, and only knocked him amongst each other, and tried to give him the go-around. I did not even like to talk to him on the diamond, which was not easy, since at the time I was still at shortstop and he was at second. Indeed, when the club dropped out of the flag chase, I did not even mind so much, for if we had become champions, Collins would surely have hogged all the kudos.

Still and all, things was not too bad. For the first time, I myself was living up to my talents on the field, and finally the club was not something to feel ashamed of. Indeed, that year we would finish all the way up in third position.

But with a fellow like Collins about, nothing ever stays easy, and just a couple of weeks before the close of the season, there was another fuss. It happened on a Pullman train heading back to Chi from Detroit. A gang of us boys was playing poker in the parlor car as we always did and all at once Collins walked in. At the time in question, I did not pay it any attention, for there was a big pot on the table, six dollars or more, and me and Happy Felsch was the only two left in the deal. Naturally I had him beat. I was sitting there with a full boat, jacks over nines, and like I say, I have seen him stay in a game when he did not even have a pair of deuces. So there I was, giving him a baby stare, and all at once Felsch drops out! Well, it turned out that Collins had been standing behind me all the while eyeing my hand and flashing Happy the "stop" sign, just the same as our coachers gave it to runners on the basepaths, and that is the only reason why Felsch had folded. I knew this 'cause Collins came right out and said so. He thought it showed a lot of wit, and could not understand why it put such a bug in my ear that I was ready to put my fist through his skull. I was in a lather for ten minutes before I finally figured out that there is just nothing to do with a fellow like this, and not even beating him silly will help, and so I shut my trap. And a little while later he beat it out of there, still smirking in that way of his.

Well, it was the very next day, back in our home park, that someone went into Collins' locker and filled his glove with shit. It was not me, I will tell you that right now. I later found out who the culprit was, but there is no use asking, 'cause I will not say. But it was certainly a fine stunt, and I heard that when Cocky stuck his paw in the mitt, he let out a howl to wake up a corpse.

The next thing I knew, I was up in Comiskey's office with The

Old Roman and Pants Rowland, and the two of them were giving
me the frosty glare, like a couple of my old teachers back in Pennsylvania. I guess I could not really blame them. Everyone in the whole
league knew that I was cutuppish and pretty fast with the donkey-
shines, and so when they started up accusing me, I did not even get
sore. The Old Roman said there was no use in me denying it 'cause
they knew it was me, and I just shook my dome and said "No, it was
not."

"Weaver, we know all about the ruckus the other day on the
train," said Pants, who was a pretty oily bird, if you really want to
know what I think.

"So what of it?" I came back. "That was no fault of mine."

"We know how you feel about Collins."

"Certainly I was miffed. Anyone else would be, too, to see someone do like he did at a poker game."

"You shouldn't be playing poker in the first place," cut in The Old
Roman.

"That's right," said Rowland, "poker is very bad for a man's
mental discipline."

So it went on like that for a while more, and finally I guess they
figured that maybe it was not me that done it, after all. For one thing
they had no proof, and for another, I don't really think they cared
so much about solving the riddle as in making a show so there would
not be such devilish goings-on next year.

So by the end of an hour, there were no hard feelings in that room
at all. Comiskey smiled and said we should let it all be bygones and
no one should stay sore at no one. Then he asked after my wife
Helen, and wished me a good winter and said I would be getting my
contract in the mail around November.

Well, for quite a while I had wanted to bring up a certain matter
to him, and suddenly this seemed like the time. "Thank you, sir,"
I said. "By the way, I was wondering what you figure I might be
worth for next season."

He took off the specs he was wearing and gazed at me quite
sincere. "Well, Buck, it's a little early to be talking of that, don't you
think? I'll sit down with Grabiner and Pants and we will send you
a figure."

"I guess it is a little early, sir," I said, "but, after all, I had a pretty good year, with my lefty swinging and all, and it seems to me I'm due for a big rise."

At that moment, Rowland slowly stood up. "Mr. Comiskey, I should be getting back to the clubhouse."

Comiskey laughed. "You just go ahead, Pants," he said, and he watched as Rowland hotfooted it out of there. See, Rowland was a fellow with the spine of a mouse and even Comiskey knew it.

"Well now, Buck," said The Old Roman, looking back at me, "just how much is it you think you're worth?"

"Well, sir, Collins is getting fifteen and I . . ."

"You never mind what Collins is making!" he jumped in. All at once his face got hard as a baseball. "He is one of the best players in the league and what he earns is no concern of yours."

That got me a bit shaky, but I did not want to leave 'til I had shot my wad to this nickel nurser. "Maybe so, Mr. Comiskey," I said, "only I cannot see that he is worth three times what I am, after the year he had and the year I had."

He leaned across his desk and looked at me close. "I am going to tell you something, young man, and you had better listen carefully. Do not worry your head about Eddie Collins. He's a college man and you are not. If he left baseball, he would earn a very fine wage elsewhere. Without baseball what could you be but a miner like your father?" He stopped. "Just ask yourself, how much would you be making in the mines?"

"I would not go to the mines," I came back. "I would go over to the Feds first!"

He gazed at me hot as fire. "Well, then, go and try. But don't come crawling back to me when they go bust."

I figured he knew what he was saying, too, for even in *The Baseball Magazine* it said that the Feds were in a pickle and this might be their last season. But I did not let on that I was in a sweat. "Well, maybe I will and maybe I won't," is all I said, and a few minutes later I blew out of that office.

You can bet I was plenty sore after that, but what could I do? Nothing, that's what! For if the Feds were indeed on the flivver, a ballplayer had better stay put where he was. The national game is a business, like shipping or something like that, and the magnates do what they please. Nor could a fellow even kick about it out in the public, for the scribes did not want to hear it.

All but one, that is, and I am talking about the famous Luther Pond. See, at that time Pond was not yet the big cheese he is today, but was still just a regular sporting writer, with the New York *Journal*. In fact, I have to say that he was not even one of the sporting writers that might make a big impression on you. He was scrawny, with hardly no chin on him, and he did not dress flashy at all. Looking at him, you would have no notion at all he was heading someplace. And on top of that, he also seemed pretty timid, which most of them scribes definitely was not. Most of them liked fun and good times. They was riding on the gravy train, spending so much of their time with other fellows and on the road and all, and they did not hide it under a bushel. But usually when you saw Pond, he was off on his own. About the only way you might guess that there was more to the fellow than shyness was from his eyes, which were little like a parakeet's and always gazing around, like he was afraid someone might be pulling something he did not know about.

But I personally did not catch on to this last part until much later. Our club only came to New York two times every year, so how well could I know him? Up 'til then, I had maybe just talked to him three times in my career. And, naturally, I figured that any fellow that was timid had to be a good egg.

Anyway, this time in New York I want to tell you about, I was pretty startled when he came up and started chatting to me. That is where we were ending up that season, playing the Yankees.

At first there was plenty of hemming and hawing, but then he said, "Buck, could I ask you something?"

So I said sure.

"Could you tell me what's going on with you fellows?"

"I don't catch what you mean," I said, for I truly did not.

At that he kind of looked away, and maybe glanced at his notebook. "I am told there's some ill feeling on your ballclub."

"I do not know where you heard that at all."

"Don't misunderstand me. Don't you think maybe someone should print your side of it?" He stopped. "Of this business between you and Comiskey."

I could not for my life figure out where this little guy had picked it up. "Well," I said, "it may be true, all right, but I sure will not talk about it with a sporting writer."

But he kept after me for a good five minutes or more, and in that real gentle way of his. He said I did not have to say nothing too strong, and that he would not put down no names if I did not want and maybe it might even do the situation some good. So at last I said "All right."

And the very next day, there it was, all right, right in the New York *Journal*. It was not a big article or nothing, littler than the one right next to it about the fine work Collins had done bringing our club up to third, but still, us boys could not hardly believe our eyes. UNREST AMONG THE PALE HOSE is what it called what was going on, and it talked all about our gripes over dough.

I do not want to make too much over this article for, like I say, it was quite short and it did not really change a single thing. After the games with the New Yorks, I went back home to York, and a few months after that the club sent me a new contract, three years at six thousand per annum, which was much less than I deserved, but I signed it anyway, and things kept on just like before.

Besides, I do not want to say too much good about Luther Pond, since in later years I got extremely sour on the guy. Indeed, I despise him like poison.

But I will tell the truth, at the moment in question, that write-up made me as happy as a pig in the poke. At last, for once, someone had put down the straight goods, and it is hard to tell you what that meant to a fellow like me.

In fact, maybe that is what caused the troubles with Pond afterward, for after that I trusted the fellow too much. But, then again, that was an old habit of mine, trusting fellows too much.

You know me Al.

Nineteen Sixteen

by George D. Weaver

Usually when a fellow is a little dim, he turns out to be a good egg. After all, a guy with gray matter upstairs can be sulky or ill-tempered and people will still pay him respect. You know how people are, and trying to change them is as easy as changing dog piss to beer. But a dimwit is like a fat person that way, if he is not good-natured, what else does he have going for him?

That is what was so odd about Joseph Jefferson Jackson of Brandon Mills, South Carolina, what a glum pot he was, for as everyone knows, Shoeless was far from a genius in the brains department. To the contrary. Yet he made no apologies for his thick skull at all, and could be as tough to be around as any man in the big show. To this day I will not say that I really understand the guy.

I personally made Joe's acquaintance, along with most of the other boys on our club, at the tail end of the '15 season, when the Sox picked him up from Cleveland. As you may expect, knowing The Old Roman, there was dirty dealings in this. See, the Feds had been chasing after the big stars harder than ever in '15, and the buzz was that Joe had an offer of eight thousand to turn traitor. That was just to be his bonus, which even today is a lot of dough, and his pay would be on top of it. Naturally, Somers, who was the magnate over in Cleveland, was pretty jumpy over such talk, for he could certainly not match it, and so when Comiskey offered up Roth and Klepfer and a load of cash for Jackson, he grabbed it fast. Well, that very day The Old Roman got Shoeless off into a hotel room in Cleveland, and

he started coming off like a father and all, the way he could sometimes. He made Joe an offer of ten grand, and told him he had better
wise up and sign a White Sox contract right there and then, 'cause
the Feds were about to do a dive, and if he signed up with them he
would definitely never play ball again. Of course, it was true what
he said about the Federals, and '15 would indeed be their finale. But
the rest of it was just yap. The next year, all the talent from the Feds
that was any good at all was right back in organized baseball, and
so if Joe had signed with them, he would have had the eight thousand
free and clear.

When us boys on the Sox heard of how The Old Roman had
hipped Joe, we were not surprised, not at all, because we knew
about Comiskey's ways, and of course had also heard plenty about
Jackson's brain. The fact is, at the time we thought it was pretty
comical. I remember that Death Valley Jim cracked a line that the
Feds should've shown Shoeless Joe the loot in pennies, and if they
had, he would've swum across Lake Erie after it.

That is the kind of dumb cluck we were expecting, and when
Jackson joined up with the club a couple of days later, we were not
disappointed. Oh, he did not look so much like a hayseed anymore.
No, indeed, after all those years in the big show he was a regular
dimestore cowboy, wearing fine silk suits that cost thirty bucks or
more for each one, and Arrow shirts that cost four bucks, and he had
even got some tooth carpenter to fix up his ivories. But, see, as soon
as he opened up his trap, you right away forgot all of that. First of
all, you could hardly get what he was saying on account of his
accent, which was thick as pitch. And once you did, you usually
wished you had not, 'cause it was such gabble.

Of course, it must be said that when he first joined us, he did not
talk all that much at all, for he was scared stiff as a board. The truth
is, Shoeless was timid as could be. Back in '08, when he was just
getting started in the big show with the Athletics, he had actually
jumped the club after just three games and headed back to Dixie, and
Connie Mack had to send Socks Seybold down there to bring him
back.

The very first day I personally spotted Shoeless in the clubhouse
at Comiskey Park, all dressed up in his new White Sox togs, I came
right over in that nice way I have and welcomed him to the club.

Well, he just looked at me bug-eyed, and nodded real fast, and beat it out to the field.

Nor was he much more cozy with anyone else. The fact is, the whole rest of that '15 season, the gink did not even suit up with us, but always showed up at the park already in his uniform. Rowland had given him the okay to do this. And after games he'd run right back to the hotel where Comiskey had him put up to get back in his civvies.

Naturally some of the boys did not like this one bit, and they said so. And what got them even madder was that this fellow Jackson, who was known wide and far for his skills, was performing for us on the diamond like a busher. In fact, he would end up hitting only .265 with us that year, which was three points under yours truly! Some of the pencil pushers were even putting down that he had caught the Pale Hose jinx.

But I stuck up for the rube. I told the boys, and Cicotte backed me up, that we should not be so fast to put the knock on him. He was only timid, I said, and not really such a sorehead as he looked, and we should definitely give a man with his talents some time.

Well, I guess The Old Roman was thinking just the same way, for when the '16 season rolled around, we found out in training that it was set up for the country jake to room with Cicotte. It made sense, too, 'cause there was surely no one else on that ballclub that could make him feel comfortable like Knuckles.

And pretty soon, before the end of training camp even, that is exactly what happened. All at once, just because he was with Knuckles, Jackson started to think he was one of the boys, and before too long he began behaving like his old self on the diamond.

That was something to see, all right, Shoeless Joe Jackson showing his stuff. These days all anyone remembers about the rube was the way he could knock the blood out of a ball, which he surely could, and to every part of the park. Joe's shots were blue ropes, as angry as any liners you ever saw. He may not have rapped too many home runs, for of course this was what they call the dead ball era I am talking about and the pill did not travel nearly so far as today, but he was a whale for two and three baggers, which was the mark of a slugger back then. But the thing not too many people know is that he was a marvel with the mitt, too, and also as smooth on the basepaths as a fox. The first day of that '16 season, against Boston, he tossed out a runner at third from his post in left field, which of course opened our eyes a little. But, see, it turned out this was a thing Jackson did all the time. I am telling you, the fellow had more natural talents than any man ever, even including Cobb and Ruth, and both of them admitted it.

Still, it was one thing playing with the guy on the field, and it was another thing having to bear him in private. For it soon turned out I was wrong in what I had told the boys. Sure he was timid, but that was only part of it. Once you got to know him, he really was a sorehead. See, Shoeless Joe could just never accept that he had no brains and leave it at that. To the contrary, he was one of those fellows who always tried to come off like he knew the score better than you did.

Now, for an ordinary witless guy to try to pull off such a thing is flukey enough, but for Joe, who had been raised in a barn, it was bughouse! The fellow did not even know how to conduct himself in public places. I mean it. For instance, even after all his years in the big leagues, he was still what we called a sword swallower, which means that the only silver he ever touched was his knife. He had as much need for a fork as you or I might for a violin. Peas, meat, potatoes, pie, it would all go straight down on that sword. Of course, no one could ever say a word about this, or crack a smile, 'cause Joe had no sense of fun about himself at all. And if someone had, it wouldn't have done no good anyway, since, like I say, no matter what situation, Joe always came off like he was right and everyone else was off.

And if that's what he was like around a dining table, you can only guess how it was trying to have a conversation with the bird. "Well, Joe," you might say, "how's tricks?" And he'd just gaze at you and hunch up his shoulders, and make some little grunt.

The fact is, he could talk more easily to his bats than to anyone else, especially at the beginning. He just adored those bats. There were about fifteen or twenty of them and every one had a name. One was called Ol' Ginril, and another was Caroliny, and his favorite was Black Betsy. Before every game, he'd sit with the one he was going to use that day, discussing with it real serious, telling it what it had to do.

In fact, before he loosened up, that was the best chance any of us had of striking up a conversation with him, by asking about those bats. It was Shano Collins, an outfielder with the club, that told me this was so, but I was not sure 'til one day in the lobby of the Bond Hotel I asked him, real polite, if his bats was okay. Well, he hemmed and hawed, but at last he said "Yeah."

"Which ones are you working with?" I came back.

At that he closed and opened his eyes a couple of times and started pulling at his ear. "Big Jim, mostly."

"Big Jim? He's a new one on me."

"Jes' a young fella, Big Jim."

"He is? Just made the big show?"

He bobbed his skull, somber like a judge. "Jes' a busher."

I nodded right back. "You got him in training, I guess."

"Yeah. He's back in my room talkin' with Black Betsy right now."

This is what it was like to chew the rag with the fellow, and I am not kidding. But it was no good trying to wise him up, for he had no use for help. Way back when he was first starting out, The Tall Tactician had even offered him to get a special teacher to teach Joe his A's, B's and C's, and later on, when he was with Cleveland, Somers had made the same offer. But Jackson had given both the brush-off. "It don't take no school stuff to help a fella play ball," is how he explained it.

I heard about those offers from Joe Birmingham that used to be the manager of the Clevelands, and not from Joe himself, who of course made like he could read like a professor. Not that him being unliterate was any kind of secret, not at all, for it had been in the papers a hundred times, but this was just Joe's way, always turning his cheek at the facts. I remember that one afternoon in Cleveland, where Joe was not so popular after the deal, there were a pair of bugs sitting behind our dugout ragging him. "Hey, Joe," one would shout out, "spell cat." "Hey, Joe," would pipe up the other one, "spell shit." They were saying it as clear as a whistle, and everyone could not help but hear it, but Joe just sat there stiff-necked, with this dumb look on his mug, like they were not there at all.

I personally thought that was a pretty clever stunt, what those bugs were pulling, and I suspect the other boys did too, 'cause I could see some of them trying to wipe the smiles off their face. But we all clammed up. You see, ever since Cicotte got stuck with the rube as a roomie, me and Knuckles and Scott and Felsch and the others in our bunch had all agreed to lay off him. Sure, once in a while, if we were off by ourselves, we might smirk about one thing or another, and even Cicotte was not above it. Like, for instance, one time he mentioned that he did not know if he would be able to throw for a while on account of injury.

"What's up?" we all said, quite worried, for of course by now Knuckles was the cream of the staff.

"Well," he came back, serious as the grave, "I woke up this morning with tusks and cow horns sticking in my ribs."

We did not know what he was getting at 'til he started smirking and told us how every night Shoeless was always eating animal crackers in bed. You see, in those days, in most hotels, roomies had to share a bed, at least the ones Comiskey put us up at.

We learned many other things about Jackson from Cicotte also, such as how fast he was with the hooch. I am not saying he was an alki stiff, and neither did Knuckles, but he always had a five-gallon jug of giggle soup with him on the road. The rube told Cicotte, who he must have thought was as big a pinhead as himself, that it was special water which he needed for pains in his gut, but in actual fact it was corn liquor and drinking it would revive a corpse. Jackson would lap it up with the animal crackers.

Another thing Knuckles clued us in on was what a Don Juan he was with the skirts. This may sound curious, on account of his dim wits and all, for you might think that any femme worth the price of admission wouldn't look twice at such a guy. But if you think that, you don't know women. First off, like I said, he dressed like a sport, and if you did not look too close, he was even something of a curlylocks, with bright blue eyes and a body like a god. And even if he had been as homely as a mud fence, it would not have mattered. After all, even little shots in the big show got all the jazzing they wanted, so why not a star like Shoeless?

But the thing was, Jackson did his womanizing on the sneak, just like his hooching. Being like he was, he just did not want other ballplayers to know his business. Now, in a way I could understand

that, since a couple of years before he joined us he had got caught
in the act by his wife, Kate. What had happened is that during the
off season, Joe had signed up with a vaudeville show called "Joe
Jackson's Baseball Girls" that travelled around the burgs of Dixie,
and he had taken up with one or two of the Baseball Girls, and when
Kate Jackson heard about it, she sent a deputy sheriff from South
Carolina to bring Joe back there. Everything might have turned out
all right, except that instead of going along peacefully, Shoeless had
brained the deputy with a bat and run off. By the time he finally
turned himself in, a couple of days later, the scribes had got hold of
it and the whole country was laughing at him.

So I guess you could not blame Joe for being careful. Only, the
thing was, such antics could have caused plenty of ill feelings on
the club. Ballplayers like to know what their fellows is up to in the
skirts department, it makes everyone feel like a brother. On the
road, guys talked about it all the time, free and easy, even yours
truly, and I did not even have much to say, being as the only time
I did the deed was in St. Loo, where Agnes had moved full time.
If you want to know the truth, at first I myself was a little squea-
mish yapping about it, especially in front of Knuckles. But pretty
soon I found out that, even though he never strayed himself and
was a friend of Helen's, Knuckles liked a good tale as much as
every man. I guess he knew that when it came down to tacks, I
was a happily married man. Helen might not have been so keen on
jazzing as Agnes, nor as interesting, but that is not what a fellow
looks for in a wife.

Anyway, getting back to Shoeless, we ended up making an exception out of him. After all, he was not fooling no one. We knew of
every movement he made. And he was right about the press, they
did have it in for him. He had been one of their favorite goats ever
since he had made the fast company, and indeed even before. Some
scribe had stuck the "Shoeless" handle on him way back when he
first began in the boonies, and he hated it like a disease. "It weren't
true that I didn't have no shoes," he complained to me one time,
bitter as a weed, "it were jes' that I did gooder barefooted."

But sympathy was not the only reason that fun-loving guys like
me and Scott and the others let the beanhead pass us by without

giving him too much chaff. No, the big reason was because of how much he helped us on the diamond. Jackson's play was like nothing you ever saw. In fact, as soon as that '16 season started, and the scribes got a load of his form, some of them even started putting down that we were the club to beat. It was not applesauce, neither. By July, with Shoeless thinking he was just one of the boys, he was hitting up near .350 and driving across runs by the bushel, and we were in the middle of the chase with Boston and Detroit for the top spot. Right there is reason enough to lay off the biggest dope on earth.

But we had yet another reason, too, and it had to do with Eddie Collins. See, with Jackson performing like he was, Cocky was bound to get less ink in the press. At the start, I don't think Collins had nothing against the rube, except of course that he was cobwebbed in the head, and Cocky had no patience with such guys. But it was not personal. It did not get personal 'til later. At first, all Collins did was give Joe the miss, same as he did all of us, and keep to his own friends, such as Ray Schalk and Dave Danforth.

I should add right here that Schalk and Danforth were not bad fellows, even despite being pals with Cocky. There are some birds that can get along with anyone, and they were two of them, and I liked them myself. I have never known a single ballplayer, except maybe Cobb, that did not have no friends at all on his own ballclub.

And the proof of that was another fellow that came over to us during that '16 season, from Detroit, by the name of Lefty Williams. Williams was a slim little southpaw that looked like he was one of them refugees from the War. He had less meat on him than an old bone, and big eyes that were sad and stupid. He was not half bad on the slab, with a big round-the-bend curver and good control, but he was nearly as empty in the dome as Jackson himself, and sulky to boot, so he was as tough to warm up to as a Philadelphia lawyer. Well, soon even he had a pal who liked him, and you can guess who it was. Joe Jackson! And Williams liked Jackson right back, that's the kind of gink he was. So all at once, we had two thickheads in our bunch, and there was not a thing to do about it.

Hanging around with fellows this dumb, you cannot just ignore them, neither, for they are forever bringing things to their own level. Especially Shoeless. If he had had the ginger to admit his warts it would have been one thing, but as it was, anyone that wanted to stay on his good side had to do unnatural things. Take the letter business. Every so often, Shoeless Joe would get a letter from his wife or some other person, and of course he would want to know what it was all about. So what he would do is always open it in front of us, and make like he was reading, and then start breaking up. "Get this," he'd explain, "it's rich." Well, to make this shorter, one of us would have to take up the letter and start reading out loud, and usually it would be about nothing more than how his wife needed a fence fixed on their farm or had gotten a visit from some next of kin.

But that was nothing next to dining out with the guy. First off, if you did not watch him like an eagle, he was sure to make a jackass of himself, drinking from the finger bowl or some such thing. The hardest part, though, was ordering your eats, for we could no longer just look at the menu and order up what we wanted. Not with that stupid sap sitting there. No, we had to sit and talk over every platter on the bill, pretending like we might be interested in it ourselves, just for his benefit. Sometimes we'd chew over the bill of fare for ten minutes before we finally got to put in our order.

Not that he knew to appreciate it. Once he had finally learned some bill of fare by memory, he would actually get short with us. There we'd be, just starting to discuss the platters, and suddenly he'd pipe up with what he was going to have and why did the rest of us always have to take so long. I am telling you, it was not easy to keep a muzzle on when Jackson pulled such a stunt.

I am not saying Joe had a bad heart. It is just that, brainless as he was, he was proud as a Turk, and so could never relax and always had a bug in his ear over one thing or another. One day he might be kicking about something he had heard some pencil pusher had put down about him. Another it could be over the bugs in the stands not giving him enough cheer.

But I guess you could say that his biggest peeve was something else, and it went by the name of Cobb. See, no matter how good Joe was going, Ty always seemed to be going a little better. The fact is, for all his fine stick work, Shoeless had never won a batting crown, for Cobb always ended up a speck on top. In '11, when Joe had hit for .408, which is remarkable, Ty had been at .420. In '13, when Joe had marked .373, Ty had hit .390. So it went every season, with Joe as the also-ran.

Well, that year of '16, as soon as Joe started talking to us, you can bet that us Sox got an earful on the subject, and especially as regards advertising. See, Cobb's advertising was Joe's biggest kick of all, since Ty was always posing for something or other. Every time a guy would open up *The Baseball Magazine*, or *The Sporting News*, or *The Sporting Life*, there would be that grinning cracker puss, talking up Bradley Knit Wear, or the Rubberset Shaving Brush, or Ide Silver Collars. Of course, there were some other ballplayers that posed too, such as Johnny Evers and old Honus Wagner, and even such guys as Moriarty and Wildfire Schulte and Marty O'Toole. But Cobb did it much more than anyone, and spotting him always put Shoeless in a lather. After all, Joe liked a dollar as well as the next ballplayer, even if he might not be able to read the numbers on it, and no one had ever asked him to be in a single advertisement.

The corker came one day in Boston. I was deep in an old stuffed chair in the lobby of the Roxbury Hotel there, glancing at *The Baseball Magazine*, and all at once Shoeless was over my shoulder, with his eyes all big.

"What's he doin' there?" he said.

I looked at the page, and there was Ty, holding a bottle of Absorbine, Jr.

"Looks to me like he's picking up some shekels the way he usually does," I said.

"But I use Absorbine more'n him. I use it more'n anyone."

"What do you do with it, drink it?"

"You're dumb, Weaver," he said. "You don' drink Absorbine, you rub it." He stopped a second. "If they was gonna start usin' somebody in adverts for Absorbine," he said at last, "it shoulda been me."

The actual fact was that Absorbine, Jr. had been using ballplayers for their advertisements for a while, including Walter Johnson and Christy Mathewson, and the only reason the rube did not know it was that before they had only printed their names and not their photograph. But I did not bring this up to him, for, after all, I was trying to be a pal.

"Well," I said instead, "I guess that's the way the old ball bounces."

That night, when I told Cicotte about this, we had a pretty good laugh on the chowderhead. So you can imagine my surprise when a few minutes later, Knuckles sat right down and started writing out a letter to the Absorbine, Jr. Company in Troy, New York.

"Knuckles," I said, "you should not do it. It's one thing to look out for the rube in public places, it is something else to do business for him."

Cicotte just smiled at that. "I only want to keep Shoeless happy, and you should, too. That guy is our bread and butter."

And I'll tell you something, believe it or not, the stunt worked. A couple of weeks later there showed up a letter from Absorbine, Jr. saying, sure, they would love to have such a fellow as Joe, especially since he used the stuff. And after Cicotte had read the letter out loud, Joe acted like it was just the most normal thing in the world for him to get such a letter.

But I really did not mind so much as maybe I sound, because I knew it was true what Knuckles had said. Joe was toting us all on his back. In fact, by September our club was right up there with Boston, scratching for the pennant, not to mention a share in the World Series dough. And there was no longer any doubt to anybody, including the scribes, about who was the chief nabob on the Chicago White Sox.

Naturally, this did not sit very well at all with Collins. Indeed, he got so touchy about it that he gave up his haughty act and started in making cracks about Joe. At first his ribbing was not so hard, and he would pretend like it was all in good fun. Most of the time he would not even do it to the rube's face, but in front of me or Cicotte or Felsch, like we were ginks ourselves for being seen in public with such a slob. For instance, one day I guess he found out that Joe always picked up old hair pins in the street, which the rube did for luck, and he started making noise to me and Scott that he had never before heard of such a cockeyed thing.

"It is not cockeyed at all," I spoke right up. "I know ballplayers that do lots dumber things for luck." Which was true, by the way.

Shoeless may have walked around everywhere staring at his feet, but there were also guys that hit their noggins against their locker twenty or thirty times before a game, and others that ran around lamp posts, and Del Gainor over with Boston, he gave his worm a good squeeze every time he stepped up to the dish. "Besides," I added, "it works, for the guy hits like Cobb up there."

"Oh, sure," came back Cocky, "he's exactly like Cobb—from the neck down." He gave a big grin when he said that, but there were certainly no laughs in his eyes.

But then, as Joe kept getting more and more kudos, Collins' ragging stopped being funny altogether. It finally got most serious of all one day in Washington, just a week before the close of the season. We had just skunked the Senators, with Lefty Williams twirling a shutout over Johnson and Shoeless doing the lumber work, and the pair of them were off together in the clubhouse, shooting the breeze. Jackson was explaining that he always took his bats home to Dixie for the winter. "It's only right," he was saying. "They don' like the freeze no more'n me."

"Well," said Lefty, "maybe you could take my mitt, too. It gets pretty cold back home in Missouri."

"Sure thing," said Joe. "I don' know about a mitt, but a bat like Black Betsy, she jes' won' work if a feller don' do right by her."

"Why not send your mitt to the Riviera," butted in Collins, all at once. "That way it can learn French." He stopped and looked over at Nemo Leibold, at the locker next to his. "Have you met these two? Tweedledumb and Tweedledumber?"

Leibold had only recently come over to our club from Cleveland, and he did not know what to say, so he said "Yeah."

"Oh, they're something, all right, those two," went on Cocky. "They sure put on a great show out there this afternoon. Why, if they could only read a book, they'd be regular Renaissance men."

Shoeless Joe and Williams just clammed up when they heard that, and got dressed real fast, and pretty soon they beat it out of there and so did the rest of our bunch.

But I was one guy who was not ready to take such a dirty dig lying down on my back, even if it had not been spoken to me. The fact is, I had heard just about enough about books from that culture-whooper Collins. So while the other boys went back to the hotel, I found a bookstore and bought a whole load of books, and that night I gave them out to the boys.

You can just guess the look on Collins' mug when we walked into the clubhouse the next day, each of us with a book. I had *Baseball Joe in the World Series* by Lester Chadwick, Knuckles had *Pitcher Pollock* by Christy Mathewson, Scott had *Jimmy Kirkland and the Plot for the Pennant* by Hugh Fullerton, Felsch had *High School Rivals* by Frank V. Webster, and Shoeless Joe and Williams had *Batting to Win* by Lester Chadwick. The two ginks had to share on account of the books costing eighty cents each.

Anyway, we all took to carrying these books around with us everywhere, and we read them, too! And sometimes in the hotel or on the train, we would get to talking about the different characters and which book was the best. For example, I thought Baseball Joe was excellent, but he did not have enough inside dope on the game. You see, he was a pitcher that was always tossing no-hit games and triple play balls, but as far as I could tell, he only had two lobs, a curver and a fast one. But Knuckles, he said that Pollock was just as real as life. And so on. And I never heard another squawk from Collins about books again.

I guess by then you could say the club was already split in two different parts. There was us guys with the books, and then there was Collins and his bunch, including Rowland. Like I say, they may not have all been bad fellows, but they were pals of Cocky, and that was enough for us.

You might think that such a thing would hurt the club, but it did not seem to. The truth is, we were only beat out for the flag on the last weekend of the season, by Boston, and with a couple of different bounces here and there we should have taken it all. That is why, after our last game with Detroit, which we won, we were all feeling pretty down. An hour after the game, our bunch was all still in the clubhouse, kind of mopey, saying our goodbyes and wait 'til next year.

Who could expect more troubles at a moment like that? Well, that is just what happened. All at once, Wilver, the batboy, ran in and said that there was a telephone call for Jackson, from long distance. So Shoeless hotfooted it up there, and a minute later he came back with a look on his map like he had just polished off a gallon of castor oil.

"Well," said Knuckles, "what's up?"

"It was Mister F. C. Lane."

We all knew who Mr. Lane was, for of course he was the editor of *The Baseball Magazine* himself.

"What did he want?"

"He wants me to make a write-up of myself." He stopped. "A whole page, from A t' Izzard."

Now, this was a regular thing in *The Baseball Magazine*, a ball-player writing up himself, but I looked at Knuckles and he eyed me right back 'cause, see, we both had a sneaking notion that it was Collins behind it.

And we were right, too, for when I asked him, Cocky said it right to my face. He said that Mr. Lane had asked him to do a write-up on himself, but he had come back that, no, Jackson was the star of the outfit now, and Mr. Lane had ought to have him do it instead. "Did I do something wrong?" Cocky told me with that smirk of his. "I thought you fellows have Jackson reading and writing."

"Well," said Cicotte to the rube, "did you say yes?"

"Sure," said Shoeless Joe. "I could do it, all right."

"Naturally you can," said Knuckles, "except for one thing. You don't know how to use a typewriting machine, do you? These write-ups have to be done on a typewriting machine."

Jackson let that bounce around in his skull a minute. "I can so."

"But you have to use one like a wizard for a job like this," said Knuckles, "and very few fellows can."

"No, maybe not," he said.

"I can!"

It was Lefty Williams that said it, and 'til this day I do not understand why.

"Well, then," said Cicotte, "Lefty and the rest of us will pitch in, just on the typewriting part."

And that is what happened. We waited a bit longer, then went on up to the press box. The club kept a row of machines for the scribes to use up there, and Williams sat down in front of one of them, and we set to working. Of course, he could not typewrite no more than a dog or some other creature, but what could we do? So we all sat there 'til it was almost night, with Shoeless Joe telling where he was born and his wife's name and such, and me or Knuckles or Scott saying it over in good American, and the sap at the machine setting it down.

"Don't forget to put in something about the deal that got you here," I said. "That is a thing the readers of *The Baseball Magazine* want to see, you talking of the deal and your hefty wages and all."

Jackson stopped and eyed me. "I ain't gonna put that in."

"Why not?"

"I jes' ain't."

"Joe, it's an important thing. Every baseball rooter already knows about it, anyway. It was on every sporting page in the country. You should just have a couple of lines on your slant."

"I ain't gonna put that in!" All at once, the fellow was in a lather.

"That's okay by us," came in Knuckles, gentle as a baby, "you don't have to put it in."

"I ain't gonna make no write-up for *The Baseball Magazine* at all!" he said. "I know how Mister F. C. Lane has mocked me before, don' think I don'." And with that, he just turned and quit the place. And the next morning he was on a train bound for Dixie, and we would not see his stupid face 'til the next spring.

After he left like that, we sat there in the press box for a long time, just taking in the autumn air.

"Well," I said at last, "there goes an odd duck for you."

"I would say so," said Scott. "He sure was hot over something." He gazed at Cicotte when he said this.

Knuckles gave a look like he did not know any better than the rest of us.

"Maybe he thinks it would sound braggety to talk of pulling down ten thousand bucks, with his people being so poor and all," I said.

There was a long silence after that one, and even I knew such a thing could not possibly be so.

"He don't make no ten grand."

It was Williams that had said it, for there he still was, sitting at the machine.

"He makes ten thousand," I came back. "Everyone knows that."

"No sir, he makes six thousand. Comiskey fibbed to the sporting writers, same as he did to Joe when he give him that contract to sign. He makes six grand and Joe told me so himself."

Back in Stowe that winter, every once in a while I would think about Shoeless Joe and how he had been took by that close-fisted magnate with his eighteen-carat lies. These days I realize how bad he must've felt inside when he found out about it, but I must admit I did not think too much about that part of it back then. See, at the time, six grand is exactly how much I was making myself and it was not nearly enough. But how the hell was I ever going to hit The Old Roman up for more than he paid the great Shoeless Joe Jackson?

Onward, Upward
with the Yellow Kid

E arly in 1894, shortly after deciding to move east from the San
Francisco Bay, William Randolph Hearst came within a
whisker of purchasing *The New York Times*. Indeed, it was
only the sudden availability of the *Morning Journal*, at the fire-sale
price of one hundred eighty thousand dollars, that saved the *Times*
from becoming the flagship of the yellow fleet.

It is, of course, no happenstance that this delicious bit of information has been all but lost to posterity; is, indeed, less generally recalled than Alice Roosevelt's White House pranks, or the fly ball
muffed by Fred Snodgrass in the 1912 World Series, or any of a
thousand other equally trivial episodes lovingly rescued from the
same era. The managers of the *Times* have, for almost a century now,
themselves been able to dictate the inheritance of future generations,
and they have always been careful to keep the record clean.

For that I do not fault them. It is human nature to display oneself,
and one's friends, flatteringly, and journalists are nothing if not
human. Were I in their position, instead of the one in which I find
myself, these memoirs surely would, like the memoirs of retired
Times men, be swollen with self-congratulations.

No, I do not fault them for that, not in principle. But what,
throughout a long life as a working reporter, I often found a good
deal harder to stomach—what, I am quite sure, ultimately left Hearst
himself believing that the unconsummated deal was the greatest
mistake of his career—was the way in which those who wrote for

the "respectable" press succeeded in stigmatizing the rest of us. After a time, I began to surmise that, as surely as certain baseball clubs sought out players of a particular mental set, so the highbrow publications—the *Sun*, the *Tribune*, the *Times*—drafted for individuals of an explicit type; men of small egos and large pretensions, men willing to remain faceless, even go without by-lines, in return for the guarantee that they were laboring in a nobler cause than their fellows. Each of our newspapers carried a boast on its masthead—"The World's Greatest Afternoon Newspaper" was the *Journal's*—but, went the bitter joke, only the underpaid wretches who scribbled for the *Times* believed theirs.

In a sense, it was hard not to feel a grudging admiration for the *Times* organization which had, after all, in a mere couple of decades, succeeded in projecting the impression that the paper was above commerce—in itself, a remarkable commercial achievement. Indeed, before long, a great many *Times* readers actually began to believe that they, too, were on the side of the angels.

Of course, Mr. Ochs knew better—knew, in fact, every bit as well as Hearst, what he was about. Every publication on God's green earth had its biases; they differed only in the subtlety, or lack of it, with which they were expressed.

Whatever else might be said of us, my colleagues and I never, at least, were dishonest with ourselves. We operated on a quite elementary assumption: that since the world does not work as described in the civics textbooks, there is no reason to pretend that it does. Flexible men—not necessarily evil, but rigorously self-serving—are everywhere around us, dominating the institutions that shape daily existence, and it was hardly our function to tamper with so intransigent a given. To the contrary, newspapers, like nations, are themselves often obliged to behave cynically as a practical matter.

This is by no means to indicate that I, for example, surrendered my ideals any more blithely than did my more self-righteous brethren. I merely happened to be considerably more intent than most of them upon getting into a position from which to act upon them. And if doing so was as much a matter of panache as perseverance—if I came to recognize that for every couple of dragons slain, another might have to be helped along—well, that was frontier justice.

In retrospect, it is more than a little surprising that it took me as long as it did to arrive at so seemingly self-evident a conclusion, for I had always been ambitious. But it was not until I had been in the business fully half a dozen years, working ceaselessly, that I at last hit my professional stride; and, then, only as a result of happening upon, as a kind of mentor, William Randolph Hearst himself.

My employer was, of course, almost as celebrated as a maker of careers as of noise—he numbered among his discoveries a score of the most prominent journalists of the day—but never, in my most fevered daydreams, could I have imagined my ascent might be so rapid; that, within months, I would be doing precisely what I was born to do; that, as we shall see, within a year I would be breaking in the reportorial techniques, even trying on the attitudes, that would make me a celebrated figure for decades to come.

The succession of events I describe began on a June evening in 1915, the occasion, as it happens, of my very first dinner party at the Clarendon, the lavish Hearst residence on Riverside Drive. Though I had often sighted the great man at 232–238 William Street, we had never exchanged a single word, and the invitation had come as an extraordinarily gratifying surprise. Indeed, for days prior to the event, I allowed myself to suppose that I had been watched all along by the single reader who most counted.

However, the dinner was not, as it turned out, an intimate one. There were more than two hundred others seated at a dozen tables in the vast, chandeliered dining room; Edith took a count. Moreover, our host was himself nowhere in evidence. As I explained to Edith, this last by no means compromised the occasion, as Hearst was beyond the fathoming even of many of those who knew him well. In addition to all the rest, this most public of men, this millionaire former congressman who, were it not for the sustained opposition of a handful of political brokers and the enemy press, would even now be sitting in the governor's mansion, was said, in a social situation, to be timid to the point of debilitation.

My wife was dubious.

"What in the world are you talking about?" she said. "There are photographs of him hobnobbing all the time in his very own papers."

"That's different," I pointed out. "He does that because people expect it."

To this she only laughed and turned away.

Edith was no fool, I'll give her that; she knew full well where I was vulnerable, and she had very quickly picked up the knack for giving as well as she got. Indeed, if she was to be believed, the circumstance that seemed to have provoked much of the difficulty in the first place—my occasional attentions to other ladies—no longer bothered her a jot. That very evening, from within her dressing room, she had dismissed my most recent friend as having "a world view that extends all the way from her fingernails to her hair."

"Maybe so," I called back, "but at least she has some respect for a man. She listens to me, she helps me make the right decisions."

Edith appeared in the doorway. Her gown, of white lace, flattered her figure, and a pearl pin glistened in her yellow hair. She looked lovely; she could still look lovely when she chose to.

"The only right decision you ever made," she said, "was to marry me. And you made it for the wrong reasons."

These constant jibes about the life I led, the people I esteemed, the things I strove for, were increasingly unsettling to my habitual good humor. How much of this could a man stand? Now, at the party, I abruptly rose to my feet and strode from the table, determined to find a toilet and a little privacy.

Instead, in a back hallway, I found William Randolph Hearst. He was sitting on the floor, cross-legged, in his evening clothes, surrounded by newspapers, one of which was spread out before him. Then, aware of my presence, he looked up and offered a wan smile.

"Good evening, sir," I said. "It is a wonderful party."

"Yes," he replied softly.

He made no effort to rise. I hovered over him for a long, painful moment.

"I am looking for a toilet."

He said nothing, merely pointed up the hall.

As I began to move around him, sidestepping the surrounding disarray—it comprised, I quickly surmised, all the following morning's newspapers, screaming, as always, of war—his hand unfolded and he offered it to me; the softest, limpest hand I had ever grasped. I released it gratefully, smiled and proceeded on my way.

But five minutes later, when I was obliged to retrace my steps, Hearst was still there. He had, however, risen to his feet, and the newspapers had vanished.

Hearst, then in his early fifties, remained attractive, even boyish, of face, but he had grown formidable in bulk; it was not for nothing that ex-President Taft's mammoth bathtub had lately been removed from the White House and installed in the Clarendon. At this moment, however, his palpable unease seemed to make him considerably smaller; stooped, economical in gesture, it was almost as if, like some forest creature, he had drawn himself in in self-defense.

"Was the fish terrine to your taste?" he asked.

"Yessir."

"And the wine?"

"It was excellent. Everything was excellent."

He hesitated. "The bathroom was satisfactory?"

This, in retrospect, having come to know Hearst's puckish sense of humor, may have been in fun, but there was no way of guessing that at the time.

"Very comfortable," I said. "Thank you."

Suddenly he half turned and leaned back against the hall wall, his large head bearing all of his weight, in the least convincing impression of nonchalance I had ever witnessed.

"My name is Luther Pond," I offered.

"Yes, of course. The sporting writer."

"Yes."

I waited for some acknowledgment of my column. There was nothing.

"I've been with the *Journal* for six years now. Since 1909."

"Yes. Is everything satisfactory?"

"Yessir."

"Good."

In fact, at that moment things were considerably less than satisfactory for me at the *Journal,* where I found myself at the end of a long one-way street. There are only so many sporting stories to be told and, though I prided myself as a stylist, only so many ways to tell them. True, I had the run of the city's ballparks, arenas and gyms. I knew full well that other men at the paper envied me that freedom. But few realized how I, in turn, had begun to ache for the chance —denied me perfunctorily by my superiors at the paper—to make a name for myself on page one.

I had, over the previous week, considered the possibility of broaching my problem at this gathering, with Hearst himself. But now, with the opportunity at hand, it seemed that no moment in the long history of employer-employee relations had ever been less propitious for the airing of a grievance. Instead, watching him there, his head against that wall, I found myself wondering, with surprising detachment, what this fellow was all about.

There were to be no answers that evening, of course. But over the next several years, observing him from an increasingly favorable position, coming more and more to regard him as a model, I would remark in Hearst a remarkable contradiction: though, far more than most men, he longed to be well thought of, by his peers, by the public, above all, by the future—was, in fact, very nearly obsessed by it—he so loathed that need within himself that he strove to appear wholly oblivious to the opinions of others. Indeed, frequently he actually seemed to court ill will. If he was to be accepted, it had to be utterly on his own terms. Convention be damned, and the disapprobation of conventional men; no one's rules were to matter except those of his own devising.

There was, to be sure, a certain arrogance in this, a recognition of the fact that most of those he encountered would be obliged to swallow him precisely as he was. But it also bespoke a yearning—a desperation to be reached out to, and grasped, and respected for precisely what he was—that a man such as myself could not but find touching.

Not that anyone else could have pushed it quite so far. So rigid was Hearst by the time I came to know him that he was prepared to accept, with outward equanimity, even the grossest misrepresentations of his character. Though an ardent democrat—and so relentless a foe of swashbuckling capital that he was regarded, in all of the appropriate places, as a traitor to his class—Hearst routinely saw himself labelled a reactionary; though, by constitution, among the most generous-spirited of men, he suffered a growing reputation as a misanthrope; though the most cultured man I have yet encountered, a collector of masterpieces from throughout the world, he was called a neanderthal. But by then I suspect he had come to regard the whole business as a kind of treacherous sport; though it would almost certainly prove a losing proposition over the long run, the playing itself was irresistible.

Of course, it is most unlikely that Hearst could ever, under any circumstances, have brought himself to behave in a manner satisfactory to his legion of critics. He frankly resented the charge that he traded in the baser emotions; it wasn't so simple as that. To him, as for most of us who found our way into his employ, the passion, the partisanship, were the glory of newspapering. The pretense of standing above the fray, *that* was a moral infirmity.

"I noticed," I said finally, "that you were looking at the morning papers before."

To this he made no reply.

"I do the same. I like to keep my eye on the competition."

"Yes."

I gazed at him levelly, trying to mask my discomfort. "Allow me to say, Mr. Hearst, if I might, that it is a privilege to work for you."

This was a mistake. The man standing before me was many things, but he was most certainly not a fool.

He raised an eyebrow. "Thank you."

"Well"—I started to back away—"I should be getting back. My wife . . ."

"Tell me, Mr. Pond," he interrupted, his high-pitched voice suddenly louder, "what do you make of the Becker case?"

"The Becker case?"

"Forgive me. Perhaps you haven't followed it in sufficient detail."

The remark was not intended to be facetious. Face to face, my employer was known to be as solicitous of another man's feelings as he was ready, if need be, to demolish him in print. Still, if anyone else had made it, I would certainly have been insulted, for the case in question was nothing less than the most sensational crime story of the decade. Like every soul of my acquaintance, I had followed it nearly from its inception, three years before, when an East Side gambler named Herman Rosenthal had been gunned down on West Forty-third Street.

The killing—the first in the city's history to feature a getaway car —had, according to eyewitnesses, been the work of four young gunmen, as Semitic in appearance as their victim, and initially it was dismissed as part of a feud among low-lifes. It quickly became apparent, however, that there was a very great deal more to it than that; that, indeed, it would lead to revelations of corruption so pervasive and so distasteful that the resultant scandal would eventually sink the entire administration of easy-going Mayor William Gaynor.

Herman Rosenthal had, as the whole city soon learned, been a most unusual thug. A fellow with a flair for public relations decades ahead of his time, he had long used the press to settle personal scores, feeding reporters for a half a dozen of the city's dailies damaging information about his rivals. Though, understandably, his enterprise had provoked some antipathy in his own circles, Herman had not been a man to flinch in the face of pressure. In fact, found in his jacket pocket as he lay dying on the pavement outside the Metropole Cafe was the following morning's edition of the New York *World*, bearing a front-page story, the latest in a series based on information provided by Rosenthal, that a large number of police, including more than a few ranking officers, were on the payroll of criminals. The *World*'s exposés had, not unnaturally, gone largely ignored—charges of police graft were as common as manure in the gutters, and, then too, one had to consider the source—but now, abruptly, they took on enormous weight.

The principal police culprit in the tale Rosenthal had fed the *World*'s man, Herbert Bayard Swope, was one Charles Becker, a hard-drinking, foul-mouthed giant of a man who was a lieutenant with the Vice Squad. It was upon Becker, described as the most notorious grafter in a thoroughly corrupt department, that the law soon cast its gaze.

From the outset, Becker, with whom the dead man had been feuding, vehemently protested his innocence, insisting that even had he been a dishonest man—for this, too, he denied—it would have been the height of folly for him to engineer such a crime. Had he not, he pointed out, gone so far as to hire a libel attorney when the *World* had begun its series? And were there not others who detested the dead man as much as he?

But his was an awkward position. Within days of the crime, the public, so it was reported, wanted police heads, and District Attorney Charles Whitman seized upon the case with a vengeance, declaring his intention to make of Becker so memorable an example that none of his brethren would ever again dare to stray so wantonly. Whitman quickly found lining up behind him a host of formidable allies, including all of those—municipal leaders, police officials,

leading members of the East Side criminal fraternity—who most
fervently desired to distance themselves from the mushrooming
scandal.

Becker's actual conviction came a year and a half later, as the
climax to the most diverting trial in memory, a spectacle that featured as witnesses for the prosecution a string of characters each of
whom appeared far more disreputable than the defendant. Though
the state Court of Appeals subsequently set aside that judgment,
declaring that the hoodlums' version of the murder—which por-
trayed Becker as a kind of honorary criminal chieftain, enraged by
Rosenthal's treachery to the point of unreason—had been related by
"men of the vilest character to save their own lives," the disgraced
lieutenant was quickly convicted at a second trial, and sentenced
anew to die in the electric chair.

If any of those newsmen covering the case had come along the
way to feel any of the same reservations as the good justices, it was
nowhere apparent in their copy. The *World*, which under the brilliant stewardship of Herbert Bayard Swope had never relinquished
its initiative on the story, may have been in bed with the prosecution
—getting inside dope on evidence unearthed and strategy planned,
even being allowed to interview potential witnesses—but every
other paper in town was struggling to hold its place atop the night
table. My own publication even had a policy on photographs; Whitman and his subordinates were to appear august, statesmanlike;
Becker, in a set of stock photos, always scowled or sneered.

How he actually looked, nearly a year after his final conviction,
was a matter of some conjecture, for he remained hidden away in
Sing Sing, awaiting his grim fate. Not that Becker had by any means
disappeared from the public consciousness. His lawyers were still
running around, filing briefs and so on, while in his wake an investigation into police graft continued apace. Moreover, Charles Whitman, lately elected governor of the state, boasted of his role in the
case to every reporter with an open pad.

"Yes," I answered Hearst evenly, "I am quite familiar with the
case." I paused. "I must say, I feel a certain sympathy for Becker,
despite myself."

"Do you? How very interesting."

On surer conversational ground, Hearst moved away from the

wall and stood erect. "And what," he added, "do you make of our coverage of the affair?"

I essayed a smile. "I would say that it has been quite strong."

"Is that so, Mr. Pond? I happen not to think so." He stopped. "And what do you make of the *Times'* coverage of the affair?"

Hearst's transformation was quite startling. The man before me was fully engaged, fixing me now with a gaze that was nearly prosecutorial. I longed for the milquetoast who had just departed.

"It certainly has not been up to the level of the *World*'s," I replied.

"No, of course not." Hearst stopped. "Wait here."

And he disappeared through a nearby door, returning a moment later with the following day's *Times*.

"Look at this."

He handed me the paper and pointed to a feature on page three, beneath the headline WIFE PLEADS FOR BECKER'S LIFE. The story, in essence a straightforward interview with Helen Becker, ran a full four columns, well onto a jump page, and it aimed directly for the reader's heart. Mrs. Becker, a Bronx schoolteacher, described her husband's prison conversion to Catholicism; and the long reflective letters he wrote her each day; and her own occasional travails at the hands of an unfeeling public.

Hearst watched impassively as I read.

"Well?" he said.

"It's quite interesting," I replied dumbly. "I've always been impressed by Mrs. Becker personally."

He grabbed the paper from my hands. "The *Times*, Mr. Pond," he exclaimed, his shrill voice rising even higher, "the *Times*."

To this I said nothing.

"This is very cunning work here, young man." He slapped the paper. "If a man is popular, Pond, you bring him down a notch, don't you? What was I thinking, I wrote that rule myself! And if a man is in desperate straits, you force the reader to care about him." He stopped. "And *they*'ll claim it's great reporting."

"People don't pay any attention to the *Times*, anyway," I said.

Hearst eyed me uncharitably. "*I* do, Mr. Pond. But we shall just have to right our course, won't we?"

We talked another fifteen minutes—he, about our faulty coverage of the case; myself in sober assent—before at last we made our way into the dining room. There what remained of the assemblage turned en masse at our entrance. So heady was the sense of being abruptly spotted, arm in arm with Hearst, by fifty colleagues, that I was wholly unaware of all else. It was only when I introduced him to Edith that I noticed that his head was tucked to his chest.

"Good evening, sir," said my wife, "I am delighted."

From William Randolph Hearst there came only a limp hand and a hoarse whisper.

By the following morning, it might as well not have happened. There I sat, at my desk in the sporting department, trapped, another deadline looming. Before me, in an untidy pile, lay several dozen scraps of paper, each bearing the fragment of a column idea. These notes to myself, each of which had seemed promising at its inception, were, in the light of morning, invariably disheartening: "A European visitor to the ballpark—find one!"; "Ban Johnson unfair to ballplayers—what about justice?"; "Thorpe follow-up"; "Rising price of pigskin/horsehide"; "Does the curveball really curve?/optical illusion?—contact scientist!"; "Verse on Walter Johnson: They come by land, they come by sea/ To see big Walter fling the pea, etc."; "New diamond rules?/ 5 balls, 4 strikes?"; "Golf—a stupid game!"

But two-thirds of my way through the pile, I came upon something I did not even recall setting down: "Jack Rose as cardsharpie —tricks of the trade."

I stopped my rifling and stared at the sliver of paper. Jack Rose! *Bald* Jack Rose! Of course. Luck, as Branch Rickey had it, assuredly is the residue of design.

Jack Rose—today remembered, when at all, almost exclusively as the originator of the cocktail that bears his name—had been among the witnesses for the prosecution in the Becker case. A gambler, self-described as an intermediary between his fraternity and an assortment of corrupt cops, Rose had, more than any other man, placed Becker in his current predicament. So vivid, so colorful had been Rose's description of the lieutenant's fury toward Rosenthal, that it had settled unequivocally in the minds of the jury the question of motive. "No beating up will fix that fellow," Rose had had the enraged cop sputtering to him, "a dog in the eyes of myself, you and everybody else. Nothing for that man but to take him off this earth—have him murdered, cut his throat, dynamite him or anything . . ."

Bald Jack had, indeed, proved himself so engagingly inventive in his use of the language—"Herman," went his description of the late Rosenthal, "was a likeable fellow, although difficult to get along with"—that, as these things go, in the days following his sensational testimony, he had been very much in the air, his peculiar turns of phrase repeated at dinner parties, his syntax imitated by those who pride themselves on doing such things. It had been during this period that I had made my notation to myself, for the singular Mr. Rose had, in addition to all the rest, advertised himself as a reformed cardsharp.

Finding Rose was no problem—his telephone number was listed in our file on the case—and persuading him to cooperate on a sporting column was even easier; out of the public eye a year now, having allegedly gone respectable, Rose clearly longed for the attention he had briefly enjoyed. He seemed, moreover, to regard himself as a member of the sporting elite, the kind of fellow who *belonged* in my column; indeed, when he showed up at the office early that afternoon, an undersized derby balanced atop his hairless skull, a cigar clenched in his teeth, he insisted in airing at length his observations on the approaching Johnson-Willard heavyweight fight. It was a full half hour before we at last got around to the matter at hand, dirty cards. On this, however, Rose was no less forthcoming.

He had not been precisely a hustler, he explained, but a "hondler," which I took to mean "a manager of people." "What counts in cards," he said, "same as everything, is how much gray matter you got upstairs. For instance, always leave guys with cabfare, or else they may turn against the game entirely. For me, guys was never pigeons, they was all pals that was not so smart as me at cards." He tapped his temple with an index finger. "Gray matter. I do not go for fisticuffs or any other manner of violent doings whatsoever."

And so he rattled on for an hour, eight or ten pages in my notepad, and it was not without regret that, in writing it up, I was obliged to take a dim view of the entire enterprise.

"Those of you who glance at other sections of this newspaper will

certainly recall the face, if not the name, of a certain Jack Rose,"
began my column. "Mr. Rose, an admitted grafter and thief, more
recently an accused perjurer, caused great merriment in these parts
last baseball season with his activities on the stand during the first
Becker trial. Of particular interest in this quarter at that time was
Rose's jovial acknowledgment that he considered himself among the
top card hustlers in this city.

"Your reporter has lately had Bald Jack up to the office to clue us
in on the 'inside game' of the hustling racket, and can now report,
without contradiction, that Rose is precisely as dishonest as he claims
to be. In fact, he is a willing dispenser of advice as to how the rest
of us might just as readily 'skin' our neighbors."

I went on to describe how Rose, all the while staying on his
victims' good side, had gone about separating them from their
money. The middle of the piece, relying as it did on Rose's own
words, was rather light in tone, and doubtless more than a few
readers were taken aback by the sobriety with which I concluded it.

"As we have seen," I wrote, "an hour passed with Bald Jack Rose
is a charming idyll. As wretches go, he is certainly a most amusing
one. That is all well—there is plenty of room for amusing wretches
in this sorry world—except for the fact that Rose has never been a
man to leave his mischief at the card table. There is, at this moment,
a man who claims to have been cheated by Jack at a far more serious
game than stud poker—the game of life. That man now languishes
in a cell at Sing Sing.

"This reporter, a mere sporting man, surely holds no brief for the
notorious Mr. Becker. But, I must say, passing a lazy afternoon with
his chief accuser would give anyone pause."

The reaction within the newspaper to this column was, from my
perspective, a rather unnerving confusion. The afternoon it appeared, I found on my desk three notes in McCullum's unmistakably
tight script, each bearing the identical message: "See Me!" When I
arrived at his office, however, he was anything but irate; sheepish,
in fact.

"Ah, Pond," he said, looking up from a manuscript. He paused for
a long moment. "You got my message."

"Yessir. All of them."

He forced a smile. "Yes. Well, it wasn't important."

"That's all?"

"Certainly, Pond, that's all."

I turned toward the door.

"Oh, Pond, I've heard from the Chief. Good show."

In fact, my column would signal an unmistakable shift in the entire thrust of the *Journal*'s coverage of the Becker case. No longer, in our relentless picking over the affair, would the doomed man be routinely savaged, nor the pronouncements of those who heaped scorn upon him be accepted uncritically. In fact, within the week we would run our own interview with Helen Becker.

None of which lessened the shock, the day after the appearance of this last, of slicing open one of the several pieces of correspondence on my desk to find a single sheet of lined yellow paper, entirely filled in pencil.

Sing Sing
Ossining, New York
July 8, 1915

Dear Mr. Pond:

I am certain you are surprised to receive a letter from me. Forgive my impudence, but I am a man with little time left on this earth, and I feel a pressing obligation to contact those few friends I shall leave behind.

I do not use the word "friend" lightly. I daresay I know the meaning of that much abused term as well as any man, and the contrary too. But I use it in regard to you without hesitation, Mr. Pond, for Mr. Manton informed me of what you did on my behalf and later I read your article myself. I thank you from the bottom of my heart. You are right, you know. That lying bum had one of the shortest lies to tell of any of the witnesses, yet his perjury was the most damaging to me.

I did not used to be a man who asked favors of any man, but I am no longer in a position to be proud. I would like to ask you one more. It now appears that my execution will occur before the end of the summer. It is not pleasant for me to state that, but I must face it squarely. It would be a great comfort to me if you, as one of the men of the Fourth Estate, along with just a few others, to have dealt with me square could be present on that occasion. I know that this is a difficult request, but I hope you will consider it. If you can see your way to being there, I am sure that Mr. Manton can help arrange it.

Believe me, there will be enough jackals present there, telling their lies 'til the very end.

May God bless you, sir.

Your friend,
Charles Becker

It is difficult, all these years later, to adequately describe the gratification I felt at that moment. When I laid the page aside, I believe my hands were actually trembling. However, I felt, too, more than a little trepidation. In my twenty-six years, I had never witnessed another human being die, not even a relative, and I did not relish the possibility.

But the unease, at least, passed quickly. So great was the professional opportunity that here presented itself—so enthusiastic were my superiors at the prospect of having two observers at the death scene while every other paper in town, even the *World*, would have only one—that all else paled beside it.

I acceded to the condemned man's request that very morning. Martin Manton, Becker's chief lawyer, may have been ineffective in court, but he was highly reliable in the execution of this task. A week later, two weeks before the event, I received my credentials as a witness to the execution.

Thus it was that late on the evening of July 29, I found myself aboard a creaky, dimly lit railway coach, rattling up the New York Central tracks toward Ossining. The car was nearly empty, the only other passengers being a dozen other newspapermen. Each of us sat by himself; following initial greetings, not a word was exchanged during the entire hour and a half trip.

That was due, I think, less to tension than exhaustion. On this day, Charles Becker's last, there had been several newsbreaks; Governor Whitman, apparently irked by the surge in public sympathy for the condemned man brought on by a suddenly soft-hearted press, had insinuated, at a morning press conference, that Becker may somehow have been responsible for the death by tuberculosis of his first wife, twenty years earlier; upon learning of the charge, an irate Becker had issued a lengthy written response; then, late in the afternoon, there had been an unexpected pilgrimage to the Governor's mansion by Helen Becker. According to my paper, her pitiable pleas had elicited not a word of response from Whitman, who, it was implied, was inebriated throughout.

The men sitting in silence around me on the train had been satisfying the public appetite for this kind of thing for over three years, but I sensed in them no relief that it was about to end; to the contrary, most of their careers had prospered hugely during that period, and life without Becker was surely, to more than a few, territory as alien and inhospitable as the frozen north had been to Commander Peary a few years earlier. When the train pulled into the Ossining station shortly before 2:00 a.m., my colleagues and I filed into the automobiles provided by the state with the solemnity of mourners.

On the prison grounds, we encountered several genuine mourners, Becker's lawyers Manton and Shay, and the warden of the prison, Thomas Osborne. Osborne, whose home adjacent to the stone fortress served as press headquarters for the occasion, appeared particularly shaken; during Becker's more than two years at Sing Sing, the warden had come to feel considerable affection for the ex-cop and, long a foe of capital punishment anyway, he had anticipated this morning with dread. He stood awkwardly in our midst in his own living room, fumbling with his bowler, offering people seats, softly restating, whenever asked by someone looking to fill time and his notepad, his horror that such an event could still occur in the modern age.

My own task this early morning was simple enough; while Crandall, our regular man on the story, ran down the particulars of the event in more or less straightforward fashion, I was to contribute a lengthy sidebar (to appear beside Becker's letter to me) describing, in exhaustive detail, the reactions of a man witnessing his first execution. This was a weighty responsibility, and the sobriety with which I conducted myself was unfeigned. In the hours before the execution, scheduled to occur precisely at 5:45, most of my colleagues were similarly grave.

The only journalist on the premises who displayed anything like relish for the task at hand was the *World*'s man, August B. Ruggles, who went merrily about, trying to elicit information from Osborne or his subordinates on the prison's history as an execution center. Ruggles had been handed the plum of covering the execution by

Herbert Bayard Swope himself, Swope being too weak from a recent
bout with rheumatic fever to handle the job himself, and he, like I,
was clearly determined to make the most of it.

When, at 5:30, we were at last led through the prison gate, across
the yard and into the cool, gray execution chamber, Ruggles hurried
to the front row, stationing himself a mere ten feet from the death
chair. The following day he would surpass all of us in the cataloguing of the ghoulish details; describing the twitch of the doomed
man's hand as he was strapped into the freshly varnished chair; and
the vigorous forward thrust of the body that came with the first surge
of electricity; and the "grayish green smoke curling away from the
scorched flesh." And afterward, after Becker had been pronounced
dead—the only cop executed in the history of the state—and his
body unstrapped from the chair, Ruggles alone would accompany
the corpse to the autopsy room, where he would ascertain beyond
question that Becker had been a magnificent physical specimen, with
a heart like that of a healthy boy, and a criminal brain "forty-five and
a quarter ounces in weight, likewise of perfect contour."

I myself was positioned in the third row of spectators, in the
corner. When Becker abruptly entered the room, his right pants leg,
the one that had been slit for the placement of the electrodes, flapping, holding in his hands a silver crucifix, muttering responses to
the litany offered by the two priests who trailed him, my pulse
quickened. Becker was a very large man, as the whole world knew,
but there was nothing fearsome about him. Indeed, with his round
face, rough features and innocent eyes, he reminded me of poor Jim
Jeffries.

I watched, in fascination, as he was led to the chair and surrounded
by five guards who, in a fifteen-second eruption of movement,
strapped him in, then stepped back.

It was only then, seeing him utterly immobile, that I was struck
by something else—the man's calm. For, in spite of what the *World*,
unyielding to the finish, would report the following day, Charles
Becker, in the last minute of his life, was fearless. He breathed easily,
there was not even a hint of perspiration on his forehead. Even while
continuing to give responses to the litany, he looked toward the
assembled newsmen, adversaries for so long, his level gaze moving
from one face to the next. When his eyes met mine, he betrayed just

a flicker of confusion; then my identity seemed to register. By now one of the guards was poised above him with a blindfold. As the material was slowly drawn over his forehead, Charles Becker smiled at me and then, this is not invention, he winked.

The special edition of the *Journal* that appeared the following afternoon was a stunning success by any standard, outselling even the one on the sinking of the *Lusitania* that had appeared a couple of months before; more important, outselling the one issued by the *American* the same day. In McCullum's office late that afternoon, Crandall and myself were actually toasted, bourbon in coffee cups, by the taciturn managing editor, who afterward clapped a hand on my shoulder in what he took to be a paternal manner.

"So the sporting page is no longer challenging enough to hold you, eh Pond?"

"I wouldn't put it that way, sir."

He chuckled. "I recall a very frightened young man who would've done anything for his own sporting column. What happened to that fellow, Pond?" He paused. "Of course, you know we can't make a habit of letting our sporting writers cover crime, can we? Next thing I knew, I'd have my dramatic critic, Mr. Lilienthal, running around in a trench somewhere, wouldn't I?"

"I would never make such a request, sir."

"No, not this week."

He pulled back and looked at me closely. For the first time in my experience, his face, which had always reminded me of the face of John D. Rockefeller, loveless and unyielding, took on a human, even a kindly aspect. "You're a lucky fellow, Pond, Mr. Hearst likes you." He stopped again. "I am going to make an exception to my own rule. Have a seat."

McCullum's proposition, to be succinct, was irresistible. I was to be a reporter at large, developing longer stories at my relative leisure. Though I of course remained under the nominal supervision of McCullum, I was free to wander in virtually any direction I chose, writing about crime one week, a sporting subject the next, the theatrical scene the one after that.

To say that I exited that office in a state of delirium would not be to grossly exaggerate. This was more than I could have hoped for, fully as much as I had imagined for myself. It was not until I arrived home, after pausing en route at three watering holes to toast myself anew, that I abruptly came crashing earthward.

Edith, alone among those in my immediate circle, had from the start expressed reservations about my role in the coverage of the execution, and she greeted the development at hand with startling ungenerosity.

"That's very nice," she said coolly. "I suppose this is what you wanted."

"Thank you," I said. "Yes, as a matter of fact it is."

"Then good for you."

And she walked from the living room, down a hallway and around a corner into her bedroom, slamming the door behind her. From the adjacent room came the sound of the baby screaming, jolted from a reverie by the noise.

I stood alone in the center of the living room, anger welling within me. Where the hell was the damn nurse? How dare this woman so belittle—so *mock*—an achievement that would, in a day's time, have half a hundred men all over the city sick with envy!

A moment later she reappeared, the bleary-eyed boy in her arms. "There's something important we have to talk about."

"Nothing," I replied drily, "is as important as my career."

"Sit down, Luther. It's time we discussed what is happening to this family."

The family again. Once—was it possible?—this woman had actually engaged my interest, my respect; now, often as not, the principal event of her afternoon was a soiled diaper.

"I talk to people for a living," I replied, heading for the door; clearly, I would be obliged to continue my celebration alone. "You should know by now, I do not believe in busman's holidays."

The truth is, of course, during that period of my life I did not much believe in holidays of any kind. Nor, it seems to me, did I believe in illness, for over the course of the several years that followed, I missed not a single workday.

If I was not precisely a man possessed—melodrama, though a

useful work tool, is inappropriate to any account of my own situation—I was certainly committed. In the aftermath of my appointment to the new post, I even went so far as to promise myself, in writing (the words, typed on the back of my business card, are in my billfold still), that never would I allow my by-line to appear over any story of which I might subsequently be ashamed. And I prided myself on my devotion to that credo. In the months that followed, while working on dozens of stories, I went about systematically developing what would come to be called the Pond style; always scratching about for the human element, for the angle that would seize the reader by the heart, or the gut—or in his pants—leaving the brainy stuff to others.

Thus was I proceeding, vigorously, very nearly contentedly, in the summer of 1916 when, quite unexpectedly, I found myself in a position to take yet another quantum leap forward.

That summer, it does not take an historian to recall, was a boom period in the affairs of men. The Great War alone produced enough headlines to sate the appetite even of the most bloodthirsty reader. At home, the political parties were about to convene, the Republicans in Chicago, the Democrats in St. Louis, to choose their standard-bearers and argue the pressing question of war and peace. A crippling, nationwide railway strike was projected. So, too, was a massive new thrust against Pancho Villa.

Yet we at the *Journal* were at a loss. Quite simply, these were not our kind of stories. As an afternoon paper, we were invariably reduced to reprinting, via the wire services, European news that had run more fully in the morning. Our national reporter—we did, in fact, have one—worked out of New York, same as the rest of us, and he was, in any case, far more adept at covering society balls than events of moment. Moreover, on the highly charged war issue, Hearst happened to be out of step with public sentiment; his latter-day reputation as a warmaker notwithstanding, the Chief, anti-Wilson and anti-Brit, strongly opposed American intervention—a policy that caused both himself and his papers no end of trouble. It was left to our more proper rivals to fan that particular flame.

Indeed, the only story looming early that summer with even a whiff of promise—and even nostrils as sensitive as my own failed to pick it up—was that of the incipient flu epidemic which, before the end of fall, would ravage the city; but even that was scuttled as a potential grabber, when municipal officials forced from the city's editors a pledge to avoid panicking the public. Henceforth we were no longer authorized to use the word "plague" to characterize the onslaught.

Under these unhappy circumstances, we at the *Journal,* and our counterparts in several other local news offices, were obliged to do what is always done in such situations—whip up some frenzy on our own. Automobile accidents, those accompanied by suitably diverting photographs, became front-page news; police graft flared anew; a half dozen beautiful blondes were slain.

But by far the most salutary emergency measure, both in terms of newspapers sold and creative needs of reporters met, was the resurrection of the white slave bugaboo.

To be sure, white slavery was not entirely myth. Although the term itself, coined by English social reformers in the last century and used to stunning effect by their allies in the London press, was hardly a precise characterization of the local phenomenon, it was known that in some of the city's more desperate immigrant neighborhoods, most particularly Jewish ones, the occasional young woman was impressed into prostitution. This was provable fact; had, indeed, been proven several times before.

This latest flurry of reportorial enterprise had as its genesis a report that had reached our office in late spring. It seemed that, with the vastly increased flow of businessmen into the city, makers of and traders in war materials, an array of con operations had sprung up to relieve them of their lucre. Among these, according to police, was a blackmail scheme based in Times Square and run by Jews. Two young women, well-dressed and well-spoken, would, in apparent innocence, encounter a pair of Western men in a fashionable hotel or restaurant, spend several days by their side and, when the moment was right, propose a weekend in Atlantic City; then, during that seeming idyll, the rubes would be confronted by a fellow posing as a New York City detective with the information that their companions were underage and that, unless a considerable sum were tendered forthwith, they would be prosecuted under the Mann Act.

This report was naturally much chuckled over within the confines of our office, and it was with some surprise that a couple of reporters learned that they had been assigned to make of it a starting point for a forthcoming white slave series. This, however, they proceeded to do, in the subsequent couple of weeks producing a string of revelations which, linked by generalization and headline, did indeed appear to indicate a pattern: a letter had lately appeared in the Jewish press from a girl who claimed to be held in bondage; a vice officer had been charged within the department with accepting payoffs from Jewish "disorderly houses"; several Jewish girls—they had allegedly "eloped"—were never seen by their families again; slum conditions, particularly in the oppressive summer heat, were, according to certain doctors, known to cause licentiousness.

So worrisome were these reports, so obviously of concern to the reading public, that, a week after our series commenced, a curious thing began to happen: one by one, other papers started assigning men to the story.

It was at this juncture that I chose to look into it myself. I understood, of course, that there was no "vice trust," not as it was now being everywhere described. But I was also aware that some rival—Schneider of the *American,* or Leech of the *World,* Carlson of the *Telegram* or Gillette of the *Times*—might stumble upon a reasonable facsimile. Moreover, I, at least, had in mind a first step as to how my particular little investigation might proceed.

Bald Jack Rose, having failed in what seemed to have been a most faint-hearted effort to go straight, now operated, among assorted other enterprises, a stuss house in back of a bakery shop off Essex Street. This had not been difficult to determine; the second peddler I approached in front of 119 Hester Street, the last address listed for the gambler in our file, looked me over and told me so.

I suppose that the peddler, a seller of notions, had himself patronized the establishment, for upon entering the place, through a narrow door beside a black pastry oven, I realized that Jack's clients were poor men, street sellers or practitioners of the needle trades. This surprised me. Never having been to such a place—and there were said to be dozens in this neighborhood—I had been prepared for something grander. *Stuss house.* The very term suggested gentility. Instead I found myself inside a single room, dimly lit, starkly furnished and, on this muggy afternoon, marked by a powerfully sour odor.

There were perhaps thirty men in the room, all shabbily dressed, many hollow-cheeked, clustered around two stuss tables, following the movement of the cards from the stuss box to the cheesecloth tabletop, wordlessly slapping down their pennies and nickels at the appearance of each new card. One of the dealers I supposed to be a pious man, for he wore a broad-brimmed hat, and long curled ringlets at his temples, and showed a fringe of shawl beneath the worn jacket he kept on even in this stifling place. The other, in a derby, smoking a cigar, was Rose.

I held back, not wishing to draw attention to myself. But this was not a room in which a man such as myself could hide. Within seconds, several pairs of eyes were upon me; then several more; then Jack's.

It was apparent that he recognized me immediately, but he turned back to the cards and finished the deal. Only when he had run through the entire deck did he pause.

"Before you, gents, is Luther Pond, the famous writer. What could a bum like I do for Mr. Pond?"

All activity in the room ceased.

"I'd like to talk to you for a moment, Jack, if I could. Perhaps we could go next door." Beside the bakery, I had noted on my way in, stood the Lefkowitz Authentic Russian Tea House. "Just for a couple of minutes."

"These people"—he indicated with a nod—"are pals of mine. Talk up."

"Please, it's personal."

He laughed loudly. "Personal, I bet." He looked around at the others with bright eyes. "From *me* he wants a favor, this bum."

It soon became evident, however, that the anger was largely sham; in retrospect, I suspect that Rose was incapable of so pointless an emotion. True, he played out the game, leading me not to the dairy restaurant but to the Lafayette Turkish Baths where, on this of all days, I was compelled to sit beside him in the steam room, surrounded by others of his faith. But, thus installed, the cigar stub stuck in his face, he proved a comparatively genial host.

"So you want to explain about before?" he began.

"Yes," I said, "as a matter of fact . . ."

"Stop!" He grinned and held a pudgy hand an inch from my face. "Just a jest. You're a bum, all right, but a bum that's heading some places. A fellow such as I makes allowances. So shut up and tell me."

In short order that is precisely what I proceeded to do; told him, at any rate, that at the moment I was poking around the white slave story and was looking for some help. We both knew, without a word being said, what was in it for him—an ear at the New York *Journal*; friendly next time. Rose listened expressionless, the sweat running down his bald dome, off his shoulders and onto his generous belly, a Hebrew buddha. It was not until we had quit that accursed chamber, showered and were dressing beside one another in the locker room that he offered a direct response.

"Gimme a pencil."

I handed him a fountain pen and watched as he slowly wrote: "Yushe Botwin. Lunchtime, 12:30. Allen Street. Rogoff Dairy Restaurant."

"Yushe Botwin?" I asked.

He pocketed the pen. "Yushe Botwin."

"How do you know he'll be there?"

"He's there every day. Just like you, he eats." He offered me a cool smile and replaced the derby atop his head. "Good riddance to you."

Botwin was there, all right, the very next afternoon, a small, graying, heavily moustached man at a corner table, stooped over a bowl of borscht. Evidently he had been told to expect me, for upon glancing up and spotting an American, he dropped his spoon and hurried over with an outstretched hand.

"Yes, yes, yes," he said, all nervous energy. "Mr. Pond. Botwin here."

His accent was heavy—I was "Punnd," he himself "Bootween" —and it would be some minutes before I would be able to fully comprehend him. But almost as soon as we sat down at the corner table he started to relax, and not very long after that I found myself being drawn in by this odd little man.

"Jack Rose, he tell me how come we talk," he began.

"For research purposes."

"Yes. Me too, I am for freedom of press. Very strong."

Though he had arrived in this country from Galicia twenty-seven years before, he went on, he had never ceased to wonder at the liberties he'd found on these shores, or the vastness of the opportunities. At this very moment, he himself had one son attending dental school, and another in university. "So I am a red and white and blue fellow," he added, "a doodle, do or die."

He himself had little formal education, of course, but I quickly gathered that he was far from an uncultured man. Early on in the conversation he explained, with profuse apologies, that he would not be able to stay long, as that very afternoon he was to attend a matinee performance of a new play by Gorky, the Russian writer.

"So we talk now," he said, "quick. One thing—you will not write my name, no?"

"No, of course not. I'm very grateful for your speaking to me at all."

He offered me his hand across the table. "You want food?"

I shook my head. "But, please, help yourself."

He did, diving into a plate of herring and sour cream, but that did not impede the conversation in the least. "My name," he began, his mouth full, "Yushe Botwin. Fifty-seven years, born Russia. By profession, *zuschiker*. Also real estate, cards, and others. Horses, too." He stopped, swallowed and stuffed half a roll into his mouth. "I know how newspapers talk, I read them all."

"What is a *zuschiker*, Yushe?"

"The fellow that delivers the goods."

"What goods?"

"Why else we talk? Girls!"

"To where?"

He shrugged. "Whoever. They pay, they get."

"I see. And how much is the girl paid?"

"Bubkis." He shrugged again. "Maybe a black eye."

I continued to gaze at him levelly, trying hard not to register all that I felt. Astonishment. Wonder. More than a little skepticism. Already, at that juncture in my career, I had run across some startling imaginations. Still, there was something most persuasive in the fellow's manner.

Methodically, I began to probe. Though Botwin was not easy to follow—both because of his limited command of the language and his apparent assumption that the commonplaces of the operation he described required no particular explanation—within an hour I had drawn from him a great many specifics of what, in fact, sounded like the real thing. As Botwin told it, hundreds of slum girls were being sold annually—often at the rate of a dollar a pound—into prostitution. Each of these girls, targeted for her good looks and her unstable family situation, would, as a first step, be seduced by an attractive, well-groomed young man known within the trade as a "cadet"; thus made ready for sale, she would be locked away for a period of further, more systematic degradation. By the time a girl was to be delivered to a house of prostitution, Botwin noted, she tended to be so disoriented, so stripped of self-respect, that she likely made no protest at all. "Human nature," he explained with a shrug.

There was, of course, a very great deal more I needed to know, but abruptly my new acquaintance began apologizing anew and rose to his feet. His play was to begin in twenty minutes.

"Might I see you again soon?" I pressed.

"Sure," he said, clearly pleased by my enthusiasm for his performance. "Okay, why not?"

"Here?"

"Yes, why not?"

"I'll be here tomorrow."

"Or maybe the next day after." With a flourish he produced a business card:

Y. BOTWIN

REAL ESTATE AND BUSINESS BROKER

Business placed in my hands receives immediate attention and treated strictly confidential

21 ALLEN STREET

"And now," he said, rubbing his hands together, "Gorky."

. . .

On returning to the office, I did not mention the encounter. My plan was to spring the remarkable tale on my superiors full blown, as it had been sprung on me, and proceed from there. It was, however, by no means easy to hold to this resolve; over the next two days, I was beset by so uncharacteristic a degree of excitement that several times I had to leave the office entirely. My rivals, all of them, were utterly lost, barking up trees a thousand miles from the forest. The *American* was running interviews with anonymous ladies of the evening, each one of whom, however, as the conscientious reader would surely note, had entered the trade of her own volition. The *World*'s man, Leech, had unearthed a certain Ruth Zimmerman, a twenty-two-year-old Bronx stenographer who, having been seduced by a married man who neglected to mention the fact, for several years thereafter handed over to him her weekly paycheck; Leech identified the married man as a white slaver. Gillette of the *Times*, whom I had disliked with mounting intensity since our meeting in Reno six years before, was in the midst of an investigation into waiters at certain plush restaurants and hotels who, with the aid of women under their control, used the old-time badger game to swindle men. Clearly, the treasure, if treasure it was, was mine alone!

When I arrived at the dairy restaurant at the designated hour, Botwin, seated at the same table as before, was already well into his plate of herring. It did not take a wizard to grasp that this was one of those men perpetually in a hurry to be somewhere else, and I wasted little time on preliminaries. The questions I carried with me had been carefully crafted, intended to elicit the sort, and the volume, of detail that might add weight to so seemingly unlikely a tale.

"Tell me," I began, "about the cadets. *Where* do they meet the girls? Where do they take them?"

"There and here," he said, his mouth full of fish. "Where else you think? In streets, in candy stores. What is hard to meet a girl?"

Following those initial encounters, he went on, things generally proceeded with comparative ease; the girls who were going to escape the net escaped at the outset. "The others"—he offered his shrug—"candy and babies." Indeed, the cadets sometimes would begin the seduction process with gifts of candy, or flowers, or books, before asking them out for a walk, or to the moving pictures, or, in the summer, in especially difficult cases, to Coney Island. For such girls,

I was led to understand, an outing to the beach at Coney Island constituted a journey as exotic as a fling on the Riviera to the rest of us.

"I simply cannot believe it is that simple," I insisted. "These fellows take a girl to the moving pictures and . . ."

"Dear Pond," he cut me off, betraying a trace of irritation, "look there." He nodded at a young waitress, rather homely, standing in the rear of the restaurant. "If each day Yushe spent for her a dollar, in five days . . ." He snapped his fingers.

"That's impossible."

"No."

"You mean to tell me, any woman can be had for a dollar a day?"

"No." He paused. "Some more, some less."

Despite myself, I was fascinated. I called over the waitress in question and asked for a glass of milk, studying her as she took the order.

"I don't believe it," I said, when she was gone.

He merely shrugged.

"It's impossible." Then, I could not help myself, I smiled. "You haven't met my wife."

He laughed. "No. Maybe not Mrs. Botwin, too."

We talked for another half hour, principally about the financial side of the operation. Although he himself had been involved in the racket virtually since his arrival in this country, he said that he did not earn especially much at it, never more than sixty dollars on a particular girl. He was merely an intermediary, working piecemeal. It was the owners of the whorehouses, he said, as well as the sellers —who often contracted to receive a percentage of the earnings of the girls they supplied—that got rich. Indeed, Yushe added with resignation, at the moment he was nearly broke, for the horses were running badly for him at Saratoga.

All of this I heard and absorbed with an equanimity that surprised even myself. "Yushe," I asked at last, "do you ever consider the morals of all of this?"

My friend seemed baffled by the question.

"I do business," he said. "Like everyone. I work hard."

"Some people would say money is your god."

"Sure. What else?"

So disarming was this response, so *refreshing*, that I was momentarily at a loss for words. That was unfortunate, for Yushe, late for a game at a local chess club with another zuschiker named Sam "The Peddler" Kirsch, seized the moment to leap to his feet.

"I'll see you again?" I asked.

"Sure, sure. Why not?

That evening, alone in my den, very nearly persuaded, I began to write, in longhand, on a pad.

"In a development so startling it reads like a page from scarlet fiction, it has been learned that there exists at this moment, in the immigrant quarter of this city, a thriving trade in degraded women, heretofore entirely unknown. According to a man intimately involved in the traffic in flesh, uncounted numbers of foreign girls, some younger than eighteen, are each year sold to the proprietors of 'disorderly resorts' and like establishments at the rate of 'a dollar a pound.'

"According to the informant, who gave his information to this reporter at a notorious East Side 'haunt,' the white slavers have little concern over police, who either ignore the crime or else are 'in the pocket' of the vice trust. 'It is easy pickings,' he says, as if speaking of an ordinary business deal, adding that capturing the human cargo is almost as simple. So steeped in poverty are most of his victims, that it seems the white slaver has only to hold out his hand to lure them astray. Once disgraced, said the informant, the fallen girls seldom have the heart to return home. 'It is human nature,' he explained."

I continued on in this vein at considerable length, examining in particular detail the role of the cadet. I touched only briefly, however, on the business side of the operation, and not only because it was less colorful; it was my intention to spread the exposé over two days, even, if I could manage it, three. In any case, there remained some questions to which I myself had not yet obtained satisfactory answers.

It was to that end that, a couple of days hence, I once again boarded a southbound subway train around noon, en route to the Rogoff Dairy Restaurant. When I stepped through the door, I saw that Yushe was at his habitual table, and that he was not alone. It was a moment, however, before the identity of his companion registered.

Arthur Gillette!

Unseen, I retreated from the place and around a corner, leaning against a wall to catch my breath and collect my thoughts. It was impossible, beyond indecency! For the first time in my life, I literally quivered with rage. For ten minutes, twenty, I stood flush against that wall, peering around the corner toward the restaurant entrance.

Finally, after more than half an hour, Botwin departed, in his usual White Rabbit rush. It was a block before I was able to catch up with him.

"Pond!" he said in surprise, his face flushing. He hesitated, then indicated his watch. "No time. I go to theatre play."

"I saw who you were with," I spat out.

He stopped and faced me, then replied with a shrug. "Okay, why not?"

"I just want to know one thing, Yushe, for my own personal information. Did he find you or did you call him?"

To this he offered another shrug. "The *Times*, Pond, the *Times*."

Gillette's story appeared the next morning, beating mine by the half day separating morning and evening papers. Noting, in typical fashion, that the report was the result of "an investigation by the *Times*," it contained all the basic information on the alleged white slave operation.

My own rewritten story was, however, anything but a loss, including as it did not only a number of shocking details, but a couple of names: Sam "The Peddler" Kirsch and Yushe Botwin.

Armed with this information, District Attorney Smith, in the tradition of his predecessor, instantly took up the case, pledging to rid the city of the unspeakable evil lately revealed. "It appears," he solemnly announced, "that the old method of serving drugged drinks has been abandoned as dangerous and fully unnecessary. We are dealing with a clever adversary." As these things go, Smith himself would dominate headlines for the subsequent month.

Not that his labors would reveal much of anything. He managed to dig up and have arrested only the owners of a few modest whorehouses, and even these he was obliged to release when, a few months hence, thieves allegedly broke into his home on 103rd Street and made off with the evidence. More to the point, the souls upon whom he had counted most heavily for information—the fallen girls themselves—were a good deal less than forthcoming. I myself received a letter from one of the witnesses sought by the D.A.'s office to the effect that, news headlines notwithstanding, prostitution beat the daylights out of laboring in a sweatshop. The letter was postmarked Sullivan County where, my correspondent informed me, she was working the summer resorts for the duration of the investigation.

Meanwhile, Yushe, dubbed the "King of the Vice Trust," credited by one paper with having been responsible for "the downfall of three thousand schoolgirls," was in the Tombs, awaiting trial, his only diversion being his periodic appearances before the press in D.A. Smith's office. At these, he would obligingly repeat his choicer stories, and appear to enjoy himself immensely. It was not until the following November, on the day that Judge Rosalsky sentenced him and his co-defendant Kirsch to fifteen years at hard labor, calling them "vipers, serpents and wreckers of women's souls," that Botwin announced that the D.A. had set him up.

"If he did," replied the Judge, "he did the community a great service."

By then, of course, I had long since moved on to other territory: had been preoccupied by eighteen or twenty other stories, a half dozen of them front-pagers; had, indeed, without a word being spoken on the subject, apparently secured for myself the right to look into any event in the vicinity brought on by nature or human folly.

If there yet remained any doubt in anyone's mind as to my status at the paper, it was definitively removed by the invitation, received just about the time poor Botwin was going before the bar, to dine at the Clarendon. This invitation was as unlike the one I'd received a year and a half earlier as was the disposition of the fellow who accepted it. This time, the Chief and I were to dine alone.

Hearst was different, too; was, in fact, very nearly at ease. Over cocktails he talked quietly about his own youth, of his self-doubts, and the hard-won successes that finally overcame them.

When, after a suitable period, he took me by the arm to lead me to the dining room, I excused myself for a moment and fetched the gift I had left in an antechamber. This I brought to the table, and he unwrapped it with evident pleasure—framed in oak and under glass, the front page of *The New York Times*, dated September 18, 1860.

I took my seat and watched as he scanned the page, most of it devoted to a report on that season's impending national election. "The Republicans," ran a particularly cogent paragraph, "have nominated a man who has rendered no services to his country, and whose highest achievement is the discovery that there is an irrepressible conflict between the North and the South, and that the whole country must be either all slave or all free; and this aggressive, wicked and dangerous doctrine has been taken up as the war cry of the Republican Party. Thankfully there are other candidates before the people, any of whom is ten thousand times preferable to Mr. Lincoln."

After a couple of minutes, Hearst laid it aside and smiled wistfully; perhaps, it later occurred to me, he already understood that, historically speaking, he was a goner.

"Thank you, Pond," he said. "This goes right up in my study, next to the Van Dyck."

Nineteen Seventeen

by George D. Weaver

W hen the 1916 season was over, if you judge by the results, I suppose you might say the Chicago White Sox was like Mister Thomas E. Dewey in the last election. We were strong, all right, but it was for sure that there was still something missing.

Like, for instance, a great first sacker.

Now, do not get me wrong, the club had had some classy first basemen in my day, like Hal Chase and Jack Fournier, who is the bird Rowland had been using there the last couple of years. I am only saying that things were not clicking with them as they could have. A champion ballclub is like a locomotive or some other machine, and every piece has to fit together, or else it is not a champion. Take Chase. For all his skills with the lumber and the mitt, and he was one of the best, he had what is nowadays called a hustle problem. Plenty of times we booted away games which we ought not have, for the only reason that Prince Hal could not be bothered to show his stuff. All at once, with the score knotted in the ninth, he was liable to let an easy one bounce by him or take a called strike three, just so he could get to the clubhouse and cool off. You could not prove this was the reason, of course, but that is sure how it seemed, and I am not kidding.

As for Fournier, he was game, all right. But, see, he was just one of those fellows that always make whatever club he played for a little bit worse. I am sorry to say that, for he was an okay egg and he had many skills, but it is true. Maybe he was a jinx. Maybe it was because he was a frog. All I can tell you is that after he left us, he played nine or ten more years, with such clubs as New York and St. Loo and Brooklyn, some of which were not so bad, and they could not win with the bird neither.

And that is how come after the '16 season, The Old Roman went out and bought Chick Gandil from Cleveland. You had to give Comiskey that, he hated to lose as bad as any gallery god in the stands. He might spend half his time jewing people, but if he learned he could get his mitts on a guy who might help him to a championship, even money was not an object.

And this Gandil was just such a guy. Indeed, at the moment he may have been the best first sacker in the league, if you do not count Stuffy McInnis with the Athletics, and you can bet us Sox was as pleased as newlyweds to see him come over.

Nor was that the only switch The Old Roman pulled off, either. For who should show up in training camp that spring but a young pheenom shortstop up from the boonies. His name was Swede Risberg, which was short for Charles. As you can guess, this made me a little itchy, since I had been the shortstop for quite a few years already with that club. It is true that I had been a little off last season, on account of a few factors, and had hit only .227, but I had not expected such a surprise. But, like I say, there was Risberg, with his ugly mug that looked like a moose, working out in my spot. Meanwhile, Rowland had me off on another diamond entirely, working out at third.

After two days of such antics, or maybe three, I decided to ask the skipper what was cooking.

"What's cooking?" Rowland came back, eyeing me like I was a worm. "It ain't your job to ask what's cooking, Weaver, it's my job."

Well, that was about as clear as mud, and it was no answer in the least. "But shortstop is my spot," I said.

"You will play where I say, same as every man on this club."

"I'm the best young shortstop in the league. Even a couple of the writers say so." Which was the facts, by the way.

He smirked at me. "You think you're still young, do you? How long do you think me and Mr. Comiskey are gonna wait for you to grow up?"

"I will be twenty-seven in August. That's not so old."

"Hurry up and get born, Weaver," is all he said to that, showing me his back. "Another word out of that trap and it'll be five smackers."

I guess maybe Pants knew what he was doing, too, for that put a muzzle on me fast. I could afford to boot away five smackers about as well as a tramp in the streets. It took the sporting pages to let me know that I was right with my suspicion and that the green pea had indeed grabbed my spot. "Swede Risberg is my shortstop until he shows me he ain't," is how Rowland put it in the *Record-American*. "As for Weaver, he'll have to fight it out with McMullin for the job at third."

I knew this last part was just gas, of course. Fred McMullin, the other guy he mentioned, was only a scrub, so how could he have a chance in a hundred against a ballplayer like me? And even if he did, it would only be a question of time before I gave him the bump.

Still, I am not the sort of fellow to rest on my laurels, and I was as lively that spring as any rookie. They do not keep records for training camp, at least they did not back then, but you can bet I blistered the ball at a .600 clip, and my glove work made me look like Pie Traynor out there. Meanwhile, McMullin played like a sandlotter. Not that it was his fault. The guy was only a ukulele hitter to start with, and ought never have been put in such a pickle.

After about a week of these goings-on, even Rowland had to face the facts. One day after I'd collected about three hits and swiped at least a couple of bases, he called me over to where he was.

"Well, Weaver," he said, "there are no flies on you these days, I'll say that. For a change."

This is the sort of bird he was, he could never just give you the straight goods.

"So I guess I made the grade, huh?"

"You are my third baseman. For now. Let's just see if you can keep it up."

Which, naturally, I did. Indeed, for the rest of that spring and right into the start of the season, the club looked like a million, clicking just like that machine I was telling about. There was not a soft spot in the lineup. Our starting pitching, with Knuckles and Williams and Red Faber, was strong as an ox, and so was our glove work. Good as the Sox had been the year before, this time we definitely looked like a champion, and I guess you might say that Gandil and Risberg and me were the difference.

It did not take long at all for the bugs in the stands to catch a dose of what they call pennant fever. By the end of May, with us already four games in front of the rest of the league, the scribes was already putting down how we was the best club anyone could remember, and all at once there was a mob waiting every time a fellow left the park, out on Thirty-fifth Street, smacking you in the back and saying how wonderful you were. This is the way fans are.

But they are not the only ones. One afternoon, a little after Independence Day, who should show up in the locker room but The Old Roman. Now, that part was not so odd, since after all he owned the club, but this time he got up on a chair, and took off his hat and started waving it around, saying he had something to say. So of course we all dummied up. "Boys," he started off, "I just want to tell you how proud I am of you. You looked like world beaters out there again today." Which we had, since we had just took a pair from the New Yorks. But looking at him up there, all red in the puss, it crossed my noggin that maybe the old gent was a little screwed. That is a thing he would never admit to, since he was a famous teetotaler and all the time was saying how much he hated hooch, but this is how he hit me. Then, all at once, his voice got real soft and he put on a fiddle face. "Boys, you all know I have not won a championship since 1906. I think you know, too, what another one would mean to me and to this town. I want you to think about that every time you go out there the rest of this season. And just to remind you, I am going to make you a promise. When we win that championship, there will be a bonus for each and every one of you."

So perhaps maybe now you will agree that there was something else in him that afternoon besides tea.

But I will tell you something funny, I do not believe many of us boys gave that bonus much thought at all. That may sound bats, big leaguers thinking that way, but it is the truth. I admit that this game of baseball can be hard on a fellow, especially in the fast company, and dough usually is on everybody's brain. But that season of 1917 was different, for that summer we played the game as perfect as any team yet, and in fact, as any team since. Sometimes, thinking of it, or even just looking at those names printed in a book, I do not know how we ever lost a game. Cicotte, Jackson, Schalk, Collins, yours truly, Gandil, Felsch, Williams, Faber, Risberg, Leibold. And every one of us in high form. Baseball was *fun* in '17, there is no other term for it. Sometimes that summer I would stand there at my spot at third, and look at the fellows around me, and then over at those happy bugs in the stands, and then maybe up at the blue sky and the clouds, and I would feel as warm in my heart as toast. It was like a pretty dream playing ball in 1917.

Not that things went so smooth off the diamond, of course. Collins was still his same old self and so were the rest of us, so how could things be better? In fact, they were even a little worse, on account of Gandil and Risberg.

See, the new boys had turned out to be a pair of rotten apples if ever there were any. The one was harder than the next. Now, on the field this was not so bad, for it is known as guts, and can help a club. That Gandil, for instance, he could get a pussful of spikes, and put some chewing tobacco on it to soak up the blood, and never even miss an inning.

But off the field, guys such as this can scare their teammates spitless, going around all the time with a scowl, and never having a kind word for nobody, and all the time ready to use their fists. It is no wonder that pretty soon no one wanted to go near either of them even with a ten-foot pole.

Including the scribes. But that did not stop them from printing all kinds of wondrous things about them, and especially Gandil. After all, with his fine play he was a hero to the bugs, so what did the facts matter? They were always writing up Chick like he was a character, telling about how he used to be a star quarterback in high school and about his adventures in Mexico when he used to play ball down there. For example, there was the time he got into a brawl during a game in a burg called Hermosillo, and the spicks had to call out three thousand soldiers just to save his neck from the home fans.

The tale was easy to believe about Chick, but I bet it was not nearly so comical as they made out. But, see, they used to put down that the only reason Chick seemed hard every once in a moon was that it helped his ballplaying. "I like to have a grouch so I can hit that pill," is what *The Sporting News* had him saying. "The first thing I do in the morning is complain about the weather. If it is warm, I try to think it's too warm. You know what they ought to do, have some guy that makes me mad to look at him."

Well, the fact is there was already a guy on the club like that, and it was Eddie Collins. For right from the start, Gandil hated Cocky as bad as any of us, and maybe even worse. Indeed, he hated him so much that he might have fit right into our bunch, except that he did not really care for any of us much, either. You might say that he only hated us less than some of the others.

That was not on account of anything we had done to him, of course. Like Chick said himself, he was always just naturally in a lather. A crab like him could get miffy over the color of a fellow's tie, so you can only guess how he was if something really went wrong. For instance, if he was not hitting for a day or two. When that happened, all at once the air would be black and blue with his perfumed talk, and bats would be flying around, and you would have to take care to give the guy the miss, or else he was liable to crown you. See, he would never take credit for what was wrong himself, but was always looking for somebody else to pin it on. Nemo Leibold once had a busted lip for a week on account of a pop fly Gandil had muffed in the field. Chick said that Nemo, who had been behind him in right, had balled up his concentration.

Then there was another scuffle he kicked up with Ray Schalk, who was his roomie for about a day. See, Chick was a fresh air fiend and could not stand to sleep with the windows closed. And Schalk was just the reverse. He hated the cold like a cat hates soap. So one night in Detroit, in April, where it can get pretty cool, Ray kept getting up to shut the windows and turn up the heat. And a little while after, Gandil would get up to open the windows and choke the heat. Well, this went on for about half the night, 'til all at once Chick knocked out a couple of Schalk's ivories.

You should have seen the way the scribes wrote up that one. You

would think they was more yuks than Weber and Fields, those two,
and especially Chick, loving the cold as he did.

But I guess at times you must put yourself in the same shoes as
a writer, and I could not really fault them. After all, most of them
were a little jittery about Gandil themselves, for scribes got skulls to
think about, same as everybody else.

I do not know for sure what they thought about Risberg, good or
bad, 'cause they did not write too much about that bird at all. He
was a clam, and kept off to himself, so how much color stuff was
there on him in the first place? And, of course, he was just a busher
that had not yet made a big name for himself. Swede had a lot of
pepper in the field, I will give him that, and he covered a lot of
territory, but who the hell would want to read about a fellow with
a moose face that could hardly hit his own weight? No one, that's
who!

But us boys on the club knew that there was much more to the
guy than met the eyes, and I am talking of his cussedness. For, like
I say, in his own way, this Risberg was definitely a bad crowd, just
like Gandil. In fact, to hear the two of them jawing together, you
would think you were in a den of cutthroats, that's how hard they
both were. One time in Detroit I happened to hear a conversation
they were having about Kid Gleason. It was raining pitchforks
outside, and a few of us were in the clubhouse, passing the time, and
all of a sudden they just started up putting the knock on the Kid.
I do not know what they had against him, for Gleason was a fine
fellow, but, then again, with those two you hardly needed a reason.

"That mutt Gleason, he couldn't coach a dogfight, if you ask me,"
said Risberg.

Gandil smiled at that one. "That back number? He's got fungus
on the brain. All he can talk about is the old days in Baltimore. That's
his notion of coaching."

"I'd like to knock his block off," said Risberg. "He has a big nerve,
telling me how to play my spot."

Of course, that was the Kid's job, giving ballplayers tips, but I am
sorry to say that under the circumstances none of us other boys in
there brought it up. So the two of them went right along, dishing
the old gent, calling him a gink and a Baltimoron and other such
names, until, all at once, good old Hap Felsch put in his two cents.

"The Kid ain't from Baltimore," cut in Happy, "he's from Camden, New Jersey."

The two lemons eyed him in surprise.

"He told me so himself," added Hap, "when we were passing through there from Philly to New York. He pointed right out the window at where he got born."

"So he's from Jew Nersey," came back Gandil, "what is the big deal in that?"

"It don't change a thing," chimed in Risberg. "He's still a moron."

But at least that got them to move off the subject, which was a relief. Pretty soon they were yapping instead about kikes, and then about burrheads, and finally about spicks, who were the bunch Chick hated worst of all, on account of his adventures in Mexico. Indeed, he mentioned he was thinking of going down there himself, to chase Villa or Gonzales and kill a few of them. "Them oilheads is happier as cadavers, anyhow," he said.

And, I will tell you, if he had not been such a fine first sacker, a few of us in that room would not have minded seeing him go.

But since he was, and since the club kept steaming along in fine fashion, even such faults as his were bearable. That is how it is when you are winning, everything is jake and no one wants to be the crepe-hanger that notices the facts. After all, life is no bargain to start with, and most of us wind up in an eternity box, so why not cut up a little while we can? This is especially true of ballplayers, for many of them never taste that winning feeling at all.

In fact, it must be said that the only true woes I had that summer did not come from baseball at all, but from my own wife Helen. See, ever since we had got handcuffed, which was almost two years, we had been living in the same place on Thirty-seventh Street where I had been batching it before. It did not seem like such a bad place to me, for we got three rooms, and they were furnished, for only forty-eight bucks a month. None of the other skirts I had had up there before had never said a word against it, but right from the start, Helen had been all hot to move on. She said that she could not have no fun where we were, on account of how just looking at the stuff in there got her sad. She said the chairs and tables and the bed were not fit for a dog, and she could certainly not have no people up there, let alone toss a dinner, 'cause she would be a laughingstock.

I did not know what to do in the face of such talk, for what could
we do? Helen had booted her job at the Starvation Army, where
anyway they were paying her beans, and there was I, working for
The Old Roman.

"We just can't move now," I finally told her. "We got the house
in Stowe to keep up with also. A man has got to watch his dough
these days."

"Ask him for a rise."

I could only shake my noggin at that one. "I can't do such a thing
during the season. I got a contract."

"But look at the year you are having."

Which I had to admit was so, but there was still nothing I could
do. "Us ballplayers is hired hands," I told her, "and that is the size
of it."

Well, all at once Helen flopped down on one of those couches she
hated so much and started to bawl. So naturally I went over, and sat
down next to her, and put my paws around her. "Don't cry, Beanball," I said. Beanball is what I called her sometimes, to show that
I liked her. "Don't cry. You'll see, things'll be fine."

But she just kept up with her bawling. I hate to say this, but that
woman could be a real Calamity Jane.

"Things'll be fine," I said again, patting her on the arm.

"No they won't," she said at last, real soft.

"Sure they will."

She stopped. "What if we have a baby?"

This was not the first time I had heard this baby stuff. Now that
she was not working, she was all the time buddying around with
Rose Cicotte, and it was her that had put all these notions in Helen's
skull.

"Well," I said, "I do not know about that. But we do not have one
yet, so why don't you get your mug out of that couch?"

She raised her head and gazed at me, all bug-eyed. "Oh, Buck, it
just isn't right."

"Yes, it isn't," I said.

"You do want a baby, don't you?"

"Sure," I said, "why not?" I paused. "Maybe you could cook
dinner now."

Helen got up on her feet. "If the team wins, you'll have some World Series money coming, won't you?"

I smiled. "Sure thing. And that is on top of the bonus Comiskey promised us."

Helen made a sour face. "Sure, I'll bet." Ever since she had heard that he made us ballplayers pay to have our own uniforms cleaned, fifty cents each time, and he was the only magnate in the game to pull such a thing, Helen had not had too much faith in The Old Roman.

"This time is different," I told her. "After all, he did not have to make such a promise."

"Well," said Helen, "the team will make the World Series, won't it?"

I laughed. "That is a promise, Beanball, and you can write it in your hat!"

And I was right on that one ten times over! The club ended up taking one hundred games that season, which was the most ever for any Sox team, including up 'til now. Unfortunately, yours truly missed twenty or thirty games in August and September, on account of Ainsmith on Washington sliding into my finger when I was trying to touch him out. But by then we were already almost a sure thing, and by the end of the season I was once again fit as ever.

Now, like I say, right from the start this season of '17 had been special, with the bugs and even some of the scribes acting like us Sox was heroes and gods, but as Al Jolson put it, we had not seen a thing yet. When we at last clinched the flag, which occurred the last week in September, suddenly the whole picture changed. I suppose not so many people remember how important it used to be to be a baseball champion, for things have changed a lot since those days. Today your average joes have plenty of other things in their minds. They have radio shows and talking pictures, not to mention other sporting events, such as tennis and golf and professional football. But at the time in question, the World Series was the center of the world, and when October rolled around, the whole country stopped cold.

And this year's series was to be even more special than usual, on account of outside events. See, America had just gotten herself into the Great War, and it was the biggest news yet. We did not have any doughboys Over There yet, for such a thing took time, but everyone was glad to have the World Series to think about instead.

I am telling you, in the days before the series, all at once us boys had our maps in every paper in the country. Usually the photo was on the sporting page, but sometimes it was in the rotogravure section, or even right on page number one, next to the war news. In the Los Angeles *Times*, for instance, and I have my book of cuttings to prove it.

But that was hardly all, for suddenly there was more scribes buzzing around than I thought could exist. There were ink slingers from New York and Texas and Florida, all of them coming up with the same pinhead questions. Of course, mainly they talked to the nabobs. Knuckles must've been asked seven hundred times what he thought about the Giants' lineup, which was the club we were to be up against, and how he tossed his famous shine ball. And Cocky kept getting asked how we stacked up compared with the Athletics when they had been champs. And Shoeless Joe was all the time having to trot out Black Betsy, and talk to it like he did, and these yapheads would hold their little pads in their paws and gawk at them, like they was waiting for Black Betsy to answer.

But after a little while, they got around to putting down some things about me, too. They wrote some personal things, such as how much I liked stogies, which I still do, as well as the name of my wife Helen, but mainly they mentioned that I was the pepper pot of the club. That is one of the best parts of the World Series, finally getting the notice a fellow deserves. There was lots of talk of how I was like a cat out there, and that Cobb himself would hardly try to bunt against me. I even have an article from some paper in New York where Pants Rowland gave me some kudos. It is right here before me now, and looking at it again I can still hardly believe it. "You can't figure out a guy like Weaver on paper," said Pants. "Pep doesn't show up. He hits 'em when they count. He is always near the top of the league in sacrifice hits and he is a flash around that third bag."

And there was plenty of other antics that went on, too, a lot of which had to do with tickets. You see, tickets for the games in Chi were all sold out the very first day they went on sale at the ballpark. And about the only ones that got their orders filled by post were the fans that had sent them in by special delivery or by private messenger, and all the others were turned down. Well, immediately a big stink went up asking where all the tickets had gone to, and all the papers were talking scandal. It turned out it was the scalpers that had got their mitts on them. Don't ask me how, even though I have my suspicions. But The Old Roman denied it all. In fact, as usual he came out smiling like roses. He told the scribes that he himself was the saddest bird in town, since he had received two hundred thousand orders that he could not meet. "In the last few days, I have lost more friends than most men make in a lifetime," he said. And he added that he would be happy to ante up ten thousand dollars to buy up the pasteboards from speculators and curb brokers, just so he could find out where they had come from and publish the names of the culprits. He never did it, of course, but it was certainly a good stall, and in a day or two it all quieted down.

But I guess that shows how worked up people were over this series. Everyone said it was to be a genuine classic, with two great clubs, one from the East and one from the West, and what could be better?

By Monday, October 5, which was the day before the series, all of Chi had the baseball bug. You could not go anywhere, indoors nor out, without spotting someone making a wager, and most of it was going our way. In the rest of the country, the betting was near even money, but in that town, it was almost two-to-one on us Sox.

I should add right here, in case you are getting any notions, that back then gambling was not yet looked at the same as now. No indeed. Betting was a big part of the game, and it was a thing most every bug did. In some towns, such as Boston, gamblers used to go right amongst the fans in the fifty-cent bleachers, shouting out odds, and when the contest was done, they'd settle their wagers right out in the daylight. There were even national baseball pools that sold tickets at thirty cents each. If a fellow could guess the scores of nine or ten games, he could pick up seventy-five grand, just like that.

Nor did even us ballplayers steer clear of the action. Maybe we were supposed to, for I guess there was some rule about it, but it was the sort of thing that everybody winked about. I know for a fact that the famous Walter Johnson, who was straight as a line, used to bet on his own games, and sometimes even did so with the scribes, twenty dollars apiece. Things were free and easy, that's all, and dirty doings did not enter into it. Why that very same season of 1917, my own teammates, including Schalk and Faber and Cocky himself, had put up forty-five dollars each and given the eight hundred fifty they raised to the pitchers of Detroit, in thanks for their skunking Boston in a big series. The only reason I didn't kick in myself is that I was out with that busted finger I told you about.

For, yes, I did indeed socialize with some gamblers myself, and I am not afraid to say it. They were sports, most of them, and 'til my poolroom had gone bust, I would sometimes see them there. And if they might ask me for some dope, such as who was heaving for us tomorrow or how was such and so's bum knee, I would go right ahead and tell them, same as I might anyone else. Why should I not? Gambling is a tough racket.

So I did not find it queer to see so much dough changing mitts in the hotel lobbies, or even right out in the streets, and I was pleased to see it going our way. It was good to know that people in Chi had that kind of belief in us, including the professionals.

And from the very first game of the World Series, it looked like they knew what they were doing, too. It was magical out there at Comiskey on October 6, 1917. After two days of dirty weather, suddenly the sun was shining like a twenty-dollar gold piece, and the stands was packed to the gills, even despite the fact that they had put in extra seats. Knuckles had McGraw's men swinging at air all day long, and Hap Felsch blasted a second-story drive and we went home with a 2–1 triumph! And then the next day we went out and did it again, 7–2, with none other than yours truly leading the heroics with a trio of one-base knocks.

From there it was on to New York, and I cannot tell you how grand it felt. By now all our fidgets were gone. We could smell that World Series triumph, and taste it, too, and even hear it, and so could our Pale Hose bugs. In fact, both the New York Central and the Pennsylvania had to run special trains from Chi to New York, that's how many true and blue fans we had. And among them were a whole load of big pokes, including Charlie Dineen, that had been the governor of Illinois, and Roger Sullivan, who was still the boss of Chi, and Mr. Field, the store owner. They all put themselves up at

the Biltmore, which is the swank inn in that burg. That is also where
The Old Roman put himself up, by the way, and he had Harry
Grabiner say a statement to the press to explain it. "Mr. Comiskey
tried to make reservations for his team at the Biltmore," said Grabiner, "but management was unable to take care of the players." That
is how come we ended up at the Manhattan Hotel.

But, like I say, by then we did not care where we stayed, and
would even have slept in a sewer. That is how full of juice we were.
All us Sox wanted was to get out to Coogan's Bluff and get back to
work. That is what they called the field where the Giants played, and
it was otherwise known as the Polo Grounds.

It was some place, too, maybe the most handsome park in all the
national game. And for the series they had done it up even better
than usual, with flags all over the place on account of the war, and
new signs in the outfield. The signs said such things as "Buy Liberty
Bonds and Knock the Kaiser out of the Box," and "Don't Let Our
Boys Fight Extra Innings," and "Join the World's Heaviest Hitter,
Uncle Sam." See, they had also set up little recruitment stands all
over the park, done in up red and white and blue, so they could sign
up the bugs on their way to the stands.

But unfortunately, nice as that place was, the Giants threw a crimp
into us there. Don't ask me why, but all at once we had a hit famine.
In the third contest we got blanked by Rube Benton, and the very
next day after that, Ferdie Schupp bottled us again. And, quick as
that, the series was all knotted up.

On the Pullman back to Chi, a few of our boys may have been in
the dumps, but I do not think so. All most of us wanted was to get
back to our home orchard, Comiskey Park, and go at them. And that
is just what happened. In game five we broke out of that slump, all
right, with a regular hit parade, and we won it 8–5. And then, two
days later, back at the Polo Grounds, we knocked McGraw off his
high perch for once and all. Good old Red Faber came through with
a neat six-hitter, 4–2, and suddenly we were the world champions.

I will never forget that contest, and neither will any of the others
that saw it, all thirty-five thousand. For not only was it our big
moment, but it featured some remarkable and famous history. If you
know anything at all about baseball, I guess you already know what

I am talking about, and it is Heinie Zimmerman's amazing boner.
What happened is that in the fourth inning, with Cocky on third and
Shoeless on first, Hap Felsch hit a bouncer to the pitcher, Schupp.
Collins was way off the bag, so Schupp threw to Zimmerman, his
third sacker. Naturally Collins went running down the line toward
home base. All Zim had to do to put him out was chuck the pill to
his catcher, Rariden. But he did not. Even though Cocky was about
the fastest guy in the game, and he himself was slow as a seven-year
itch, what he did was start running after him. And he chased him
all the way across the plate, which turned out to be the run that won
it for us.

Well, of course, for weeks after that, the whole world was talking
of Heinie's mad dash, and who could blame them, for it was the
marbletop play of all times. Indeed, happy as us Sox were to be
champions, we could not stop smirking about it ourselves. On the
train back to Chi, it was just about all anyone could think to speak
of, including the scribes. Parker was there from the *Times*, and
Willingham from the *Record-American*, and Joe Farrell from the
Tribune, and this one time, they nearly fit in with the ballplayers,
laughing, and guzzling brew and acting cutuppish. We must have
spent at least an hour just chasing one another up and down the
parlor car, pretending we were Zim and Collins.

Not that Cocky himself would join in the festivities, of course. As
usual, he stayed off on his own. We did not even spot his mug 'til
we were halfway to Chi, at which point he strolled into the parlor
car, and gave us the once over, and turned right around.

"Hey, Ed," called out Joe Farrell, for naturally he did not know
the swellhead as us ballplayers did, "let me show you my imitation
of Zim. I want it to be authentic. Make like I'm chasing you."

Collins turned and eyed him in that way of his. "I think we should
let poor Zim be. It wasn't even his fault."

"Wasn't his fault?" Ten guys must've said it all at once.

"The plate wasn't covered," said Collins. "Under the circumstances, he made the only play he could."

"What do you mean the plate wasn't covered?" said Joe Farrell,
smirking right back at him, and good for him. "What ballgame were
you at?"

Cocky gazed at him, smug as ever. "You were in the press box,

I expect. I was in the middle of the play. And Rariden was out of position."

"Like fudge he was!" came back the scribe, for I guess he could tell that Cocky was only trying to puff up his own self with such talk, making like he had suckered every Giant on the diamond away from his spot. "Not only was Rariden there to make the play, but so was Schupp."

Which naturally we all agreed was so. Collins jawed with us a bit, but pretty soon he gave up, and shook his noggin like we were all dimwits, and went off to another car.

But the rest of us just stayed on for what seemed like hours, and probably was hours, painting that place red. I remember that at some point, Knuckles cooked up the notion that Zim had pulled the bone on purpose. So we all started up laughing again, and asked what did that mean.

"After all," explained Knuckles, "how would it look, things being like they are, for a German fellow to be a hero. Especially against the *American* League champs. I figure Heinie was trying his darnedest to be the goat. Otherwise someone might've turned him in to the secret service as a spy."

This was a silly notion, all right, and no doubt about it, but it had us rolling around in the aisles. See, at the moment in question, it was indeed not very healthy to be a kraut, or even friendly to the krauts. To listen to the papers, the Teuts had spies all over the place. Just that week the Feds had nabbed a big one named Bernstorff, and the buzz was he'd had a hundred more working for him alone. No one could escape suspicions. There was a story in the papers that very day about the literary editor of the *Evening Mail*, who went by the name of Wright, being turned in by his stenographer, for dictating something nice about some kraut in a letter. And Professor Cattell in Columbia University had just got canned from the Chair of Psychology, just on account of something he told his students in a class. This is what it was like right then, and that is how come Knuckles made his crack.

"Well," spoke up Lefty Williams, "who knows, maybe Heinie *is* a spy."

We all turned and looked at him to see if he meant it. He did not crack a grin, so I guess he did. There was a long pause.

"Did you hear that some sport named Maines has offered a hundred bucks to the first doughboy that captures a Fritz?" said Farrell finally. "What do you say we all turn in Heinie?"

We were all having a few more yuks over that one, when all at once the door opened up again, and who should step in but The Old Roman. And behind him was Grabiner, toting a wood box.

Comiskey looked at all of us, and gave us one of his big smiles. "You boys look like you're having a grand old time. Good. No one deserves it more." He stopped. "You might remember that a few months ago, I promised you something special if you came through. Well, I don't forget my promises."

He nodded for Grabiner to put down the box, and open it up, which he did. And what do you think was inside? Champagne, that's what! And not even champagne from Over There, but champagne from somewheres in New York state. Finger Lakes was the name on it.

Comiskey made a big show of opening up a few bottles, and pouring some of us boys drinks, like we was guests at one of his fancy parties, and about ten minutes later he wished us all luck and made a quick fade back to his own car.

Well, after he was gone we all just looked at each other in wonder. This was the bonus? A case of champagne that tasted like stale dog piss? Even the boys that knew him best of all, such as me, would never have guessed such a thing.

But it was queer, most of us did not get miffed, not even for a minute. For one thing, we had our World Series winnings, which was pretty hefty. Each of us was to get over four thousand bucks, which is plenty to get a new place to live, and send a guy's wife down to State Street for new furniture. But it was not only that. It just seemed not to matter enough to spoil our fun.

Of course, Risberg, being the sort of fellow he was, got as red as a kidney bean. He said that he did not like no one making a fool of him that way, and Gandil agreed with him. But the rest of us kept our tongues. We told them to never mind, 'cause that was just how things was, and we could not change them.

That afternoon at four, our train rolled into the La Salle Street station in Chi. There were five thousand bugs there waiting for us, and two bands playing, and when we started to get off, the bugs broke past the law, and crowded all around us, and lifted us up in the air, shouting our names and so on. It was a spectacle like I had never been a part of before, and have not been since, and I will admit that it touched me right to the heart. Having all those people adore you that way, people you do not even know, makes all the slights in the world seem worthwhile.

I know that may sound odd to you, for it does to most, but I do not care. Do you know, can you even guess in your dreams, how it feels to win the World Series?

Nineteen Eighteen

by George D. Weaver

There are fellows who will tell you it is not so delightful being a hero. Some film actors out West are all the time saying it, and even some ballplayers. Christy Mathewson, old Big Six, for instance was one such. All you ever heard from Matty was how being a hero was such a big responsibility. To listen to the bird, you would think that tossing the ball around was as important as running a rail line, or being president, or some other thing. A hero such as himself, he would say, could never louse around, not even a little, 'cause if he did he would fall down in the eyes of the public, and especially the kids.

Well, he was off his nut. I know what I am saying, too, for that winter of '17 and '18 I was a hero myself, and a pretty big one. I could not show my puss anywhere, without some fellow running over and hitting me on the back and maybe even buying a drink. This was true everywhere I went, even up in Michigan when I went hunting there for a few days, for the World Series is not exactly a secret, even in the littlest burg. But it was truest of all in Chi. After all, I was the guy that had batted .333 against the Giants, which was second best on the club, and that was enough to make me a king in that town.

Which is one of the reasons me and Helen did not bother to go back to Stowe at all that winter. Oh, certainly there were a couple of other reasons also, such as us getting a new place to live, and fixing it up, and me helping Helen's brother Carl get set up in his new drugstore. But mainly we stayed on account of glory. I cannot recall how many times we did not even have to cough up for our eats in restaurants. Some bug would spot me in there, and call over the waiter, and tell him, real hush-hush, to never mind me springing for the bill, 'cause he would do so. Not to mention all the people that wanted my john hancock, and not all of them were tykes, neither.

Well, you tell me how any guy would not get a boot out of such things.

Indeed, by the time I got down to Texas to start training for the '18 season, I admit that I had a bit of a swollen cranium, and so did many of the other boys. It is no big responsibility being a hero, I tell you that, but it certainly does slow a fellow down. For one thing, I had put on some lard, at least eight pounds, and for another, none of us boys felt like working as we had once done. Why should we, that is what we thought, being the champions of the world? So I guess you could say, if you're being honest about it, that the job in front of Pants Rowland that season was not as simple as it looked.

But, the way it turned out, he had plenty more on his shoulders than that, and so did The Old Roman, and so did all the other magnates. Of course, I am talking about the War. See, by now there were already plenty of doughboys Over There, and there were more getting on the boat every day. You could hardly turn around without hearing about the Somme, or Armentieres, which is where the girl later came from in the song, or Blackjack Pershing. We were making the world safe, that's what it said in the papers, and everybody was supposed to cut the comedy and do his bit. Out in the streets, fellows were trying to get you to spring for war bonds, and other fellows were trying to get you to sign up. And there were people coming by your house asking for clothes for the little orphans in Europe.

And that was only the top of the iceberg, let me tell you. They had started daylight saving to help the war effort (which was a thing I did not get at all), and ladies were no longer supposed to buy wool, but let the doughboys have it, and some stores had even begun printing their adverts in frog, such as John Wanamaker, to show what good scouts they were. There it would be in the papers every day, "Prix Speciaux," or "Dernier Confort," or "Ventes de Mai," and you will pardon my steam if I say it was cracked. But this is how it was, and there was no getting away from it. Even in the motion picture houses, just when you were starting to relax, there would

come a one-reeler of the newest horrible stuff the krauts had just
pulled in Belgium. Indeed, I could not even lose it in my own house.
My own wife Helen had signed up with the Red Cross, and before
I knew it, she was running around asking guys to hand over some
blood.

Not that everybody was so glad about this War as it may sound.
Things are rarely so clear as that. See, for all the shouting and the
patriotic song contests that were always turning up in the papers,
plenty of people were also grumbling to themselves, and it was
mainly on account of the draft law that Uncle Sam had set up. It was
a brand new thing, this business of Congress sending fellows across
the seas, and naturally everyone wanted other guys to go and not
himself. In fact, when they first started it up, almost every bird they
looked at claimed exemption. One guy would say he had feet as flat
as a pancake, and the next guy would say his family needed him for
work reasons, and the next would open his trap to show his rotten
ivories. It was so bad that the papers would even have an Honor Roll,
district by district, listing the fellows that had *not* claimed exemption. Indeed, that is how we found out how many rabbit hearts there
were in the first place. For instance,

DISTRICT 61, SOUTH SIDE

Number Examined.	335
Physically Unfit and Aliens.	28
Claiming Exemption.	220
Not Claiming Exemption.	89

So finally they just decided to get harder, and let's take every slob
we can get our mitts on, including aliens. And that is what they did.
By the time I am talking about, which was the spring of '18, if you
were as much as five feet high and weighed in at a hundred and ten
pounds, you were as good as in, and no questions asked. Even if you
were deformed, it did not matter. A nose like a banana, such as some
fellows have, was just not enough anymore.

But, like I say, you did not see any of the anti-draft stuff in the
papers, except if you count those lists, and now that I think of it, it

is a wonder that even they got in print. For there was another new law going around called the Trading with the Enemy Act. It told the scribes what they could do and what they could not do, and what they could not do was knock the president, or his pals, or the Army, or the war effort. If a paper did not put down all the rah-rah stuff and that slackers were yellow-livered, it could get shut down fast, as some of them were.

This is what had Comiskey and the other magnates so jumpy, for there were those that were starting to say that baseball was a slacker itself. It was nothing official, not yet, for President Wilson had given the game the "green light" on account of it helping morale. But when people said such things in those days, you could not just dust it off.

Baseball answered back, of course. You could not hardly open up a baseball magazine in those days without spotting a write-up about how grand tossing a ball around was for the nation's spirits. To listen to these articles, you would wonder why the krauts would bother to try and lick us in the first place. One of them in *The Baseball Magazine* even went right out and called itself "Baseball Will Win the War." "One of the leading faults of the Teutonic mind," it explained, "has been its absolute lack of good sportsmanship. As a race the German peoples have not taken kindly to Athletic sport. This failure has narrowed them, made them unfair in business and ruthless in war. But we Americans are blessed with baseball."

Now there may have even been a thing or two to what that article was saying. I don't know, being only a ballplayer and not so bright as some others. But I do know that the magnates had a problem in their hands, and all the articles in the world in *The Baseball Magazine* would not cure it for them. Not that they were thinking of closing the game down, not as long as there was still a nickel to be grabbed. But they knew they had to do something. You might say they wanted to have their cake and also eat it. So what they did is to make us start pretending like we were soldiers. This is true what I am saying, every word. Down in training camp, when we ought to have been doing our work, hitting the pill or getting the old wing in shape, they had us drilling on the diamond, only using bats instead of guns. And as soon as we started up playing games in front of bugs, that is how we would have to show up on the field, marching in lines.

Nor did we play real training games, such as a ballplayer needs to get ready for the season. No sir, instead they had us touring to Army bases, such as Fort Bliss in Texas, and Camp Meade, and Camp Upton, and other faraway places. The Clevelands came with us, and at each of these places we would have to put on a show for the doughboys there. In the fourth inning of every one, Germany Schaefer would pinch bat, and our twirler was supposed to walk him, and then we would let Schaefer steal second and third. Then, suddenly, he would make a dash for home base, just as Cocky had done in the series, and the third sacker, which was me or McMullin, would chase after him, making like we was Zimmerman. Naturally, this always was delightful for the doughboys in question, I will admit that, but I ask you if it was baseball. No, it was not. It was hijinx, that is what it was!

And such dumb things kept up even after the season got started. Not only did we have to march on the diamond, but when we got there, they started up playing "The Star Spangled Banner," and we all had to stop playing pepper and stand there, stiff as a week-old cadaver.

Now, do not get me wrong, I do not mean to come off like maybe I am. I am a good American and always was. But my business was to play ball, which is the American game, and not march about with lumber on my shoulder and such, just so some magnate might look good. If I wanted to join up, that is what I would do, but I was there to play ball.

A lot of us boys had thought about doing that very thing, by the way. I remember right at the start of training camp, a few of us had sat on the bench during a rest period from marching, adding up the cons and pros. Jim Scott was the one most hopped up about getting into the scrap. He kept saying that this was the time to be a patriot, and that it was no time to be a no-man. He even toted around with him an article saying what old Teddy Roosevelt, who was his favorite guy of all times, had said about the subject. "Germany has reduced savagery to a science," is how he put it, "and this great war must go on until the German cancer is cut clean out of the world body."

"Well," I said to Scott, after he had finished reading that to us and folded it back up in his pocket, "I guess pretty soon it'll be 'o reservoir' to you."

That stopped him, but just for a second. "I am considering it," he said, "I am considering it awfully hard. You are looking at one fellow that does not want to miss out on the glory."

"There isn't any glory anymore," came in Knuckles.

We all turned to gaze on him, for what he was saying sounded a little bolsheviki and un-American.

"Certainly there is glory," I said. "It's in all the papers."

Cicotte just shook his head. "What do you think, Buck, it is still like San Juan Hill? You don't fight anymore, it's all automatical stuff. A professor on your side draws a circle on a map. Then they aim the big guns toward the circle and they shoot. Those big guns will hit the mark from sixteen or seventeen miles, some of them. That is in the papers, too."

"That is not all there is to it at all," said Scott.

"Sure it is. Unless you are looking for glory in the trenches, or in no-man's-land."

"Well, then," spoke up Hap Felsch, "how do you know who wins?"

Knuckles smiled. "That's easy. If your professor hits more circles than their professor, you win."

We all sat there and turned that around in our noggins for a while. "Well," I said finally, "I wonder what it would cost to get a professor to draw a circle with The Old Roman inside."

But I will tell you something, just a week or two after that, Jim Scott did go and join up, just like he said, and without even getting drafted, and a few weeks later he was in Camp Upton, watching the rest of us play ball. And he was not the only one, neither. By the time that season started, five guys on our club had got into uniform, birds like Jenkins and Kieser and Payne. And it was the same way on all the other clubs. All at once, fellows was signing up as fast as a horse could trot. On the Philadelphia club alone there were ten, and Detroit had eight. The magnates were all pushing them to do so, too, especially if they were not regulars, as almost none of them were. Indeed, there probably was more glory for such guys in this than on the diamond. Take Hank Gowdy, who was a guy with Boston in the other league. Just because he had been the first ballplayer to join up, you would think Gowdy was Cobb or somebody, that is how much his mug got in the papers. And this was a fellow that had hit only .214 in '17!

Meantime, all the scribes started poking around, wanting to get the scoop on the rest of us that had not gone. You can believe me, pretty soon it got tough to bear. No one was left out of this, and they even went snooping after some back numbers that were not in the game no more. Even poor old Ed Walsh was made to account for himself. "I have a wife and a home to look out for," is what Big Ed told to the *Tribune*, "and am not my own master as I used to be, or as some of these other fellows are now. If I were in their shoes I would be over in those trenches right enough, and my only question would be how soon could I get to the front."

Well, I suppose that is just about how I felt about it myself. Even though Helen said she would not mind if I went, and would like me to, I could not leave her there by herself. What would happen to her if I came home in an eternity box? She would be in the soup, that's what.

I did not mention this to any of the writers, of course, for some of the ballplayers that were heading over there were in the same boat, and how would it look? Nor did I remark to them why weren't they Over There themselves, instead of asking pea-brained questions, which I thought of doing. A ballplayer had to watch his yap in those days, or he would wind up in the bad. So all I told them was that I was thinking about it real serious, and, who knows, I might be in France any week now. That turned the trick pretty good.

Though the truth is, the scribes did not bother with me about it nearly so much as some of the other guys. Swede Risberg was one, for he was only twenty-two and not yet married, and Hap Felsch was another. But the main one they chased after, the one they drove mad as a loon, was Joe Jackson.

Now, this might seem strange, since Joe was no youngster. He had thirty years on him, and of course he was also hitched as tight as any man in the game. Plus, he had three brothers that was already in the ranks. All of which is how come the rube had been put in Class-4 in the first place. But when Uncle Sam started getting tougher, his exemption board down in Dixie suddenly advanced him to Class-1, and it was then that the writers took after him. After all, putting the knock on a big star like Shoeless, who had just been a hero in the World Series, was a sure bet to get them a big story, which is always the main item in their heads. And this was especially so when the guy they were after did not have the wits to answer back.

Joe was hitting up a tornado at the time, the best since he had joined the club back in '15, but all at once that did not matter at all. Chowderhead that he was, though, it took Joe quite a little while to catch on to the fix he was in, and I do not think it really hit him 'til one afternoon in Washington. Joe had just had a big day at the dish, cuffing around the Nats for a pair of three-baggers, and afterwards, in the clubhouse, he sat himself down in front of his locker with that stupid grin of his, all set to tell about it. But, see, that very same day the doughboys in the AEF were right in the thick of their first scrape, and they were not faring too well, and the whole town was sick over it. But what did Joe know of that? To Joe the war was like a mystery.

"You can watch this if you want to," said Knuckles to me, eyeing the scribes as they hotfooted it in there, "but I'm going back to the hotel." He was already in his civvies, on account of being a pitcher.

Well, as you might guess, there was not a single query about the contest that had just been played. First they asked Joe why he had not yet joined up, being Class-1 and all. The dimwit turned all pasty and did not say nothing. So they just kept after him that way. "Do you know how many Americans died in the latest casualty report from the front?" asked one. "Two hundred and eighty-three! What do you think about that?"

Of course, Joe did not know. "It is too bad," he said.

"Do you love your country?" asked a scribe.

"The good ol' U.S. of A?"

"Enough to fight for it?"

I can't tell you how much it ouched me to listen to this two-faced ballyhoo, and I did not stick around for much more of it. As for Joe, in the days after that he just went hermit. He started showing up at the ballpark already dressed in his baseball togs, same as before, and leaving the same way. And the worst part was that for once us other boys could not do a thing to help him.

Not that we did not try, for by now I guess we had a sort of liking for the gink, after all the heroics we had gone through together. A week after that time in Washington, me and Knuckles turned up at his room in Boston. Lefty Williams, who was his roomie, let us in. Shoeless was looking even dumber than usual, lying on the bed, wearing his shoes and all, staring up at nothing. That is where we took a seat.

"Well, Joe," started off Cicotte, "we haven't seen you around too much lately, have we?"

"He ain't been around," answered Lefty.

"That's what I am saying," said Knuckles. "We know how much chaff you've been taking, and we want you to know we don't think it's right."

"What about me?" said Williams. See, he had just got put in Class-1 himself, from his board over in Missouri, though it seemed to me that the scribes had not hardly given him no chaff at all.

"You also, Lefty," said Cicotte. "It is a tough nut, what's going on."

"Well," I chimed in with a laugh, "I suppose things could be worse. Did you boys hear about that fellow in Illinois that got strung up?"

Shoeless turned his head real slow and gazed at me. "Strung up?"

"It was no big thing," said Cicotte, "just some socialist. A bunch of coalminers did it to him."

"For gol'brickin'?" You could hear the fidgets in the rube's voice, and all at once he was pale as marble, laying there.

"No," said Knuckles, "for disloyalty. He was trying to get them all to beat the draft. They tied old glory around him and strung him up." He paused. "Don't worry, the only ballplayers I ever heard of that got strung up, they were in effigy."

Jackson shot straight up in bed. "Where?"

"Effigy," said Williams. "Effigy, Ohio." He looked at us. "We got no need to worry, that's a long ways from where me and Joe is goin'."

"Oh, yes," said I, "and where is that?"

"Delaware. It's all fixed up. Me and Joe is gonna work at the shipworks there. It's as good as joinin' up."

"Jes' as good," said Joe.

It was true what they were saying, too, only not exactly. See, a fellow that jumped to a job in a war industry, such as building ships or guns, did not have to go Over There, even if he was able. It was the law and that was that.

But Mister John Public is not the fool some people think he is, not always, and everyone could see the dodge for what it was. Many of these companies had teams in baseball leagues where they were, so they were pleased as songbirds to sign up fellows that jumped from the big show. In fact, sometimes they even sent bird dogs to sign them up, which is what had happened to Joe and Lefty.

The place where the two ginks were headed was called the Harlan and Hollingsworth company, and their team played in the Steel Baseball League, five games per week. I guess it was really not so different from working for us Sox, except that you worked in more peace. The competition was pretty fierce, and most of the stars, such as Joe, got paid pretty good dough, a few hundred a week. Plus, he would not have to look at Comiskey's puss, nor Pants Rowland's, nor Cocky Collins'.

It is no wonder that before too long, a bunch of other boys on our club began doing just the same thing. Byrd Lynn, who was our catcher behind Schalk, went over to some place in Pittsburgh that made steel. Then Red Faber jumped to a shell-making outfit, and a bit later, Risberg followed him. Then, around June, Hap Felsch, who had been taking so much yap from the scribes lately that it nearly cured him of his grin, announced that he was quitting the national game altogether and heading home to Milwaukee. He said he had war work there with a gas company, and from now on he would play only semi-pro ball on Saturday and Sunday.

I could not blame any of them, and if I myself had been Class-1, I might have done the same thing. But I was not. I do not know the reason for sure, except maybe that I was the fellow that had put Stowe on the map and the board down there did not want to risk me getting stiffed, for that might wipe them right off the map again. So I just stayed behind, doing my bit, keeping up morale with my work at third base.

Still, it was no pipe for us boys remaining with the Sox, neither.

Even though we were not slackers, not even by stretching the imagination, and most of us had the papers to prove it, the scribes just kept
after us with the same old queries. And after a while, some of the
bugs started getting on us, too, especially in certain towns. Boston
was the worst. There were a bunch of fans behind the bench at
Fenway Park, and some of the things they came out with were as
blue as the sky. One day I was at shortstop, which is where I had
gone back to since Risberg left, and McMullin was at third, and these
warts started up, and one guy above all. He had lungs like Caruso,
this mutt, and the whole park must've heard him, including skirts.

"Hey, rabbit heart," he shouted, "even your fucking toenails are
yellow." "Hey, fuckhead, kill a kraut, why don't you?"

Now, it was hard to know who he was talking to, me or McMullin, but we both started to take it pretty hard, for it went on this way
most of the afternoon. Then, around the sixth inning, a ball got
batted in the hole right between the two of us, and though we both
made a dive, it went through clean for a base hit.

"Hey, fuckhead," spoke up our pal, "lose that mitt and grab a
rifle, why don't you? You don't know what to do with the glove,
anyway."

Well, that did it. All at once me and McMullin got the same
notion, and it was that there'd been enough grape juice diplomacy.
As soon as we were on our feet, we both went running toward the
wiseacre like a bull. Fred got there first, being as he was playing
third, climbed into the stands and got on top of the guy. He was not
a big fellow, neither, but runty, and though he sounded like a young-
timer, I would say he was at least forty. "It is *Mister* Fuckhead to
you," yelled McMullin, right into the guy's puss.

Now I do not like to kick a guy when he is down, but this one
time, I could not help myself, and I gave him a boot right in the leg.
"It is Mister Fuckhead," I joined in.

"*Mister* Fuckhead," he agreed, real quiet.

But by then the law was all over us, and some bugs too, pulling
us back out on the field, and naturally we were both tossed out of
the contest. And the next day the ink slingers made a big incident
out of it, saying that the fan, who went by the handle Augustus J.
McNulty, had every right to say what he did, or else what were our
boys Over There fighting for? There were even a couple that said

me and McMullin ought to get the bounce out of the game for kicking up such a row.

Pretty soon, though, it all blew past, like almost everything does. The next time the club was in Beantown, which was the start of August, we had to show up in court to explain away our antics, but Augustus J. McNulty did not show his face. So that was the end of it.

But not really. For more and more, the fans kept after us ballplayers with such digs. Indeed, it started to happen even in Chi, especially as the club began to do a fade in the standings. After all, with all the talent we had lost, we were not the outfit we had once been, so how could we play like we were? By the middle of the summer we were already twelve or thirteen games down, and slipping more every day, and you almost did not want to come out to the ballpark no more. I guess you could say we had become clock watchers out there, and were just waiting it out.

And then there was more personal things going on, and some of them were of such a cruel nature I do not even want to get into them. For example, my dealings with Agnes. Now, I had been stopping by to see her every time the club was in St. Loo for four years already, and we was a pretty fair duo. Maybe she had a few other beaus too, I am not saying she didn't, such as a boy dancer, and a doctor, and even a fellow that worked in a bank. That is just the kind of girl she was. But she was hotter on me than all the rest, that is what she told me after we won the series, and might even consider changing her way of looking at things and marrying me. She said that as though me already being hitched up to Helen did not add up to nothing, this is how cocky she was!

So here it is, just a few months later, and all at once she goes into the woodwork. We blow into that town for a weekend series and try as I might, I cannot get her on the telephone, only the maid. And finally, when I do, just before we are set to leave for Chi, she tells me she cannot see me no more. When I ask Why not, she tells me she is in love with another. I say Har-de-har-har, I do not believe it! And then she admits that no, the real reason is because her old man does not want her to, on account of me being a slacker. And she feels the same way, too. And a minute later she says she has some stuff to do and hustles off the line, never to be heard from again. Which really taught me a lesson, you can believe that. And Agnes used to make out like she was a bolsheviki, and that no one should ever fight in wars!

But do not get me wrong, I do not hardly have the right to kick, for others had it plenty worse than me. Look at Joe Jackson. Even though he was way off in Delaware, out of sight, the papers kept right on cutting him up. After a while, it seemed like he stood for every slacker in the land. And maybe he did, being such a famous hero. The New York *Herald* printed that Joe had "conscientious objections to getting hurt in defense of his country and to associating with patriots." And in Chi, the *Tribune* even came out with an editorial about the rube, which is a thing they usually only do about war, or peace, or finances. In this editorial they may as well have pegged Joe as Hindenburg's kid or something, 'cause that is how you were supposed to feel about him when you finished reading it. It started with some wind about Shoeless being a bird "of unusual physical development, and presumably would make an excellent fighting man, but it appears that Mr. Jackson would prefer not to fight." But then it got even meaner. It said that Joe was certainly a fine ballplayer, all right, but under such conditions as we had then, that did not mean a thing. For, good as he was, one day the public would have their say about him, and "good Americans will not be very enthusiastic over seeing him play baseball after the war is over."

Those were brutish words, and it was not too nice spotting them right in our home burg. But even that was not the worst thing that happened to Joe. For before long, Ban Johnson, who was the president of the American League, decided it was time for him to spout off, too. "I hope that the provost marshal yanks Jackson and these other evaders from the shipyards and the steel works by the coat collar," is what he said. "I hope they are all sent to cantonments to prepare for future events on the western front."

And what about Comiskey? Did he back up his star ballplayers? Did all the balloon juice about Joe and the rest of us get up The Old Roman's Irish, like it did mine and Knuckles'? Ha, tell me another! For one thing, he and Johnson hated each other like snakes from way back, ever since they were both green kids, and he was certainly not going to let such a guy get a leg on him now. And for another, as usual he was only thinking about his pockets. So Comiskey joined right in the attacks, and even harder than the others. As soon as Johnson made that speech about the rube, he called a mob of scribes into his office and told them that, so far as he could see, Shoeless and those other jumpers was hardly better than socialists, and maybe that notion the *Tribune* had suggested made a lot of sense. "Gentlemen," he said, "I want you to know that there is no room on my club for players who wish to evade the army draft by entering the employ of shipbuilders."

You can probably guess by now that I no longer lost too much love on The Old Roman, and had not for a while. When it came to salting away dough, he was a regular Hetty Green, and when the talk got to contracts, he was always as slippery as an eel in lard. But this was the worst yet. For here he was, queering his own ballplayers, lousing up the season and maybe our lives, and he did so without even batting an eyelash.

To the contrary, in spite of baseball's woes, Comiskey seemed to feel pretty fair that summer, and maybe even better than usual. The reason was that he was having some book written about him, and everywhere he would go, even amongst us boys, this writer would trail after, putting down his words. The writer was G. W. Axelson, the same bird that had been with us on the round-the-world tour, and you never saw a fellow lay on the banana oil as he did that summer. He was all the time telling The Old Roman how wonderful he was, and how wise, and other such pap, and Comiskey would puff out, and say it wasn't so, and then come across with more hot air about his own self. We must have heard a hundred of his tales that season, some of them a few times, for you could just not shut him up on the subject, even in our clubhouse or around the batting net during warm-ups. A lot of what he said could just about make you ill, too, for naturally he was always pointing up how much better guys were in his days compared to modern ballplayers. And especially than this bunch he had working for him now.

For instance, one tale I heard at least two times was about how the year before, The Old Roman had got a telegram from the owner of the Chicago *Record-American* asking if he would give over ten percent of the club's gate receipts to the American Red Cross. At that point in the tale, Comiskey would make like he was stunned. "Is ten percent enough?" he would have himself saying. "I don't think so.

I owe this country everything, and it can call on me for all I possess."
Then he would stop a while and gaze at us boys that were on the
scene, all of us wishing he would choke to death on his own words.
"But I guess it's different for young men today, isn't it?"

This is the kind of stuff we had to bear every day that season. As
a matter of fact, it got so rough that around the middle of the
summer, by which moment we were definitely out of the pennant
chase, a few more guys actually did go and join up. And one of them
was Cocky Collins. Personally, in his case, I think it was The Old
Roman himself that made him do it, for he was his pet on the club,
and how did it look for a college boy like him to be a slacker like
the rest of us?

Not that Collins made it Over There, of course. By then the war
was just about done, as everybody knew, and all he had to do was
dress up like a Marine and watch some warehouse in Philly. And
naturally play a load of games for the Marines team. But to hear him
talk of it after he'd got out, you would think he'd won the whole
thing on his own. He was all the time saying how proud he was to
have been a Marine, and how rough and tough they were, and how
it had changed his whole way of looking at things. When the club
got together for the next season, he even hung up a big Marines
plaque by his locker.

Meanwhile, Joe Jackson, who was doing just about the same thing
in a different uniform, remained a bum. None of us boys with the
club had gotten a load of him for some time, of course, but knowing
the rube like we did, it was not hard to guess how he was taking it.
Nor would Comiskey lay off of him. Right up 'til the end of that
season, every time someone would say his name, The Old Roman
would point out that why would he want such a fellow back with
his club. He said it so much, that even yours truly started to buy it,
and I had not believed nothing that fellow had said in years.

Some of the other magnates believed it also, such as Frazee with
the Red Sox and Ruppert with the Yankees, and they started making
offers for the dimwit.

The Bostons ended up taking the pennant that year, by the way,
in case you give a hoot, and also the World Series. Babe Ruth won
twenty-four games for them as a twirler, and at the same time also

led the league in four-baggers. That is an amazing feat, if you think about it, but at the time in question, almost no one did.

In fact, it might be said that that whole baseball season was one big fizzle. The magnates were doing so lousy at the gates that they even shut down the game a month early, at the end of August. Us Sox ended up working only about a hundred and twenty-five contests.

Then, being like they were, they pulled something else, and it was as crooked as a dog's hind leg. Since our contracts had it that they had to cough up our salaries for the whole season, they went and released every one of us. That's right, every man in the big show got canned, just like that. Only, of course, they had agreed between themselves that each magnate would hire back his same players the next year, if it looked like there was to be a season.

And was there a single thing for us to do about it? Of course not, especially since the magnates made like they were pulling it all for the war effort. So we all just went back to our homes, meek as kids.

Well, it is a well-known fact of history that just a couple of months after that, in November, the war ended, and our side won. And then, the oddest thing of all happened. In a wink, everything that had gone on that season was forgotten. I mean it, it was like all the talk about slackers and rabbit hearts had never gone on. The dirty digs in the press stopped, and that winter we all got our contracts in the post, same as usual. And the next spring, which was 1919, all the same old mugs was back in training camp. Me and Felsch and Cocky with his Marines plaque, and all the rest. Including Jackson. And all the big pokes in the game was acting like everything was oke, and thank heavens.

When we got up to Chi that spring to play our first regular contest, the park was filled to the beams, just like the old days. And when each of us went out for our first trip to the dish, all thirty thousand bugs got up on their feet and started whooping and calling our names. If a fellow closed his eyes, it might have been the World Series all over again. And the biggest yell of all went up for nobody else than Shoeless Joe Jackson. There was even a band in the stands that day playing for him, and around the fifth inning, the bugs in the rightfield boxes dropped down a bedsheet. On it, in big black words, it said JACKSON ROOTERS!

But, of course, it was not really the same as before, not at all. For though it is true that most things blow past, some things do not. The magnates might have thought so, for that is the way you think when everything always goes your way, and also the scribes. Who could blame them? But some of us ballplayers could not forget such things so fast, let alone forgive.

Who knew it at the time, but maybe by then the dice had already been thrown.

Nineteen Nineteen

by George D. Weaver

Nineteen nineteen. There is that word, and I already know what is going on in your skull. I suppose I cannot blame you, for it is the same with everyone. It is almost like saying 1776 or some year like that. But just one time I would like to hear someone say "Nineteen nineteen, wasn't that the year all them nabobs and kings got together in Versailles?" Or "Nineteen nineteen, wasn't that when old man Ford started up the Model-T?" Or "Nineteen Nineteen, wasn't that the time the Babe got dealt to New York?"

But I am no sucker, and I gave up waiting for such events a long time ago.

I bought an automobile myself that year, by the way, in case you're interested. It was not a Henry, but a Studebaker, which was even better. That was Helen's idea. Me, I did not care what sort of machine I drove in, so long as it got you there. I had had a Ford once before, and I was all set to get another one, for it only cost six hundred and ninety-five dollars. Anyway, the whole country had Forditis right then. But Helen said how would it look for a star like me to run around in the same machine as all the little shots. She said if I was going to do a thing I should do it correct.

So that is how come I showed up in Texas that spring in my Studebaker. Some of the boys were a little stunned by this, and especially Knuckles. See, he was always telling us how we had to mind our dough, and just 'cause the public thought us ballplayers was rolling around in clover, that did not make it so. Especially not us fellows working for Comiskey. And, of course, the year before had not exactly been easy on our bankroll. Knuckles himself had put his money in a farm in Michigan, which I have to admit made sense if you were thinking of future years. Which once in a while I did also, even if it did not look like it.

"I did not get this machine for kicks," I explained to Cicotte. "A fellow like myself needs a gas buggy. I have been wanting one for years."

"Maybe that's so," he said, "but it seems to me it was a dim idea to buy such a spiffy one just now."

"No," I came back, "this was the right time, all right. And would you like to hear how come?"

He rolled his eyes in his head. "I'm standing here, aren't I?"

"The reason is that I was down and needed a lift. After last year, I mean."

At that, he could not stop himself from grinning. The fact is, nearly every guy on the club probably had felt just as much in the dumps as me. Including Knuckles.

"Well," he said, "if I were you, I would think about buying some automobile insurance. Otherwise, you might crash it up, and where will you be then?"

I told Knuckles I would do just that thing, but I am afraid that between one thing and another thing, I never did get to it. It did not matter, though, for I did not crash up that automobile, after all. In fact, I did not even drive it too much. After training was done that spring, the club let me drive it home to Stowe, where I garaged it. The next winter, I mainly stayed in Chi. And the winter after that, what with my troubles and on account of needing dough, I sold it for six hundred. So maybe Knuckles was right in the first place, for there is no question I got soaked in the deal. Indeed, I felt like such a chump over it that I have never bought another car since.

But only a genius could've guessed such a future at the time. The truth is, at the start of that season, I suppose I was hoping for bygones. There we all were, the same bunch from '17, and there was no reason we could not be champions again. And if we were, we would tote off enough World Series loot to buy three Studebakers!

In fact, things looked even brighter than ever, because we had a new manager, and his name was Gleason!

That's right, the Kid himself. Now, this might surprise you, as it did some of us, since everyone knew that him and The Old Roman were not exactly chums. To the contrary. Being a little fellow, the Kid had always had to be a tough bird, and he would hardly ever take yap from nobody, even Comiskey. Things had gotten so rough amongst him and the old man that Gleason had not even been with the club the year before as a coacher.

But maybe that is why he was back with us now as brains-in-chief. After all, with the club having sunk like lead the year before, The Old Roman needed someone besides himself to be the goat, and naturally Rowland was the guy. And, wanting to win bad as he did, he needed another fellow who had the real stuff, even if he could not stand his map. And that guy was Gleason. It was all beeswax to him.

But as far as us ballplayers was concerned, we did not ask no questions. It was enough just to have that little Celt back with us again, for there was no grander fellow in the game, and not too many with more upstairs. They even said that back when he was with Baltimore, it was him that hatched up the intentional walk. It is odd to think of someone inventing such a thing, for it is as common as water, but that is what they said.

But, most important, Gleason did not keep favorites, like Rowland or Callahan. Not even Collins. Oh, the Kid was kindly enough to Cocky, all right, and even made him team captain (which did not mean a thing on that club and, anyway, if you ask me, it was Comiskey's work). But, the thing was, he was just as straight with us other boys. In fact, the guy on the club that he maybe liked best of all was nobody else but Knuckles. Of course, they had known each other quite a while by now, ever since they were Runts together.

So, like I say, I was pretty happy about the looks of the club that spring. Comiskey had even made a couple of moves in the pitching department, where we hardly needed help to start with. My old pal Scott was gone with the wind, and in his place were some young soupboners. One was Roy Wilkinson, who we had got from Cleveland, but the best of them was Dickie Kerr. There is no doubt that, added on top of Cicotte and Williams and Faber, this gave us the most wonderful herd of twirlers in the league.

This bird Kerr was tricky as a convention of ambulance lawyers out there on the hill. Looking at him, you would not guess he had too much stuff, for he was a little mite, and just a bag full of bones. But he had a noggin that worked overtime. He was one of them rare guys that was born thinking. After three weeks in the big show, he knew as much about the enemy batsmen as some throwers that had been around for years. He only had a ten-cent fastball, but what does that matter if you know a fellow's weaknesses. He would set up that little fastball with his curver, which was the flukiest I had seen on a young pitcher in a while, and he would change speeds so nice that lots of times fellows would fall right down trying to swat his tosses.

But, aside from watching his work on the diamond, it was tough to figure out how the guy ticked, for he did not break out at the mouth too much. This may be because he was timid, but I do not think so. Guys that have lion hearts on the mound, usually are not scared around other guys. No, I figured that, being so heavy in the bean, he just found out fast what was up on that club, and he did not want no part of it.

Nor could you blame him, though some of the other guys did. For example, McMullin thought he was cold as a fish. But, the actual fact was that spirits were even worse amongst us Pale Hose than before, and only a numbskull would want to jump in the middle.

Naturally, this was not something you could put your fingers on from the outside. John Fan thought things were just dandy on that club, and why not? The ink slingers certainly never wrote of such problems, and right from the start of that year, our work on the diamond was up to par. Every man on the club was coming across as planned, especially the pitchers, and by June we were in front of the pack. Under such circumstances, why should anybody notice that in warm-ups not a single one of us in the infield ever tossed the ball to the second sacker, who was Collins, and that the only time Cocky ever touched the pill is when the catcher Schalk would give it to him? Or that guys stayed away from Risberg and Gandil like lepers? Or that some fellows hardly talked to anyone at all but themselves? It was ballplayer against ballplayer on that club, not to mention ballplayer against nabob.

I guess you might say that everything that had gone on over all those years was like an ugly stain, and it would not come out.

Of course, this was not an easy situation, day in and out. I am not saying all of us went around glum-faced, not at all. We still had plenty of high times, same as everyone in the big show, pulling stunts on guys, or even just hanging about, shooting the gas. The thing was, even at the best of times, even if there was yuks filling the air, you could not really get away from the ill feelings.

And, naturally, sometimes you just could not stop it, things popped right into the open. One time in Boston, this was in late June, a bunch of us Sox were in the lobby of the Hotel Somerset, waiting for the wagon to fetch us to the station. See, we had just ended a series with the Red Sox and were headed for New York. Anyway, the papers that day all had write-ups that Fatty Arbuckle, who was a famous baseball bug, had just bought himself the Vernon club in the California League, and some of us were shooting the breeze about it.

"Hey, Knuckles," said Hap Felsch, "how'd you like to work for old Fatty?"

Cicotte grinned. "It'd be oke by me. I'll bet meal money would be better than with this racket." See, The Old Roman only gave us three bucks a day for eats, instead of four like the other clubs.

"Sure," I joined in, "and he could probably show you a thing or two about life, too. Did you boys catch *Fatty at the Beach*? I'll bet the stands there in Vernon are gonna be full of them Bathing Beauties."

Being like he was, Knuckles turned a little red at that one. "That'd be oke by me, too," he said.

And that is how it went on for a bit, with us boys making fun like ballplayers do. But then Risberg came in.

"I'll tell you one thing," he said, "any owner'd be better than the one we got."

"That's right," agreed McMullin. "At least that movie oaf probably pays out a living wage."

Now, this was certainly so, for Fatty was indeed the prince of good fellows. But it was not the sort of words to be said in front of a crowd, especially not that one, for Harry Grabiner, the club secretary and Comiskey's stooge-in-chief, was sitting right there. Not that such a thing would stop these fellows.

"Say, Swede," spoke up Gandil, "what d'you figure you'd be worth to a straight-up owner?"

"Who knows?" said Risberg. "I ain't met up with one yet."

This was just about enough for Grabiner, though you could not tell from what he said. "All right, all right," he piped up, real meek, "let's hold it down."

Gandil gave him a frosty glare. "Shut your own trap, Harry, this is a free country."

There was a long pause. Nobody had ever heard no one speak up to a nabob, or even an assistant nabob, in such terms.

"All right, boys, just let it lie," said Ray Schalk finally.

"You dummy up, too, squirt," came back Gandil, "let him hear what is where for a change. These are the straight goods."

"Mr. Comiskey will have a report about this," said Grabiner, still kind of soft.

"Oh, yeah, who's gonna tell him?"

"Straight goods, my eye!" All at once Cocky was on his feet, next to Grabiner. "You earn what you deserve, Chick. Why don't you grow up and cut out your grumbling?"

Now it was Gandil's turn to be stunned. In fact, Risberg had to answer back for him.

"You sonovabitch," said Swede, "you make fifteen grand. You know what we earn?"

"I don't give a hoot," said Cocky, calm as ever, "it's none of my business."

At that, Risberg turned red as a tomato. "You fucking egghead, you think you deserve *five times* more than me? You think you're *five times* as good as me?" For it was the truth, that was all Swede was pulling down, less than three grand.

But Cocky only smiled. "I guess you can't argue with the numbers, can you?"

And that did it. First Risberg went after him, and then Gandil, and in a moment that whole lobby was like a saloon in the moving pictures. A few guys were standing up for Cocky, such as Faber and

Leibold, and other guys were trying to yank everyone apart, and a few of us were standing on the side, whooping it up. It must've gone on like that for four or five minutes, before the Kid himself finally showed up and put a lid on it, and by then I guess there were a couple of lamps that had got broken, and also some nice chairs.

That ruckus got a lot of ink at the time. Of course, the scribes just put down that some of the boys had been hitting the hooch a little, and a good time was had by all, and there was not too much more about it. But the next time the club came to Beantown, we got put up at the Buckminster, which was not nearly so swank, instead of the Somerset.

Still, like I say, most of the time, most of us kept our feelings to our own selves. For instance, you may notice that Joe Jackson did not even join in that incident. In fact, Shoeless did not join in hardly anything at all that season, not even in our gabfests. Some of us even used to laugh about it. How could he have been a slacker, we used to say, for here he was, "shellshocked."

I suppose, though, that thick as he was, maybe Joe had a point. The milk was already spilled, so why keep crying over it? You could not forgive the cheapskate, of course, but getting miffy does no good, either. Finally, if your noggin is on right, all you feel is scorn, and it turns in your stomach like a bad supper.

I know that is how I looked at it. There I was, a star in the national game for many years already, and I was making six thousand per annum, while on other clubs, bums that were not half so skilled were making ten thousand, or even more. Indeed, that summer *The Baseball Magazine* printed a list of salaries from the old days, and it turned out that even some of them ancient timers had got more than me. For instance, back in '88, there was a second sacker on the Pittsburgh club called Fred Dunlap. If you listened to *The Baseball Magazine,* and why shouldn't you, even a little cheese like him, that no one had heard of since, was earning seven thousand. And that was when a dollar meant a thing or two!

And, on top of it, The Old Roman's book, the one he had done up with Axelson, came out at just around the same time, and the thing was loaded with gas about him being a big spender. All the other magnates turned up in there saying how generous he was, and how he was in the game for sport and not bucks. Naturally, us slaves were supposed to adore him. "Comiskey has less trouble with his players than any other owner in the game," is how it put it. "The player depends on him for a square deal. If he delivers, he knows that he is going to get everything that is coming to him." And The Old Roman adored us right back. "It has been a habit with Commy, when some of his veteran players start to slip, to offer them their choice of some minor league club. 'Go out and pick you a club and I will back you,' is his injunction. 'If you make any money, it is yours; if there is a deficit at the end of the season, I will make it up.' "

Most of us just had to grin and bear that, same as all the rest. For, of course, the ones that kicked up a stink would just end up getting even more mud in their eye.

Like Gandil and Risberg. Maybe it was because they were still a little new with the club, maybe it was on account of their disposition, but the two lemons would just never accept things as they were. Around July, they even got the Kid, who they could not stand behind his back, to go up and see Comiskey about giving them a rise. See, before the season, The Old Roman had made a rule nixing all rises in pay, and his excuse was how low attendance had been the year before. He said we should just be glad he did not cut us, for he could hardly make his own ends meet. But, now, here we were in the middle of '19, and attendance was higher than ever. So up went Gleason to see him—and, naturally, half an hour later he came back to the clubhouse empty. Which got Gandil and Risberg huffier than ever. They started making noise that enough was enough, and we all had to put our feet down together, making like me and Cicotte and Felsch and the others were all on their side. In other words, they were talking strike.

Of course, such gabble was crazy as a drunk nigger, and it was plain to see. But the two of them would not listen. For a whole day they kept up with it, and finally Knuckles had to have them over at his own home, over eats, and go over the ins and outs, which were that if we struck, we would all be out of the game on our ears. And that would be that, the bad with the good. That is what it took to shut those two off.

Probably no one else on that club could've done it, either, except Cicotte. I am telling you, I had known the fellow five or six years by now, but I never stopped getting surprised by how wise he was in the head. Most of the boys felt the same way. The fact is, he was in a worse fix than any of us, for he was thirty-five years old, with maybe only a year or two left in his wing, and he had those kids of his to think about, plus his wife Rose, not to mention the mortgage on that farm of his in Michigan. But did you ever see Cicotte on a soapbox? Not once!

I am not saying that he let The Old Roman walk on top of him, not at all. He just knew what could be pulled off and what could not. Indeed, just the winter before, when he had gotten his own contract in the mail, and saw it was only for six grand, he had pulled a thing of his own. He journeyed to Chi from his place in Michigan, and went to see Comiskey, and told him he would not gripe about the wage. But then he asked The Old Roman how would he feel about giving him a bonus if he won, say, thirty games for the club? Well, at that Comiskey just smirked, for, of course, such a feat was nearly impossible. Not a single twirler in the league had done it for many years, not even the great Walter Johnson, let alone an old guy like Knuckles. He did not even mind when Cicotte mentioned the number ten thousand dollars. The Old Roman just said "Sure, it's a deal," and wrote it right down in Knuckles' contract.

Only, the thing was, here we were in the middle of the season, and Cicotte looked like he might just upset the dope. By the end of July, he already had eighteen wins in his belt, and when September rolled around, he was up near twenty-three, and still going like a million. The fact is, it was his great pitching that was carting the rest of us on his back, for, great as we were, without all those victories, we might have been in the middle of the pack.

Even as it was, Cleveland was still giving us fidgets, and with a few weeks left in the season, we were still in a scrap. Things were so tight that when Gandil started crabbing about pains in his kitchen, and the sawbones told him it might be appendicitis, The Old Roman would not let him quit the lineup. He said he should freeze it, and go ahead and play, and they could operate after the season.

Which is why what happened to Knuckles was such a tough nut to bear. He just kept on throwing gorgeous for us, just like he had all year, and with about ten days left, he got his twenty-eighth, 4–1 over Detroit. But that same afternoon, the Clevelands lost to Washington. And the next day after that, while Williams was winning for us, they booted away a doubleheader. And suddenly, all at once, us Sox started to look like a dead cinch. This naturally made us pretty happy. But, the thing was, when Cicotte's next turn came around, he did not pitch. He was ready and all, but his name was not on the lineup card. Nor was it there the next day.

It was not so hard to figure out what was cooking, of course, but Knuckles just could not believe it was so, not after all his hard work. And after the second day, he went to see the Kid.

Gleason gave him the straight dope, all right, you have to give him that, and no beating around the bushes. When Knuckles came back into the clubhouse after that little talk, the look in his eyes was like some corpses I have seen. I did not even get to pop the question.

"He says he's sorry," said my best pal, very soft, "he's very sorry. But he's got a family to think about, too." He stopped. "I can't blame him. How often does a fellow get to bring a club into the World Series his very first year?"

He really did not blame him, either, I am not kidding. Not even when it came out in the papers that he was being kept out on account of a pain in his shoulder. And when, at last, the last week of the season, in Beantown, Comiskey let him back in the lineup, so he would be in shape for the series, what did Knuckles do? He tossed a beauty, that's what, 4-0, for his last win of the regular year. His twenty-ninth.

It was in Beantown that we clinched the flag, by the way. But after that, we still had to go to New York, to finish up with a couple of contests with the Yankees. Well, you can believe me, if you had been on that train, you sure would not know that the fellows beside you had just grabbed the championship of the American League. And if someone had said so, you'd have said he was loose in the nut. This is how sober we were.

I personally was sitting next to Eddie Cicotte, the star twirler of that club, and for four hours we did not speak hardly a word amongst us. Except once or twice when he did a backdoor trot to the can, he just gazed out the window at nothing. In fact, about the very first thing he said to me was "Excuse me."

I thought he was planning to take another leak, and did not pay no attention. Except, instead of heading to the back of the car, he just moved up the aisle a little ways and put himself down next to

Gandil, who as usual was sitting on his own. From where I was, I could see the two of them jawing a little while, real earnest, and then Knuckles got up and came back to his place.

"Can you come up to Chick's room tonight?" he said.

"What for?"

"Nothing special. After supper, around eight-thirty."

The hotel we stayed at that season in New York was called the Ansonia, and it was quite a nice place. It was right on Broadway, the biggest avenue in that burg, just in case you don't know geography, and there was always plenty doing around there in the way of shows and eats. But the night in question, I had no time for such antics. The train did not get in 'til around four, and as soon as we got to the inn, I hit the slats for a nap. By the time I was up again, it was already seven-thirty, and my belly was kicking up a row, so I went out and had some fast eats around the corner at the Uptown Cafe.

Anyway, what I am getting to, is I made it up to Gandil's and Risberg's room, number 421, just a little bit late, maybe ten minutes. And when I got there, I had some surprise. For there was our whole bunch—Cicotte, Felsch, Jackson, Williams and McMullin, plus the two lemons. As soon as I got there, everybody gave a nice hello, except for Chick.

"You're late, Weaver," he said.

"I guess I am," I came right back with a grin. After all, what could he do with all my pals right there?

"Well," he said, "next time you got an appointment with me, you'd best remember to get a wiggle on."

"I'll try and remember, Chick."

But for once Gandil had other things in his head besides putting the knock on people, and a moment later he let it out. He said that while we were in Boston, he had met up with an old friend of his called Sport Sullivan, who was a gentleman and a gambler, and this Sullivan had made a proposition to us Sox. Gandil said he himself figured this proposition was solid, and he thought us other boys would, too. He paused for a second. "What he wants us to do is not win the World Series."

That is how it was posed to us, simple as that, the stunt that would change the history of the national game. Nor were any of us in that room shocked over it, even for a moment. Why should we be? Talk

of fixes was pretty normal back then, and even actual fixes themselves. Every guy there knew that Hal Chase had probably been
booting away games for years, and we had a sneaking notion about
a few other fellows, also. The idea was not even new to the World
Series. Back in '12, there had been lots of talk that a nabob with the
Giants had gone out and tried to buy up the umpires, Klem and
Johnstone. Who knows, maybe he had even done so.

So, like I say, none of us batted an eye as Gandil went on. "Now,
I have already talked to some of you about this. Swede. Knuckles.
Fred." He nodded his noggin at them, one at a time. "I know you're
interested. As for the rest of you, the terms are pretty simple. We
lose the series, Cincinnati wins, and each of us gets ten thousand
dollars."

Now, you might be curious to know how come McMullin got in
on it, being only a scrub. I know I was, and it turned out there was
a comical tale there. See, what happened was that when Gandil told
the deal to Risberg in the clubhouse, thinking they were alone, all
the while Fred was lazing on a bench on the other side of some
lockers. And when they'd done talking, he suddenly popped up and
wanted to be cut in, and what else could they do? Even though he
would maybe just pinch hit one or two times for his ten grand!

After Gandil had told the rest of us the terms, he stopped again,
like he was an actor on the stage, or some such nonsense. Believe me,
he did not have to pull any theatrics to get fellows that worked for
The Old Roman interested. To us, ten thousand sounded like a
million.

"When would we get the loot?" piped up Hap Felsch.

"In advance. I told Sport it had to be in advance or no go."

"Well," said Hap with a smile, "sounds easy enough to me. What
am I supposed to do, trip over my own feet on the basepaths?"

Right there, that broke up the ice. All at once, guys started calling
out humorous ways we might fall down on the job, running into walls, or letting balls bounce on our heads, or making heaves
downtown.

"That would not be so hard for me," I joined in. "I do it plenty
of times by accident."

The fact is, we all knew it would not be so tough to put over a fix, especially not with Cicotte and Williams with us. All a twirler has to do to blow a game is get off a couple of fat slobs at the right time. As for us others, we could pitch in by running just a shade slower than usual, or making a foozle on a tough chance, or hitting out in the pinch. It would be pie, and not even a diamond veteran could spot it.

"Listen," added McMullin, "I got an even better idea. Why don't we take the dough and then go out and win anyhow? The winner's pot this year is gonna be pretty big."

Which it definitely would, since after the big year baseball had had in attendance, the magnates had come up with the notion of making the series the best of nine contests, instead of seven. That would make extra profits for one and all, especially themselves.

But Gandil put a lid on that one fast. "Don't even kid about that," he said, sharp as a pin. "These are not small-timers I am in with on this. You don't sting these fellows. Don't even kid about that."

We got sober, all right, and quick. But I do not think a single one of us left the powwow that night in a sweat. I myself certainly did not feel that I was getting myself into any kind of a hole. First of all, it was only a proposition, and Gandil still had a lot more yapping to do with Sullivan. And even if we did go on with it, what of it? The national game was full of sell-outers, just like any other business. It is a thing of life.

But over the next few days, I admit that I started to have a few other feelings. It is an odd thing, but baseball could do that to you sometimes. When we got back to Chi from New York, there were thirty thousand bugs waiting for us at the station, even more than in '17. And then the World Series frenzy started up all over again. The scribes were once again all over the place like fleas, with their dumb queries and their talk about us Sox being the wonder of the sporting scene, and such events can make a ballplayer feel excited as a tyke. But it was not only that. You see, what happened is that all at once most of us guys that were in on the racket started acting queer. It was not something you could tell right off, but suddenly, amidst all the fuss, we was quietly giving each other the miss. And when we could not help but bump into each other, for instance at practice, we would be real short, and usually not meet eyes.

Believe it or not, this happened even between Knuckles and yours truly. At practice, a few days before the series was to start, I walked into the clubhouse and there he was, lobbing the bull to some writer from the sticks on the subject of booze. "I am not a prohibitionist," he was saying. "I enjoy a glass of beer as well as the next man, but I think . . ."

"You bet he does," I cut in from the side, in that way I have, "unless the next man happens to be named Bugs Raymond. Hey, newsboy, talk to me if you want the straight goods on that one."

But Knuckles did not even make a grin. "But I think a man has to keep to a schedule," he went right on. "Personally, I always eat well and sleep well. I am a believer in good sense."

Naturally, I did not risk another peep. And a minute later, when the scribe had taken down enough bull, my pal just turned around on his heel and walked away.

Not that I got miffed at him. No, the truth is, I did not want to socialize with them much more than vice versa. There was just a foul badness in the air that whole week, and you could not duck it, especially not around that crowd. If only that meeting had never happened, then we might be able to go about our work.

But it had, and I could not bury my skull in the dirt about it. Like it or not, judging by the facts, it seemed that the fix was in, at least to some. Namely, the world of gamblers. Now, I do not know how it had come off so quick, but suddenly it seemed like everywhere you looked, even there in Chi, heavy money was going down on the Cincinnati Reds. From the outside, this surely looked quirky, for everyone knew the Reds were not half the club we were. They had some fair ballplayers, all right, such as Roush, and Daubert and Greasy Neale, and their manager Moran, known as Whiskey Face (and if you looked at him you would know why!), had plenty of smarts, but there were three or four teams in our league that were stronger. Which is how come the odds had started out eight-to-five in our favor. But now, just two days before the series was to start, those odds had fell all the way down to even money. And as they fell, rumors of a fix began blowing around like hot dog wrappers on a windy Saturday.

Still, not a penny had yet changed mitts, so how could anything be for sure? Indeed, I had no idea at all what was up. Finally, after our last practice at Comiskey, I cornered Gandil and put it to him direct.

"Just hold on to your beanie, Weaver," he said. "As a matter of fact, I have set up a meet this evening at the Warner Hotel. In Risberg's room. You'll get your answers, don't worry."

"I'm not so sure about this whole deal," I said. "I'm not sure at all."

Chick almost stopped breathing, and his eyes got hot as an oven. "Don't you go gooey on me, Weaver," he said in a whisper. "You get cold feet, and you will regret it."

I was at the Warner Hotel that night, too, you can bet on that, and so were all the other boys. I am not saying that most of them looked much happier than me, but they were there.

And so were a couple of other birds that I did not know. One turned out to be Sport Sullivan, who was indeed a sport, right down to his gray spats and such. The other was named Nat Brown, who was a friend of his. As soon as we were all in there, Sullivan got on his feet and made the intros. He said he was really happy to make our acquaintance, being as he had always admired our work, and what a pleasure it was to be amongst us. But then Brown took over and he was a little rougher. He mentioned that him and Sullivan had come all the way from New York, representing a whole load of gamblers, and they wanted to make sure we were going to put over the deal as planned. He said under no circumstances did he want any trip-ups.

None of us ballplayers had said a word up 'til then, but Fred McMullin changed that.

"We were supposed to get the dough in advance."

At that, Brown just looked at him. "That's very nice. And what do I get as collateral?"

There was a long pause.

"My word of honor."

It was Gandil that said it, and even a couple of us boys had to smirk. But not Brown. He seemed to turn it around in his noggin a couple of times, then he spoke up again. "All right, you'll have some of it in advance. Not all eighty grand, but some of it."

Then Sullivan said that they had a train to catch, but he would see us again soon, and what a pleasure it had been, and him and Brown beat it out of there.

That left just us Sox, with Gandil in the middle. "Okay," he said, "you all satisfied?" And the meeting broke up.

But, at least for some of us, the doubts could not fade so fast. Indeed, to see us leave that room, you would think our mother had just kicked the bucket. I would say that of the eight of us, the only ones that had any excitement over the deal were the two crab apples and McMullin. And I guess maybe you could say that Cicotte was still hot for the dough.

But for the rest of us, we were just stuck in a jar of jam, with no way out. Nor was there anybody to talk to, certainly not each other, and probably no one else. Consider my own wife Helen. First of all, she was a woman, and would not understand. And if she did, how would it look to her, her husband titty high in woes, and about to lie down on the job?

These are the kinds of thoughts I was having as I got off the elevator and started across the lobby. But all at once, who should I spot there but Luther Pond!

To tell you that this bird had changed in recent years is not to give half the tale. It was not only that he was dressing better, which he definitely was, and that he was already getting pretty famous, but that even his mug looked different. Before, he was such a hangdog that you would almost feel sorry for the guy just by looking at him. But now, believe it or not, he was suddenly all big grins and glad hands.

He saw me the same moment I saw him, and in a flash he was out of his big soft chair and pumping my paw. This is what he had become like.

"Well, Mister George Weaver. It's been too long a time."

"Yes, sir, it has."

"My congratulations on your season."

"Yes, the club played pretty fair, all right. You don't get in the World Series on your pretty face."

He laughed. "I meant you personally. You ended up over .300 again, didn't you?"

".296. I was skinned a few times by the scorers."

"I'll bet you were." He laughed again. "C'mere, Buck, I want you to meet somebody."

And before I could speak a word, he was hauling me off by the arm to where he had been before. There was another big soft chair there, and in it was another gent in fancy duds, puffing a stogie. He was older than Pond, at least forty-five or fifty, but when we got near his eyes lighted up, and his map got cut in half with a grin and he bounced up on his feet like a jack-in-a-box.

"Buck Weaver," said Pond, "meet George M. Cohan."

"It is my pleasure, young fellow," said Cohan, sticking out his hand. "I've admired your play for a helluva long time, Buck." He grinned. "Though, I must say, you and your friends have cost me quite a bit of change over the years. I don't seem able to break the bad habit of betting on New York teams."

"I've heard about you, also," I answered back.

"Well, how often does a simple song-and-dance man get a compliment like that?" He gave me a bow. "I thank you."

"You're welcome."

"So," he added, "I expect you fellows are in shape for the series. Or are you planning to cost me some more money?"

"No, we're in shape, all right."

"George and I are heading down to Cincy tomorrow ourselves," explained Pond. "I figure the World Series ought to be good for a column or two. Especially having George M. Cohan as a sidekick."

"Sure thing," said Cohan, with a wink. "The fish that'll get wrapped in it can't wait."

Which I have to admit was fairly funny. But there was no putting this fellow Pond down, not really, for by now you could tell he definitely had the real stuff. No longer was he just a regular scribe. In the few years since I had seen him, he had got his own column in that rag back in New York. Nor did he have to write only sporting stuff, but he could scribble about anything in the world he cared to. This had puffed up his name quite a bit. Of course, he was not yet as famous as he was going to get, not by a long shot, but he was already a big enough shot to make other fellows his own age feel like late risers. Even a famous ballplayer such as myself, who had known him back when.

Me and them made a little more chatter, about this and that, and then I looked at my pocketwatch and said I had to cut out. It was a lie, naturally, but that is what people say when they wish to do a Houdini.

"Just wait one sec, will you, Buck?" said Pond. He turned to Cohan. "Excuse us, George, there's something I have to tell my old buddy here."

And before I could nix it, he had me by the arm again, yanking me to a quiet spot in the corner. When we got there, he leaned real close and gazed at me with his baby blues.

"Say, Buck, what's this I hear about the series being in the bag?"

I guess I might've turned pale as a girl. "What are you getting at?" I answered finally.

"It's just chatter, of course," he said, perfectly calm. "There are always rumors around World Series time."

"Sure there are," I said. "Just the other day someone told me that President Wilson had croaked." Which was true, at least that I had heard it.

"So you don't know a thing about it?"

"Why should I?" I paused. "I have got to get packing for the trip to Cincy."

"I guess we'll see you there." He took my paw in his and shook it, real sincere. "I've always been straight with you, isn't that true, Buck?"

"Sure," I said, for it was.

"Good. I just want you to remember one thing. If you hear anything, I'm the guy."

At last he let go of my mitt.

"Well," I said, "see you in Cincy."

"We'll be at the Sinton, same as you."

The Sinton was about the nicest hotel in that town, that's what people said, and when the club showed up there the next morning, it looked like it was so. They had big crystal lamps in the lobby, and rugs from China, and also pictures of China on the walls. The hitch was, the place was so loaded down with rubes gawking at us that who could enjoy it? There must have been five hundred of them waiting when we walked into that lobby. They were all yelling our names, and holding papers out for our names to go on, and standing up on tippy toes, and what with all the hubbub, we were lucky to get out of there in one piece.

When we finally reached our rooms, they were pretty high class, too. But we could not enjoy that no more than the lobby, for in an hour, Gleason wanted us over at Redlands Field for a workout. That is where the series was to begin the next day. I am telling you, that is the part of the World Series the average bug never hears about, how the ballplayers get pushed and pulled around like a fat lady's girdle.

Nor was it easier even when we got over to the ballpark, for the place was lousy with scribes. Every time a fellow got a couple of minutes to take a few swings at the dish, or practice spearing grounders, some new pencil pusher would come up with a list of queries. Normally, the manager would stop these bums from acting so, but not that day. Maybe since it was his first time as the brains in the series, the Kid was lapping it up. Or maybe The Old Roman had told him to kiss up to the press. I do not know. I can only tell you that there was nowhere in that place to do your work.

Finally I just gave it up, and walked out to the outfield fence, and took a seat right on the ground. And that is where I was, thinking my own thoughts, chewing on a piece of grass, when I gazed up and who should be there? Luther Pond! ·

"Trying to dodge the gentlemen of the press?" he asked.

"Yes."

"Not an easy task." With that he laughed and, without me even asking him, plopped his skinny self down next to me.

"How's it going, my friend? I missed you at the hotel."

"Fine."

"You feeling fit?"

"Sure, why not? I'm all set for this World Series, and no one can say I'm not."

He put that down in his pad.

"Had any more thoughts about what we talked about?"

"No."

There was a long silence. I spat out the piece of grass in my mouth and picked another one.

"Listen, Buck, there are sports all over town giving odds on the Redlegs. Now how do you explain that?"

This bird could get on a fellow's nerves, and no doubt about it. "Maybe," I answered back at last, "they think Knuckles still has a sore shoulder."

"Does he?"

"No. And maybe he never did." I started to get up to my feet. "Excuse me, I got some work to do."

"Okay, Buck," he said, with a harder voice, "why don't we cut the comedy? You've heard the whispers, same as me."

I looked down at him there, all smug as a bug. "Let me tell you something. I do not know at all if there is a scheme or not. And if I did, I would not say. I am not the sort of a fellow that does such things to pals."

But that did not stop him in the least. "That's very admirable," he said, with a little grin, and he started right up mentioning the names he had heard about. Cicotte. Williams. Gandil.

I told him again I did not know nothing, so he might as well save his wind. "Anyways," I added, "if there is such a thing, it could be anybody. How about Cocky Collins?"

And with that, I turned and trotted off into the clubhouse.

But even that was not the end, for there was to be no peace the whole rest of that day. When we got back to the hotel, around dinner hour, the place was still as loaded with yokels as before. All I wanted was to get to my own hole and crawl in, but instead I stayed there for two hours and handed out my john hancock. This is the sort of decent fellow I have always been. And as I was doing so, I had to make chin music with them, just like everything was peachy.

It must've been at least nine when I at last got up to my room, and I was weary as death. I just fell down on the bed and lay there and tried to add things up. Was we really going to pull this thing? Here it was, the night before the opener, and everything was still up in the air.

Not that I was alone with such thoughts, of course. After just fifteen or twenty minutes, the telephone rang. It was Gandil on the line. "Get over to my room double quick," he said, sharp as a serpent's tooth.

"I can't now," I said. "I've just ordered up some eats." This was true, lamb chops and cabbage and potatoes. "Anyway, I need my rest."

"Don't give me no stall, Weaver. We're waiting on you!"

And they were, too. All the boys were there, except Shoeless, who I guess they had not been able to collar so quick. Plus, there were a couple of other fellows on hand, not Sullivan and Brown, but two others. One of them was called Sleepy Burns, who used to be a twirler with Detroit when I first came up. And the other was Abe Attell! Once upon a time, this Attell was a famous boxer.

After the hellos, it was Attell that stood up and started yapping. Naturally, we all listened to him with respect.

"Now, I know some of you boys are nervous," he started off. "That makes sense. I was always nervous myself before I stepped into the ring. It's smart to be nervous."

But then, a second later, he added that there was no cause to be nervous at all. He said he was fronting for a big shot from New York named Rothstein. Sullivan and Brown were out, he said, but this Rothstein was going to make the bargain stick, and then some. In fact, because we had been so patient up to now, we were going to get one hundred grand instead of just eighty—twenty after each contest we dropped.

Then he stopped, almost like he was waiting for a comeback.

"We were supposed to get the money in advance," said Gandil. "That has been the deal from the start."

"That's what Sullivan said," came in Felsch.

"Forget Sullivan," said Attell, "it's Rothstein in charge."

"How do we even know this character is good for it?" said Risberg.

At that, Attell looked over at Burns, and they gave each other a big smile, like it was all a joke or something. "Listen," said Attell, "Arnold Rothstein is a goddamn walking bank." He stopped and looked around at us. "Do you hear me doubting you boys? No! We're not even asking you to lose any particular games. Throw them in any order you please. All we ask is that they add up to five." He smiled again. "Take it from The Little Champ, you'll get your money."

He was plenty smooth, there was no question of that, and before too long, he had a few boys agreeing that it made sense. After all, with all the money they had already wagered, we had them as much over the barrel as they had us.

I did not say nothing myself, for there was no point. It was easy
to see how the wind was going in there, and one guy could not
change it.

But there was one curious thing that went on in there, and it gave
me some hopes. Cicotte had not spoken a single word, neither.

So when the meet was over, I trailed after him, and cornered him
outside his room.

"I don't like this, Knuckles," I said. "I feel bad about this."

He nodded. "I know, Buck. Me, too."

"Me, I'm not gonna go ahead with it. I ain't gonna take a red
nickel."

He put his hand in his pocket, got out his key and stuck it in the
door. "Goodnight, Buck. Get some sleep. We got a World Series
tomorrow."

"You don't have to go through with it, too, Knuckles."

He stopped and gazed at me, weary as a grandpa with a twenty-
year-old wife. "I already got mine, Buck. In honor of starting the
first game." He patted his jacket. "Ten thousand, just like I had
coming." He gave me a sad smirk. "I'm thirty-five years old. And
I don't think Comiskey is going to hand me a minor league club."

When I got back to my own room, there was the eats I had
ordered, outside on a tray, cool as a cucumber. But I ate it up
anyway. Then I lay me down to sleep and, fast as that, still dressed
in my civvies, I was out.

Now, I am not the sort that normally recalls a dream. In fact, I
almost never do. After all, they are not real, so what good are they?
But the one that came to me that night was different. Indeed, even
now it remains as clear in my head as morning. It took place in some
old, rickety ballpark, the kind they used to make of wood instead of
iron. Us Sox were playing in a very big game, and we were losing
bad. But, all at once, we sprung a big rally and started catching up.
Our runners were circling the bases like crazy, and the bugs in the
stands were yelling out their lungs and so was I. See, in this dream
I was not a player, but a coacher, and I was standing behind the dish
with the umpire. And there was another odd thing—there were no
batsmen, only those baserunners. It was real foggy out there on the
field, and how they would score is that all at once the pill would
shoot out of the pea soup in the outfield, and we would see it for just

a second, and then it'd sail by the catcher, and I'd be waving in another runner. You probably know how dreams are. Anyway, this went on for quite a while, 'til finally I sneaked a gander at the scoreboard and saw that we had tied them up, 17–17. Naturally, by now everyone in the place was on their feet, asking for more. And, sure enough, another ball flies past the catcher, and there I go, waving in another man from third. And he slides, and he's safe!

But here comes the funny part. All at once I notice that he is not one of our boys at all. He is wearing a gray NEW YORK road uniform and no spikes. And I realize that this fellow has scored the winning run for *them*. And I look over at their bench, and it is *them* that's whooping it up. And, though I know there is definitely something fishy going on, there is not a thing I can do about it.

Well, that was my dream. I am not saying it makes sense, for what the hell was that guy doing on the bases when it was us at bat? But I will tell you something, when I woke up I was as wet as Niagara Falls. For a long time I just lay there, turning it around in my skull. Then I reached out for the telephone and told the hello girl to give me Kid Gleason.

The Kid was out dead when I got him, and could not hardly talk. And when he could, what he said was no lullaby to my ears.

"Weaver?" he started out. "What in hell do *you* want? What time is it?"

But when I quickly mentioned that I had to see him, and I was serious, he hotfooted it over to my room in five minutes. When I let him in, he looked pretty odd, for he was wearing the pants from a suit and the tops of his peejays, and his hairs was all mussed up, but the look he had on his puss would've put a muzzle on a hyena.

"All right, Weaver," he said, "this had better be good."

"I guess you didn't expect to hear from old Buck at this late date, did you?" I told him.

"No." He sat down on my bed. "Well?"

For a moment I did not know how to put it.

"You're feeling okay, aren't you?"

"I don't know about that."

He leaned forward in earnest and looked at me with them sleepy eyes. "How come? What's wrong?"

"My leg ain't so good. I think maybe the hamstrings might be acting up again." See, I had been out for a week with this back in August.

"What'd you do to it? You do something today in practice?"

"I guess so."

"Why didn't you tell me then?"

"I don't know." I stalled a minute. "It just started to pinch right here in bed."

He breathed in deep and then breathed out again. "Can you play on it?"

"That's what I wanted to talk about. I don't know about it."

He got off my bed and began walking around. He made a big circle before he stopped.

"You heard the talk that's been going around, Buck?"

"What talk?"

"There are some people saying some things about the series not being on the square. Have you heard that?"

"No. Why would I?"

He shook his head. "I don't know, I don't know." He paused. "I want you to play tomorrow."

"Sure." My heart was down at my toes. "You know me. I'll play my hardest out there, same as always. I thought maybe you'd wanna know, is all."

He bobbed his skull. "I appreciate it. We'll have the doc look at it. I want you in the training room first thing."

"Okay, Kid."

"And if you hear anything fishy, clue me in, will you?"

"You know me, Kid."

"Good." He opened the door. "Good. Now get some sleep."

It turned out that me and the Kid were not the only ones that did not get so much shuteye that night. Knuckles was out walking around in the streets. And Gandil, he kept getting woken up by itchy gamblers on the horn. And I later found out that Shoeless Joe actually went up to see The Old Roman and asked him to be pulled out of the lineup. The rube told him that he had pains in the gut and could not play.

But he played, all right, and so did I. 'Til the day I start helping the daisies grow, I will never forget how it was, standing there at Redlands Field with my mitt on my heart, while Sousa's bunch played "The Star Spangled Banner." The stands were loaded to the beams. The flags were blowing in the breeze. The sky was blue over our noggins. It was a thing to behold, the national game at its finest, with two great clubs about to go at it, and the whole world jumpy with excitement. And all the while, me knowing it was only a skin game.

It did not take long to find out just how sorry it was to become. Being the visitors, we batted first, and did not score. Then Cicotte walked slowly to the hill. I stood there at my spot near the third bag, looking and waiting, hoping for a little miracle. Then my old roomie Morrie Rath, who was now their second sacker, stepped up to the dish. He looked out at Knuckles, the arty and craftiest twirler in the game, and you could see he had the fidgets. In a tough pinch, Rath was always a nervous worm. Cicotte swung into his famous windup and delivered the pellet. Strike one. My pal took the ball back from Schalk and wound up again. The pitch was a curver—and it hit Rath smack in the middle of the back.

As the little bum trotted toward first base, and all the Cincy bugs started screaming for joy, I just closed my eyes and wished I had never heard of this game of baseball in the first place.

I do not want to go into too many ugly details, for they are not news. The whole world saw how Cicotte pitched that day, and that we got beat 9–1. And that the next day, Lefty Williams, who that season had walked less than two batsmen per game, walked three in one inning, which caused us to lose again, 4–2.

The third game was another thing entirely, and if you know your history, you know how come. See, Faber was benched with a sore wing, so the busher Kerr started for us. And he won, too, with yours truly providing the punch, 3–0. This did not seem like such a spectacular feat at the time, of course, but later, when it came out that half the guys on his side had been trying to boot the contest, Kerr got to be a hero for it.

But the next game, Knuckles was at it again, losing 2–0 on account of his own two misplays. And in game number five, with Williams on the slab, we got skunked once more, 5–0.

By now, if you were keeping count, you would know that we were behind four contests to one, and amongst our teammates, only a moron would not have a few suspicions. Gleason was steamed up, and so was Schalk, who had been sitting there behind the dish for a week, watching the aces of the club toss like second-raters. Not to mention that Gandil would hardly even bother to run out a batted ball.

Finally, Schalk and such other guys as Leibold and Faber could just not stop themselves, and started popping off. They could not cut loose with everything they thought, of course, for where was the proof? But by the end of that fifth game, on the bench, they were openly ragging the sell-outers about their lack of vim. And the ones that were playing consumption came right back with a few Sunday school words of their own, telling them to shut their lousy yaps and hoe their *own* potatoes. For the truth is, some of the boys that were cleanest of all, including Leibold and Cocky, were playing even lousier than some of the ones doing a dive. I am telling you, before long, it was as fierce on that Pale Hose bench as the Ardennes. I had never seen no team ride the enemy this hard, let alone themselves!

And, like I say, Gleason was as angry as anyone. After Williams had booted away his second one, letting in those five runs on just four hits (but three of them were in one inning!), the Kid knew that he could not stay mum no longer. He called a meeting in the club-house in Comiskey.

"You've all been hearing the talk," is how he began, "and so have I. I may be old, but I'm sure as hell not deaf." He stopped and gazed right at Cicotte. "And if there's anything to it, anything at all, I want you to speak up fast."

Well, naturally Knuckles did not open his trap. But Gandil sure did, and about as quick as Gleason wanted. The lemon said that sure he had heard the rumors, who hadn't, but it was pure applesauce. He said that someone was just trying to smear up honest ballplayers. A few guys were not playing as good as hoped, that's all, but that was baseball. If we all pulled together, the club might still win this World Series yet! And as soon as he stopped talking, our whole bunch piped up to agree with him.

I guess that is just about what the Kid had wanted to hear, for he let the matter lie right there. Nor would we hear any more questions about the fix inside our own club for a real long time.

It was the same way with the scribes. I guess at least half of them had a notion that foul things was up, and quite a few of them also had a few facts. How could they not? The facts was as easy to get in that World Series as half beer. Look at Pond. Or Hughie Fullerton with the *Herald and Examiner* there in Chi, who I heard actually had a line to some of the gamblers.

But, see, they were in no more rush to get it out than we were, or Gleason, or The Old Roman. And neither were their editors. This is the way things are in the business of baseball, with everybody looking after his own skin by scratching backs. No one wanted to kill the national game, and that is what a big scandal might do. Besides being rooters themselves, without baseball a lot of Americans would stop buying newspapers, and those writers would be out on the dole. Plus there was the matter of friendship. The big pokes that owned these papers was all pals with the magnates. They were always cooking up business deals, and going out on the town, and their wives was always tossing bashes for each other.

And so, the stuff that showed up in the papers during that World Series was not the crooked rumors at all, but the same old gabble as always. "Any team looks bad when they are not hitting," is the kind of thing Lefty Williams had to say. "In five games we have scored one earned run," said Eddie Collins, "and you're not going to win many games on that margin." "Tomorrow is another day," chimed in Gandil, innocent as an angel.

But it was an odd thing, what Gandil said turned out to be true. The next day, Kerr worked for us again, and though he did not have his best stuff, he showed lots of grit. We beat them in ten innings, 5–4, with myself marking the winning tally.

I have not mentioned this before, for how would it look, but now I will come out and say it. From the very start of that series, I had done beautiful work. In the field, I made nary a bobble, and, along with Shoeless, I was the club's star batsman. In fact, it was rare that I had powdered the ball so regular, and with such power. You can ask anybody that saw it. It is no wonder that of all the lists made by the scribes (just for the fun of it), of possible sell-outers, Buck Weaver was not on a single one. I was not on Gleason's list, neither, nor even on The Old Roman's.

In fact, the day after that, in game number seven, I starred once again, with a two bagger and a single.

But, even more important, on that afternoon, which was October 8, back at Redlands Field, the great Eddie Cicotte looked like his old self. He went the whole route, and smothered them with ease, 4–1.

After that contest was over, I did not speak to him in the clubhouse, that is how crimpy things had got between us. But I could not miss the big grin on his puss, like he had just eaten a whole apple pie on his own. In fact, there were grins on maps all over that clubhouse. And why not? All at once, there we were, trailing in the World Series by only four contests to three. If we could just take two more games, we would again be champs.

Indeed, it looked to me like maybe the whole scheme had done a fizzle. I could not say for certain, for since the start of the series, with me playing so fine, Gandil did not have a thing to say to me. But that is certainly how it looked, especially with Knuckles coming across like he had.

Then, for another thing, there was a whole batch of new rumors going around, and one had it that now some of the Reds was on the take. If you listened to the buzz, some of the gamblers that had got left out of the first fix, had got to the Cincy twirlers, and those birds was trying to hand us the series on a platter, which you could believe if you had got a look at some of their fat lobs.

But, at the same time, there was another rumor, which seemed even more possible. It was that Attell had not come through as promised and só, at last, our boys had got fed up and were out to double-cross him. That sounded like our boys.

But it was not to be so. The very next day, in game number eight, Lefty Williams took the hill for our side. And he settled things for once and all. He was gone in the first frame, in fact, after retiring only one batsman—and letting in four runs. And that did it. We would not get close to them the whole contest.

Now, to be fair about it, it later came out that Lefty had been told before the game that there was a rifle aimed at his back. But that is not an out, not to me. And if the lowbrow had to lose, he at least could have looked a little smarter about it, instead of making like a hunk of TNT. After a series like he had, it is no wonder people might have had some doubts. To this day, Lefty Williams is still the only pitcher ever to lose three games in a World Series.

As for me, I do not mind saying that it was pretty tough for me during that last game. I have always been a prideful fellow and, seeing how things were going, and knowing how come, at moments I felt like bawling. I also knew how it was going to be in coming days. The papers would be full of the Redlegs spouting gas, all of them telling how they had pulled off the miracle, and explaining that they had really been better than us American Leaguers all along, and it was about time people had finally wised up. And us White Sox would have to swallow it all down without a peep.

As a matter of fact, seeing how things turned out anyway, I wish I had pulled one last thing. It would have made some stunt. After we made our last out, and those Redlegs started jumping all over each other, like dogs on the make, I wish I had run right into the middle of them and given that nice grin of mine. "Hold on a second, boys," I would've said, "don't you know we weren't even trying?"

Success and
Its Liabilities

O ver the course of a long career, I was pleased to be often
praised as a wordsmith. Indeed, more than a few of the terms
I coined—eyeballing, small potatoes, two-timing—eventually found their way into certain iconoclastic dictionaries.

Their breeziness notwithstanding, those creations, most of them,
did not come easily; glibness for me was almost always a matter of
sweat. But, as it happens, the single most memorable expression ever
to spin out of my typewriter came about by happenstance.

"White Sox my eye!" read the note I received from "Ex-Baseball
Bug" in October 1920, just as the investigation into the previous
autumn's baseball scandal was reaching its height. "Those crooks
have black hearts, and everything else is black, too, sox included!
They have been traitors to the whole public."

Thus it was that several days hence I introduced a new phrase into
the national idiom, one so appropriate to its subject it soon replaced
the actual title entirely. Henceforth, those eight sorry souls who
came so close to destroying the institution that had brought them
recognition and financial reward far beyond rational measure would
be as conveniently pigeonholed as scoundrels as were the Rough-
riders as heroes; and, more importantly, I myself would be forever
associated, on the record, with their undoing.

I have never ceased to regard that association with pride. But it
is a curious thing, the eight or ten month period of my life of which
the Black Sox case was the centerpiece was anything but a happy one

for me. I was, in fact, in a state of agitation throughout much of it. What should, by rights, be a time treasured in memory—for it was the time I at last achieved so much of what I had so earnestly sought —was instead one which, above all, evokes memories of depression and self-doubt—mostly fostered by the mean-spiritedness of others.

Still, no longer do I regret the ordeal. For in the end, it rendered me more suitable to my task, battered me into fighting trim. The emotional adjustments forced upon me right at the start—the realization that, in fact, a man in my position cannot expect to have real friends—was to prove as invaluable an asset to my career as my connection with the Black Sox story itself.

All of which leads us, in an old man's roundabout fashion, back to October 1919, and the tainted games themselves. I hasten to point out I was hardly the only observer present at the World Series to surmise early on that something was amiss. The initial contests in particular were so marked by sloppy play on the part of the White Sox, especially their pitching stars Cicotte and Williams, that from one end of the press box to the other, the goings-on, at first taken as bizarre, were finally, reluctantly, seen as suspicious.

In retrospect, even that seems generous. After all, in the several days prior to the start of the series, the odds had, for no good reason, shifted dramatically in the direction of the Cincinnatis, to most minds the inferior collection of athletic specimens on display that week. Virtually every member of the sporting press had personally witnessed, in his own hotel lobby, sporting men on the prowl for Chicago money. Then, too, those of us with even a glancing familiarity with human nature could *sense* something odd about the White Sox that week. The mirthless, almost mournful way they proceeded about their task, in the locker room as well as on the diamond, bespoke a great deal more than traditional series butterflies.

But newspapermen, like almost everyone else, are cautious, and timid, and prefer not to rock boats owned by those bigger than themselves. In the aftermath of the games, the queer plays dutifully set down for posterity alongside the stirring ones, the vast majority of my colleagues gratefully moved on to other, smaller concerns. For those few who saw life in terms of moral obligations, there was reassurance; the matter was to be reviewed by those most immediately concerned—the directors of the White Sox themselves. Indeed, no less formidable a figure than Charles Comiskey had let it be known that he intended to see to the integrity of the game. Nor did it have to be announced, for the benefit of the would-be investigators lurking in the wings, that not only did Commy have at his disposal an impressive assemblage of libel attorneys, but he happened to be a friend of most of the country's most influential publishers.

Even I, at that juncture, was less aggressive than I might have been. I operated under no illusions. I recognized how very unlikely it was that even the most assiduous investigation would bear fruit.

If, from this distance, such an attitude strikes one as improbable, I can only assert that it was based on a good deal of experience. Only a minute percentage of the great deceptions perpetrated upon this society are ever revealed to anyone other than the associates of those most immediately involved, and far fewer still find their way into the newspapers.

And when, indeed, at the start of the subsequent baseball season, I at last resumed poking around the story, there was frustration aplenty. While my research was hardly dogged—unlike the several others, sportswriters all, who joined the hunt around the same time, I was driven by nothing so dramatic as indignation, or rage—I went about my work with no lack of diligence; on every one of those occasions when, in the course of other reports, I found myself in reasonable proximity to baseballers, I renewed ties to old acquaintances, and vigorously attempted to elicit their views on the previous fall's events. All this line of endeavor managed to do, however, was to reaffirm a lesson of the Federal League fight: that, in times of crisis, sporting types can be as mutually protective as the most committed Wobblies.

And, there could be no mistaking it, in the doubts raised about the American League champions, there *was* a threat to them all. They knew, and so did I, that gambling had been a part of the game decades longer than peanuts or crackerjacks. I was personally aware of half a dozen pitchers who had long supplemented their income by wagering upon themselves. It was, indeed, not without a feeling of some foolishness that, in conversations with men I had known throughout my career, I now went about raising the subject as an issue.

Which is why I was more than a little taken aback to hear, one evening in early June, while on assignment in Chicago, from a player with an intriguing bit of information to impart. The individual in question was not, alas, a member of the hometown White Sox—to a man, as surly and distant a crew that season as any I had ever encountered—but one Dutch Leonard, a lefthanded pitcher with the Detroit Tigers.

Like the hapless Tigers, who were playing a weekend series against the powerful White Sox, I was in Chicago just then on what seemed a fool's errand. Having, three months before, signed on with the New York *Daily News*, I had learned soon thereafter that it was my new publisher's fervent wish that I cast my eye upon the political arena—and the Republicans were about to convene on the banks of Lake Michigan for the purpose of selecting their presidential candidate. The catch was that I was not much interested in politics. In fact, so lightly did the obligation at hand engage me, that I had actually passed up that day's municipal luncheon for the press to visit Comiskey Park and press forward with my baseball probe—once again, with unsatisfactory results.

But that evening, as I was about to depart my hotel room for dinner, the operator put through a call.

"Luther Pond?"

"Who's this?"

"Dutch Leonard. I'd like to talk to you." A moody man, a pitcher whose once considerable skills were in sharp decline, Leonard was among those with whom I had conversed, briefly, earlier in the day.

"Certainly, Dutch," I said. "I'm at your disposal."

"Can I come to your room? I'm right down here in the lobby."

Three minutes later he was perched on the edge of my bed, eyes downcast, his oversized pitcher's hands kneading one another, telling his tale. It dealt, I grasped immediately, with a rush of disappointment, not with the World Series at all, but with his own team. During the last week of the previous season, Leonard said, it had been arranged for the Tigers to be handed a victory by the Cleveland Indians.

"What was the point of that?" I asked.

"The White Sox had already clinched the pennant," he explained, "and Cleveland had sewed up second. But, see, we still had a shot at third place money. We needed that win. So they got paid for it. Five hundred bucks."

"I see," I said, without enthusiasm. It was, after all, not uncommon at the time for hungry teams to attempt, through financial inducements, to influence the outcome of games crucial to their chances. Repeatedly over the years, there had been reports of rewards proffered by contending clubs to also-rans for knocking off their rivals.

"Were there gamblers involved?" I pressed.

"Not professional ones." He paused. "After it was fixed up, a couple of boys put down some of their own. One of the fellows that works at Navin Field, Fred West, he laid down the bets."

"Uh huh." I was not sure I had very much more to ask. "This occurred when?"

"September 25, 1919. Boland was on the hill for our side, and Myers for them. We won it 9–5."

"I see." I made a notation.

"You can't print my name, though," he added hurriedly, then looked up at me with a sheepish grin. "See, maybe I made a few bucks on it, myself."

"Of course not." I stopped. "Well, I appreciate this very much, Dutch, I really do. But, you see, what I'm basically looking for is information about the World Series. That's what . . ."

"Ain't you gonna ask who set it up?"

"Sure. Who?"

He gazed at me steadily. "Cobb and Speaker."

For a moment I made no reply. The mention of the two most venerable stars in the game was intended to startle, and it did. "You know that for a fact?"

"I heard 'em plan it myself, under the stands there at the ballpark. Ty asked Tris could he get his boys to lay down, and Speak said sure, why not. Then they shook on it, and that's just how it happened."

"Tell me, Dutch, why are you telling me this?"

He smiled. "You're the first one that asked, that's why. I woulda told anyone, but no one asked."

. . .

Of that I was quite certain. The game in question was even more meaningless now than when it had been played. It bore not at all upon the issue of the tainted World Series. Moreover, there was little reason to suppose that Leonard was telling the truth, and good reason to suppose he might not be; like every other man in a Detroit uniform, he despised Ty Cobb.

It is, indeed, an indication of my regard for the tip, as well as for the business of covering a political convention, that a day later, when I learned that Joseph Bowne Ellwell, society man and best-selling author of *Ellwell on Bridge*, had been discovered in his New York brownstone with a bullet hole through his handsome head, I forthwith issued a request that I be allowed to drop all else and return home. My interest in the Ellwell story, I explained to my publisher, was not only professional but intensely personal.

"Stay where you are," he snapped over the long-distance line. "Maybe you'll actually learn something."

How he guessed that I never knew. Then as now, for sheer volume of mediocre humanity, nothing in this world beats a hall-ful of delegates, dutifully bent to their task. But, in fact, this convention *would*, in a backhanded way, prove both historic and immensely instructive. For, while democracy's drama lumbered along, while the forces of General Wood and Governor Lowden and Senator Johnson paraded their banners, sang their songs and made their speeches, the nominee was being chosen (as his own manager, Harry Daugherty, so engagingly put it) "in seclusion around a big table, by fifteen men, perspiring profusely and bleary-eyed with loss of sleep. Just a nice bunch of fellows cutting a deal."

I would, in fact, eventually come to see that 1920 Republican Convention, as much as the fixed World Series itself, as a harbinger of the approaching age, not only in the manner its business was conducted—noisy fun masking audacious sleight-of-hand—but in the kinds of men, determined yet flexible, self-interested yet endlessly engaging, who gave it its character. Even the nominee himself, soon to be president, was as radical a departure from his predecessor as two men of the same generation and profession could conceivably be. While Woodrow Wilson, straight-laced and implacable, remained even now, in mortal illness, incapable of compromise, Warren Harding compromised reflexively, by instinct; he was, in fact, as the world was to shortly discover, prepared to dicker away *anything*.

Alas, the political reports I filed out of Chicago were marked by no such insights. In large measure, this was a function of inexperience; over the course of that week, during which I ended up having as fine a time as I'd had in years, I came to like Harding and the men around him far too much for my own good. Even three years later, upon their slapstick fall from popular grace, I would find little cause to denigrate them in private. But, more than that, like so many of my colleagues, I became caught up in the political moment that produced them. For what was at hand, what in a curious way they represented, was the political response to the revolution of mores and outlook that, all of us knew without saying, had been quietly reshaping the American soul since the end of the Great War. And —need it be observed?—in revolutionary times one tends not to be particular.

The quality of the change then in progress has, of course, been endlessly remarked upon in the years since—has, indeed, been reduced to a visual cliché by the relentless newsreel footage of flappers, and packed ballparks, and pole sitters, and Wall Streeters gone berserk—but it is nonetheless difficult to communicate from this distance the sense of being in its midst. It is certain that never before, in the entirety of human history, had any culture not rent by war or revolution undergone so thorough a transformation so quickly. Those who like the sound of such things are wont to observe that this was the instant when Americans lost their innocence; it was, more precisely, the time when they stopped being embarrassed by it. Abruptly, in a hundred tiny ways, millions of ordinary people were behaving, *thinking*, with an unmistakable abandon—often in ways that a half dozen years before would have been beyond imagining. Within months of Prohibition, numberless good burghers were blithely breaking the law. All at once, hitherto conservative men were rushing their savings into beach property a thousand miles from home. One memorable afternoon, my own landlady, Mrs. Zaretsky, turned up with her hair bobbed.

Quite simply, we found ourselves at the edge of an era in which many of the precepts with which we had come to maturity, and virtually all of the constraints, would abruptly be antique. There is,

I realize, today a powerful nostalgia for the values discarded in the shuffle—in moments of weakness or uncertainty, I feel a certain yearning for them myself—but, the truth is, at the time only the most solemn of fuddy-duddies mourned their passing. For this new age was electric with promise, crowded with opportunities for the grasping; a time in which a daring man's expectations for himself rose as fast as hemlines in the streets.

All in all, it is hardly a coincidence that I myself had lately taken the single most dramatic step of my professional life. Nothing had impelled me to do so. I was comfortable at the *Journal*, and as content as any man of my temperament has a right to expect. Moreover, the task I had agreed to undertake at the *News*, to—and the hell with false modesty—go about inventing a new journalistic form, was one which, in that other, more settled time, would certainly have filled me with trepidation. My reputation notwithstanding, I am not, by nature, an uncautious sort.

But in February, 1920, prudence had suddenly seemed out of the question. It was, you see, as if life's stage had been redecorated exactly to my specifications.

The *Daily News* was but half a year old at the time, its initial sixteen-page edition having appeared the previous June, and had my colleagues at the *Journal* suspected I was considering joining its staff, they'd have been struck dumb. An unapologetic imitation of London's notorious *Daily Mirror*, packed with more pictures per page than most papers featured in an entire issue, all but devoid of bona fide news, aimed directly at the semi-literate, the *News* was regarded as a kind of pseudo-journalism, an aberration unworthy of serious consideration. It was even strange to the touch, being only half the size of the city's other dailies. Women complained that the ink from its grimy front page smudged their gloves.

Indeed, during the first several months of its life, its proprietors, the young cousins Joe Patterson and Robert McCormick of the Tribune Company in Chicago, had themselves seemed to place little faith in its chances. Having hatched the paper while on duty in France—reputedly, atop a farmyard manure pile—both retreated to the safety of hogtown, leaving others to run the sheet on a day-to-day basis out of a corner office rented from the *Daily Mail*. The paper's editors, led by one Arthur L. Clarke, appeared so frankly at a loss during those early months, that they gave themselves over to an orgy of experimentation unparalleled in memory. One day a photograph of the Albanian king, of no discernible news interest, might occupy the front page, followed the next day by word of a "Love Balm Suit," and a promotion for the paper's own beauty contest the one after that; a literary page came and went; so did a dozen reporters; on one particularly bizarre morning, shortly after the paper had inexplicably dropped the word "Illustrated" from its title, there actually appeared, beneath the headline ELLA WHEELER WILCOX SPEAKS FROM THE SPIRIT WORLD, a "composograph" depicting the lately deceased poetess cavorting in the beyond.

Under the circumstances, it was not at all surprising that, before the end of the paper's first summer, the little world that I inhabited was rife with happy speculation of its imminent demise.

But even then I had my doubts. From the *News'* first appearance, I had been watching it closely, each morning laying down my two cents at the newsstand at William and Fulton Streets and flipping through it at my desk; the habit was, indeed, much snickered at within the office.

That did not bother me. Certainly the *News* was ill executed, any half-wit could see that. But, at the same time, I saw something else —that this rag had within it all the elements to be the newspaper of the age. Never, in all my days, had I run across a publication that so aspired to serve the mass sensibility. If the *News* was undersized, that only made it easier to manage on the subway. If it catered to the diminished attention span, so did the moving picture, and the comic strip, and every other modern popular form. If, above all, it chose to define as noteworthy only the titillating and the curious, well— as every man laboring on William Street should have known—that is precisely how most of *our* public had always defined the term. Were it to hit its stride, none of the rest of us could even hope to compete with a sheet so embodying the dictum set forth by wily old Jamie Bennett half a century before: "The newspaper's function is not to instruct but to startle."

So when, one bitter cold morning in early February, I had received a call from Colonel Patterson himself inviting me to drop by his office, I did not hesitate to accept. And once there, I listened as closely as I had to anyone in months. The *News* was planning a new column, tentatively entitled "Tattle and Prattle," which would be a compendium of news items relating to the famous. Since I was not only an established stylist, but a reporter with lines to the worlds of theatre, of business, of politics, of crime, I was being offered first crack at the job.

"You're very kind," I said.

"I am not kind at all," he demurred, "I'm a good businessman."

"It's an interesting thought. I will certainly think it over."

"Take your time. Take a week or two."

In fact, the decision took less than a day. That very evening at home, I settled into a soft chair, took up a scratchpad and set down the words that had been rattling about within my head all afternoon: "What's up, pal o' mine?"

But astonishing as it seems now, I was very nearly as absorbed by something else I had learned at the meeting. It seemed that four months earlier, Patterson had received a surreptitious call from none other than Arthur Brisbane, Hearst's most trusted comrade-in-arms and his most renowned syndicated columnist, offering to personally take the *News* off the Tribune Company's hands. "There are," Brisbane had assured the publisher, "too few charwomen in New York for the paper to make a go of it."

But the great journalist had waited just a little too long. Had he turned up even a month earlier, noted Patterson, he might have been believed; such was his reputation for integrity. But already the paper's fortunes had turned stunningly. By Christmas, its circulation exceeded one hundred fifty thousand; now, as we spoke, it had as many readers as thirteen of the town's eighteen other dailies, and was already bearing down on Hearst's *American*.

However, Brisbane's maneuver aroused in me no indignation. In fact, in the months ahead, it was to be a source of considerable comfort. No other single act could more effectively have given the lie to the vicious charges—of duplicity, of disloyalty, of ingratitude —that were to be so persistently levelled at me. For if, in doing what I was about to, I had acted dishonorably, then the entire profession was dishonorable; and business itself. I in fact wondered at the time whether, in their rage, my detractors within the Hearst organization had actually forgotten, or merely set aside, the fact that it was the Old Man himself who had pioneered the practice of pirating journalists.

Still, I do not deny that the slanders hurt, and a very great deal.

It is not too presumptuous to maintain that, by that juncture, Hearst and I had come to regard each other as friends, and this in a world in which each of us could number his friends on a single hand. We dined together with some frequency, and spoke on the telephone as often as twice a week. Though the relationship was certainly grounded in mutual respect, it was by no means a sober one. The man's weakness for comedy was legend—it was a standing order to all of his editors never to print an unkind word about Weber and Fields—yet, alone among the younger men in his employ, I approached him without reverence.

I knew very well that Hearst had plans for me; he had intimated as much in my presence. The problem, finally, was that no longer did they coincide with my plans for myself.

I confirmed this for myself beyond question soon after my meeting with Patterson. Stopping by his office one late afternoon, I announced that I had a notion for the *Journal* that was a can't-miss: a column, to be called "Out of School," devoted exclusively to the doings of the celebrated.

Hearst's reaction amounted to no reaction at all.

"It was my understanding that you'd had your fill of columning," he observed testily, before agreeing, finally, to the very minimum— to take the matter under advisement.

This I willfully supposed to be a temporary setback; the idea not being even remotely his own, he wished only to add a few twists to it before handing it back. Over the course of the next two weeks, however, he was to utter not another syllable on the subject.

I knew well the likely consequences of my defection. Hearst and his principal lieutenants scorned all competitors, but their hatred of the Tribune Company was very nearly pathological. It may even have been justified. Before the war, in Chicago, Hearst's *Herald-Examiner* and the *Tribune* had engaged in a newspaper war so murderous that it was subsequently held responsible for launching gangsterism in that city; in its wake, no fewer than half a dozen newsstand dealers and truck drivers lay dead.

But that, I came to recognize as I approached my decision, could no longer be my concern. The matter at hand had to be considered soberly, as a business proposition, and the sober truth was incontestable: Hearst was fading. His reputation for daring notwithstanding, he had never been so much an innovator as a sly adapter of already successful formulas—and he was no longer even that. Having, for example, had every opportunity to himself launch the tabloid on these shores—having, as I subsequently learned, gone so far as to equip a tabloid plant at 55 Fulton Street—he had let the moment pass, as now he had failed to grasp the possibilities inherent in my proposal.

Sentiment aside, was there any justification in staying with the man?

When I phoned up Patterson with my decision, his delight was unfeigned. How soon, he demanded, could I begin? Would I be able to meet with him the following day?

However, at the agreed-upon hour, when I arrived at the *Daily News* offices, I learned that the publisher had been summoned back to Chicago the evening before.

"It was damn urgent," observed Managing Editor Clarke, the man assigned to meet with me in his stead, in reply to my request for specifics, "that's all I know. That's all you need to know, too."

The first indignity I was willing to swallow; it is a publisher's right to be unavailable. But Clarke's manner, so typical of underlings allowed a whiff of authority, I took as an affront.

After a few perfunctory words, he led me to his cubicle, sat me down and leaned across his desk. Had I yet informed Hearst of my intentions, he wanted to know.

"I don't see that that is any of your concern," I replied curtly.

"Mr. Pond, in Mr. Patterson's absence it is very much my concern. Are you prepared to sign a contract with us?"

"I haven't yet decided. I haven't decided even whether I shall leave the *Journal.*" Though, in fact, my letter of resignation was in my breast pocket.

Clarke looked at me in surprise. "Mr. Pond, we are here, as I understand it, to work out the terms of . . ."

"And I understood," I cut him off, "that I would be discussing this with Colonel Patterson."

"I have the authority to . . ."

"That," I said more insistently, "was my understanding. Now, I am prepared to tell you exactly what I am looking for. You may relay what I say to Chicago."

To my surprise, he made no objection, merely sighed and sat back in his chair. This I took as acquiescence.

"I want two hundred seventy-five to start. That is for two columns a week. The salary will of course rise if we decide I am to appear more frequently. Patterson knows about this already."

"So I have been informed."

"I will need a telephone line entirely my own. Also access to a photo taker."

He nodded.

"My column will not be edited. There will be no changes whatsoever without my approval."

I paused a moment. "Those are the main points."

"All of that is acceptable."

"Good. I would like it set down in writing. I don't want there to be any misunderstandings."

"There is no danger of that."

"I would like it in writing."

"Fine. Done."

"Good. One more thing." I hesitated; I did not much like the sound of this myself. "I might need a little help running down items."

He shook his head. "I'm afraid that is out of the question."

"You've got a dozen picture chasers!"

"We're a picture newspaper, Mr. Pond. That's why people look at the *News*."

"That," I assured him, "was before I got here." I paused. "Well, you just take it up with Patterson."

"The matter has already been discussed." Clarke did not smile, but he certainly relished the moment. "We shall ruin one man at a time."

I did not take particular offense at the remark; one must consider sources. But neither did I approach the undertaking with the sense of assurance it at the time seemed so necessary to convey. To the contrary, the possibility that the column might become the force that it did—that, indeed, I would even remain with it any longer than I had the other waystops along my career path—was so remote as to never have occurred to me. For days after I tendered my resignation at the *Journal*, I was plagued by second and third and fourth thoughts. Successful though it had been, my professional life to date had been marked by a restlessness that approached the self-destructive. Had I this time gone too far?

My initial effort appeared a mere twelve days later, on March 30, 1920. The title of the column had been decided upon at the last possible moment, following fevered consultations with a handful of colleagues located in the vicinity of my bare new office: "Hoopla."

What's up, pal o' mine? Listen close . . .

So you want to know what's doing on Old Broadway, do you? Seems that George White, the famously known producer, is fixing to fill up his fall Scandals with brand new faces, not to mention brand new . . . well, you catch our drift. Girlie, does that mean *you*???

By the by, pretty little Mary Graham, now hoofing it up in *Happy Days* at the Hippodrome, figures to get her Big Break in this one. First billing! Says who? Says she—and she's no white fibber!!

Meantime, Max Corvin, the big textiles cheesecloth, is head over spats for showgal Edwina Tyler, late of Mobile, Alabammy. Why, he's even shaved his whiskers just to please li'l ol' her.

It's a boy at the Whitney Sages. Huzzahs!

Listen closer, pal. There's nothing at all to the breeze that Mister I. Berlin's new show has pfffed! As we speak, he is pianoed up at home, in-co-mo-no-ca-do (except to your pal!). Bet your do-re-mi it'll be tin pantastic!!!

Got an express report from John McGraw that his Jints are a cinch for the World Series this year. Funny thing, Hug says the same thing about his Yankees! And Uncle Robbie about *his* Brooks!! Gonna be some mob out there in the field come October!!!

And so it went for another forty or so lines, concluding—why not?—with a rhyme.

> We're the new kid on the block
> A pal beneath the skin.
> Short on manners, long on sock
> So keep on looking in.

I recognized that this was hardly the stuff legends are made of. I certainly did not need Clarke to inform me that it "seemed a trifle soft." The damn thing was softer than custard, and only slightly less bland! What small consolation I could find in it—that the stylistic devices I had devised, the breathlessness, the word playfulness, were serviceable—did little to lift my spirits.

I was no amateur. I understood that a newspaper column does not simply spring to life full blown. But I had also come to understand that the undertaking at hand presented difficulties entirely original in character, ones that no other columnist had yet faced. The problem was not in running down material with a bite; I had as many sources as any man in town, and at any given moment, most every one had something on someone. No, it lay, more than ever before in my experience, in getting the grittier stuff into print. There was, you see, a tradition of newspaper column writing in this country, one much respected even by my new employers. A man in my position was expected to conduct himself with decorum; to be—and even then I detested the word—a *gentleman*. A columnist, far more than a reporter, was expected to have his facts in order. Nor was that expectation without a certain pragmatic basis. Readers would not identify with, would, indeed, soon turn their backs on, the mud artist.

But not, I knew, as readily as they would desert a bore. By the end of my second week on the job, in something akin to desperation, I elected to give the column an entirely new feel. The technique I would employ to that end, I regarded at that moment strictly as a stopgap measure; a version of it had, after all, been used for years by edgy political writers, and never, I thought, satisfyingly. No matter how many twists and spins I gave an item, no matter how tantalizing the tease, who in hell would care about a report with no names attached?

Which, I suppose, is just about the spirit in which the wheel was invented. The analogy is not inappropriate. The blind item has, by now, become so much a commonplace, so much a fixture of the social environment, that to the younger than elderly it must seem ludicrous that it ever had to be launched at all. I can only assure them that at the time, and to my own surprise, it was in some quarters viewed as an innovation as daring and as outrageous as the shimmy. Indeed, when Clarke spotted the first in print—"It has come to our attention that a certain show gal is now carrying more for her married producer than just a torch"—he was incoherent with fear.

What, in his panic, he failed to recognize was something I had suspected from the start: that, legally, the technique was foolproof. Who in the world would volunteer, under oath, that he was the party so named? And if the sorry soul did step forward, what was to prevent me from professing never to have heard of the wretch?

What it took me slightly longer to appreciate was the impact of the blind item on the reader. Used judiciously, properly crafted, it turned out to be every bit as effective as the most scrupulously researched report; often, even more so. The aura of mystery generated by a single sentence could be very nearly irresistible. When I queried "Which act at the Palace is shelling out for hecklers to bury which other act at the Palace?", people *wondered* about it. When I noted that there was major gambling action in the back room of a certain swank eatery off lower Madison Avenue, everyone who had been anywhere near lower Madison the previous month felt special.

It is an odd thing about success in the newspaper business; though it is very difficult to measure, it is almost impossible not to sense. And it came at me now in a tidal rush; in the way strangers reacted to my name; in the deference of other reporters; in the flood of tipsters suddenly at hand; above all, in the way I was catered to by those who saw themselves as potential objects of my attention.

However, almost simultaneously I became aware of something else, something for which I was utterly unprepared: that many of the performers, producers, politicians, sportsmen, society types who courted my favor viewed me with suspicion, even outright loathing. In a sense, of course, their attitude was not wholly displeasing; as a favorable mention by Pond was likely to boost a career, so a slam could be a devastating setback. This is the way I wanted it, the way I designed it to be.

But I was not a gratuitously cruel man, nor an unfeeling one. Almost without exception, those assailed under my by-line wrote their own tickets; I rarely invented their trespasses, I merely reported them. And it alarmed me that no longer was I being measured by the same yardstick as other men.

It was in this atmosphere, at once heady and unsettling, that I chose to take my boldest step to date in my inquiry into the 1919 World Series; to wit, that several days after my return from the Republican shindig in Chicago I made known to my sources within the city's criminal fraternity my interest in the matter. As I had supposed, these were more eager than ever to find themselves in my good graces. In less than a day I had in my possession a name that I had been assured was of value: that of Abe Attell.

I knew all about Attell, of course. A decade earlier, as my career on the sporting page had been picking up steam, his as a stylish and popular featherweight had been drawing to a close, and several times in subsequent years, with deadlines bearing down upon me, I had had occasion to write him up. As luck would have it, my prose had not been gentle. Upon leaving the ring, Attell, like so many in his misbegotten profession, lacking (as I once put it) "the will and the skill of an honest bricklayer," had aligned himself with the unsavory elements moving to control the sport. I had, indeed, actually been moved to rechristen him "The Little Tramp," suggesting that if Charles Chaplin had any objection, Attell doubtless stood ready to fight him for the title. "Abe," I wrote, "has always been a sucker for sure things."

Who could ever have imagined that there would come the day when I might *need* the man?

I was, under the circumstances, most gratified to learn that Attell had agreed to meet with me. Being an instinctively pragmatic creature, I reassured myself, he was certainly not inclined to dwell on ancient slights. And, indeed, when I spotted him at a back table at Lindy's—Bald Jack Rose had set up the rendezvous—he waved and offered something very like a smile.

"Thanks for coming, Abe," I said, taking a seat across from him. "You look good. You look like you could step into a ring tonight."

"With Charlie Chaplin? And you, Pond—you look like garbage."

"Well," I replied, "I suppose I don't take very good care of myself." This was not going well at all. "Listen, Champ, why don't we forget all that? Maybe we can help each other."

"*You* help *me?*" He laughed metallically.

"I don't care if you like me or not, Abe, that isn't the point."

"I *don't* like you. I . . ."

"Good."

"Don't cut me off, wise guy. I only showed up to give you something you had coming a long time."

I tried, and failed, to appear nonchalant. "I'm not going to fight you, Abe."

"You wanna bet, chump?"

And, before I had time to react, he was on his feet, letting fly with a punch to my jaw powerful beyond reckoning. I must have blacked out for a moment, for I recall no sound—not glasses smashing, nor chairs overturning, nor my own head walloping into the plaster wall. When, after a few seconds, I was once again semi-lucid, I was aware of blood in my mouth, and of a throbbing at the temples, and of the tiny man hovering above me menacingly, his face a picture of scorn. "And this," he added, offering a brutal kick to my side, before striding toward the door, "is for what you wrote yesterday about Sid Gottfried."

I have come to recognize, of course, that this last was comical. That a man like Attell would take it upon himself to defend a renowned gladhander against the assertion that he'd been party to a "marital splat" was the kind of screwball thing that, in later years, I'd have dined on for weeks, or perhaps even have inserted into the column.

But it is a measure of my emotional state at that moment that it did not amuse me in the least; that, in fact, as I sat at home nursing severely bruised ribs, it aroused within me feelings of intense indignation and self-pity.

Throughout my career I had, you see, been able to remain on relatively cordial terms with the rest of the world. Now, it was daily becoming more clear, that was forever behind me. Abuse, as much as sycophancy and invitations to dinner, came with my new territory.

And, in case I was in need of even more evidence, barely a week hence I found myself in the midst of an even more dispiriting situation, one involving my late friend Joe Ellwell. Indeed, in its wake I would even be moved to briefly consider surrendering the column. No longer, it seemed, were even my most selfless impulses—those involving loyalty and gratitude—immune to challenge.

It would be imprecise to say I had known Ellwell intimately. Though we were both members of the Studio Club, though we ran in more or less the same circles, though we resided within blocks of one another, we had had, as it happened, only one conversation of any length during the entirety of our association. Still, so memorable had that encounter been that it was without hesitation that I characterized him, then as now, as considerably more than an acquaintance.

The conversation in question had occurred almost precisely a year earlier, on the evening of June 30, 1919, at the bar of the Hotel Breton Hall. I recall the date with certainty because it was the date itself that had drawn me there, along with the rest of those who packed the place; at midnight, this bar, like every other legal watering hole in the land, would close its doors.

It was not until I had placed my order that I remarked on the identity of the man beside me, elegant in pinstripes and spats, calmly sipping a gin and tonic.

"How are you?" I slurred. Though I was a man not given to reckless excess, the significance of this instant in the social history of the realm had been much advertised, and I was giving it its due.

"Very well, very well." Ellwell smiled. "Quite well."

"Hot time in the old town," I observed.

"Yes," he agreed, with an indulgent smile, and offered to pay for my next drink.

Ellwell's smoothness was entirely in character; this was, after all, the fellow who had parlayed skill at cards into a home in Palm Beach and a string of racehorses. The several times I had dealt with him previously, his superciliousness had, in fact, struck me as faintly unattractive; or perhaps those of us obliged to sweat our way through life need to feel that way about ease. In any case, at the moment, in the midst of the desolation that surrounded us, the quality was actually reassuring.

That perhaps is what led me, as the evening progressed, to unburden myself of another matter, one which in recent months had lain far more heavily upon me than any issue of public moment; the matter of my association with my wife.

The problem was no longer simply one of impatience with the woman. She had become, rather, an incessant irritation, a permanent cloud in my midst. The difficulty between Edith and myself was not something we spoke of; we spoke only when absolutely necessary.

Only once in recent months had our situation been alluded to, then only obliquely. Edith had just returned from a suffragists rally in Albany that, I had learned via the wires, had turned into a virtual riot when local college students released ten thousand mice amongst the gathered females.

"Say," I remarked good-naturedly, "did you bring home a mouse for dinner? Or am I supposed to forage for myself again?"

"Catch one yourself," she hissed. Then she paused. "Why do you make a gag of everything?"

To this I made no response.

"I know you have contempt for me. Why don't you just say so?"

The answer to that, quite simply, as I pointed out to Ellwell, was tact. Where I grew up, certain things were not said, even in the arena of domestic relations, and other things were not done. My own parents had endured a marriage quite as unrewarding as my own, as silent and as painful, and would, I supposed, in the end, not have wanted it otherwise.

Ellwell grinned at this. "These are modern times, Pond."

"That's easy for you to say, a gay bachelor."

He laughed. "I'll let you in on a secret. I've got a wife, all right. She lives right across town. Only I haven't had to look at her in five years." He nudged me with an elbow. "Once a woman gets past thirty, there isn't so much to look at anyway."

"It's not just that," I said. "I've got a little boy. He's four years old now."

"So do I, Pond. Well, not so little—he's fourteen or fifteen already." He paused and raised his glass in a mock toast. "Here's to Florence. I am told she's doing a splendid job with him."

He leaned close. "Stop *worrying* so much, for heaven's sake. Think about yourself a little."

It was, I confess, somewhat startling to run across an individual for whom things truly were as simple as they seemed, a man seemingly immune to regret, who blithely sidestepped the moral dilemmas placed in each of our paths. But it was also, in a curious way, inspiring.

I will not say that my decision, shortly thereafter, to move out of the house had its genesis in this colloquy; that determination had been years in the making. Rather, for a time the encounter was for me a kind of touchstone, something to be referred back to in moments of reflection or doubt.

And now, abruptly, in June of 1920, I found myself in a position to render him a service in return—and at the moment when the poor fellow most desperately needed it. In the two weeks since his murder, you see, Joe Ellwell had become notorious. Day by day, as every soul the dead man had known was descended upon, the specifics of his remarkable existence were becoming public, and seldom had the headline authors had more to work with. According to Ellwell's chauffeur, for instance, no fewer than seven young women, perhaps as many as twelve, possessed keys to his brownstone on West Seventieth Street; a number of these were said to be very comfortably married. A friend revealed that the wives of prominent businessmen regularly held "bridge parties"—the term was understood to have been used loosely—in his private quarters. Others spoke of his predilection for virgins. "Joe always cast off a girl when he got tired of her," chimed in the dead man's estranged wife. "I can't imagine the promises he must have made." Then, too, there was Ellwell's vastly complicated business life, and the intimations of dirty card games, fixed horse races, even rum-running.

The Ellwell story was, in brief, one of those very occasional pieces of life designed to delight the most adamant reader of fiction. It did not lack even for comic relief: found (alongside a blackjack and a pink silk negligee with the monogram removed) in the bedroom closet of the man described by one former lover as having "possessed a manly beauty so great it was enthralling," was a trunk packed with "first aids to masculine beauty"—several pairs of false teeth and forty wigs.

However, my own Ellwell piece, composed while I was still smarting from Attell's assault—a week before I was to depart for the Democratic Convention in San Francisco—did not mention the wigs, or the negligee, or horses, or businessmen's wives. Entitled "Ellwell—The Way I Knew Him," it described a decent and thoroughly misunderstood man.

So starkly did this piece stand in counterpoint to the prevailing clamor, so convinced was I that I had served my subject admirably, that it was not until it saw print that I came to grips with a horrifying fact: that, as far as the rest of the world was concerned, the way I knew Ellwell had been hardly at all.

Perhaps I overreacted to this; overreaction was certainly in my nature. But I was instantly seized by the notion—to me it was a diamond-hard certainty—that all those many souls who wished me ill would pounce upon this chance to humiliate me. And, indeed, over the next twenty-four hours it came to my attention that the piece *was* being widely snickered over; that even some of Ellwell's friends had been taken aback by it; that it was being used to denigrate all the rest of my work. One of the few Hearst men with whom I was still in contact informed me that McCullum was, in fact, considering excerpting a paragraph or two of the column for inclusion in my former paper's daily Ellwell roundup.

On the morning I obtained this intelligence, hemorrhaging within, I almost instinctively abandoned my desk and began heading uptown, in the direction of the Polo Grounds. Long before I had discovered the therapeutic properties inherent in attending a ballgame: nowhere in the vast metropolis was a man under pressure more likely to find a semblance of peace; nowhere, certainly, would I be able to submerge myself within so vast an assemblage of souls so unconcerned with the small, bitter world I inhabited.

Then, too—for even in distress I was no idler—I had a bit of unfinished business on the premises. On hand to play the hometown Yankees that Thursday were the Tigers of Detroit, who had, by way of Cleveland and Philadelphia, followed me to town.

My intuition had been faultless. Within minutes of parking my car in the lot at 157th Street and Eighth Avenue and attaching myself to the throng heading toward the stadium Speedway, I was already feeling better about things; within half an hour, my troubles were very distant, indeed. By the time I caught sight of Ty Cobb, sitting on the visitors bench during batting practice, leisurely working a wad of chewing tobacco and picking his fingernails with a penknife, I was very nearly chipper.

"Hey, Ty," I said, approaching him, "how's tricks?"

It had, it is true, been half a dozen years since he had laid eyes upon me. Still, to my mind, we had parted on cordial terms, and I was surprised to elicit no response but a glance and a nod.

Eyeing the object in his hand, I took a seat a dozen feet from him on the wooden plank. "I saw you the week before last out in Chicago. Against Kerr."

"Yeah?" He spat a wad of gummy brown saliva at my feet.

"Three hits that day. Felsch robbed you of number four."

"And I saw what you wrote in the papers yesterday. You really believe that crap?"

Baseball was, at that moment, in the midst of a revolution of its own—one launched by Babe Ruth and his home run bat—and it was being bandied about in the press box that Ty Cobb had adjusted to the game's altered circumstances. No longer, in an era of power, could Cobb hope to be the diamond force he had been. Already in his mid-thirties, perhaps a step slower, he was said to have eased up on the world, perhaps even on himself.

Now, seeing him in the flesh, I knew it was a lie.

"I knew the man, Ty," I said with some irritation. "Did you?"

"Don't tell me," he sneered. "I know a crumb bum when I hear about one."

He rose to his feet, folded his knife into the pocket of his flannels and trotted off in the direction of the visiting clubhouse, deep in left centerfield.

I followed him, and five minutes later found him sitting before his locker.

"I'd like to talk to you about something, Ty."

"I got a game to play. Make it fast."

"I mean afterwards. It's rather important."

Abruptly, he was up again, moving briskly across the room and into the trainer's area, off limits to the press. But a moment later he peered out at me, tobacco juice dribbling down his chin. "After the game you take me back to the hotel in a taxi. I'm gettin' too old to ride the damn team bus."

We were clear of the ballpark traffic and moving down Broadway when I posed the question. Cobb was at the wheel of my Chalmers, a strategic move on my part.

"What," I said, "do you make of the World Series rumors?"

He cast me a hard look. "Nothing."

"Nothing? You mean you haven't heard that . . ."

"Can't you get it through your thick skull I ain't gonna talk about it? Why the hell don't you bastards let them White Sox be?" He paused. "You can print *that*, if you got the guts."

"That's all you have to say on the subject?"

"That's it, Mr. Big New York City Reporter."

I hesitated a long moment. "There's something else I'm curious about. There's some talk that maybe your club has been mixed up in some things, also."

I had edged far into my corner before saying it, and placed a hand upon the door handle, but there was no outburst.

"Who told you that hogwash?" he said emphatically.

"A couple of fellows."

"Who?"

"I can't tell you that, Ty. But fellows in a position to know. Ballplayers."

"So you believe it, that's what you're telling me?" There was, faintly but beyond question, a hint of distress in the question.

"I don't know, Ty." I stopped. "The game I heard about was last September. Against Cleveland."

There was a long pause as this registered. And then the facade crumbled. "I get what you're sayin'! *You're sayin' Ty Cobb did something crooked!*" He stepped on the gas pedal and the automobile lurched forward. "That's what you're sayin', ain't it, you fuckin' lily-liver?"

"Not exactly, I . . ."

"Ty Cobb, who *worships* the game! That's what you're sayin', ain't it?"

"I'm only telling you what I . . ."

"Why would I do that? You think I'm dumb or something?"

But the fact was inescapable, the man was no longer protesting the point so much as pleading with me. And, as we drove down Broadway, his sense of urgency only seemed to increase. Indeed, by the time we arrived at his hotel—the Ansonia, on Seventy-fourth Street —there were tears in his eyes.

This I was not aware of until he shut off the engine and turned to face me. The sight was frankly embarrassing.

"I never bet on a game in my life," he said.

"Take it easy, Ty," I said softly.

"All the Cobbs cry easy." He dried his eyes roughly on his sleeves. "So what's this all about? You gonna print this, are you?"

"I don't know yet." I paused just an instant. "I'm still looking for help on the World Series."

Odd as it may seem, this development was a source of only limited comfort at the time. I had not lied to Cobb; I seriously doubted whether I could, in fact, risk accusing baseball's greatest star of even the most minor transgression. More to the point, the Ellwell business was nowhere near concluded. I had, you see, in an act that might well be seen as lunatic, begun the column I'd handed in that very morning with a blind item suggesting the identity of my late friend's mysterious "Pink Pajama Girl," the owner of the famous negligee. My intention had been to reestablish my reportorial credentials on the story. So strikingly at odds was this report with the tone of my earlier Ellwell piece, however, that it served only to compound the original gaffe.

The debacle was such that even Clarke was moved to a certain sympathy for me. Never again, I swore to him, as the latest reaction washed over me, would I fall prey to the easy sentiment that had landed me in this fix. Never again would I forget what my readers expected of me.

"*Your readers,*" he sneered. "Tomorrow, what you wrote yesterday will be as hazy to your readers as the Civil War."

I looked at him uncertainly.

"You're going to be in California for how long?"

"A week."

"Your first trip?"

"Yes."

"Why don't you lose it," he said, the soundest advice I'd heard yet, "and have yourself a decent time for a change?"

And so I might have, had it not been for a very nasty run-in out there with the writer Ring Lardner.

I do not mean to go on in this vein. I am not, and certainly was not then, a bellyacher; to the contrary, I have always looked upon the breed with a special contempt. Obviously I was a fortunate man. In a world that stands in awe of even modest celebrity, I was rapidly becoming a luminary. Moreover, at that moment I stood on the threshold of one of the great coups of my career.

Still, to find myself misunderstood, *maltreated*, by a man such as Lardner was another object lesson, and one of considerable force. Lardner was, you see, as unlikely an instructor in the ways of the world as I was a pupil. Reed-tall and gaunt as an El Greco, possessed of a manner at once sheepish and solemn—was it Robert Sherwood who so aptly compared it with Buster Keaton's?—he was as inoffensive a sort as one was likely to encounter.

Lardner's work was, of course, hugely celebrated at the time, but he had not even a writer's arrogance. In fact, that he was so widely touted as a popular genius—his witticisms much repeated, his style compared by critics to those of Twain and Ade—served only to embarrass the man, and to deepen his already profound sense of cynicism.

I liked that about him. It is the exceptional fellow who is able to view with dispassion his place in a razzmatazz world. I like to think it is as I would have been, had I been in the same position.

I had been acquainted with Lardner almost a decade, our paths having initially crossed on our respective baseball beats, but his extreme shyness and hangman's demeanor had been formidable obstacles to intimacy. Still, even then, five years before he would be well known, he had interested me. I vividly recall, on a visit to Chicago, running across a Lardner column describing, in most personal terms, his depthless affection for the national game; it resided, he wrote, in the fact that it was the only institution on this woebegotten continent in which a man rose or fell strictly on his own merits. The piece gave me goosebumps. That was precisely as I felt!

His baseball reportage had, in my opinion, been the best work he had ever done, far more heartfelt than his much-praised fiction. But he was past any kind of honest labor now. These days, he had but to pound out words, and spruce them up with an occasional "Lardnerism," and a large check in his name would be dispensed forthwith. Thus had he assumed his place among the nation's literary elite; thus was his already low opinion of contemporary standards, and of himself, regularly confirmed.

As it turned out, Lardner was on just such a hack errand at the moment in question. I discovered this at the convention's opening session when, from the press stand, I spotted him across the convention floor, gazing mournfully toward the rafters.

"Hey," I poked my neighbor, "look who's down there. Ring Lardner."

"Sure. He's here for the Bell Syndicate."

"Otherwise"—I rolled my eyes—"known as Bell's Palsy. Christ, what a life!"

But I was, in truth, quite pleased to see him. The business of covering an extravaganza—a convention, a World Series, a championship fight—is unwieldly for any reporter, but for a man charged with conveying a *feel* for the event and its principal players, it is doubly vexing. Years before, I had hit upon a technique for use under such circumstances that had served me admirably: to attach myself to a single notable individual and allow the reader to ride on his back. This time the pickings had looked slim—but, all at once, I had my boy.

Lardner was not averse to the proposition, but he was not exactly amenable to it either. True to form, he heard me out, his sad black eyes fixed upon my eager blue ones, then announced his decision—"I guess it'll bother me less than it'll bother your readers"—and made good his escape.

San Francisco was not, in my view, the paradise its boosters were already so incessantly proclaiming it to be; I was in full agreement with the observation of Tammany boss Charley Murphy, who, having endured an hour of such chatter from a local whilst trapped aboard one of those vessels that roam its harbor, at last cut him off with a terse "I *see*, it's a big bay." But the city was extraordinary in another respect. Barely sixteen years past the disaster that had left it a ruin, it had been reborn as the most thoroughly modern dot on the national map. All around us were striking new edifices of limestone or brick. A handsome electric transport system was in place. There were more motion picture palaces in the downtown alone than in many cities twice the size. In the convention hall, too, were to be found a dazzling array of twentieth-century wonders; a loudspeaking system, a bank of telephones specifically designed for long distances, noiseless typewriters. Even as we sat watching the candidates —McAdoo, Palmer, Smith, Cox, Davis—being placed in nomination, even before one raucous floor demonstration had flowed into the next, the news was being sped to the world via a telegraphic setup hitherto unimagined.

Yet there we sat our first day together, Lardner and myself, for almost ten hours, exchanging not a word.

Eventually, inevitably, I found myself wondering: how had I offended this remarkable fellow? Had I done something in the old days? Did he regard me as an interloper? Had he, perhaps, seen something in my column slighting someone he knew? This last, I concluded, after giving the matter considerable thought, was it. Several weeks before, there had appeared a blind item about the nocturnal wanderings of the producer Morris Gest. Goddamn it, talk about lousy luck, my companion had once worked with Gest!

It was with a sense of resignation that I filed out of the hall beside him that evening, a pair of glum pots in a sea of animated faces.

"Well," I gave it a feeble try, "who do you suppose it will be?"

Lardner did not reply for a long moment. "The question," he said at last, his voice so soft it was barely audible above the din, "is which compromise candidate intends to compromise himself the most."

And right there I had my answer: the fellow had been anxious to please all along, he simply had not wanted to disappoint me. It had never even crossed his mind that I had been out to steal his thunder. Indeed, it turned out that his disinterest in the proceedings was almost total. Never mind that arrayed below us was the most varied menagerie of political animals in memory: Ku Klux Klanners and would-be anarchists; Bible-thumping Prohibitionists and big city saloon keepers; public men ranging in age and outlook from William Jennings Bryan, who had carried the party's standard twenty-four years earlier, to Franklin Roosevelt, who would carry it twenty-four years hence; and, for the first time ever, by the hundreds, sedate and whooping it up like veterans, women. But never mind any of that. Lardner was planning to devote his initial column to Mrs. Uda Waldrop, the convention organist, whose incessant rendering of "Dixie" over the loudspeaking system had nearly routed him from the hall.

My own first effort, which I telephoned into the office the following morning, read as follows:

SAN FRANCISCO, JULY 1   What's up, pal o' mine? Listen close . . .

"This burg's been cockeyed since the big shake and burn," says
Ring Lardner, "and you can quote me on it!" Ring's sporting a Palmer
boater, a Cox watch fob and a "Mac'll Do" pin all at once 'cause, see,
he's been doing his own lobbying job—against the rule forbidding
smoking in the convention arena! "Hooch was one thing," says Friend
Ring, "but now they've taken away the air I breathe!"

But there's fire around here even without the smoke. Confirmation
of the Cox divorce rumors has his men in a sweat and a half. But that'll
be just the start. Come closer, pal. Any minute now it'll break that one
of the other front and center runners has been stepping out on Missus
Front Runner. The fem delegates, bless 'em, ain't gonna go for *that*
one little bit. . . .

Not that that'll faze the animales in attendance. Word around here
is that there are two varieties of male delegate around here: some are
at large and the rest have their wives with 'em!

Who can say where it'll end? Not your Gov, and mine, that's for
sure. Seems Our Al got a wire from a certain Broadway Big—initials
A.J.—asking who to put his dough on. "Tell *me*, wise guy," sped the
reply East. . . .

Say, Gov, try on this derby for size. A couple of your own bosses
on the floor are giving their all behind the scenes for the darkest horse
of all: Woodrow Wilson!!

Not that the Hearst press cares about *that*. No, sireeee. Since no one
seems to want him on the ticket, local boy Willie has gone sour on all
donkeydom. In the *Chronicle* out here, Warren Harding's name now
comes with a comma attached, as in ". . ., *our next president* . . ." The
main *Chronicle* headline for the opening day of the convention?
"Three Die In Blazing Airplane" . . .

. . . But, then, this is California, where fruits are borne or bread.
Every Eastern jaw is agape. On the beaches here, bathing costumes are
a new thing in the altogether, and wait'll you get a peek!!!! At the
dance halls here, people move in ways we never heard about back
home. And Volstead? Who's that? Why, there's so much hooch
around here that the dry plank is waterlogged. We hear that half the
delegates are planning to return home via Canada—and not for the
scenery, either. Guess all that tsk-tsking about that famous back room
in Chicago builds up a healthy thirst! . . . By the by, they're talking
up our own Gov as the Great Wet Hope. Must've gotten a look at that
nose, huh Al?

The cheeriest news yet comes from a psychic named Louis Benjamin. Abe Lincoln has gone over to the Dems! Seems Abe got Lou over the psychic phone and spilled the beans—he's all hot for the League of Nations!!!

Now there's the kind of item that gets our pal Lardner's attention, and fast. "Sure thing," says Ring. "But what I want to know is where does he stand on the smoking issue???"

When I showed Lardner a copy of my effort, he read it carefully, then offered me the politest of smiles. "Didn't you used to work for Hearst?"

"Yes." I smiled back. "Emphasis on 'used to.' "

He studied me a moment. "That's what I thought."

If, at that juncture, the ice between us was not yet broken, it appeared, at any rate, to have cracked. Over the next couple of days, sitting beside one another in the hall, as the presidential balloting began, and then moved into a stalemate, I actually sensed a certain rapport—of the marooned sailor variety—developing between us. "I am seriously thinking," I recall him deadpanning on the afternoon preceding the July fourth recess, "of dropping out of the race."

It was against this backdrop that I dared to suggest that we take advantage of the free day for an outing.

"I have a couple of bottles of scotch in my room," he said. "That's my outing."

"I had in mind Santa Cruz or Monterey. One of those Spanish places. It'll be on the *Daily News.*"

"My favorite is Los Gatos. The Cats." He paused. "It's on the Bell Syndicate. We both feel better when I spend their money."

How Ty Cobb discovered my whereabouts in San Francisco I still have no idea; I know for a fact that no one at the *Daily News* passed him the information. Indeed, when the telephone girl at the Hotel California gave me the message—that I had missed a long-distance call, but Operator Number Six in Detroit, a Mr. Keeney, would put me through to my party—I allowed myself only the faintest hope that the caller might have been Cobb.

But with the first syllables over the transcontinental line, all doubt vanished.

"Who's there?"

"It's Luther Pond, Ty."

"I thought so. Get out your pad."

"I've got it right here."

If Cobb remained troubled by his performance at our previous encounter, the fact was far beyond my not inconsiderable powers of detection. Never, in my experience with him, had the man been more self-possessed, never had his tone been more glacial.

"These," he said, "are the ones that were in on it. Cicotte. Gandil. Felsch. Williams. Jackson. Risberg. Maybe Weaver and maybe McMullin."

"How'd you find that out?"

"That's for me to know, Mr. Reporter. I got friends. You want me to do all your work for you?"

"How much did they get?"

"That's all you're getting outta me," he said, with unmistakable finality. "I got nothing else to tell you. And if my name is anywhere near this, you're gonna pay, you hear me?"

"It won't be, Ty." I paused. "I wish I could shake your hand."

Even all these years later, I can hear the snort on the other end of the line. "Just you don't ever bother me again, you sonovabitch!"

After I had hung up, I sat for a long while on the edge of the bed, then called up for dinner in my room, then read a bit of fiction. I was altogether calm. But somewhere within, I was certainly dealing with the information, sorting it out and weighing it, for when I at last switched off the bedside lamp, I was so agitated that I was unable to find sleep for five hours.

In truth, my role in the unravelling of the Black Sox case would result almost entirely from that brief conversation. Over subsequent months I would, of course, continue to ask questions and pursue leads, and I would stumble upon a few ancillary facts that would, eventually, serve to flesh out the affair in its human dimension. But I would come up with nothing that would make the case against the criminal ballplayers the slightest bit more convincing to the average newspaper buyer; nor would any other newshound. The fuller story would, indeed, only emerge when drawn out of the culprits themselves, by subpoena and outright threat.

I realized, however, that first evening in San Francisco, that the value of the information in my possession was beyond measure. I did not need corroboration. Virtually alone among my colleagues, I was at liberty to *suggest* elements of the story. It remained only for me to decide precisely how to do so, and when.

I was still alive with excitement when Lardner stopped by the Hotel California at eight-thirty the next morning in a rented Mercer sport. What was astonishing was that he appeared to be in spirits nearly as high as my own.

"Where to?" I inquired, sliding in beside him.

He grinned. "A place called La Tassajara. I like their come-on in the *Chronicle.*" He tossed me a copy of the previous day's paper, folded back to the resorts page. One ad was circled in thick pencil: "La Tassajara. Mountain Fun. Good Eats. (No Tuberculars.)"

"I think," said Lardner, pulling away from the curb, "we are in for one of those fabled California days."

And so we might have been. As we motored south, our hair flaring in the wind, a bonded bottle between us, we talked as easily as we had yet. The subject, which I had raised with rather less nonchalance than I'd have liked, was baseball. At the wheel, Lardner was increasingly animated as he reminisced about assorted diamond characters he had known, and particularly dramatic contests he had witnessed. "I am," he noted at one point, "appearances notwithstanding, one of the very few men who can tell you honestly that he's achieved his ambition in life. Growing up, that was all I really wished for, to see all the ballgames I wanted."

But after a very pleasant hour thus passed, I am afraid I went a wee bit too far.

"You covered the Hitless Wonders, didn't you?" I prompted during a lull. The reference was to the remarkable White Sox championship team of 1906.

"No, that was a couple of years before my time."

I paused. "I guess you know this current bunch pretty well, though."

Silently, I cursed myself; this of the most famous White Sox rooter in the nation, a man known as an intimate of Gleason and Cicotte and half a dozen others.

"Yes," he replied blandly. "Pretty well."

I waited a beat. "You've heard the rumors, of course."

"Yes."

For several minutes we drove on in silence, my companion once again wearing the stricken look one associates with the graveside.

"It's a tragedy," I observed at last, softly.

He made no reply.

"How many do you think might have been involved?"

"I don't know."

"Cicotte?"

"I don't know." He momentarily took his eyes off the road and looked at me; what I saw within them made me distinctly ill at ease. "Are you," he said, with unexpected sharpness, "interviewing me?"

"No, of course not."

"Good."

But Lardner had even less stomach for confrontation than did I. After several minutes he suddenly began—if this is an appropriate characterization of the sound—to sing. The melody belonged to the popular number "I'm Forever Blowing Bubbles," but Lardner's rendition, deep and terribly, terribly slow, in fact had the quality of a dirge.

> I'm forever blowing ballgames,
> Pretty ballgames in the air.
> I come from Chi,
> I hardly try,
> Just take my swings and fade and die.
> Well, fortune's coming my way,
> That's why I don't care.
> Yes, I'm forever blowing ballgames,
> Pretty ballgames in the air.

I was flabbergasted. Was it conceivable Lardner did not know who I was? What sort of reaction could he have anticipated?

"That's wonderful," I enthused. "Any more to it?"

> I'm forever blowing ballgames,
> Pretty ballgames in the air.

My feet are lead,
My arm is dead,
(About my heart, the less is said.)
Still, I'm a happy loser,
Who am I to whine?
For I'm forever blowing ballgames,
And the sports, they treat me fine.

It was harder than one might imagine to keep those lyrics straight in my head; for the next half hour I was, after all, obliged to make conversation with their author. Even now I cannot say with utter certainty I got them down absolutely right. But I did my damnedest. When we at last stopped for gasoline in the town of Gilroy, I excused myself forthwith and hurried off to the men's room.

It was there, in an open stall, that Lardner found me, pants down, pencil in my hand, my pad open upon my knees.

"I just wanted to write it down," I explained. "For my own information."

For a long moment he simply stared at me, seemingly less angry than perplexed.

"While it was still fresh," I added.

He did not budge.

"Ring, what are you doing?"

"Me? Just trying to get what makes you tick."

"What's that supposed to mean?"

"Is there anything at all that embarrasses you? Is there anything you could do that you couldn't justify to yourself?"

I do not easily take offense, and I tried not to now. But I had my limits. I knew full well what I was about; with myself, especially, I do not dissemble.

"You don't know the first thing about me," I replied.

"Sure I do. It's men like you that run the world."

"I am only doing my job," I snapped, "same as you."

"So I see." He moved toward the door; obviously, he would be returning to San Francisco alone. "Be sure to flush when you finish doing it."

The most unfortunate aspect of the incident, in retrospect, is that it was so wholly unnecessary. I certainly meant Ring Lardner no harm. To the contrary, at the time I had every intention of continuing to flatter him in print.

And, indeed, three and a half months later, when I had occasion to spring his little ditty upon the world, the item did his reputation every bit as much good as it did mine. This I pointed out to him in the note I sent accompanying the item. But he did not even have the good grace to answer back. And I never saw fit to give him a favorable mention in the column again.

I can only hope that eventually, upon reflection, he came to understand that the loss was far more his than mine.

Nineteen Twenty

by George D. Weaver

Y ou know what they say, sometimes it pours instead of just rains. Well, that is exactly what was about to happen to your pal, Buck Weaver. And it has not really stopped raining on me yet.

I guess I may be sounding a little sorry for my own self here. Usually I do not, but sometimes a fellow just cannot stop himself. For when I get in that certain kind of mood, just thinking about what has happened gets me miffed and sorrowful all at the same time. That is just the way it is.

The queer part is that for a while, I thought '20 was going to be a wonderful year. And not only for yours truly, but for all Americans. That is how it was advertised. After all, here we were in a brand new decade. The war was passed, business was hopping, we was even getting to vote in a new president. As for baseball, people said we was smack in the middle of a new age of gold. Never before had there been such a mess of big stars all working at once, including Cobb, and Ruth, and Shoeless, and Johnson, and Sisler and Speaker. And that is only talking about the American League!

And us Sox was to be one of the main parts of it. Indeed, looking at it from the inside, things looked even brighter to us Pale Hose than ever. For the club no longer had a big bully named Gandil hanging around, giving you the jumps. What had happened is that after that '19 season, when he had got his contract in the mails, with its usual small terms, Chick had tore it right up. He wrote to Comiskey that he wanted ten thousand per annum or no dice. Well, naturally The Old Roman figured it as a bluff and would not give it to him. But when the '20 season got started, Chick did just what he said, and stayed home in California.

You can bet that stunned a lot of other people, too, besides Comiskey. Even the scribes could not believe that a guy only thirty-one years young would quit, just like that. Of course, they did not know how much Chick had bagged back in October when we was blowing the series. It was thirty-five thousand dollars!

Do not look again, your peepers have read it perfectly correct. See, when the gamblers had at last paid off, from their winnings, Gandil had used his slot as master of ceremonies to skin the other boys. Except for Knuckles, who of course had already got his ten grand, and Risberg, who ended up with fifteen, not one of the fixers got paid as promised. Some of the fellows collected five thousand, and a few got none at all. As a matter of fact, this was probably another reason why Gandil flew that coop.

But, all in all, if you add in the pros with the cons, it was good riddance to him. Shano Collins, who took over his spot at first, may not have been so strong with the lumber, but at least you could grin around the guy, or make a little joke, without someone barking your head off.

I am not saying that suddenly it was hearts and roses around the club. The ill feelings in that bunch stuck out like a canker sore on an engaged girl's lip. I am only saying it was a relief compared to before. That may not sound like much to you, but you were not around before.

Personally speaking, I started off that season of 1920 in high style. This was my ninth year in the fast company and, no questions about it, by now I was definitely one of the crackerjacks of the game. Day in and out, I showed hustle out there, and smarts, and enough guts for an army. At the bat, I could swat the pellet to any part of the field I wished, with power or without! Running bases, I was like a weasel, and like a cat in the field. Maybe it had taken a little while, but there I was, on the top of the heap!

Nor from the looks of it, did the team miss the lemon even a little, for we were winning as regular as ever. Most of us fellows had played together for so long, that by now we worked together as smooth as any nine that ever put on a uniform. Including those '27 Yankees people are always getting sappy over. They might have had Ruth and Gehrig and Meusel and Lazzeri, but they also had a few bums, whereas us, we had no weak spots at all. Not one. Even Cocky Collins, who has spent the whole rest of his life putting the knock on us so-called Black Sox, had to admit that that team was the greatest in all of history. If it had not been for what happened, you know how many of that bunch would have landed in the Hall of Fame? Six, that is how many! And I am not even counting in such guys as Felsch, Risberg and Williams, that had not yet played enough seasons to show all of their stuff.

But I know it is dumb to talk that way, or even to dream of it. It did not happen. And I guess I knew right from the time of that '19 season that it would not, and that our days had numbers.

You may think I am spouting bull when I say such a thing. How could I know in advance when nobody else did? And it is true that when the series was done, most of the suspicions went away with it. Oh, there may still have been a few rumors here and there, but what does that mean? Even The Old Roman, who at first had held up sending out the World Series checks to the players that looked fishy, just in case they got nabbed, went ahead and sent them out.

Indeed, the only writer who continued kicking up any fuss at all was Hughie Fullerton, here in Chi, and all he could find to print was that there had been lots of low types hanging about the series, and perhaps something foul had gone on. In other words, it was so mealy-mouthed that only a simpleton could take it serious. Right away, Comiskey called in the other scribes, and laughed, and offered ten grand if anyone could show the series had not been one hundred percent on the square. Naturally, he had no takers.

Meantime, the other scribes jumped all over Fullerton. "After each World Series," as they put it in *The Baseball Magazine*, "the public is deluged with wild stories emanating from writers, whose real duty it should be to aid baseball, instead of trying to destroy the confidence of the public by yarns about gambling made out of whole cloth." And that was just the start. "President Charles A. Comiskey," said a scribe called Obenshain, in *The Sporting News*, "has made a proposition that ought to mean pretty pickings—if the peddlers of scandal can make good. Because a lot of dirty, long-nosed, thick-

lipped and strong-smelling gamblers butted into the World Series—
an American event by the way—and some of said gamblers got
crossed, stories were peddled that there was something wrong with
the games that were played . . . Comiskey has met that by offering
ten thousand dollars for any sort of a clue that will bear out such a
charge. He might as well have offered a million, for there will be no
takers, because there is no such evidence, except in the mucking
minds of the stinkers who—because they are crooked—think all the
rest of the world can't play it straight. What Commy should have
done was to offer *twenty* thousand to any of the accusers who would
meet one of the accused face to face and make the charge. There
wouldn't have been any takers, unless some of the scandalmongers
are a good deal better with their fists than they are with their brains."

And he had it right, too, that scribe. Us ballplayers could get as
touchy about such rumors as a Barrymore on the sauce. Take
Knuckles. He might not have busted Fullerton in the chops, like that
scribe said, for he was fairly puny, but if you got him on the subject,
he could be plenty miffed. "Could you imagine," as he put it to
Mister F. C. Lane, "that I would be such a fool as to sell out my
reputation, the good will of my friends, the respect of my family, my
job and my good name as the oldest player in point of service in the
American League for a *few dirty dollars?*"

And, of course, he was right, such a thing did not make no sense
at all. Not unless you knew all that went on behind it. Maybe that
is how come the talk faded away so fast, and why by the time the
'20 season got started, it was all forgotten.

So, you are probably asking again, how come I knew all along that
there was still troubles ahead. Well, I cannot give you a simple yes
or no answer. Sometimes a fellow just feels a thing, the same way
I usually knew before a ball was hit that it was coming my way. Such
a thing is called instincts, and I have always had them.

There was another thing, too. You see, for some guys the dealings
with the gamblers had not ended with the World Series. Gamblers
are not the sort of fellows that let easy deals fade away, nor some of
my teammates, neither. They had all found out how simple it was
to toss a ballgame, and how much dough was in it, so why should
they quit now? For they also had learned that nobody was in a big
hurry to stop them.

At the start of 1920, I did not yet know this. Since the series I had been in bad with all of the old bunch, and I no longer knew a thing that was up with them. Nor was their dirty work on the diamond very easy to see, even to an old pro. The club was playing fine ball, and if once in a moon somebody booted a game on a foozle, what of it? But after a month or so, questions started to get asked. On May 18, for instance (I am no almanac for dates, but this was my brother Luther's birthday), we were up against the Clevelands. Jim Bagby was going for them, and Kerr was on the hill for our side. The contest was as tight as a hook's dress, with both clubs getting goose-egged for seven innings. In their half of the eighth, their first bats-man got a hit, and Ray Chapman, their shortstop, tried to bunt him along. Kerr fielded the ball to Risberg at second—but Swede made a real Nick Altrock play on it. The ball hit right in his palms and bounced away, as if he forgot to hold on. Then, on the very next pitch, Speaker hit a pop-up to short center, which Hap Felsch short-legged into a two-base hit. Well, when the stanza was over and we got back to the bench, I have never seen Kerr so hot. "If you fellows are trying to throw this game," he said, "why don't you just let me in on it?" And the rest of us just looked at the dirt and kept our traps shut, for it looked like he was right.

After that, I had as good an idea of what was up as anyone. Lefty Williams looked to be in on the racket, too, and Fred McMullin. And, more and more, when something flukey would happen, other guys would pipe up with a dirty dig.

Indeed, one time I even got accused myself, and by who do you think? Cocky Collins! It happened in Washington. I happened to be at the bat when Collins got tossed out trying to swipe second base. It was the last out of the inning, so I grabbed my glove out of my butt pocket and started walking to my spot at third. But suddenly the egghead was blocking my path.

"What the hell's the matter with you," he said, "didn't you see my hit-and-run sign?" Which meant that I was supposed to take a swipe at the pitch when he started running.

I did not say nothing, just continued around him.

"What do you think," he repeated, "that I do not know what you're up to out there? Well, I do. And so does the Kid."

I turned around quick as a cat and looked him between the eyes.

"Don't you use me to alibi for your own thick baserunning!" I said. "To hell with you!"

But, of course, damages had already been done. If Gleason didn't have suspicions about me before, he surely did now, and probably so did the others.

And I will admit that things were not helped by my fielding record that year, for I was making a few more misplays than the year before. That was normal. The type of fielder I was, who reaches balls other guys can only dream of, almost never shows up too great in the numbers department. In fact, it was the year before, when I had not made a bushel of misplays, that was not so normal. But at such times, who thinks about such details?

Perhaps you might think by what I say that, as that season of 1920 rolled along, I was getting troubled. If so, you would be correct. There I was, deep in the soup, and all alone in the world. I had no more pals on the club. My friends were all back home in Stowe. I certainly could not talk with my own wife Helen.

But that is a whole other tale. You see, the winter before, Helen had gotten a book called "Vivilore" by Doctor Mary Ries Melendy. It was Rose Cicotte that gave it to her, and 'til this moment I will not forgive her. Me and Knuckles were not even talking no more, and the wives go out and buy presents! Or maybe it was Knuckles that put her up to it. Anyway, this book was supposed to have in it all the right ways for ladies to live. I did not pay much mind to it at first, of course, for Helen looked at plenty of books, and I was busy with other things. But one night, I sat down to supper and the vegetable soup was as cool as the weather outside.

"Why is this soup cold?" I asked. "You got it out of a tin. All you have to do is hot it up."

"It is not cold," she said. "Why do you always have to look at the dark side of everything?"

"Taste this soup yourself!"

"If it has no bright side," she came back, "don't look at it at all. Look at something else."

That was one of the rules out of this book. Never getting miffed was supposed to make a lady grow beautiful. You should never think bad thoughts, or speak evil of someone, and look for good in everyone, even a bad egg like Gandil. Well, how the hell is a guy supposed to have a conversation with someone like that?

But that was not the worst part. The worst part had to do with screwing. See, it also had in this book that a woman should only get screwed one time a month, or maybe twice. Before, me and Helen had had relations any old time I wanted, which was quite a bit. But now, in the book, it said people could turn into morons doing such things.

Helen was so strong on this that she copied some words right out of the book and stuck them up on the bedroom wall. "The sexual act should never be indulged in at a time when either participant is tired or debilitated. Children conceived at such a time would be lacking in vitality; and the coition would also add to the exhausted condition. A genuine man never obtrudes, but instinctively waits 'til invited."

Then she went out and bought a big dresser and stuck it between our beds, so I couldn't even look at her puss no more.

Now, I am a square guy and I want to be straight here. It could be that Helen was provoked. It could be that she had a couple of gripes against me after all these years. After all, I had not paid her feelings much attention, the way a woman likes. And it was fairly important to me to do things my way instead of the other way around. And there was no doubt that she had heard a few whispers about Agnes, which was another present from Rose Cicotte. But what could yours truly do about such slights at this late date? Nothing, that's what!

All I can say is that it was lucky for me there was something else to busy my head about, or else I might have gone bug house. Namely the pennant chase. You see, suddenly it had turned into the greatest chase in years. There were two other clubs scrapping it out with us, Cleveland and New York, and both were plenty game. The Indians had not only Speaker, who was having his greatest season ever, which is saying a thing or two, but also such batsmen as Elmer Smith and little Larry Gardner, plus a mound corps that was near as strong as our own. Bagby would wind up winning thirty-one games for them that year, and Coveleski twenty-four, and Slim Caldwell twenty. If you add that up, it is just about all you need to grab the flag right there. As for the New Yorks, they now had Babe Ruth, and after that what else did they need? Before he came along, the league record for home runs had been sixteen, which was knocked up by Socks Seybold back in '02. Well, this year the Babe was about to hit fifty-four! And drive across one hundred thirty-seven, which was also a new record! And hit for .376 on top of it! I am telling you, I have never seen a show like he could put on at the dish, not since or before. I would almost have paid money to see it.

So, in between those two clubs, our mitts was full from the opening gong. Indeed, it was not 'til the end of August that I began to think we would make it. It was still tight and all, but at last we could take a breath. We were about two games on top of Cleveland, and maybe three on the Yankees.

Right there is the moment that hell busted loose.

The club was home in Chi when it happened, September 4, 1920. "A day that should live in infamy," as FDR might say. All at once, for no reason at all, a letter showed up on the sporting page of the Chicago *Tribune*, where I had never before spotted a letter in all my days in that burg. And this was no ordinary letter, it had a big box around it, so it hit you right in the head. It was from a guy called Loomis, that was a big shot businessman in that town. Loomis said that he had heard some yap about dirty doings in the national game, and he was waiting for actions. Real baseball bugs such as himself was fed up, he said. There was a grand jury right there in Chi, why did they not look into the rumors?

Well, this letter was a new thing entirely. Another fellow might have told himself that it would blow by, same as usual, but not me. I could read the writing as plain as a nose on a face. And with us about to meet Cleveland in a big series, too!

It did not take long to find out I was right. That letter kicked off the biggest flood of woes in the world. Thousands of baseball rooters wrote in to agree with it, not only to the *Tribune*, but also to the other newspapers, and it did not take long for the baby kissers to get the message. Just two days later a guy named Hoyne, who was the State's Attorney and up to get reelected, announced that the grand jury of Cook County would indeed start sniffing around the baseball business.

Most of us Sox were in the clubhouse when we heard about it. We had licked Cleveland about an hour before, but we were still sitting around there, naked as a peeled apple, the way ballplayers do, when Al the clubhouse boy came in with the happy news. No one said a word for a long time. Everyone was trying to keep his eyes to himself, but all of us kept sneaking a little glance at Knuckles and Felsch and Williams, who were the sell-outers in there. However, all the three of them looked as calm as a clock, probably from all the practice they'd had putting on airs. But then I spotted Knuckles' hose. And, as I watched, it got littler and littler, like someone was sucking the blood out of it or something. Then someone made a crack about how Hoyne ought to investigate himself instead, and we all smirked, and that broke up the gloom a little, and a lot of the guys started hustling out of there.

But not Knuckles. A couple of minutes later, I went over to him. This is the sort of fellow I was, a good scout, and still am. He was still sitting in the same spot, only he had stuck a towel over the private part.

"Well," I said, "that was some news, all right."

He looked up at me and tried a grin. "How are you doing, Buck?"

"Good, Knuckles. And you?"

"Fine."

I stood there for quite a while before we spoke up again.

"You're having a great season," he said.

"Thanks." I stopped for a second. His season was going okay, but not as great as expected. "You also."

"Thanks."

"Well," I added, "I guess I will be getting home to Helen."

I started off along my way.

"Buck . . ."

I turned around. "What?"

"Good luck to us both, huh?"

But there was not much good luck at all. No, indeed. For the very next day, who came back into my life but Mister Luther Pond!

He was now working for another paper in New York, a brand new one. It was the New York *Daily News*, which is famous now, but at the moment in question I had never even heard of yet. I heard about it that day in September 1920, though, and in spades! Indeed, when my pal Aaron Ward of the Yankees read me Pond's little story over the long-distance phone, I almost tossed up my breakfast of ham and eggs right there.

"What's up, pal o' mine?" is how it started off. "Listen close . . . That grand old jury looking into the grand old game out in Chi is sitting on a volcano. Ready for this one, pal? If they bother to sniff in the right places, they're going to find that last year's World Series stinks like at least half a dozen rotten eggs. Those games were signed, sealed and delivered, exactly as ordered—and we have it from the inside . . ."

That did it. All at once, a slew of other scribes crawled out of the woodworks and started saying the same thing. From the looks of it, they did not have a bit of evidence, but have such details ever stopped such fellows? Of course not! They was only after the glory, same as always. But you can bet the grand jury was paying attention. Suddenly all the stuff that was going on in that investigation, which was supposed to be secret, by the way, in case you don't know, was showing up in the papers. Every day there was scribbling on the front pages about where the grand jury was sticking its snoot, and the witnesses that had showed up and whose names had popped up.

Still and all, for a while some of our boys managed to keep up their hopes even despite this. See, for all the yap, it looked like that grand jury did not have any line at all about what had gone on in the World Series. For weeks, almost all the talk in there was about the baseball pools, and gambling in the stands, and such matters as those.

But I am afraid I must tell you that at last that changed—and it was thanks to Ban Johnson.

Like I say, this Johnson hated The Old Roman as much as any guy that had ever played for him, and had for many, many years. I cannot say how it started between them, but you know how nabobs are, proud as a nigger in shoes, and once it got going, it could not be patched up. There was a story that one time Johnson had tried —he had gave Comiskey a big fish that he had caught himself. But The Old Roman took that fish and heaved it right out the window, and said, "Am I supposed to play that in left field?" See, I guess I forgot to mention that a little while before, Johnson had suspended his leftfielder.

Anyway, from that day on, all Johnson wanted was the skinflint's blood. And now, at last, he could smell it. When he saw that after

almost a month the grand jury was still off hunting wild geese, he
went to visit Judge MacDonald, who was in charge, and gave him
a whole list of fellows he should get as witnesses—ballplayers,
nabobs and gamblers.

Speaking of which, our goose was cooked right there. The very
next day, the witnesses started showing up, beginning with The Old
Roman himself. Comiskey did not tell them much, of course, except
how honorable he was himself and that Ban Johnson was a skunk.
But after him came Buck Herzog, the Cubs shortstop, and Rube
Benton of the Giants, and Charlie Weeghman, who used to own the
Cubs, and all of them had some solid info that ballgames had been
tossed. Including World Series games. In fact, Weeghman came
right out and admitted that before the '19 series, a gambler he knew
had told him that seven White Sox were laying down.

A day after that who should show up but George M. Cohan!
Naturally this got me plenty jumpy, having met the guy and all, and
I was not disappointed. Cohan said that he had gone to the series all
set to bet on the Sox, but once he got to Cincy, he had got a solid
tip that the games were in the bag for the Reds.

And who gave him such a tip? he was asked.

He could not say for sure, he came back, for he had never met the
gent before. But he was a gambler.

I am sorry to admit that that was not the end of it, either. No, sir,
for the very next day, Luther Pond was at it again.

Since that first little story of his, he had continued to kick up
trouble, of course. Every day there would be something or another.
But, see, after a while it began to look like he was just as big a hot-air
artist as the rest. He did not have no inside info either, for if he did,
where the hell was it?

But then this next little thing came along.

"SPOTLIGHT ON THE SERIES SCANDAL . . . That Chicago grand jury
was so dazzled by the bright lights of the White Way, pal, they
forgot to ask our Yankee Doodle Dandy some very important questions . . . By the by, Judge MacDonald, for your information (and
'cause we're weary of you getting it wrong), there were not six, not
seven, but EIGHT White Sox a-laying . . ."

After Ward had read it to me a couple of times, I had him read
it once more, real slow, and I wrote it down on a piece of paper, so

I could look it over myself when I got off. Which I did. For half an hour, I sat in this same chair where I am sitting now and gazed at those words. Then I picked up the phone again and told the hello girl to put me through to Luther Pond, at the *Daily News* in New York.

"Pond, here," he came in, five minutes later.

"Mister Pond, this is Buck Weaver!" I was trying to keep the old voice from shaking. I had a few things to say.

But he did not even give a pause. "Say, Buck, what can I do for you? You got a tip for me?"

"No, I do not have no tip! I am phoning up over long distance about that story you put down today!"

"Yes . . ."

He was so pleasant about it, it made it seem like what was I getting into such a lather over? "Well," I said, "what about it?"

"Say, Buck, didn't you tell me yourself you couldn't swear the series was on the up and up?

"Maybe I did. But who says I was in on it? I told you I was not!"

"Certainly you did. Did someone say otherwise?"

"You said there was eight fixers."

He laughed. "Listen, Buck, it could be anyone. Even Cocky Collins. Now, you don't think I . . . Hold on a sec, will you, bub?" He went away for a minute, then got back on again. "Listen, something's come up here, can I get right back to you?"

"When?"

"Right away." He started to get off the line.

"I will give you this number. It's Decatur 806 . . ."

"I got it." And the line went dead.

Unless you are a chickenhead, I do not have to tell you that he did not ring me right back, at all. I waited in that house 'til it was past eleven, at which moment I had to go to the ballpark. And in the days after, every time I tried to nab him at the *Daily News*, which I did at least seven times, he was invisible. Some flat tire would get on the line and tell me that Mister Pond was out, but he would certainly call me back. Which still has not happened yet. I know the old brush-off when I see it.

Anyway, by the time I got to the ballpark that morning, it was quite late, and I had missed hitting practice. That was fine by me, for to tell you the truth, I did not feel like working. First off, I was weak as a pup, for while waiting for the ink slinger to call back, this time I had went right ahead and tossed up my breakfast on the floor. And lately, Helen had not been the sort of wife to fix eats two times in one morning. To add to it, it had rained pitchforks the night before, and my spot at third looked like a gang of pigs could live there.

I guess the Kid knew what was coming off, for he looked at me sort of sidewise. But I did not say nothin', nor did he, and when it was time to play ball, I made like I was keen as mustard. That is all everyone ever expected of old Buck Weaver, and it was always what they got. I went out and knocked three bingles that afternoon.

But after the contest, I had no more obligations to no one. All I wanted was to get off on my own to Ma Cuddy's Tavern and dip my beak. However, I had not even finished two brews before a scribe smoked me out. He wanted to know what I thought of what had gone on that day over at the grand jury.

"I do not know and I do not care!" I answered. "Why should that concern me?"

Well, this scribe said, Rube Benton had been back in the box, and he had said plenty about the '19 Series. "And," added the scribe, "he named names."

"Oh, yes," I said, "and who might that be?"

It turned out that it was not me at all that had got named, but Knuckles and Lefty and Gandil and all the others that any fool with a pair of ears already knew about.

"I do not believe a single bit of such talk," I said.

But he just kept up pestering me.

"Do you have any comment on the rumors about yourself, Buck?" he asked, real sincere, like he was my best pal. This scribe was a green apple, just twenty-three or four, and I had not seen his mug more than once or twice in my whole life.

"I did not do a thing that was not on the up-and-up," I shouted at him. "Why the hell don't you take a look at my record?"

The noise must have shook him a bit. For a minute he choked his questions and let me drink in peace.

"Will you appear before the grand jury yourself?" he piped up finally.

I gazed at him. He held his little pencil above his notebook, all bright eyes, like what I was going to say was the most important thing in the whole world.

"Yes, I will!" I came back. "Buck Weaver has nothing to hide!"

Of course, I did not have an intention of doing any such thing. Why should I? I was as honest as the day, and why should I travel to some courthouse for no good reason?

But, in the end, it did not matter, for people seemed to care very little if I squawked or not. They could get their facts elsewhere. Just a day later, a gambler in Philly by the name of Maharg broke out at the mouth in one of the papers there, with all of the details of the fix. And, like it or not, I was one of the men he accused.

I did not learn of this turn of events until after our ballgame that day, against Detroit. When we got back to the clubhouse, there was the clubhouse boy again, with a copy of the Chi *Herald American* in his mitts. It was hard to miss the title: EIGHT SERIES FIXERS NAMED. And standing right next to him was Charles A. Comiskey.

The Old Roman was not in a rage, as you might suspect. To the contrary, he looked about a hundred and ten years old, all bent at the shoulder and with his noggin hanging low, and his white hairs all mussed up. And when he spoke, you could hardly even hear him.

"Well, boys," he said, when we got to our spots by our lockers, "the jig is up. The seven of you still with the club are suspended, as of this moment. Without pay." And very slow, so slow it looked like he was not moving at all, he walked out of that room.

No one else made a peep. In such circumstances, words are just a waste of breath. But all at once there came a queer sound from the side of the room. Lefty Williams had his skull in his hands and, soft as that, he was bawling.

The very next day, Eddie Cicotte showed up in front of that grand jury and opened up his guts. Indeed, if I did not know the fellow as I did, and still cared for him, I might have thought he was the lowest worm in the ground, the way he handed out the sob stuff. It was not enough for him to say he had done the deed. No, he named other fellows, too, stopping every once in a while for a cry, all the time saying how he did not know how he could have done such a thing to Comiskey.

Just hearing of it was enough to turn a man's belly. What did I need this for, on top of the rest?

But I am running a little ahead of myself here, for I want to talk some more about that day The Old Roman gave us the bounce. The scribes was waiting for us outside the clubhouse, of course, yelling out queries that I did not even want to think about. I just walked past them like I did not see them, out to Thirty-fifth Street. I suppose you might say I was in a daze. I walked for a long time, all the way over to the Loop. Then I went to see a moving picture. It was called *Belly Up* at the Broad Street Theatre. I looked at it two times. By then my brains was working again, trying to figure out what to do next, and how to pull it off. But I could not find any easy answers, so I went to yet another picture show, with good old Hoot Gibson.

By the time I made it to my own home, it was far past bedtime hour, and I went into the house like a mouse. I certainly did not want to bother my wife Helen. And when I got into my own bed, I might have sobbed a little. I will admit it. This is how sorrowful I felt.

But just a little after I started, there was a paw on my shoulder, and it was Helen. She got into the bed next to me, and for a long time she held me tight as a skin.

And then she let me jazz her as good as I had in months.

Nineteen Twenty-One

by George D. Weaver

After Knuckles had sprung his leak, there was no stopping the other boys. Panic was in the wind, and in such conditions even guys with fine brains can act like saps. Not to mention guys like Joe Jackson, who was the very first to follow Cicotte in front of that grand jury.

This was such a funny sight, the hick in there, that you could almost have laughed at it. There he was, all done up in his Sunday duds, honestly thinking he could get himself out of this scrape. Of course, all he ended up doing was digging himself a hole about a thousand feet deep. In fact, he even crabbed that he had not gotten all the dough that was due him! I suppose he figured this'd make the whole world feel sorry for him.

Well, no such thing! Tell me how John Fan could respect a ballplayer after a thing like that! And, on top of it, when he had left the jury room, he went right over to the mob of scribes and admitted a few other things. He said he was glad he had squawked, even despite the fact that Risberg had warned him that bad things would happen to him if he did so. "Swede is a hard guy," he said.

Next came that weasel Lefty Williams, and it was the same song all over again, about how the fix had got set up, and the powwows with the gamblers and the ins and outs of how the contests got booted away. And, once again, yours truly got mentioned, right along with the actual crooks. In fact, it almost seemed like he went out of his natural way to stick it to me. Yes, he said, Buck was at this meeting, sure thing, Bucko was at that occasion, too. Well, I ask you, what is the big news in that? Of course I was at those meetings! I will say it myself! I have been at many meetings in my life, and listened to plenty of propositions. But did I or did I not come across on the diamond? That is the question that no one even asked!

I had never liked Williams, and I guess he liked me just about as much. But Hap Felsch, he was a genuine letdown to me. Hap did not pull an act for the grand jury, at least I will say that for him, but what he did was almost as bad, for Hap spilled his guts in ink, to a scribe for the Chi *American.* And, once again, I got yanked right into the midst of it. "I'm going to see Buck Weaver," he said at the end of the article, out of left field, "and get him to see the State's Attorney with me."

I suppose Hap really thought I would go, too. Why not? Once so many guys had gabbed, what was there to lose? The only dummies left were the hard apples (if you count McMullin with them, which I do) and myself.

In fact, that same afternoon that Hap popped up in the *American,* I got a telephone call at my own house from Mister Alfred Austrian asking me to do just that. Austrian was the lawyer for the ballclub, and he was just about as slippery as you might guess from his handle. Hitler is an Austrian, too, in case you didn't know, and not just a regular kraut. Why don't you come right over to the club offices for a little chat, he said. Believe me, he said, you will feel a lot better when you get stuff off your chest, as your pals have.

But me, I remained calm as a lake. "That is very interesting, Mister Austrian," I said, "but the only thing is, I do not feel too bad in the first place."

He chuckled at that one. Well, why did I not just come over anyhow, and we would see what he could do for me.

The way he was talking, candy would melt in your mouth, and I mean it. So I had to hem and haw for a couple of minutes. "No," I told him finally, "I do not think I will do so just now. But I will certainly ring you if I have a change of mind."

Which I would not have, of course. And if I did, I sure would not let some cloak and suiter that worked for The Old Roman in on it.

But, I will tell you the truth, at that moment I did not know what to do at all. The situation was getting as tight as a sailor's knot, and there I was in my living room. Do not get me wrong, I am a clever bird, and had proved it many times on the diamond. But, you see, this was a different thing. So after I got off with Austrian, I got right back on the line and told the hello girl to get me the State's Attorney.

"Replogle!" he answered, for that was his name, Hartley Replogle. Do not ask me how he got it.

"Mr. Replogle, this is Buck Weaver."

"Hello there, Buck. Good to hear from you."

I stopped. "Have we met someplace before?"

"No, no," he came back, with a twinkle in his voice, "just a figure of speech."

"Oh."

On my end, my wife Helen came into the room. She gazed at me and moved her lips, real hush-hush. "Who are you talking to?"

"What can I do for you, Buck?" said Replogle.

"I have got something to say to you. I want the truth about me to come out in this grand jury. I do not have any things to hide."

"Who are you talking to?" said Helen again, only she was a little louder about it, spitting through her ivories like a cat.

"Never you mind," I told her. "This is my business."

"Pardon me?"

"Nothing, Mr. Replogle, I was talking to my own wife."

"Replogle!"

"Well, Buck, that's good to hear. I'm sure we can work something out. I expect that the grand jury will be quite favorably impressed by what . . ."

But, all at once, Helen grabbed that telephone cup right out of my ear and put it back in the holder.

"What the hell are you doing?" I screamed. "That was the State's Attorney."

"If you do any talking, Buck, you get your own lawyer first."

"You cannot act that way to the State's Attorney." I paused. "Anyway, I do not have any lawyer. I do not even know a lawyer!"

"My brother Harold knows a lawyer. I talked to Harold about it myself."

And, to make the story a little shorter, that is how Tom Nash got to be my attorney.

Nash was a little guy that was always smoking a cheroot and

thought he was a card. He was all the time pulling stunts, such as putting a whoopee cushion on a fellow's chair, and then he would laugh for about half an hour. But for all his antics, he was as slick as grease. Just a couple of days after that, I was in his office for the first time, which was a big place right on State Street, telling my tale of woe, and right off the bat he had a line on the whole business.

"It sounds to me," he said, "that you're in this mess only because you refused to squeal on your friends. Is that it?"

"Yessir. I am not no squealer and never have been. You could ask anyone."

"You know what the State's Attorney's going to say, don't you Buck? That it was your duty to the game to tell what you knew. What do you say to that?"

"Duty to the game!" I had never heard such a shovelful of palaver yet! "Lots of other people besides me knew that that series was on the bum," I said. "Including Comiskey! And some of them scribes. One of them I told him myself, by the name of Luther Pond. Go ask him."

"Would you be able to prove in a court of law that you played up to your capabilities in the World Series?" he asked.

Even though he was a brainy guy, like I say, this was a thick-headed query, and there is no other way to put it. "I guess you're no baseball bug," I said.

He grinned. "I suppose that answers the question, then. No, I'm afraid I'm not." He made a clip-clop noise with his tongue and pretended with his hands like he was yanking some reins. "I like the horsies."

"So do I. This ain't a one-or-other world, you know."

He laughed and bit off the end of one of them stogies of his. "You think you could get me a reputable baseball man or two to vouch for your performance in the World Series?"

"Certainly I could!" I could not stop a smile. "How's about the whole pitching staff for Cincinnati?"

He bobbed his noggin up and down real slow. "Good. That would certainly help."

But Nash saw right off what the big problem was, and after he explained it to me, so did I. In fact, after a little while I started to think that if I'd had a few more years in school, maybe I might've made a lawyer, too. The problem was that John Public was after blood, and he was getting even madder with every day that went by. And who could blame him, the way the boys kept shooting off their traps? The way me and Nash looked at it, my ex-pals were acting like they wanted to get crucified some more. Indeed, not one of them had even yet thought to get himself an attorney. They were all counting on Alfred Austrian, which was like letting chickens sleep with a fox. It was Austrian that had got Knuckles and Shoeless and Williams to go to the grand jury in the first place, same as he tried to do with me. And it turned out that before doing so, he had told each of them what to say, and what to leave out, and then he had got all of them to put their john hancock on a paper saying that later on it could all be used against them.

The reason that Austrian was sneaking around in such a way was pretty clear to me and Nash. Him and Comiskey wanted to fix it up that us deck hands would be the goats, while the big pokes would never even get mentioned.

Nor were they alone in this scheme, not judging by the newspapers. As soon as events started to bust open, the articles started in the press about what a fine old gent Comiskey was, and how excellent he had always been to his players, and that it was a tragedy that a gang of dirty ballplayers would do such a thing to him. Meanwhile, The Old Roman kept such talk coming with his own actions. First he sent out telegrams to all the guys that had already got suspended telling us that we were suspended all over again, and gave a copy to the scribes. "If you are guilty," is how it ended, "you will be retired from Organized Baseball for the rest of your lives if I can accomplish it. It is due to the public that I take this action, even though it costs Chicago the pennant."

Which was a laugh if I ever heard one. Not the part about us costing the club the flag, for there was no doubts about that. Us guys that had got the bounce made up four everyday starting regulars, plus the team's two top twirlers, and without us the White Sox was bound to blow it. Which is just what they went ahead and did. To the Clevelands. But this business of Comiskey sniffing around for kudos was the limit! He would rather have ate a pile of shit than lose that pennant, but he just did not have any other choices. Otherwise a bunch of ballplayers that the whole world knew was dirty were about to play in the World Series all over again.

These are the actual facts I'm giving here. But did even one scribe in a million print them? And you can guess how they lapped it up when the skinflint pulled his next stunt, which was to give all the guys that were still with the club a check for fifteen hundred bucks. See, this was supposed to be the extra dough they would've got if us others had played it square and won the '19 series.

But, I will tell you something, even such showboating could not end his troubles, nor those of the other nabobs, for the truth is, by now all of baseball was up a tree with us "Black" Sox. After all, every bug in the land had seen what was up with the national game. They had heard the tales of rottenness and greed, not to mention other problems, and it was not too hard to figure out that the owners had not exactly knocked themselves out to put a stop to such doings.

And so, before too long, the owners saw that they had to come across with more than the usual applesauce. Otherwise, there was a chance that the public would put their feet down, and drop baseball like a potato. Oh, it might keep going for a while, all right, but less and less people would give a damn, until finally it would end up like tennis or wrestling or some sport like that.

That is when a guy called Albert Lasker had the bright idea to get a commissioner. Lasker was one of the owners of the Cubs, as well as being a buddy of Comiskey's, so he was pretty excited at the time. See, there also happened to be a few suspicions floating around about some of the Cubs players being on the take, and Lasker knew there was plenty to them. So he told the other big shots that they had to get someone to watch the store that the public would trust. And that guy would be the commissioner.

Well, of course, some of the owners had trouble swallowing this, and so did Ban Johnson. In fact, it almost made Johnson puke. For many years, since the league had gotten started, he had been the boss and he felt why should he give it up? So he fought back like an angry old horse.

But, at that instant, no one cared about his gripes. They knew that Lasker was right, so right after the '20 World Series, which Cleveland took from Brooklyn five games to two, in case you're interested,

they came up with the guy they were after. Kenesaw Mountain
Landis.

This was all the scribes needed to start hollering that baseball was
fixing up its own house and the crisis was over. Why not? If you
were worried about the public's relations, Landis had everything
going for him. Ten years before that, he had stood up to John D.
Rockefeller himself, and announced that Standard Oil was a trust.
Then, in '18, he had put all the leaders of the Wobblies in the slammer
for being against the war. So, of course, everyone except Ban Johnson agreed he was wise and fair and stern, just like a commissioner
ought to be. He even looked that way, with all that white hair, and
them beady eyes, and skin like old leather. It is no wonder that earlier
that same year, the Republicans had thought of running him for
president, before they came up with Harding, who looked almost as
good.

But the best part about Landis, if you asked the owners, was
something the newspapers hardly went into at all. See, back in '13,
when the Feds had tried to sue baseball as a trust, the case had ended
up in Landis' courthouse. And instead of giving a ruling, Landis just
sat on top of that case. That's right, he just sat and sat for more than
a year, and he kept on sitting 'til at last the Feds went bust. So, the
nabobs knew they could count on him, and no questions asked.

As for yours truly, I was doing nothing at all except laying low.
I did not like it, for I am a man of actions, but Nash was the brains
of the outfit. He said it was a delicate moment, and I had better not
gum it up. See, his notion was to get me separated apart from the
other boys legally.

But then, all at once, things changed. On October 22, 1920, the
Grand Jury gave its indictments: Cicotte, Gandil, Jackson, Felsch,
Williams, Risberg, McMullin, a couple of gamblers—and Buck
Weaver.

I cannot say that it was a big surprise. But you know how it is
sometimes, when such a thing happens, even if you have been waiting for it, it is like a fist in the kisser. I am made of flesh and bones,
just like other fellows, and this was too much to just smoke in my
pipe.

But I am no pinhead, neither. When the scribes came running
around to my house to ask me about getting indicted, I kept my head.

I told them, real friendly, that I was clean and, wait and see, my name would get cleared. But then I may have made an error. It was on account of the way they were acting, pushing me this way and that in that way they have, looking for color stuff and not giving a damn who they stepped on to get it, and finally, for a second, I did lose my wits. "I don't want any of you to put down that Buck Weaver is broke up over this," I said. "I know your ways. Why don't you tell the facts for a change?" Which I guess was a mistake, for the next day they murdered me all over the place.

Not that it really mattered by then. Like it or not, I was going on trial, and so were the other boys. The rest was just icing on top of the cake.

The first time I actually went in the Cook County Courthouse was on February 14, 1921. I was calm, thanks to Nash. He had told me that it was like a big ballgame, and having the fidgets just made a fellow bobble the ball. Besides, this was only a thing they call the arraignment, which is not the same as a trial. We were getting arraigned for conspiracy to mess up the national game and wreck The Old Roman's business. This last part would not have been such a bad idea, but unfortunately no one had thought of it.

Believe it or not, it made me feel better just to be in that court-room. It was better than just waiting in my own house with no one to talk to but the walls and Helen. Nor was it all starchy in there, the way I expected, for the place was packed to the gills with baseball bugs. And the moment us boys showed our faces, they started up yelling and cheering, just like it was the ballpark. I am telling you, it sent pimples right down my spine.

And then there were the lawyers. Nash was grinning like an ape. That did not surprise me so much, knowing the fellow as I did, but, see, so were the other lawyers for our side. There were three of them, by the name of O'Brien, and Short, and Ahearn, and people said they were about the best money could get. To see them standing there, full of vim as a pack of schoolkids, you would think we had already taken the contest. I must admit, it crossed my skull to wonder how my ex-pals had gotten the smarts to hire such a fine bunch.

Speaking of which, all seven of them were there also, together again like peas in a pod. And it was like we had never been apart. I was not on talking terms with them, and they was not on talking terms with me. I even tried to sit apart from them on that bench. This was Nash's notion, to show the people there that even though I had not gotten a separate trial, I was not amongst them in my heart. Gandil, who had come back to Chi from his new house in Texas for the occasion, was not talking to nobody, neither, except Risberg and McMullin. The way he looked at it, this whole stink would not be happening in the first place if Cicotte and the others had not started gabbing. Seeing him there, with eyes as cold as February, I really believe that if he could, he would have took a blade and cut open their gizzards right on the spot. But, of course, under the circumstances, he could not.

The lawyer for the other side, Gorman, who was the Assistant State's Attorney, did not look so happy, neither. He took one look at that mob of fancypants defense lawyers, and immediately asked the judge to delay the trial. Why should I do that? asked the judge, and I agreed with him. After all, if the trial got over quick, I would still have time to take a little trip with my wife Helen and then get down to Texas for training camp. But then Gorman pulled a surprise out of his sleeve. He said that the confessions that Knuckles and Lefty and Shoeless had signed back in the fall had disappeared out of his files.

Well, that stopped everything cold. The judge said okay to the delay, and hit his hammer against his desk, and that was that.

There was not a thing to be done. Us ballplayers would just have to sit on our ass while the season got started without us! For the first time since I was a tyke (and there I was, thirty-one years old), I would not be putting on a uniform in the spring.

This might not sound like much to you, but how would you know? Outside the weather got warmer and hotter, until finally a fellow did not even have to put on an undershirt, and there I still was, sitting on my ass. By the time that trial finally started up, which was the end of June, I was as jumpy as a hen without a head.

The other boys did not have it quite so bad. Except for Cicotte, who had become a real hermit in the eyes of the public, they all *had* been playing ball. They had got up a team called the Major Stars, and had been playing contests against semi-pro clubs all over the Chi area, and making pretty fair loot at it, too. So when I spotted them back in that courtroom, they were as loose and merry as ever, with tans on their faces and big smiles. Even Gandil. It was enough to make an innocent man wish he was guilty.

But, I must say, over the next days, as things went along, I found myself warming up to some of them scoundrels. There is nothing a fellow can do about that. It is all in the emotions. After all, we were all in the same fix, sitting there day after day, and after a while I said a few words to them, and then a few more, and pretty soon we were back sharing eats together. At first it was a little tense, of course. I watched my tongue like a hawk, and so did they. We would mainly make gas about the national game, how fine the Babe was doing, and what a bunch of stiffs the Sox were without us. But before too long, it was on to wives and tykes, and finally we got around to more important matters.

Not that I would talk to any of them about the fix. I was still plenty touchy on that one, and with good reason. Not one of them birds had yet come out and said the truth about me, which was that I had played in that World Series like gangbusters! Not even Knuckles. But, sure, after a while I would yap to them about what was going on in that courtroom. Why the hell not? Like I say, no man is an island.

One day, for instance, a bunch of us were loafing in the clubhouse, which is what we called the room next to the court where sometimes we'd eat our lunch out of a paper bag. It was our wives that fixed up the bags, so that a man would not have to rub against the ink slingers when he was trying to digest. Anyway, we were shooting the breeze about whether or not it would be a brainy move for the lawyers to get all men on the jury and no skirts. Some thought yes, some thought no, and some did not think about it at all. Namely Shoeless.

"Why would we want skirts?" said Felsch. "They do not know a thing about baseball. Not even my wife."

"That is not the point," answered back Knuckles. "A woman will judge you on your face. Look how they all went for Harding."

"Oh, yeah?" cut in McMullin with a smirk. "Then it's a dead cinch Hap here would get convicted."

Cicotte shrugged him away. "Everybody knows that a woman has a kinder heart than a man. It's a natural fact. Isn't that so, Buck?"

See, me and Knuckles had been talking amongst ourselves on this very subject just a couple of days before.

"Certainly, it is true," I agreed. "But I think you're wrong about having skirts on this jury."

Knuckles gazed at me in surprise, for I was singing a brand new tune.

"Oh, yes? Why's that?"

"Tom Nash told me. He said that you just cannot trust a girl to do what she is supposed to. Logic is with us in this case, so we want a jury that gets logic. If we did not have logic on our side, then you would fill the jury with skirts."

They all thought that over for a second.

"Why is logic with us?" asked Felsch.

"Because," I came right back, "the charge against us is for conspiracy, and how can you prove conspiracy if no one else can testify against us except us?"

Which they all had to agree was so, even Knuckles, for he came out and admitted that maybe I was right.

"Don't any of you fellows ever talk over such matters with your attorneys?" I added a minute later.

"Why 'n hell should we?" spoke up Jackson, all of a sudden. "That stuff don' make no difference anyway, long as we win."

"What else are you paying them all that dough for?" I said. After all, I myself had had to borrow three thousand bucks from Helen's brother for Nash.

"Look," said Felsch, "they don't ask me how to play centerfield, do they? Anyway, who says we're paying them?"

"You're *not?*"

There was a pause as heavy as one of the Babe's bats.

"We were going to," said Cicotte finally, and you could tell he was a little sheepish about the whole thing, "but then we were told not to bother. The tabs would get picked up."

"By who?"

He did not answer, just shrugged up his shoulders. But I guess I knew anyway. And later, when I thought about it, it made sense. If we won the trial and could play again, they would have to thank The Old Roman for sticking by them in thick and thin, and would go right back to the Pale Hose. And if we did not win, these lawyers could at least make sure that Comiskey's name did not get mussed up in that courtroom. It was a streak of genius!

And, sure enough, just a few days after that, The Old Roman himself showed up in court to give his evidence. And did any of those defense lawyers ask him what he had known of the fix? Not a word! The old fake was allowed to just sit there and tell his stories about all the things he had done to help create baseball, and what a fine character he was, like it was 1913 all over again, and the whole bunch of us, ballplayers, scribes, lawyers and spectators, were with him on the deck of the *St. Albens,* going through the Suez Canal or someplace. I am not kidding, he yakked more about 1890 than 1919. And when he was done, he was so pleased, you could have popped him like a balloon.

But that was just the start. It was the same way when Kid Gleason dropped by, and Schalk, and Kerr, and Cocky Collins, the right queries just did not seem to get asked. And if they did, one bird or another would shout Objection, and so it would not get answered.

Well, every time it happened, it was like they were sticking another nail in my flesh, not to mention my coffin.

I do not mean to sound smallish, I know that this is how the laws work. But just tell me what else this trial was supposed to be about, if not what went on on the diamond. My job in that World Series was to hit the orb, and run the bases, and field the number three bag, and I had done so like a champion! What does it matter what was said in some hotel room? It got so that you would think us ballplayers never quit those hotel rooms at all.

And I will tell you the worst part of all, after hearing about those meetings day after day, it starts to fiddle up a man's thinking. I knew I was not guilty of a thing, but hearing it said in such a way, my actions were starting to sound fairly evil, even to myself. This is what happens in a courtroom, where a man is not allowed to speak normal, but can only reply to questions from highbrows that were not even there. And it got to sounding worst of all when Sleepy Burns hit the stand.

Perhaps you remember about Burns. He was the other gambler at the Hotel Sinton in Cincinnati besides Abe Attell. Well, Ban Johnson, who was working like a big-city nigger for the other side, so that he could grab the glory instead of Landis, and also do in Comiskey at the same time, had tracked him down in Texas, and had personally brought him up to Chi to squawk.

This is the thing they call irony. Here was Johnson, trying his best to wreck The Old Roman by wrecking a bunch of guys that hated him as bad as himself. He did not give a damn about us, of course, but that does not stop it from being irony.

Anyway, this Burns ended up shooting off his mouth in that courtroom for three whole days, acting like he was born there. After a while, he even started cracking gags, much to the delight of the fans. And murdering us defendants all the while. In fact, a couple of times, watching him, I got sick in the guts and almost had to puke. I could not even make myself turn and smile at my own wife, who was sitting behind me in row number three (in honor of third base), as I had done throughout the trial.

After Burns' first day up there, I did not even go over to see Helen, but rushed right over to Tom Nash.

"I have got to talk to you!" I said.

"Here?" He laughed with his eyes, for we were right in the middle of the court, in front of the judge's spot, and guys was bustling all around us.

I did not say nothing in reply, so he took me by the arm and led me into the clubhouse.

"Now, then," he spoke up, "what's the problem?"

"*What's the problem?* You heard that fellow today."

"What did you expect, Buck? We both knew what Burns would say."

"I did not like hearing it," I said. "I did not like him putting me in with the others that way. I am an innocent man!"

Nash smirked at me in a friendly way and placed his paw on my shoulder. "Trust me, Buck, I know it's unpleasant, but Burns is nothing to worry about. They can't prove conspiracy without someone to corroborate Burns' testimony. I don't see much chance of that"—he gave a little laugh—"unless you would like to volunteer for the job."

"That's what I was thinking, I would."

He stopped, quick as that, and gazed at me. "Would what?"

"Like to go up there and talk for my own self. I want to tell the real facts, as they were."

He shook his head. "You can't do that, Buck."

"Why not?"

"Don't you know that we're winning this case? There's no way on earth they can convict with what they have. But if they get any of you players on that witness stand, it's another story. If you tell anything approaching the truth about those meetings, you're finished. That's why we worked so hard in the first place to invalidate the original confessions."

I did not have to think about that for more than an instant. Naturally he was right, such fellows always are. "But I am not like the others. I played square in that series."

"For purposes of this trial, my friend, I'm afraid you are." He said it stern, to get me to shut my beak. He probably had to take a leak, or go out hobnobbing with some big shots.

But, see, I had been thinking of something else for quite a while, ever since The Old Roman had done his act in that court, and this was the moment to unload it off my chest. "Anyways," I said, "I thought we was going to get experts to say how great I played."

"It's immaterial. This is a conspiracy trial."

"How could it be? It's the most important thing."

"Buck, we wouldn't even be *allowed.*"

"How about Comiskey?"

He let out a big sigh. "What about Comiskey?"

"Why didn't you get him to tell how he covered up the fix? Like we planned before?"

"Dammit, Buck, it's immaterial. Comiskey's not on trial, you are!"

His voice was getting pretty loud, for he was not a guy used to getting talked at this way. But yours truly has lungs also.

"Sure, but you're working for me, not him!" I stopped. "Or maybe you're working for him, too!"

He stared at me red-hot for a second and was about to say something, but instead held onto himself, and in a moment he was frosty. "I'm not even going to dignify that with an answer," he said, then turned on his heels and walked out of that room. And, I will tell you something, to this moment I do not have an answer.

But, of course, Nash was dead right about how the trial was going, for no one ever denied he was a fox. And before too long, others on the outside started figuring it out, too, even the scribes. All at once

the rags began printing how things looked good for us, and that the
state had hardly no case at all. And guys that had not touched us with
a pole for months were suddenly charming again. Including baseball
men. It did not matter that some in our bunch had already confessed
to the crime. Such things as right and wrong do not matter to most
people. All they care for is their own selves, and what other jackasses
think about them.

Not that I was kicking about this at the moment in question, no
indeed. I liked that they all wanted to be my pal again. Why not?
My plan was to get back into the big show, no questions asked, and
things were looking bright as a new penny. Especially on July 31,
1921, which was a Sunday morning. For who should I bump into on
Randolph Street that day but John McGraw. Not that this was a
coincidence, of course. I may have bumped into him, but he had not
bumped into me. He had come looking.

But, like I say, I did not give a damn why or wherefore, so long
as things stacked up okay. So we shot the breeze there on the street
for a while, about the Giants' chances that season, and then he said
it was pretty hot out there, and why did we not go for a cool
lemonade. Which we did. And then he stopped beating around the
bushes and came to his point. He told me he had long admired my
skills, ever since the trip 'round the world, and if you asked him, I
was the best third sacker in the game. "And you're a great manager,
Mr. McGraw," I answered back, that's the way I was brought up.
So he said thanks, and then he asked, "How would you like to play
for the New York Giants?" I said I would like that just dandy. In
fact, I would even be ready to join him this year, for I already knew
many of the twirlers in the National League from training games.
He laughed at that, and said next season would be fine. And then we
shook on it. "Don't worry," he said, "we will work out the details
just as soon as things quiet down."

Well, if you have ever seen a puppy kicking up his heels, or else
a baby goat, you can guess how I felt. Full of beans! And, sure
enough, just two days later, on August 2, things got even better, as
if that was possible. For on that night, the jury did their work just
as predicted. Not guilty, not one of us!

You should have seen the goings-on in that court when it got
announced, too! In a flash, us ballplayers jumped all over each other,

and then on the jury, and even on the judge, while the bugs in the stands were whooping it up like it was the last game of the World Series. And pretty soon they had hoisted us all up in the air, and the whole mess of us moved right out into the streets and started a little parade.

Through all the hullabaloo, I kept looking for my wife Helen, but I did not find her 'til an hour later at the bash one of the bugs was throwing for us and the jurors at the Little Capri restaurant. All us boys were there, and our wives, as well as plenty of other happy geeks, and it got to be some high time. Personally, being so jolly, I did not have much of a stomach for eats, but I had more than Knuckles. He just sat in a corner with his wife Rose, quietly crying from joy. He had turned out to be a first class crybaby, that fellow.

It went on this way most of the night, 'til after it had started to get light outside. Me and Helen walked outside, holding onto each other like kids. Then, at the corner of Thirty-fifth and Halsted, we spotted a newsboy, hawking the *Tribune*. We gave him two bits and let him keep the change, all set to read all about it. And there it was, all right, and in big letters. WHITE SOX ACQUITTED. But there was something else in there, too. "Regardless of the verdict of juries," said Commissioner Kenesaw Mountain Landis, "no player who throws a ballgame will ever play professional baseball."

I suppose, looking at it today, you might maybe say that I had not been so bright all this time as I thought. Perhaps I was not even so bright as the other seven. At least they had the smarts right off to believe what it said in that newspaper, that they would never play in the big leagues again, and leave it at that. Most of them just dropped away from the scene quiet as a cat and the public never heard another peep about them. Oh, they kept up playing ball, all right, where they could. That very season, the whole mess of them signed up with a thing called the Continental League, which a guy called Lawson had put together. This fellow's notion was that he would have white men and niggers all playing on the same diamond. "The Continental League was planned in the trenches," he liked to put it, "and colored men were also there as comrades." Which you will have to agree was a dim idea, and it is no wonder it flivvered before it even started up. Maybe it would've worked Over There.

Then some of the boys got up their own team, which was named The South Side All-Stars. They played a little while with that, mainly against semi-pro clubs, after which they split up and went different ways, playing in different parts of the land, such as out West and down in Dixie. Wherever they might make a dollar.

But, even though they did not make no waves, they still had plenty of troubles. See, right at the start, Landis had thought up a rule that no guy would be allowed in Organized Ball who had ever played *against* one of us Black Sox. So lots of times, when other players saw one of us coming, they would run away like we had a social disease.

This is how Landis was, little-hearted as a flea. But old Buck here, I just would not believe the doors was closed. Indeed, I wasted many years waiting for the judge to give me justice.

I am not looking for excuses, not at this late date, but I guess part of the reason I kept hoping was on account of Landis' personality when you saw him up close. In snapshots he may have always looked like he was about to bite you, with those beady eyes and angry look on his mug. But, see, that was only an act. As some scribe put it, Kenesaw Mountain Landis showed how far dramatic talent can carry a man in this land, if only he has the sense not to go on the stage. And I kept getting took in.

When I had my very first powwow with him, which was just a little after the trial, he was so friendly I thought he was going to have me to his place to meet Mrs. Landis. He welcomed me into his big office, and told me to have a chair, and asked me did I want a chew of tobacco. Then, I am not kidding, he started up telling me gags, sticking me in the ribs at the comical parts. Some of them gags were as blue as anything we ever said in the clubhouse, too. This went on for a good half hour before we got around to business. But then, at last, for the first time, I got to tell my side of the fix, just as it was.

"Judge," I said, "I never went ahead with no crooked deal. I played my best in that series and I did not take one dirty penny."

He bobbed his skull, real sober, like he knew just what I was talking about. Which I was sure he did. After all, by then there were already plenty of feelings going around that I had got a raw deal. There had been petitions, and statements by some big pokes in Chi, and even some nice words in the papers. So when I left there that afternoon, and he pumped my paw real earnest and said he would give me his decision shortly, I had all the hopes in the world that I was about to be in Giants togs.

But he did not call me at all. Instead, ten days after, I read his decision in the papers. "Birds of a feather flock together," he said. And a couple of days after that, when I happened to mention to a scribe that I had talked to McGraw about a spot with the Giants, McGraw piped up immediately to deny it.

And that is how it has been ever since.

But, like I say, I just could not get myself to accept it. In fact, for a long while, whenever some outlaw club would proposition me to play for them, I would get snitty. I'd tell them that I was just waiting for Landis to reach his senses so I could go back to the big time. Waiting was pretty tough, being the sort of fellow I am, but I kept busy in my brother-in-law's drugstore, jerking sodas and selling stogies and such, and also getting out my petitions, so it was not so bad. I was doing very fine in the drugstore, my brother-in-law Harold told me so himself, and never mind if every once in a while some customer made a dirty crack. I knew I would show him when I got back in the big show.

However, after three or four years, it got a little harder to fool myself. I was already thirty-three or four years old, and maybe my skills were already fading. Nor was I a wealthy man. I had started up a court case against The Old Roman, who refused to ante up on the back pay from my contract, but who could say what would be coming? So at last, I did like the others. I went down to Louisiana with Knuckles, Shoeless and Risberg and hooked on with a semi-pro club in a burg called Bastrop. I changed my handle to George Thomas so nobody would know me, and played ball as hard as I could. I still had it, too, that was a relief.

And for the next ten years, 'til I was past forty, I kept up with it. I am not saying I gave up hopes of clearing myself. Every chance I got, in every town I played in, I would talk myself over with the mayor or some other bigwig, or at least write a letter, and a couple of times I even got Landis to turn me down again personally. I kept this up for a long time.

But finally I had to look the facts in the eye, which was that people no longer gave a damn about Buck Weaver's woes, not even some people I knew. As time went by, I was just one of the Black Sox, no different than Gandil or Risberg. Even my lawyers gave up the fight, who I could not hardly afford to have in the first place. They told me there was no point.

I guess the other boys thought I was loose in the bean to keep up with such actions as long as I did. All they wanted was to get forgotten as fast as possible, and one by one, when their playing days ended, they went back to where they came from and did a disappearing act. Knuckles ended up home in Michigan, where he signed up as a game warden at three and a half bucks a day. Later on he got a job with the Ford Company, helping bust up some of the strikes they had there. Hap Felsch went back to Milwaukee, where he was from in the first place, and after Prohibition landed a spot jerking beer. They say he is as happy and gay as ever. Gandil went to California as a boilermaker. Shoeless went back to Dixie and opened up a clothes cleaning store with his wife Kate. Once in a moon, since he used to be such a star and all, you still see a write-up on him. For instance, a few years back he was planning to manage a team in the Greenville Industrial league but, this was the point of the write-up, Landis heard about it and put a stop to it. Believe it or not, Risberg turned out to be a farmer in Minnesota.

But now I will give you another little dose of that irony. Things did not really work out very much better for the other fellows on the old club, the ones the scribes used to call the Lily White Sox. Not with The Old Roman still alive and breathing, which he continued to do until around '33. Schalk played a few more years with the club, and even got to be manager, but when the team went sour, he got booted right out of the organization. They was even less grateful to little Dickie Kerr. In '21, after he had won nineteen games for a team that finished in seventh place, Comiskey refused to give him a rise in pay. "Even five hundred bucks," Dickie told the press, "would do something for my self-respect," but when he could not get it, he ended up sitting out the '22 season, same as the crooks. In fact, he played against Gandil, Risberg and Felsch on a barnstorming tour that year, just to make ends meet, and in '23, when he wanted back in Organized Baseball, he got blacklisted by Landis for having done so. Which was pretty much the finish of his career.

The last of the old Sox to quit the game was Red Faber in '33. He was forty-five years old, and with that flukey knuckleball of his, and a soupbone like a rubber hose, he might have gone on five more years. But, see, he had had a lousy season in '32, and the club was trying to cut him by twenty-five hundred dollars.

Indeed, the only guy that ended up with a smile on his puss when the White Sox got through with him was the famous Eddie Collins. But I guess that is not news to you, not if you know anything about the national game, for Cocky is now one of the owners of the Boston Red Sox.

I am not complaining, mind you. Not at all. My job at the track, taking bets, may not be so dazzling, but I am not doing so bad, and I do not want you to say your goodbyes thinking so.

As for baseball, like I told Shoeless on the telephone, it is no longer my concern. Naturally, I would still like to get my name cleared up. Why wouldn't I? When they get around to hiring a new commissioner, maybe I shall even drop him a line. I am considering it.

But it does not occupy my head as it once did. I am certainly not going to let my heart get broken all over again. Why should I, things are not so bad for me. I like my job just dandy. I do not have no kids, but I got my wife Helen, and quite a few pals, which they are always saying is one of the main things in this life. I got my health, too.

Indeed, you would probably be stunned if you could get a peek at me, that is, the sort of shape I am still in. Here I am fifty-four years old, and people think I am no more than thirty-eight. It is not just my baby face, neither, which I have always had. See, I still have amazing skills. I can still keep my legs stiff as a stake and touch the floor with my mitts fifty times. And I can still do seventy-five push-ups. I do so every night, before I hit the slats. And, when I want to, I can still pick up a ground ball as slick and easy as any man in the big show.

Maybe you think I am bluffing about this, but I am not. Come over to the softball diamonds at Grant Park any Saturday afternoon. That is when I am there with my girls. Any old time you want, I will show you.

Addendum

I n the aftermath of the Black Sox story, my place in the world
was secure; I would not relinquish it—would, indeed, continue
to see my influence grow—throughout much of the five decades
to follow. But were I not to make brief mention of one subsequent
episode, the tale I have told on these pages would be less than
complete.

When, just before Christmas, 1926, charges of corruption were
levelled against Ty Cobb and Tris Speaker, I learned the details of
the story in the same manner as every chump in the street—from the
newspapers. Rarely had I experienced such frustration. Had there
been heads at my disposal, other than my secretary's and my own,
someone's surely would have rolled. Not only had I once had the
inside track on the story—hell, I had *owned* it!—but as recently as
three months before, when both players had abruptly been dropped
as playing managers by their respective clubs, I had made a mental
note to look into it anew—and then failed to do so.

It was small comfort at the time that this ghastly oversight was the
result of something quite the opposite of negligence. The preceding
months, starting in late August, when Rudolf Valentino unexpectedly breathed his last, had, you see, been the most frenetic since I'd
taken on the column more than six years before.

"Even in death," mourned the producer Mark Hellinger, as The
Great Lover's fans stormed the Campbell Funeral Church, "there is
no peace for Valentino"—but no one commiserated with those of us

who were obliged, for weeks hence, to spend all our waking hours striving to wring yet more titillation from the Italian ex-gardener's tedious life; or who, when at last the Rudy mania began to subside, found ourselves with Peaches Heenan, a fifteen-year-old out of Washington Heights, and "Daddy" Browning, the fifty-one-year-old real estate millionaire who had wooed her, wed her and now taken her to court over her reluctance to perform in ways he considered essential to marital bliss; or who, once "Daddy" got his separation and strolled back into obscurity, were almost instantly in court again, as witnesses to the Hall-Mills trial, the latest Trial of the Century to roar down the pike.

This last, at least, was diverting, featuring as it did not only lust, blood and lucre, but a generous dollop of religion. Then, too, I had something of a personal stake in its outcome. The Reverend Edward Hall and his choirgirl sweetheart Eleanor Mills had, in fact, been shot and slashed to death four years before, but Hall's widow Frances, wealthy and severe, had only now been charged with the crime—as the result of an exposé in Hearst's new tabloid, the *Daily Mirror*.

Thus it was that I made it a point to be in regular attendance at the Somerville, New Jersey trial which consumed much of the fall, and that I gave the spectacle even gaudier play than I ordinarily would have. Love letters—Eleanor addressed the Reverend as "Babykins" and spoke unceasingly of her naked body; the Reverend liked to compose poetry to his "Gypsy Queen"—turned up in my column before being introduced as evidence; so, too, did the "Pig Woman," the female swineherd, terminally ill and bed ridden, who claimed to have witnessed the massacre.

These and a half dozen other coups I engineered not only through the power of my name, not simply because sources who dodged other newsmen cooperated with me gladly, but because I was constantly on the scene, working furiously. When the new baseball scandal broke, there were those, especially in the Hearst press, who made much of my having missed the story. Another man in my position, it was said, would never have allowed an item so large to quietly slip through the cracks. Perhaps they even believed it. But, then, no other reporter *was* in my position, and from without few could fully appreciate the character of my labors. It had assuredly not been carelessness, or indolence, that had gotten me, already, into more than sixty papers nationwide; that would, within another half decade, establish my name even among illiterates via the airwaves. On the Hall-Mills story there had been three hundred competitors on the scene; *The New York Times* alone had four *stenographers* in the courtroom. To have been elsewhere, even in spirit, would have been to place at risk not only my exclusives, but the kind of feel for the event that my public had come to expect of me.

The last exclusive I obtained on the story, incidentally, was the most satisfying of all. A week after her acquittal, Frances Hall, whose vigorous champion I had been from the outset, announced in my column that she was suing the New York *Daily Mirror* for libel.

So, no, disheartening as it may have been at the time, I certainly no longer fault myself for the apparent lapse. In fact, so fully were my attentions otherwise engaged that even when a break in the baseball story was imminent, I failed to heed the obvious signs. It was not until December 20 that I learned beyond question that something major was brewing at the game's highest levels—and on the twenty-first, the story busted on the nation's front pages. On the basis of material provided by Hubert "Dutch" Leonard, announced Commissioner Kenesaw Mountain Landis, Ty Cobb, Tris Speaker, Joe Wood and Leonard himself had been formally charged with having arranged the outcome of a game in 1919. Though none was any longer in the employ of a major league organization, each would, if the charges held up, face stiff consequences—presumably banishment from the game for life. The investigation was continuing apace.

I was, as one might surmise, nearly as confused as I was demoralized. In my long-ago encounter with Leonard, Joe Wood—the former pitching star who, after a severe arm injury, had signed on with Cleveland as an itinerant outfielder—had not been mentioned; nor had the large sums—betting money—that were now being cited in the headlines.

But in reviewing the evidence made available by the commissioner's office, the discrepancies quickly sorted themselves out: in speaking to me, Leonard had obviously been trying, with a ballplayer's guile, to obscure his tracks. Only now that his career was definitively at an end—after sitting out two seasons, he had attempted a comeback before being released, in his managerial capacity, by Ty Cobb—had he come forth with a fuller version of the fix. He had been as culpable as the other three, Leonard now conceded, and no other ballplayers had been aware of the scheme at all. "Speaker," he said of the Cleveland manager, so crucial to the plan's success, "told us he'd go in there and pitch himself if he had to." As for the betting angle, Cobb had agreed to put down two thousand dollars on the game's outcome, Leonard himself fifteen hundred, Speaker and his pal Wood a thousand apiece.

However, admitted Leonard, considerably less than that had actually been bet for the players by Fred West—a total of only six hundred dollars, and none of it had been Cobb's. The Georgia Peach had, at the last moment, allegedly claimed he was unable to raise the money.

Intriguing as they were, all of these charges would undoubtedly have been dismissed even more readily by the authorities than they had once been by me, had not Leonard, this time, simultaneously made available a couple of remarkable documents: letters addressed to himself, in the immediate aftermath of the alleged fix (for, his own season having already ended, Leonard was en route home to Missouri when the suspicious game was played) by Joe Wood and Ty Cobb.

"Dear Friend Dutch," began the missive from Wood, since his retirement the baseball coach at Yale.

> Enclosed please find certified check for sixteen hundred and thirty dollars ($1630.00). The only bet West could get down was $600 against $420 (10 to 7.) Cobb did not get up a cent. He told us that and I believed him. Could have put up some at 5 to 2 on Detroit, but did not, as that would make us put up $1000 to win $400.
>
> We won the $420. I gave West $30, leaving $390 or $130 for each of us. Would not have cashed your check at all, but West thought he could get it up at 10 to 7, and I was going to put it all up at those odds. We would have won $1750 for the $2500 if we could have placed it.
>
> If we ever have another chance like this we will know enough to try to get it down early.
>
> Let me hear from you, Dutch. With all good wishes to Mrs. Leonard, I am
>
> Joe Wood

Cobb's note seemed equally unmistakable in intent. After a few opening amenities—his baby girl was fine but Mrs. Cobb was only fair—he proceeded with dispatch to the business at hand: "Wood and myself were considerably disappointed in our business proposition, as we had $2000 to put into it and the other side quoted us $1400, and when we finally secured that much money it was about 2 o'clock and they refused to deal with us, as they had men in Chicago to take up the matter with and they had no time, so we completely fell down and of course we felt badly over it.

"Everything was open to Wood and he can tell you about it when we get together. It was quite a responsibility and I don't care for it again, I can assure you. . . ."

So striking were these pieces of evidence that, in fact, the continuing inquiry seemed the merest of formalities. "Both Cobb and Speaker saw the handwriting on the wall," announced American League President Ban Johnson the day the scandal broke, "and that is why they decided to pull out. Neither will ever return to the American League in any capacity." According to my sources, Johnson, who had actually heard Leonard's charges before Landis, was now aching for a share of the credit.

This I could understand as fully at that moment as anyone on the planet. Yet somehow, instinctively, I myself knew to hold my peace. My silence was not a matter of resignation; I had botched other stories in the past and recouped afterward. Nor did it have to do with the much publicized fact that Leonard, having already endured a visit by Landis to his grape farm outside Fresno, was resisting requests that he appear in Chicago before the official inquiry, offering only the tart explanation "They bump off people once in a while there." I had it on reliable authority that Leonard did indeed fear for his safety. Ty Cobb was in Chicago.

No, it was, finally, the force of Ty Cobb's personality that aroused in me such uncharacteristic caution. More than any of my brother newsmen—probably as much as Dutch Leonard himself—I was acquainted with Ty's capacity for fury; and right from the start, I surmised the manner in which he would fight back.

As it happened, Cobb counterattacked even more forcefully than I had supposed he would, and with far greater speed. Though his explanation for the damning words above his signature strained credibility—he was, he maintained, aware that Leonard had bet on the game, and had merely been relaying Wood's information to him as a favor—he advanced it to Landis with an urgency that was almost convincing. Then, leaving the hearing room and finding himself besieged by half a hundred reporters, Cobb surveyed the throng and launched his campaign in earnest. "My conscience is clear," he began. "I've got nothing to hide, no matter what any smear artist says. I have never bet on an American League game."

If this seemed somewhat beside the point—no one, Leonard included, had maintained otherwise—rest assured that Cobb was just getting started. "I have played the game as hard and square and clean as any man ever did," he said, in what over subsequent days would become a familiar refrain, "and every real baseball man knows it. I will rest my case with the American fans."

Cobb's case rested on a handful of premises: that Leonard had concocted his tale, a mass of half-truths and outright fabrications, in retaliation for having been released by Cobb in his capacity as Detroit manager; that the letters had been entirely misconstrued by the authorities; that, in fact, Cobb had resigned as manager of the Tigers, not because of any impending revelations, but because, true to his character, he no longer wished to be associated with a club with no chance of winning the pennant; that Leonard, in refusing to appear at the hearing, had himself been revealed as "a lying, gutless cur dog."

A good many members of my trade were taken aback by Cobb's audacity—Speaker, after all (although he too maintained his innocence), was ready to go quietly—but almost no one said so in print. For, in fact, it was almost instantly apparent that the public *was* rallying behind the beleaguered star. Two days after the initial revelations, Cobb, back home in Augusta, held an impromptu press conference, and there displayed more than ten thousand letters expressing confidence in his integrity.

"The people out there know Ty Cobb," he said. "Hell, if that bum Leonard had anything on me, do you think I would have released him? I am guilty of only one thing—of fulfilling a promise to a friend."

"Ty may have his faults," concurred Mrs. Cobb, standing on one side of him, "but dishonesty is not one of them." "There exists," added the president of the Augusta City Council, standing on the other, "a conspiracy on the part of baseball to defame Ty Cobb."

The lords of the game, observing the scene from Chicago, would certainly have shrugged off so improbable a suggestion, had not the theme been so readily picked up elsewhere. All at once, civic groups from Boston to Portland, Oregon were issuing proclamations in Cobb's defense; so were the Philadelphia Sports Writers Association, and the American Boys Commonwealth; and, as a unit, most of the Detroit Tigers of 1919. A dozen individuals, independent of one another, offered rewards for information proving that the Detroit star had ever been a party to any conspiracy; one wealthy Cleve-lander offered to subsidize Cobb in his legal fight as far as he cared to take it. Unmistakably, the attitude was in the air. "If those fellows have been selling out all these years," as Will Rogers observed in his syndicated column, "I'd like to have seen 'em when they wasn't selling."

Cobb had never been one to let such an opening go unexploited. Having engaged as his attorney the eminent James O. Murphin, former Circuit Court judge and now a regent of the University of Michigan, he filed a damage suit against Leonard. Then, with Speaker in tow, he set out for Washington.

This last had, as far as the Commissioner was concerned, to be far more ominous than all that had come before. Already, Cobb had found some support among public men; "Landis has fouled his own nest in his desire for sensationalism," said Chicago Municipal Judge E. J. Jeffries, speaking on behalf of a collection of judicial colleagues; Detroit city officials had launched a petition drive calling upon American League officials to proffer charges of incompetency against the commissioner. But Washington was different. It was only through the indulgence of Congress that baseball was permitted to operate beyond the anti-trust statutes. When, on the morning the ballplayers arrived in the capital, Georgia Senator Harris and South Carolina's Smith vehemently put themselves on record in support of Dixie's proudest son, and Indiana's James Watson, soon to be the majority leader, lined up behind them, declaring "I do not believe the charges against Cobb and Speaker," a chill went through the baseball world.

At last, Landis was obliged to act—discreetly. On the day after Christmas, he allowed it to be known, via "sources within his office," that there would be no guilty finding against the accused men; that, since all had retired from the game, no determination in the case was necessary at all. But this was no longer good enough for the legion of Cobb supporters—certainly not for the aggrieved Peach himself. On December 28 it was announced, by Senator Smith, that a special committee of the Senate would shortly be commissioned to look into "the manner in which the game polices itself."

Through the first week of controversy, the editorial writers, ever cautious, had generally remained silent. Now even many of these began to evince sympathy for the accused ballplayers, indicating that, at the very minimum, their rights had been abridged.

Indeed, quite suddenly, with Landis uncharacteristically continuing to avoid public gaze, only his rival Johnson, who had spoken out too early and much too imprudently, seemed to be holding his ground. Over and over and over again, the League President asserted that none of the men would ever again be permitted in the game. In fact, as the possible consequences of his behavior dawned on him, Johnson's denunciations of the deposed stars only grew more shrill.

It certainly had to have been desperation that moved him, on the final day of the old year, to usher a wholly unexpected personality onto the stage: Swede Risberg. Swede, a bit older than when last we had seen him but perhaps even less wise, had been unearthed by Johnson in rural Texas where, in the aftermath of the initial revelations, he had been quoted in a local paper as saying that he had the goods on *twenty-five* former colleagues; these, he claimed, had, on Labor Day weekend, 1917, participated in a four-game series that Detroit had thrown to the White Sox.

By the time Johnson got him up to Chicago to testify before Landis, the number of alleged conspirators had grown by ten—and, over the days that followed, a great many of the accused showed up in the hearing room to denounce Johnson's star witness in the most vividly uncharitable terms. Nor was Johnson's position strengthened when he called upon two more of the notorious Black Sox, Chick Gandil and Buck Weaver, to corroborate their cohort's tale; Gandil did so gladly, but the jug-eared Weaver, professing ignorance of any 1917 plot, merely seized the occasion to plead, pathetically, for his *own* reinstatement to the game.

Though, in fact, the "Risberg series," as it was already mockingly known, had no direct bearing on the allegations by Leonard, it proved to be a pivotal point in the affair. In its wake, Cobb's witchhunt charges were infinitely more credible. And, too, for the first time, supporters of the commissioner and Cobb's determined friends had the opportunity—at Ban Johnson's expense—to make common cause.

It was at this particular moment that I chose to break my own silence on the scandal.

What's up, pal o' mine? Listen close . . .

So, you've been wondering about that mess Dutch Leonard's been kicking up? Well, let me tell you, no more than old Kenesaw Mountain over in Chi . . . Seems the longer things roll along, the worse they look for the Dutchman, wouldn't you say? But he ain't heard nothin' yet. Fred West now says he never bet an alleged cent, red, white or blue, on any ballgame. "I put down Joe Wood's money on a horse" —and that's from the mouth of the horse himself. He'll tell it to Landis tomorrow . . . It looks like the only one who still believes Leonard's tale, aside from Ban Johnson, who'd *better* believe it, is little Dickie Kerr. "It still sounds on the mark to me," says the ex-former-used-to-be-could-have-been star. Say, Dick, when you gonna get over being so sore at the grand old game?

Here's a scoop and a half for you pal, with a cherry on top. Around here, we had our hands on Leonard's lukewarm tip a long time ago. But you didn't read it here, now did you? How come? Everybody knows we like to go a-huntin', and the better the game, the bigger we like it. Remember us, Fatty Arbuckle? Hey, there, Jolie. And we didn't get any Christmas cards from Sister Aimee this year, either, or from Snotty Fitzgerald, or from . . . But in this racket, a fellow hears a *lot* of things, and he'd better learn fast who's on the square and who deserves the old heave-ho. Now Billy Evans, the umpire, there's a fellow we'd trust with a good friend's life. Well, listen to what *he's* got to say about friend Dutch: "As a pitcher, Leonard was gutless. We umpires had no respect for him, for he whined on every pitch called against him. He refused to face the tough teams and he picked the soft spots." ... And now we find old Dutch hiding from the toughest team of all, the Chicago Questioners!!

As for Tyrus the Great, we hear he might have a quirk or two himself. Mrs. Tyrus hears the same thing. But once you've had an eyeful of the bird in action, on the diamond or anywhere you please, you don't need to know a thing more about a little item called character. (Now, if you're looking for *a* character, pal, that's Ban Johnson.)

A personal note. We happen to know of a certain incident, twenty or so years back, that touched Ty deeply. His beloved father was involved, and his mother, and a revolver. But we'll spare you details. Suffice to say that Cobb triumphed over that terrible adversity, as he is on his way to overcoming this one. The author of these words is proud to know him.

By the by, only one statement by the Peach in this whole business fails to check out like a whistle, ten thousand percent. *Never* bet on a ballgame, Ty? Tsk tsk. We have it that you bet, all right, and in 1919, too—on the *White Sox to win the World Series!!!*

Speaking of wagering (and normally we ain't that kind of guy), we'll lay you ten to one right now that come spring, both Ty and Tris will be right back where they belong—on the diamond. And—sorry, Ban—wearing American League uniforms.

There is, I like to believe, a moral in the Cobb-Speaker affair, and it is this: that if you are very good at what you do, even your most inept moves will generally turn out all right.

On January 23, the eight American League owners, convening at the Blackstone Hotel in Chicago under the chairmanship of Charles Comiskey, relieved Ban Johnson, league founder and president, of his duties. Upon hearing the news, Johnson collapsed and had to be hospitalized. Frank Navin was appointed acting league head.

Four days later, on the twenty-seventh, Ty Cobb and Tris Speaker were formally exonerated of the charges levelled against them by Dutch Leonard. "These players," read the commissioner's statement, "have not been, nor are they now, found guilty of fixing a ballgame. By no decent system of justice could such finding be made."

When, early the following spring, the two stars signed on with

new clubs for the 1927 season, Speaker with the Senators, Cobb with
Connie Mack's Athletics, I instructed my secretary to forward a
copy of that most prescient of columns to Ty at his Augusta home,
accompanied by the following note: "Looks like we both come out
smelling like roses."

After I'd thought about it a bit, however, I told her to forget it.

ACKNOWLEDGMENTS

The source material that went into the making of this book is far reaching. Among the works that I found of particular use were *Eight Men Out*, Eliot Asinof's seminal account of the Black Sox scandal; *Of Me I Sing*, Malcolm Bingay's wonderful depiction of turn-of-the-century newspapering; the books of Lester Chadwick; *Baseball As I Have Known It*, by Fred Lieb; Andy Logan's *Against the Evidence*, on the Rosenthal-Becker case; *The Lawless Decade*, by Paul Sann; and assorted biographies, principal among them works by Donald Gropman (Joe Jackson), Herman Klurfeld (Walter Winchell), John D. McCallum (Ty Cobb), Scott Meredith (Ring Lardner), Lyle Stuart (Winchell), Al Stump (Cobb), W. A. Swanberg (William Randolph Hearst) and Jonathan Yardley (Lardner).

I am deeply indebted to those who aided me during my long labors at the Baseball Hall of Fame Library in Cooperstown: Betty McCarthy, Jack Redding, Edith Ruhmshottel, Donna Cornell and Clifford Kachline; to my agent, Jay Acton; to Bob Gottlieb, my editor, for his skill and superhuman patience; and to Marty Bell, David Black, Marcelle Clements, Donald Fagan, Stanley Hertzberg, Elisabeth Johansson, Lucy McCullough, Frank Rich, Ray Robinson, Cary Schneider, Tony Schwartz and, above all, Priscilla Turner. Their input was invaluable.

ABOUT THE AUTHOR

Harry Stein has written for *The New York Times Magazine*, *Playboy*, and *New York* magazine, and he has published a collection of his essays, *Ethics (and other liabilities)*, based on his column in *Esquire* magazine.